Magnolias
in
Paradise
A Novel

LEONARD SEET

Excelsior Publishing

Published in the United States by Excelsior Publishing

ISBN-10: 0-967-49374-9
ISBN-13: 978-0-967-49374-9

Seet, Leonard

Magnolias in Paradise / Leonard Seet.

p. cm

1.   Magnolias

2.   Paradise

3.   Leonard Seet

First Edition

2016935445

Praise for *Magnolias in Paradise*

"Leonard Seet brings his intelligence and wit and gifts as a writer to a broader audience in *Magnolias in Paradise* in a gritty, realistic novel. Seet has reinvented himself as a writer in his evolution from his deeply rich, engaging and inspirational books about spirituality to the rough ride on the mean streets of *Magnolias in Paradise*. ...you'll definitely be engaged by this novel."

> - David Lentz, author *Bloomsday: the Bostoniad*

"The book is immensely readable and is packed with fast paced actions, and cliff hanging chapter endings."

> - Ashok Shenolikar, author *What Did You Say Your Name Was?*

Praise for *Meditation on Space-Time*

"Meditation on Space-Time is a strong pick for those seeking a metaphysical twist..."

> - Midwest Book Review

"Great lyrical novel... A rich, intricately plotted story."

> - Mike Bresner, author *All I Want for Christmas*

"Literary, Metaphysical, Thought-provoking."

> - Mallory Heart Review

Acknowledgement

I would like to thank my wife for her support. I would like to thank Silvia Curry for proofreading the manuscript.

CONTENTS

CHAPTER 1 - ERNST

The baby slipped through his arms. Falling and wailing, its heart-shaped pendant dancing in the air. Ernst shouted a name. Awoke from his dream and opened his eyes. He sat in a train, sweat dripping down his forehead. The seat squeezed his back and buttocks. Cold air blew from the vents above, but heat seeped through the window and scraped his face and neck. His arms embraced not a baby but a courier bag and through the nylon the stacks of cash pressed against his belly. Fifty-thousand dollars.

The train stopped at the station. On the platform, travelers young and old fanned their faces, some carrying suitcases, others knapsacks or handbags. The clock above the sign *Welcome to Paradise* clicked to 1:25 p.m. Ernst had dosed through the twenty-five-minute trip from Charleston.

"My dear lad, it's alright." The middle-aged lady behind him, who had introduced herself as Elizabeth McDonald when boarding, patted him on the shoulder. "Only the train coming to a halt."

"I say, the bloody driver should learn to stop a train the proper way." Mr. McDonald propped his chin on Ernst's headrest and, after smoothing his mustache, checked the time on his Mickey Mouse watch.

Ernst left his seat, still hugging the courier bag. *Hurry up.* After bidding the McDonalds farewell and an enjoyable vacation, he grabbed his backpack, felt for the snow globe inside, and rushed down the aisle toward the exit. The door opened. The air hot and humid slammed into his face and he coughed for several seconds before stepping onto the platform.

1

He struggled to breathe and his heart thumped. After easing his breathing, he headed toward the depot. By the time he passed the poster for the gun show, sweat poured down his back and his head weighed on his neck. He struggled past the advertisement and reached the entrance.

When he opened the door, a draft refreshed him and he entered the waiting hall. The sweat on his face and back cooled, and a chill slivered through his body and goose bumps sprouted on his skin.

Before he took out a napkin to wipe his face and neck, a girl to the right slapped a flyer into his hand and said, "Re-elect Mayor Davis this fall." He was about to read the flyer when a boy to the left stacked another flyer over the previous one and said, "Re-elect Sheriff Perry in November."

He shuffled to a bench, where a homeless man lay snoozing. The stench of sweat and urine vexed his nose. On the TV against the wall, a broadcaster announced the police had dug up more body parts from thrill kills.

Ernst clenched the courier bag and pressed the stacks of cash against his chest. Those body parts didn't belong to Lee-Ann, no way. After dropping onto the bench at the homeless man's feet, he slipped the campaign flyers between the vagrant's heels. He had brought the money to ransom Lee-Ann and he had to hold her hands and kiss her lips.

No young man wearing a Harley-Davidson T-shirt and holding a magnolia. Mr. and Mrs. McDonald squeezed through the door, the husband in a safari hat and the wife in a bonnet and both wiping their faces with handkerchiefs. A boy about ten years old, a beggar, his face smudged and his hair stringy, approached them holding out a Starbucks cup. Mr. McDonald rummaged through his wallet and dropped a bill into it. The boy walked away. When the McDonalds passed Ernst, he again bid them a pleasant trip.

Still no one in a Harley-Davidson T-shirt. He tapped the bag, which he had put down on the bench, while the homeless man continued to snore.

As he was shooing away a fly, the boy approached and begged for change, but slipped and fell before reaching the bench. Ernst stooped and grasped his arm. He lifted the beggar. The boy thanked him. As Ernst was taking out his wallet, the fly buzzed around his head and annoyed him. The bag flew from the bench. He couldn't grab it. The boy snatched the bag and sprinted down the aisle toward the exit. The homeless man kicked away the flyers and cursed the beggar for waking him up.

"Stop. My bag." Ernst leaped up and ran down the aisle. His ponytail swinging. His feet thumping on the tiles. His hip knocked down a trashcan. Ignoring the pain on his side, he dashed toward the beggar and took out his phone.

No, not the money, not the ransom, not Lee-Ann's life.

The beggar, having passed the benches, shoved aside the McDonalds and charged toward the revolving door.

Mrs. McDonald, after faltering, twisted around and clutched the beggar's T-shirt. The boy raised one arm and then the other, switching hands to hold the courier bag, and he slipped out of the rag and ran half-naked through the front door. Ernst, phone in hand, took a photo of his ugly face.

Mr. McDonald said, "Stop." But the beggar turned right and disappeared.

Ernst kicked aside a soda can. Ran past the McDonalds and pushed through the revolving door. He plunged into the heat and again struggled to breathe. Ignoring the nausea, he dashed down the sidewalk snapping another photo, and crashed into a young man. They fell onto the sidewalk, the man dropping a magnolia and a Harley-Davidson helmet.

"Jeez, watch your freaking steps. Boy, check your eyes before you leave your dump." The young man, his heart-shaped pendant dangling in front of his Harley-Davidson T-shirt, leaped up, seized Ernst's collar, shoved him against the wall.

"Oh, it's you. Hey, hey, it's me." Ernst tried to free himself from Rick, the man who had called about the kidnapping.

Rick stopped before his forehead landed on Ernst's nose. "You're Ernst, the Yankee, the Bostonian?" He released the collar, straightened his T-shirt, pushed back his hair, and picked up his Harley-Davidson helmet. "Where're you bolting to, man? You're supposed to wait for me. And where's the dough? We need it to rescue Lee-Ann. Damn it. If you didn't bring it, what the hell you loafing down here for?" He slipped the pendant inside his shirt.

"The ransom—" Ernst pointed down the street.

"Do you think kidnappers down here just *veg* out and if they couldn't get the ransom, just shake your hand and let you go? Just because this ain't Chicago, think we're cushy?" Rick said. "Do you know some butcher's been chopping up body parts and dumping them in landfills?"

"That beggar—"

"Don't lay it on the beggar. If you donated the dough to a beggar, then you're more stupider than those damn deer. I want the dough. You hear me?"

"But I have—" Ernst turned to look for the beggar, but Rick's helmet blocked his view.

Rick's phone jangled. After putting his helmet on a Kawasaki Ninja ZX-6R parked under a no-parking sign, he took out his phone and checked the display. But didn't pick up the call.

"Damn Jo-Beth." Rick dropped the phone into his pants pocket. "Never mind the call. From a witch I wish I didn't know. Probably wants me to tell her if she should have hamburger or cheeseburger for lunch. If I answer, I'll probably tell her to stuff herself with chicken chow mein."

When Rick first contacted him, Ernst had suspected that he was living with Lee-Ann. The thought gnawed at his stomach for two days. He couldn't enjoy his breakfast or lunch or dinner. Couldn't sleep for more than two hours the past two nights. But now, the woman calling had to be Rick's lover. Not Lee-Ann, but another woman.

"A stinking beggar snatched the money," Ernst said.

Rick cursed and smashed his fist into the mayor's poster and knocked a thumbtack off the bulletin board. When he spotted the half-naked beggar running down the sidewalk beside the train station, Ernst pointed and said, "That's him." Without waiting for Rick, he took off and charged through the hot wind while the boy swirled to avoid an old lady.

"Shit," Rick said. "That's freaking Al, jackass-of-all-trade."

Ernst struggled to breathe. As he passed the old lady who staggered and leaned against the wall, the beggar reached the end of the train station and turned right along the building. Rick shouted after the beggar. His footsteps thundering on the sidewalk. He passed Ernst.

"Come on, move your sluggish ass," Rick said. "Lee-Ann's life's on the line."

Lee-Ann's name boomed in Ernst's ears. The two syllables drove him forward. How her body rested against his. By the time he reached the end of the train station, his legs were slowing down. He turned right. He ran down the pathway beside a parking lot toward the train tracks. Al was gone. Maybe he wouldn't retrieve the money; maybe he couldn't save Lee-Ann. He twisted his ankle and almost tumbled. He had dropped the baby. In the dream. But not a dream. No, he mustn't fail Lee-Ann as he had that baby. Lee-Ann, his love, had to hang on. He would bring the money. He would rescue her.

Rick dashed ahead. The pendant swinging before his chest. He cussed and said, "I'll check out the tracks and the station. You comb the parking lot. Don't let the freaking shit head make a getaway."

Ernst swirled into the parking lot and tripped over a man's eyeless head bouncing on a spring. What a God-forsaken town. No wonder Lee-Ann wanted to escape from this hell. The scent of blood nauseated him and he staggered into an Accord, but kept his eyes on the hollow eye-sockets. *No, no, not Lee-Ann, not her head.* Just a middle-aged man's head, with the number 66 carved on one cheek.

Ernst was backing away from the head when two men holding hands entered the parking lot. "Are you B?" the man with green earrings said. "The one who knows where Luc is?" But the other pointed at the head on a spring and pulled out his phone.

Ernst turned around and fled. His knees trembled and his head spun. After one step, he slipped on a magician's wand and tumbled onto the ground in front of the Accord.

Both men were shouting for the police.

Ernst grasped the Accord's bumper but his palm slipped and his forehead hit the hood. He was groaning in pain and cowering behind the sedan when a motorcycle roared into the lot and skidded to a halt. Rick must have come to help him. But the masked biker was riding a Honda Gold Wing rather than a Ninja.

Just as the two men stopped shouting and Ernst prepared to run toward the tracks, the biker sprayed Mace into one man's eyes. While the man screamed and doubled over, his partner shouted and tried to grab the can, but the biker back away and sprayed it into his eyes. When the two men crashed into each other and fell down, the biker lifted a pickax, its blade gleaming under the sunlight.

No, no, for God's sake. Ernst collapsed behind the Accord. His arms convulsing. His mouth cursing his fate. Blood pulsing in his head. After the first thump, one man groaned. When the other screamed, a second blow silenced him. Then the ax thumped and thumped and thumped. Ernst covered his ears with both hands. He wouldn't survive to find Lee-Ann. He wouldn't live with her in the Boston suburbs.

The biker whistled and approached the Accord.

The sedan's window shattered. Its front tire popped. Shards clinking and blood spreading around the men's bodies.

Ernst was falling down an abyss, the light fading and the darkness engulfing him. He hung onto the moments with Lee-Ann: lunching at Faneuil Hall, strolling in Harvard Square, picnicking in The Common and making love in his Arlington apartment. Scenes and memories shattered with the car windows.

The ax would land on his neck; life would flee from his body. But no, the killer stopped in front of the head and tapped the pate with the ax handle. The head bounced on the spring while the killer hopped on his Gold Wing and rode out of the parking lot.

Children screamed. Heels clacked. A crow landed on the Accord's side mirror.

He was alive. He could still marry Lee-Ann in Las Vegas and they could still buy a Colonial in Newton.

Minutes later, footsteps approached. Ernst got up, treaded on glass shards, and ignoring the scribbles beside the pools of blood, ran toward the tracks.

On the platform several travelers huddled against the building, but no Rick. In the lounge a kind-faced man in an aloha-shirt cowered under a bench, but no Rick. Outside, the police sirens blared, but no Rick or Al. Ernst sprinted down Angel Road toward a spire in the distance. Lee-Ann had to be in a cellar or a warehouse waiting for him and the ransom and praying for a second chance at life.

CHAPTER 2 - PERRY

Sheriff Todd Perry had been smoking a cigarette and watching Grace sleep naked under the lamplight when he noticed her turquoise floral dress on the floor missing a button. He snuffed out the cigarette in the ashtray and picked up her bra and pantyhose and he searched under the bed and around the drawer and found the green button under the divan.

After picking up the button and the dress, he took out the sewing kit from his briefcase, and in the divan glanced at Grace, a lock of blonde hair caressing her cheek. He set an hourglass on the nightstand and the sand tunneled from the upper bulb to the lower. From the kit, he took out a needle and a spool of thread and while checking its color against that of the green button, he lamented at his astigmatism. After cutting off two feet of thread, he wetted the tip with his tongue and threaded the needle, sliding the strand through the eye and tying the ends. He removed the dangling threads from the sleeve, put the button in position and checked against the buttonhole. Then, pushed the needle through the cloth and out of the button. Up and down; up and down. He matched the rhythm of Grace's breathing with that of his stitching.

The phone rang and startled him. He got up, put the dress on the divan and picked up his cell phone. His deputy had found more body parts, this time in the cemetery on Melchizedek Street. He still hadn't identified the psychopath who had dismembered the Georgian girl or the bigot who had axed the New York gay couple at the train station. Now, another dismembered body.

7

He returned to the divan to stitch the button while humming to Grace's even breathing. When finished, he laid the dress near the bed's edge, parallel to her body.

Stay in bed. Soak up her breathing and her fragrance. His desire for her grieved him. But he couldn't imagine her as a wife and a mother. Not when his mother kept undressing before a customer. He could still hear their panting and moaning. Perhaps, Grace, her body's warmth would purge that image and those sounds. No, he had to leave, even if his deputy hadn't called about the body parts.

As the last grain of sand reached the bottom bulb, he put on his shirt and pants in front of Grace. After stroking her hair and kissing her on the cheek, he put the sewing kit and camcorder in the travel bag and walked to the front door. He inhaled, opened the door and stepped into the hallway. He wouldn't see her again.

Several days ago, she was walking in Davis Municipal Park toward the Town Square. Her floral dress, merging into the surrounding landscape, brushed against her ankles as she glided through the wind. Her face plain yet pristine… He had been young, but never tasted youth. He had laughed, but never soared into the air.

Billy McGee, the local clown with a branded cross on his forehead, and his drinking buddies emerged from the bushes near the statue of Mayor Gus Davis and surrounded her. They reached for her but she retreated.

Todd thanked Billy for giving him the chance to save her. The fear in her eyes almost healed his soul. Almost. He got out of his cruiser, adjusted his hat and approached the opposite sidewalk. He swung his baton as he whistled a tune and mulled over how to rearrange Billy's monkey face.

But before he reached the sidewalk, a man—a stranger, a foreigner—marched along the walkway toward the gang. Todd studied the calm eyes, the pressed lips, the steady gaits. This man would thrash Billy and his gang, and might even deliver Todd from his hell.

Might he be the one?

Todd stepped behind a tree, blossoms on the branches swaying in the wind. His heart beat like that of a lady gazing at her Prince Charming.

The stranger strutted past the statue toward the posse. One loser after another turned to face the man. They froze. The man marched through the group. They backed away, opening a path for him to reach Grace. She turned toward him. He held her hand and led her away.

Walk up and greet the man. But he despised Billy and the gang too much to face them.

"Hey, Mohammed, where'd you think you're going?" Billy scratched his groin.

The man stopped. The muscle beneath his left eye twitched. The crease on his face deepened. Billy retreated. He stepped on a peach stone and flopped onto the ground. Todd gripped his baton and waited for the man's fist to land on Billy's red nose. The man would probably land three punches before Billy groaned.

"My name is Wolfgang, as in Wolfgang Amadeus Mozart," the man said as he turned and left the park with Grace, her dress sweeping against his trousers.

"Who the fuck's Mozart? You aiming to be funny?" Billy shouted after the man had left.

This Wolfgang's poise betrayed his mental and emotional strength. An Interpol agent searching for human traffickers, a treasury agent investigating the mayor's finances, or at least a bounty hunter.

The next day when Todd walked into the Akdeniz, a Turkish restaurant, for the grand opening, this Wolfgang welcomed him. In the dining hall filled with patrons sampling the cuisine, Todd's dream dispersed. He should strangle the proprietor for trampling on his hope of salvation. Still, after finishing his meal, he complimented the food and gave the server a five-dollar tip.

#

After collecting his *consulting fees* from Benjamin's Fight Club, Todd drove down Main Street as the wind whispered in his ears and tried to whisk him into a dream. But he had to examine more body parts. He parked next to the other police cruisers at New Heaven Cemetery and inhaled the warm evening air, reeking of dirt. He bought a cup of coffee from the food truck whose owner always followed the officers to crime scenes and would earn about fifty dollars before his competitors arrived. Todd sipped the coffee and greeted his men at the gate, with two iron gargoyles. He sniffed their breaths to check whether they had been drinking in the local bar. At the nearest plot, he stroked the headstone of his former deputy whom a deranged veteran had gunned down last year. Along the cemetery's edge, rows of headstones faced the fence and Melchizedek Street. Amid the din and the spotlights, his officers were hovering around several spots, some stooping down while others pointing their flashlights. The coroner had arrived and was kneeling near a headstone that was reclining toward the fence.

The night reeked of decaying flesh, which had become familiar in the last month. He straddled the tape and crossed the police line. His deputy, who was kneeling and pointing his flashlight at a dirt pile, raised his head and said, "Boss, check out the cut."

Todd set the cup of coffee on a headstone and put on plastic gloves. He examined a hairy arm in a plastic bag. A clean cut at the end of the humerus had severed the arm from the shoulder blade. No hesitation marks.

"My butcher wouldn't have done a better job." The deputy rubbed hand-cream onto his palms and covered his nose.

"A surgeon?"

"Not the sick bastard who diced up the girl." A month ago, the police found a Georgian high-school girl's body parts. But a power saw, not a scalpel, had cut through the flesh and bones. Todd suspected Mitch the Vampire, the mayor's son and a local gang leader, of slaying the girl but hadn't found evidence to implicate the delinquent.

"But it's not yet Halloween." Todd turned the bag to study the cut. The killer had severed the arm in three cuts. He had to agree with his deputy: a cleaver wouldn't have made a cleaner cut. The killer had even sealed the plastic bag to avoid contaminating the soil.

Hours ago, at the train station, someone killed a gay couple from New York and wrote antigay slurs on the ground next to the bodies. More body parts would only complicate his investigations. Different cut marks and tools, different techniques and killers.

"Never expected this town to have so many sickos," the deputy said.

"Scalpel, number 36 blade."

"Must've gotten bored in the operating room."

"May belong to that bobble head we found earlier at the train station."

Todd left the arm and smoked a cigarette. The killer probably enjoyed cutting up the body. What prevented him, Todd, from crossing that line? He read several epitaphs before approaching another body part. An upper leg cut at both ends of the femur in a plastic bag. Similar cuts. Probably no fingerprints, but he directed the crime scene unit to collect hair for STR tests. Todd was examining the smooth edges of the severed leg when his deputy informed him a Yank asked to talk to him. He raised his eyes as the deputy shrugged and pointed his thumb toward the police cruisers.

"Do I look like I'm bored and want to yak with a tourist? Is he looking for direction to the local museum? Should I give him a tour of Paradise?"

Near the flashing lights, a man in long-sleeved striped shirt next to a police cruiser was stroking his blond ponytail.

"Boss, the Yank insists on seeing you."

"Does he know who butchered this man?"

"Do you want me to shoo him away?"

Todd grabbed his cup and walked through the headstones toward the parking lot. He had come to this cemetery hundreds of times to mull over evidence and assemble cases and always found the place refreshing. But now, some psycho had desecrated the holy ground. Could he still organize his thoughts here? A breeze drifted across the cemetery, and magnolia's fragrance soothed him, but the lights and sirens still irritated him just as they were probably disturbing the dead. He passed a seven-foot headstone with the inscription *the richest man in town.* When would Mayor Davis remove it? He crossed the police line to face the scarred cheek with a ponytail.

"You on Prozac or what?" Todd said.

"I'd appreciate your help. I lost—" the *Ponytail* said.

"Hey buddy, do you know what I have here?"

"It's very important."

"I have body parts here. Like an arm, a leg and half a chest. Do you hear me? What's so important that you've got to look for me down here? Did you lose your cat or what?"

The deputy crossed the police line and told him some beggar had stolen the man's bag. Todd rubbed his forehead as the man scratched his scalp.

"To me, it's very important," the man said.

"Not as important as that man's life was to him." Todd pointed at the torso the coroner was examining. "Of course, he can't whine. Not anymore."

"I'm sorry."

"I have body parts here and you're asking me to look for your missing purse? Are you kidding me? Listen, pal, can't even spare a jiffy, unless in your purse you've got a hand or a head."

"Sure sounded like Al the dirty Mouse," the deputy said. Todd ordered the *Ponytail* to file a report at the sheriff's office. Al would loiter around malls and parks and train stations to filch wallets, bags and jewelry from tourists, and Todd would have to double his staff to keep up with the beggar.

He gulped down the coffee as a lieutenant crossed the police line and handed him a badge an officer had found in the pile of clothing beside the body parts. An FBI agent's shield.

"Shit." Federal agents had descended into the town without informing him. But a psychopath, probably a local gangster, had thumbed his nose at the Feds. The agency would be sending a squadron of goons to capture the killer, and disturb Todd's dominion.

CHAPTER 3 – JO-BETH

Jo-Beth kicked away the swinging doors and stepped into hell's kitchen where the diner's chef was barking at his assistant for sprinkling too much salt into the bland mash potatoes. She dumped the dishes into the sink, the slime swirling and devouring the plates and half-eaten under-cooked pork chop. She leaned against the counter and for the third time she called Rick. The assistant flashed his middle finger when the chef turned the other way. Another waitress, a gold-digger, dumped dishes and utensils into the slime and splashed coffee onto Jo-Beth's floral apron. God damned dumb ass. She raised a fist. The phone rang but Rick didn't answer her call.

Come on, sweetie pie. Pick up the phone. Let me hear your voice.

The customer hadn't left any cornbread, so she stuffed leftover French fries into her mouth and paced around the stinking sink while the chef declared the assistant a mega-moron of the nth order.

Right, like you're Einstein. Jeez, how much longer?

A waitress smacked five orders on the counter. The chef cussed and swung his hand across the counter as if to sweep the orders onto the floor. Instead, he stopped midway and cussed again.

What a loser.

Before coming to work, Jo-Beth had gone to the gynecologist, who told her she was two months pregnant. Like with a baby. Was he hitting on her? But he showed her the ultrasound, and she hugged him and kissed him.

She was gonna have a child with Rick, her sweetheart.

Not the baby she'd given away twenty-two years ago. And certainly not Lucy-Jane, whom she couldn't suffer another God-forsaken day. But Rick's child: an angel who'd bless her and bind her to her lover, forever.

When her first husband divorced her for having an affair with Gus Davis, who'd become mayor, she celebrated at a bar, with a Screwdriver or maybe a Manhattan. If only he'd taken Lucy-Jane with him. But if Rick, who could have any woman in town, left her, God forbid, she'd take a bottle of sleeping pills to end her miserable life. In her nightmares, he'd have affairs with the models at the New Hollywood Model Agency or run away with Lucy-Jane or the fast food restaurant cashier Lily-Rose. She gave him money to spend so he wouldn't have to work, so he couldn't meet any sluts. She bought him the Kawasaki Ninja so he would take her on rides through the town. Though she feared falling off the motorcycle and breaking her neck. She'd bought him the latest gizmos so he wouldn't think about harlots.

After swallowing the carbohydrate and saturated fat, she dodged a waitress rushing through the kitchen with two trays of dishes and went to the mirror beside the lady's room. The wrinkles at the corners of her eyes, the hair on her face and the lump under her chin, they taunted her. Just like her daughter's ivory skin and silky hair. She cursed Lucy-Jane. Rick must be having affairs with younger and prettier women. She almost dropped her phone.

Would he dump her just as her mother and Gus Davis had?

When she first worked as a waitress, the male customers would flirt with her and she let the generous tippers pinch her buttocks while refusing to serve the cheapskates. But this morning, a construction worker, after scrutinizing her, requested another waitress. He didn't want the *hag*. She should smash the plate on his freaking skull. But no, she needed the money to support her beloved Rick.

"Where the hell do you think you are? In a beauty parlor?" The manager shoved her finger at Jo-Beth's cheekbone. "Get your ass out there before I fire you."

Jo-Beth recoiled as spittle showered her cheek. Stepping away, she crashed into the chef who shoved her aside and said to the manager, "This ain't gonna work. Get me a new assistant."

Bitch, I'll get you fired one of these Goddamned days. Or I ain't Jo-Beth McIntyre.

She apologized to the witch and left hell's kitchen. In the dining room, a man in a ponytail was waiting at the door. She picked up a menu, but before she claimed him as her customer, *Gold-Digger* wiggling her sluttish behind, seized him and led him to her lair. After sitting down, the man showed Gold-Digger a picture and mumbled some words, sounding like a New Englander.

Damn whore.

The next order—a club sandwich with French fries and a chicken fried steak with green peas—she delivered to the customers who promised to complain about her service. While trying to figure out where Rick had gone, she almost knocked the plate from another waitress's hand. The fat brunette shouted at her and stepped on her precious toes.

Jo-Beth staggered as pain upset her balance. The Northerner reached out of the booth, showed her a picture and asked whether she'd seen the man, but she ignored him and limped to the greasy counter and leaned against a pole. The first time Rick had come over he peeped at her daughter. Lucy-Jane, that slut, if she wanted Rick, would seduce him just as she had Gus Davis.

She called Rick again.

Oh, Ricky, please answer the phone.

Had something happened to him? She should've expelled her daughter from the house before bringing Rick home. Or given up Lucy-Jane for adoption just as she had her first baby. She wiped her forehead and pinched her chin to smooth the wrinkles.

The Northerner, after talking to the fat brunette, waved at her, but she just waited for Rick's call.

When the manager came out of the kitchen, squinting at her staff, Jo-Beth ended the call. She picked up another order—a double cheeseburger with ham and bacon—and rushed to the table near the front door, not daring to face the witch.

She'd worked at Jacob's Café since coming to town. Nineteen years and two months. Through four owners and more than a dozen managers. She'd outlast this witch just as she had the other tyrants.

Someone pinched her buttock as she put down a plate of overcooked fried chicken on the greasy table. She turned around to smile. A geezer pulled away his hand and she raised a plate to strike his baldhead. But down the aisle the manager was greeting several customers at the door so Jo-Beth just poured a bottle of Tabasco sauce on his fried chicken.

At the booth next to the Northerner, she picked up the tips the customers had left. Two-dollars and twenty-three cents.

God grant me the serenity to accept the things I cannot change…

She grabbed the glasses and the napkins and was returning to the kitchen where the *brilliant* chef was still barking at the *dumb* assistant.

The picture in the Yankee's hand.

Ricky.

She dropped the tray onto the table and seized the man's shirtfront and said, "What happened to Ricky? What have you done to him?"

"Do you know where he is? I've got to find him. It's a matter of life and death."

"What'd you mean life and death?" She pulled the man off his seat. An image of Rick crashing his Ninja into a semi flashed through her mind. But the man didn't know where Rick was. So she shoved him back onto the seat and called Rick.

Busy signal.

CHAPTER 4 - RICK

Rick curled up inside the janitor's closet, chewing spearmint gum, covering his ears. While the annoying siren clamored and adults and kids screeched. When a migraine, a throb behind his right ear, rammed his brain, he dropped his head between his knees and cursed the racket. He sweated, waiting forever for the *party* to end. He had to jump off a cliff. After what seemed like a century in hell, after the train station had hushed, he sneaked out of the building and drove his Ninja along the train track. Away from the blood and the bodies. Away from the head bobbing on a spring. Never mind that freaking homicidal maniac. Rick sang, "Goodness is the vice of dopes." And just like that his migraine faded away.

Rick passed the town's *penal colony*, the sheriff's fiefdom, where the vines on the walls reminded him of a haunted house. When the snub-nosed deputy sheriff wobbled out of the building and into a police cruiser, Rick slowed down to avoid the wrath of the law. After he'd passed Heaven's Way, the deputy blasted hell's siren and chased him through a red light.

Shit, what the hell? Which freaking fiat had he just pooh-poohed on?

Maybe the deputy had fought with his mistress over the toothpaste cap and had to vent his anger. As Rick slowed, the police cruiser whizzed by him, the siren numbing his eardrums. The clunker almost hit a stray pooch. Not braking, not even swerving. The beast leaped onto the sidewalk to avoid dog heaven.

Rick pulled the motorbike to the sidewalk outside Davis Municipal Park. Near the gate, a little girl was goading a blonde lady into asking

"Uncle Wolfgang" to take them to the botanical garden. He bought a beer from the one-eyed hawker. If only his father had taken him to rock concerts, instead of football games. He never liked those armored gladiators thrashing one another. After swallowing the warm flat liquid, he phoned Al the freaking Mouse, his scheming errand boy during the past year. The fifty-thousand dollars belonged to him and Lucy-Jane. Their ticket out of Paradise, away from Jo-Beth and her dead-end life. That spineless rat had to cough up the money.

"Hey," said Al, "Rick my man. Just the man I'm looking for. Remember I said I'd buy you a finger-licking steak."

Rick spat and said, "I want the dough."

"You mean you don't care none for the steak and rather have the moolah? Wow, you must be in the ditch."

"Cut the crap. I know what you did, you toothless mouse."

"Chill out, man. Guess we got off the wrong when I greeted you. Okay, let's rewind. Ahem. Hi, Rick. How's-it-going? Isn't-this-a-fabulous-day?"

"I'm giving you an hour to cough up the dough. You hear me? One hour. It's one thing swiping from a Yankee. It's another thing swiping from me."

"Oh, bad hair day, eh? Maybe—"

"No maybes. Choose between the fifty thousand and your life." Rick drank the beer while mulling over how to ferret out the beggar.

"Hey, man. You're beginning to piss me off."

"Cut the crap and meet me—"

"Hey, wait a second. Who the hell you think you're? If I— Hey, hey. Who invited you in here? Get the hell— Hey, hey, what're you—"

Al screamed. Rick said, "Stop the damn act." A second scream farther away. A third scream. Silence. The call ended.

CHAPTER 5 - ERNST

Under the noon sun wisps of steam rose from the sidewalk and distorted the buildings, cars and pedestrians. For an hour, Ernst walked down Main Street from City Hall showing photos of Rick and the beggar to every passerby. But, no one had recognized them. Most men and women smiled and skirted around him. He had left a message for Rick. But no reply.

He passed a foreclosed mansion where two men were playing minigolf in the front yard. A man in a shirt and tie shouted for him to repent of his sins and accept the Righteous Way before the world ends on New Year's Eve. When the preacher peddled a pamphlet that would prepare him for the end, he thanked the doomsayer and walked away, ignoring the cussing, hoping the man wouldn't chase him with a club. He had to save the three hundred dollars in his wallet.

After he had passed City Hall, bazaar music drifted out of St. Davis Square. He paid ten dollars to enter. Amid the music, he approached a senior, but the man just played with his water gun. Near the merry-go-round, he showed the photos to a child, but the boy just ate his cotton candy.

When he left and walked down Abraham Boulevard, still under the bazaar's folk music, footsteps closed in behind him and a gun barrel poked at his back, just behind his heart.

"Don't yell. Don't panic," a woman said. "I prefer not to have to kill you."

"My wallet's in my back pocket." Ernst cursed his birthday. He had lost the ransom and would lose the rest of his cash. Perhaps he couldn't even return to Boston. The woman's voice calm and peaceful and the gun barrel firm and steady against his back. Had the kidnapper located him to extort money? But he only had several hundred dollars in his pocket.

"Step back and go into the alley."

"Just take my money, please."

"Hey, chicken, just shut up and do as I say."

Ernst hesitated. The photos trembled in his hand. Sweat soaked his palms. He backed toward the alley where glass shards paved the ground. The woman was wearing a ski mask but her left hand sported a brass ring with the initial K.M.L. Was she going to shoot him? Just one more chance to hold Lee-Ann, before heading toward the big vacuum.

While his heart pounded and his legs trembled and his thoughts churned and churned, a siren blared in the distance.

"If you want to see your girlfriend, then come with me."

"Where is she?"

Sweat dripped onto the photos in his hand. He called Lee-Ann's name. But no sound came out of his mouth. He cussed.

He had to rescue her. He had to show her his love.

"Just keep standing there and talking and you'll never see her again."

"Don't harm her. I'll give you the money."

Just as Ernst raised his left foot, a little girl ran across Jerusalem Avenue where a minivan sped toward the intersection to run a yellow light.

The girl screamed. The minivan tires screeched.

"Don't even think about it." The woman pressed the barrel against the back of his head.

Ernst cussed. Exhaled. Shook his head. He dropped the photos. Ran past the parking meter. Slipped between two parked cars. Dashed toward the girl. A bullet was probably coming at him. Then in his mind, the baby was falling and crying, falling and crying, and he faltered a step.

Where's the bullet?

"Ida."

He mustn't fail.

The rubber burned. A woman shouted the girl's name. Ernst reached the girl. Lifted her. Dodged the vehicle. He embraced the girl as he had the courier bag. A gust cooled his back while the minivan's side mirror cleared his shoulder.

The bullet hit him. No, a pebble bounced off him and dropped to the ground.

He put down the girl and grasped the parking meter to slow his breathing. A blonde lady ran across the street and ran toward the girl. She tripped over the curb and almost hit the parking meter but she reached the girl and embraced her.

The minivan stopped at the intersection but the driver didn't get out. When the traffic lights turned green, the vehicle left. He picked up the photos to check whether he had wrinkled them.

The masked woman near the alley had gone, leaving behind footprints among the glass shards.

I'm here. Take me to Lee-Ann. He had lost the chance to sacrifice for Lee-Ann, but he had to save the little girl. He'd just have to look for that voice and that ring.

"Kerstin Becker." The lady shook his hand and thanked him. Her eyes blue and shining, her movements graceful without airs. The girl, face pale, smiled.

When Ernst showed the photos, the lady said, "I'm sorry. We're visiting, a friend. We've just arrived two days ago."

He thanked her and pocketed the photos. No miracles in this inferno. Never believed in them anyway. The girl thanked him and gave him an apricot Danish.

"But our friend may be able to help."

"Would he?"

"He owns a restaurant, just down there." Kerstin pointed down Jerusalem Avenue. "We are going there. Come."

Across Abraham Boulevard, in St. John Square, restaurants and shops surrounded a water fountain and children were chasing each other on the cobblestone paths. Ida scattered the wobbling pigeons, while he followed Kerstin along the arcade past a restaurant, where the aroma of barbecue vexed him.

Lee-Ann relished barbecue ribs. So on a Saturday afternoon, just two weeks after meeting her, Ernst bought spareribs, barbecue sauce and a grill, and he barbecued the ribs on his apartment balcony while a March wind chilled his bones. They hovered around the grill to warm their hands as her laughter warmed his heart. On most weekdays, after returning from work, he would prepare the meal and, whenever the weather permitted, eat dinner on the balcony. The children would play hide-and-seek around the common area and couples would bike along the trail beside the apartment complex. He would work on his projects: tuning the parameters of his discounted-cash-flow spreadsheet to value a target company or checking a firm's liquidity or leverage to understand the risk in buying it. Or just fill a crossword puzzle. He had never barbecued on the balcony until he met Lee-Ann—the first visitor to step into his apartment after his brother had died on 9/11.

#

The Turkish restaurant faced Jerusalem Avenue. Ottoman miniatures decorated the door and windows and on the sign above the lintel, a tughra followed the word *Akdeniz*. A menu stood behind the stained-glass window.

Inside the restaurant, amid the aroma of roast lamb, an Oushak carpet covered the floor in the waiting area. At the bar to the left, a six-foot tall, broad-shouldered man in a pink shirt was arranging roses in a vase. After finishing the arrangement, the man put the jug on the counter and said, "What'd you think?"

"Show off," Kerstin said.

"Don't forget, you promised me a duel." The man entered the dining hall and put the vase on a table beside the floral-patterned wall.

"I don't wish to eliminate Wolfgang's right-hand man."

"Don't worry. You know I won't harm my boss's girl." The man grabbed a menu and approached Ernst. "We got the best pilaf in town. Genuine Turkish cuisine."

"He came to see Wolfgang," Kerstin said.

"Oh, Uncle Isaiah, I want the Nohutlu Pilav." Ida climbed onto a stool and tugged the man's jacket.

The man filled a glass with orange juice and handed her the drink. "One Nohutlu Pilav coming right up. Just give me a sec."

After Kerstin had taken Ida across the dining hall to the back of the restaurant, Ernst took the menu, sat at a table beside a partition wrapping around the room's back corner, and ordered the Nohutlu Pilav also. Relishing the jasmine's fragrance while he waited.

The man brought him a glass of beer and showed him how to arrange the flowers in a vase.

"I'm Ernst Niebuhr."

"Ah, so. Do you believe a nation, like an individual or a church, can be a martyr?"

Who was he speaking to? No one else was in the dining room. "I believe in profit margins," Ernst said, "in Excel spreadsheets and in discounted cash flows." He took the glass of beer, thanked the philosopher-florist, and drank it.

"Reinhold Niebuhr."

"Not related."

"But do you agree or disagree?"

"Never read his stuff."

"But it's a moral dilemma."

"I've got enough personal problems."

"I'm Isaiah Jefferson. As you can see, I don't look like our third president. But rumor has it… well…" Isaiah opened a copy of Norman R. Shapiro's translation of *Baudelaire* to "The End of the Day."

In all its raucous imprudence
Life writhes, cavorts in pallid light,
With little cause or consequence;
And when, with darkling skies, the night.

"I'm sure you feel a kinship," Isaiah said.

"I'm looking for someone."

"We're all looking for someone."

Isaiah flipped to "The Taste for Nothingness" and pointed to the line *Dead soul, gone now your thirst for victory!* Ernst drank the beer. Thirst, yes, thirst. He thirsted for Lee-Ann.

"I hope you'll run into him or her," Isaiah said.

"I will. I have to."

"Maybe the person was never lost."

"Then I'm lost."

"Then maybe you've come to the right place."

Ernst pulled out Lee-Ann's photo and pushed it across the table.

"Pretty girl." Isaiah examined the photo, tracing his index finger around Lee-Ann's head. "May want to go to Eden's Joy. Of course, if you want a real drink, you better stay here." He went to the bar to clean the tumblers.

"She wanted to escape from Paradise." Ernst said, "She wanted to go to Hollywood and become a movie star." Lee-Ann was going to leave the backwoods, escape from the *witch* and build a new life.

"Sure, and end up a waitress in a diner just like a zillion other girls."

"Better that than rot in Paradise."

"Okay, you got a point there."

"Never should've let her return to Paradise."

A day after meeting him, she checked out of the motel and went to his apartment. He slept on the living room sofa and let her have the bedroom. In Paradise, she lived in a trailer with her mother and had only hallucinated about living in a single-family house. So he drove her around Newton to show her the Colonials he was looking to buy and afterward, they lunched in an Indian restaurant in Lexington. In Burlington Mall, she ran from one store to the next, trying on dresses and rummaging through handbags. She just kept talking about the perfumes and the sweaters and the massage chairs. At night, he took her to the Wang Center to watch *Phantom of the Opera*. He urged her to stay, but in the end, she returned to Paradise.

Isaiah returned to the table and put down the floral arrangement. "Regret is one of the most overrated emotions."

When the waiter served the pilaf, the boss still hadn't come out. Behind the dining room, Ida was laughing.

"I've been thinking about how to overcome *facticity* and *throwness* to disclose possibilities and arrive at understanding," Isaiah said.

A poster of Walden Pond hung on the opposite wall. Ernst had picnicked with Lee-Ann in Thoreau's refuge before she left. He would leave Paradise as soon as he found her and would return to Boston and revisit Tupelo Point and forget about the kidnapping and this inferno.

"How do I reconcile *already-in-a-world* and *ahead-of-itself?*" Isaiah accepted a cup of chai from the waiter and took out a piece of paper with words, circles, arrows and question marks.

"Just wish I could figure out *who-the-hell-stole-my-money?*"

"Well, it's your local banker."

"Where's your boss anyway?"

"He likes to take his own sweet time. Unmoved by the joy and grief of this world."

"I need to get back the money."

"You may be better off going to the police station," Isaiah said. "You know, I'm working on a book call *The Philosophy of Suffering*."

"Forget about the book. Help save a life and relieve someone's suffering." Ernst got up, ready to leave.

The door flung open. A leathery-faced man with thinning hair charged into the restaurant and cussed at the door. "What the hell's this here place? I ain't got wind of it nowhere." His breath reeked of alcohol.

"Maybe you got a problem with your ears," Isaiah said.

"Hey, how come you to let that ponytail in here?" Thin-hair pointed at Ernst and spat on the floor. "Is this here a queer bar?"

"Okay, it's your drunken mouth's got the problem. I can fix that." Isaiah cracked his knuckles and moved aside a table. "And as a bonus, wipe away that cross from your forehead."

"I don't need the entertainment," Ernst said.

"It's on the house."

"I'm fixing to bust your queer jaw or I ain't Billy McGee." Thin-hair raised his fists and charged through the dining room.

Isaiah sidestepped to the left and stuck out his foot. Thin-hair tripped and flew into the partition, knocking it over. Behind the screen, a man on one leg, his palms together before his chest, was facing a poster of Lake Louise.

"Now, you're in deep shit," Isaiah said.

Billy scrambled to his feet. Backing away from the man. Crashing into a chair. Falling onto the floor. He got up. Rushed toward the doorway. Tripping over a trashcan. He crawled to the door. After grasping the handle and climbing onto his feet, he ran through the doorway and scurried down the sidewalk.

"I think you scared the pants off him." Isaiah shut the door and after returning to the bar, poured a glass of iced-tea.

The man's aquiline nose was just like Reza's. After his brother had died in the South Tower on 9/11, Ernst couldn't sit down with his friend Reza to discuss his pain, anger and hatred until two months after the tragedy. Reza had also lost a friend that day and Ernst had abandoned his friend when the latter needed a hand on his shoulder. Though they vowed to overcome the barrier with love and kindness, his friendship with Reza deteriorated through the years. He shouldn't have transferred his anger to Reza, who couldn't even speak Arabic, but he did. His friend's face would remind him that on 9/11 he had lost his brother, his only family since their grandmother passed away three years earlier.

Ernst tasted bile. His chest scorched and his stomach churned and sweat wetted his palms. While the man gazed at the lake's still reflection.

"Eh, you can stop showing off. Your visitor's probably impressed with you scaring off that cockroach. Right, Ernst?" Isaiah finished his iced-tea and continued to arrange the flowers, putting some lilacs against the daffodils.

After paying for the pilaf, Ernst walked to the entrance and grasped the doorknob but didn't turn it. He had to find the money. He had to ransom Lee-Ann. And this man could help him.

CHAPTER 6 - WOLFGANG

A month ago, Agent Wolfgang Demir stepped out of the car and into Paradise's heat and humidity. If he had taken the assignment in Toronto, he would be having dim sum in a restaurant on Dundas Street instead of serving pilaf in Paradise. But several weeks earlier, he had received a note with a red rose insignia.

If you want to find out who killed your father, come to Paradise, South Carolina.

He had to seize the chance. He had to find his father's killer. He had to capture the Red Rose. He had to get rid of the nightmares. Arriving at the restaurant, he touched the Ottoman miniatures on the door. He had visited Istanbul two decades ago and was going to take Kerstin and Ida there. When he entered the dining hall, Isaiah pointed out the Oushak carpet and lectured about its origin. He still preferred dim sum in Dundas Street, but after entering the office with the floral arrangement, he thanked Isaiah, booted up his laptop and reviewed the surveillance videos that had captured several missing women's last activities.

#

Wolfgang turned from the poster and Lake Louise's calm and faced the man who years ago had beaten his father to death while he lay across the alley, lips bleeding and left leg broken. Even in his dreams, he would hunt down that man through the streets of Frankfurt. With the specter from his past beside Isaiah, the nightmare again emerged. But the killer was in his sixties by now. Not this man. Still, he shut his eyes to avoid the face that had haunted his dreams.

The note from the Red Rose. This man who looked like his father's killer. Not a coincidence.

"I can see you two would get along real well. Yeah, just real well." Isaiah finished his floral arrangement whose colors and shades matched those of the dining room frescos, a harmony that Wolfgang lacked in his soul.

The man's face no longer twitched as he rubbed his face with both palms. Wolfgang flung away the images of his father lying in the alley and picked up the partition while Isaiah put the pot on the bar's counter where Grace had eaten the pilaf.

"Boss, how's this? Pretty decent, eh?"

Wolfgang praised Isaiah's floral arrangements, whose colors and symmetries evoke a tranquil lake that reflects peak and sky. He pushed the partition against the wall and rolled up the yoga mat. Ida's laughter drifted into the dining room.

"Just to let you know, this isn't the local lost and found. Won't find here any missing cats." Isaiah picked up the chair Billy had knocked down and pushed it under the table. Once behind the counter, he poured two glasses of iced-tea. "But don't worry, at least we got to yak about what-the-hell-ness." He handed Ernst one glass and Wolfgang the other and strolled into the kitchen.

"It's a matter of life and death." Walking up to Wolfgang, Ernst pulled out his cell phone and showed him the photo of a half-naked young beggar fleeing through a revolving door. Then downed the liquid in three drafts.

"Go to the police station." *He has the same eyes as Father's killer.*

"I lost my brother on 9/11," Ernst said.

Shove him out of the restaurant for looking like Father's killer. Wolfgang turned to the Lake Louise poster whose stillness again calmed his mind. Five years ago in New York, he had met a man willing to befriend local Muslims despite losing his wife in the World Trade Center and the man's face had always encouraged him.

He also wanted to forgive his father's killer.

"My best friend is a Muslim."

"I have Muslim friends also. Does that mean I should help you?"

"I lost fifty-thousand dollars."

"Go to the police station."

"Kerstin said you're a good man and you'd lend me a hand."

"Did she? A good man?" Wolfgang turned toward the back of the dining room where a corridor leads to the restrooms, his office, and the gymnasium. No voices or laughter. But Kerstin and Ida were waiting. He had made a tiramisu to celebrate Ida's birthday, a rare day when joy would shield the shadow of evil.

What is a good man?

"I believe her."

"Why?"

Two days ago, when Kerstin showed up in Paradise, Wolfgang reproached her for straining Ida's body through the flight across the Atlantic. But the girl had asked to celebrate her birthday with him before undergoing chemotherapy for her leukemia. Had searching for human traffickers become more important than her birthday?

"You're my last hope," Ernst said.

"For your sake, I hope not." Wolfgang couldn't prevent the racist from beating his father to death and he couldn't stop the rapist from violating his sister. Perhaps, he had joined the FBI to compensate for his failures and to alleviate his guilt. He liked to think justice drove him to corner criminals. But no, more often, the faces of the racist and the rapist fueled him.

And he was supposed to be good man?

From the counter, he picked up a menu and scanned the dishes. Would running a Turkish restaurant and making pilaf fulfill his life more than chasing psychopaths? He could make a decent Nohutlu Pilav.

"I don't bear grudges against Muslims, even though sometimes when I see one, I'd get steamed up." Ernst scratched his scalp and grasped his ponytail while his chest rose and fell.

"Thank you for your confession, but I'm not a priest." Wolfgang had lost an agent after just two weeks here and would have to tell the wife about the man's death and face her tears and sobs and accusations. But he had to center his mind and heart, and focus on the criminals.

No more cursed mistakes.

He would rather stop human traffickers from raping innocent girls and selling them into prostitution than locate Ernst's fifty-thousand dollars. Any time of the day and any day of the year.

Perhaps, just an excuse not to help this man?

"Doesn't matter if you don't like me." Ernst put the glass on the table beside the bar and wiped his forehead. "You can still lend me a hand even if you hate me."

"What made you think I hate you?"

"Will you lend me a hand?"

"Fifty-thousand dollars."

"Like I said, life and death."

28

Ernst's vein pulsated on his forehead as sweat rolled down the ridge of his nose and hung at the tip.

Life and death for the young women who might fall into the human trafficker's traps.

When Ernst's breathing brushed against his neck, Wolfgang returned to the poster of Lake Louise for wisdom.

"Here's what—" Wolfgang said.

"Thank you."

"What for?"

Wolfgang should show him the young women who might be raped and sold into prostitution, and compare them with his money, but he only said, "I can't spare the time."

Ernst took out a handkerchief to wipe the sweat from his forehead. He picked up the glass. Put it down again. Opened his mouth as if to speak but shut it and put the handkerchief into his pocket. Two young women passed the restaurant and their giggles echoed in the dining room.

Wolfgang took out a photo and dangled it in front of Ernst. "I want some info on this woman." He put the photo on the table between the glass and the saltshaker. His agent had died while tracking Grace, who was to meet this Mary-Lou Kensington, New Hollywood Model Agency's owner. He had to locate her and find out what happened and her role in the human trafficking ring.

If only he had handled it himself, perhaps Tom would still be alive and Grace…

That day, Wolfgang put a tracking device in Grace's handbag and assigned Tom to follow her. When she was crossing St. John Square, he should've gone with her. But he had to analyze the Georgian girl's autopsy report. In the office, he monitored her moves on the screen. She entered Eden's Joy. Tom followed. Then they disappeared. She left her handbag on the stool and her shoe on the floor, a strand of blonde hair inside. Grace had chestnut hair. He sent the strand for DNA testing. Still, a passerby rather than the kidnapper might have dropped the hair into the shoe. He couldn't stop the criminals when his father was beaten and when his sister was raped and he couldn't when Grace was kidnapped.

A leaf was swirling outside the restaurant's front door and it hit the windowpane but continued to dance in the wind. Wolfgang walked toward the door but before he opened it, the leaf flew across the square and disappeared behind the water fountain. He waited. But it didn't come back. It wouldn't come back. He had to look for it. He had to go after it.

Or he would lose it forever. When the wind tossed a lollipop wrapper in the air, he returned to Ernst.

"I thought you're helping me." Ernst studied the photo while his lips and his voice trembled.

"Take it to the Church of Paradise and inquire about her, check if anyone has seen her in the last few days."

"Doesn't the Mafia have an extensive network of henchmen to track the local citizens and dig out dirt from their lives? I thought you could even tell me what I ate for breakfast yesterday."

"Look for Dick Wadlington, a local homeless man."

"Why should I lend you a hand? And why are you interested in a homeless man?" Ernst held his head in both hands to study the photo.

"I'm not. You are."

"Not a homeless man. A young beggar."

"Dick Wadlington is more connected than Facebook when it comes to the slums of Paradise. Knows every beggar, every prostitute, every homeless man or woman. Find him and you'll find your beggar. I'm going to give you his *usual* hiding place, but in case you couldn't find him, I'm sure this minister would know of his *top secret* hiding places." Wolfgang gave Ernst a hand-drawn map with diagonal chicken-scratches.

"Then, maybe you should go and ask him about this Mary-Lou Kensington."

Wolfgang gave him the church address and the worship time. "Since tomorrow is Sunday, you can worship there."

"For your information, on Sundays I don't go to church." Ernst took the photo and left the restaurant.

Wolfgang walked down the hallway beyond the dining room and adjusted Gandhi's framed photo he had bought in London while visiting Kerstin and Ida. In his office, he sniffed the lilies on the shelf and picked up the laptop on his desk beside several files. Outside the window, a couple was embracing next to the water fountain and two girls were chasing each other around St. John Square. As the draft flowing out of the air conditioner vent cooled his face and neck, he took out his agent Tom's gun, which another agent had recovered near the severed head. What would he say to the newly wedded wife?

After the police had found Tom's head at the train station and his body parts in New Heaven Cemetery, Wolfgang practiced kendo with Isaiah and broke the shinai, smashing it onto his friend's *men* or mask. He then strolled on the walkway in Bliss Park, this time without Grace. Her voice and her harmonica's notes still warmed his heart as two sparrows landed on a sycamore branch and chirped. Their song vexed him. At the edge of the park, he faced the ocean. He would rescue her. After Isaiah had located the agent's mark in the Church of Paradise cemetery, he investigated the connection between the criminals and the church. Now, he had to reassess his strategy and tactics and his options.

He would solve this problem just as he had the others.

Several days ago, he was making Nohutlu Pilav when his female agent returned from New Hollywood Model Agency and, after thanking him for the food, reported that Mary-Lou Kensington refused to take her as a model without a letter or tell her how to get such an invitation. He was tracking down an invitation but now Ernst might help find the link between the model agency owner and the human traffickers.

What madness had kept him going all these years? As he locked the gun in the desk drawer, Isaiah entered the office and shut the door. He lowered the blinds over the windows and, after transferring the vase from the shelf to the desk, he sat in front of the desk and pulled the chair toward Wolfgang.

"What the hell were you thinking?" Isaiah pushed back the foliage in the vase, pulled the lilies out of the floral foams and inserted them at an angle, his hands moving like a sculptor chiseling out his masterpiece.

"I won't allow another agent to be killed," Wolfgang said, "and I won't allow another girl to be kidnapped. Ernst, who had just arrived and lost his money, wouldn't draw suspicion when asking around."

"Let me go to the church. I certainly look like a foreigner."

"When they see you, they would think you're either a secret agent or a mobster. And then they would clam up."

"At least they'd let me in. You, they'd call the police, thinking you're a suicide bomber."

"I would like to have some chrysanthemums, green and white, not the yellow ones."

"You're becoming more like a bureaucrat."

"I'm a proprietor now and counting my pennies."

"Come on, we joined the FBI to kick butts. Not to sit in a restaurant serving food."

"Not we, you. Don't drag me into your ulterior motives."

"Your emotions are clouding your judgment. You want to save those girls from the snare, but—" Isaiah adjusted the lilies and pushed the vase to the side.

"Are you questioning my judgment?"

"That girl, Grace."

"He's a new face in town and the locals wouldn't suspect him."

"He's an amateur and you're risking his life."

Wolfgang dropped the photo and leaned forward. "I assessed my options and their risks."

"The girl reminds you of your sister. Your frustration at not being able to save her gets mixed up with your guilt." Isaiah kicked down the trash bin and left the office.

Wolfgang took out Grace's painting of the magnolia tree. The dark-gray bark, the conical crown, the oblong green leaves, the white blossoms. She had left a part of herself on the canvas, but he had failed her even as he was holding a part of her. He traced the leaves' curvatures with his finger. Would the hand that had drawn those lines also sketch the seascape beyond Bliss Park?

After Wolfgang had rescued Grace from the thugs in Babel Park, they strolled in Bliss Park beside the ocean and while the wind cooled his face, she took out a harmonica and played "Jesu, Joy of Man's Desiring." The day in Frankfurt that he lost his father, the same tune, from a church organ, had drifted into the alley and it continued to haunt him in many still nights.

While they were strolling under the sycamore trees, Grace told him she had learned to play the harmonica and the piano from a choirmaster in the church. When she first attended her best friend's church and found herself the only white girl in the worship hall, she asked to leave the service. When the members treated her like the other girls, she stayed and made friends. Soon, the choirmaster taught her music theory and Baroque music. As Wolfgang listened to her story, he imagined the melodies of *The Well Tempered Clavier* mixing with the waves' rhythm beyond the park.

She came from Mississippi with an invitation to the New Hollywood Model Agency but she didn't aspire to a modeling career. Her younger brother had brain cancer. Her father repaired roofs and her mother kept the books for a bike shop, and they didn't have health insurance. Grace would earn enough money to pay for her brother's treatment.

After the walk, they returned to Akdeniz for lunch, and she sketched the magnolia tree beside the restaurant, then gave him the drawing and left.

If only he hadn't let her go. If only he had protected her and prevented the human traffickers from taking her. But his regrets wouldn't bring her back.

CHAPTER 7 - RICK

Rick gulped down the stale beer and cursed Al. That ruse, he'd used years before the Mouse could yelp. He downed the beer and threw the can into the gutter, then sped toward Eden's Joy, Paradise's most popular pub, to find Al's latest hideouts.

Late afternoon in the bar, the barman was shining the glasses and arranging the bottles of booze on the shelf. A waitress at a table was taking a drag and studying a tabloid. He bought a San Miguel and asked about Al. The bartender hadn't smelled the freaking Mouse since tossing his butt out of the bar two weeks ago. After paying for his drink, Rick dropped into the booth next to the dance floor, the same on which he'd pledged to deliver Lucy-Jane from Paradise. He rang his honey.

"I made barbecue ribs. And bought a bottle of champagne to celebrate. When will you be back?" Lucy-Jane said over the phone.

Go home and chow down those tangy ribs. But not yet. He sipped the beer and told her about the damn flop at the train station. While the tune of George Michael's "Careless Whisper" reminded him of his first time here with Lucy-Jane. He'd ferret out the Mouse, and retrieve their meal tickets, he promised. Some guilty bystander must've bumped into Al. Rick would prowl around the dumpsites and landfills and dig through the garbage and dirt. And he would flatten that snout.

"Oh, we need the dough to leave Paradise, this hell," she said.

"I love you."

Money would pave the way to their castle in the sky, in America and in the Bahamas. No two ways about it. He'd suffered and she'd suffered more than enough and they'd earned their Eden. They'd leave Paradise as soon as his fingers touched those bills and he'd crush any thief or dunce blocking the way.

"No way, never again. Never. Not you or me." Nothing more to do with either Mayor Davis or Jo-Beth.

"I wish—"

"We create our happiness, not wish it."

"Okay, I'll drop by Jo-Beth's pigsty to pinch some money. Hope she's got some stashed away."

"Check in the pipe behind the toilet bowl," he said. "Be careful. You'll have to unlatch the pipe." He should go grab the dough but he had to find Al before the Mouse disappeared.

"We'll be in the Bahamas next Sunday, sipping margaritas on the beach."

"The bitch. Have to leave a video to show her how we make love at Devil's Point."

"Love you."

"Forever."

On the anniversary of the Great East Japan Earthquake, Rick was kissing Lucy-Jane in this seat, the very same, while a band covered the Beatles. Several couples were dancing on the floor. When her lips left his, she said, "I've got to leave Jo-Beth that bitch and Paradise this hell. Let's run away to the Bahamas and live off those well-off womanizers."

He'd take her away from her nightmare, he promised. And end his affair with Jo-Beth, especially after the hag had hinted at marriage.

He'd spent sleepless nights in the landfill brewing a plan. The trash's stench nourished his pain, charged his mind. His motorbike sped along the ramp the tires burning rubber, lifted off into the darkness, turned upside down, and somersaulted above trash dunes. The exhaust gyrated and his brain churned and churned and the air whipped his face, but his migraine prevented him from coming up with a game plan. Then, one night, New Hollywood Model Agency's owner Mary-Lou Kensington stepped into the landfill and after listening to his dilemma, enlightened him. She showed him the picture of his childhood neighbor, Ernst Niebuhr. Lucy-Jane would have to play an innocent girl and work the dupe, easy enough for her. Then he would contact Ernst and lure him to Paradise to pay a ransom. Ernst was the perfect dupe. He said, "How'd you know Ernst? How'd you know we were neighbors? And why are you strolling in a dumpsite at night?" Kensington bade him success and left, humming, "Sunshine on My Shoulders Makes Me Cry." She was scheming for her own gain but he didn't care, as long as he got the money.

Though Lucy-Jane had slept with several rich men, he still suffered from knowing she'd give herself to a dupe. He'd sworn to smash the sucker's head once he grabbed the money, reward the lecher for sleeping with Lucy-Jane.

Goodness is the vice of fools. And this damned Yankee was the greatest one.

After leaving the pub, he searched and searched the rat holes for several hours without finding the freaking Mouse. At three o'clock in the morning, he returned to his apartment to the aroma of barbecue ribs and found an unopened bottle of champagne on the table. Lucy-Jane wasn't in the living room, the kitchen, or the bedroom. She should've returned to the apartment after stealing the money. He should call her, but she might be sleeping in the trailer.

Don't wake her up. He hoped Jo-Beth hadn't caught her.

He ate the ribs. After taking out Paradise's map, he checked the dumpsites, landfills, alleys, and abandoned warehouses where he might locate Al. He should talk to Pastor Cassidy in the morning. Al had been going to the church for freebies almost every week and probably told the pastor about his stunts. And the pastor enjoyed the beggar's tales and would plagiarize the material in his sermons.

He waited in the living room for Lucy-Jane, but dawn arrived and she still hadn't returned. He called her. She didn't answer the phone. *Go to Jo-Beth's trailer and check on Lucy-Jane.* No, he had to talk to Pastor Cassidy first.

At nine o'clock, he left the apartment for the Church of Paradise. When he drove his motorbike past the farmer's market on Abraham Boulevard, shoppers were cramming between the stalls and picking tomatoes, carrots, peaches, and strawberries. Last Saturday, he and Lucy-Jane had gone there to buy peaches and squash and spent half a day just strolling among the stalls. Yesterday, they'd planned to go there and buy some strawberries. At the red light, he held up the phone to call her, but the light turned green and he continued down Abraham Boulevard. A young couple crossed the street hand-in-hand and he honked at them.

The phone rang. Damn Jo-Beth was calling again. Maybe about buying a green dress or a blue one. Sure, he liked her depending on him. But damn it, she couldn't even choose between an apple and an orange.

The car behind honked at him and his head throbbed in pain on the upper right side and he grunted and held his head. He groaned and fell onto the ground, the motorbike almost crushing his leg. These damn migraines he had ever since a child and had looked high and low for a cure or at least for relief. Then one day he followed some boys and jumped off the cliff into the river and sure enough as he plunged through the air and into the water, the pain stopped haunting him. And he shouted for joy at the remedy. Sure, the migraine would return. But every time he plunged into the water, he'd escape the headache for days. Of course, as the remedy became less effective, he had to dive from ever-higher cliffs.

Last July, several days after arriving in Paradise, he entered Jacob's Café with Jo-Beth's wrinkled picture and his last ten-dollars. His father, Collins, after divorcing his mother Isabella, had married and then divorced Jo-Beth. He'd milk a few thousand dollars from this woman while looking for a wealthy widow. When a middle-aged waitress with a turkey chin walked up to take his order, he was going to drop his scheme and shoo away the hag. Until he peeled the last bill in his pocket. When the hag flirted with him, he smiled and asked her about life in Paradise, as if he cared.

In the evening, he had dinner with Jo-Beth, not sure where. After dinner, he borrowed fifty dollars from her and went to Eden's Joy, where he met Mayor Davis's wife.

Rick began an affair with Mrs. Davis and stayed in a condominium she owned, a unit facing the ocean and he ignored Jo-Beth's calls, except to kill time. But the affair with the mayor's wife only lasted for a month. A thug, the mayor's personal assistant, showed up one day in his building lobby and warned him to stay away from her if maybe he valued his hands and legs.

Mrs. Davis had given him enough money to live in a penthouse for about six months, but he saved the money for his retirement. After enjoying life for two weeks, he returned to Eden's Joy to find the next Mrs. Davis. Sure, he met several rich women but the affairs never lasted.

After hesitating for three days, he showed up at Jacob's Café and reluctantly asked Jo-Beth to go out for dinner, and they began the affair. He would take her on his motorbike and pretend someone else was riding behind him. Hell, he enjoyed speeding down the highway and scaring Jo-Beth to death. But he wouldn't kill her. He had to get her money.

He continued to go to Eden's Joy and seduced a few rich lonely women, but no relationship lasted and he only milked a few thousand dollars from them. In the end, he had to stay with Jo-Beth. Soon, he met Lucy-Jane and found love and hope. Now, he just looked forward to recovering the ransom and welcoming the Bahamas. The hell with Paradise.

#

Rick waited for half an hour in the apse smoking and reading magic books while Pastor Cassidy performed magic for schoolchildren in the sanctuary. When the cross on the wall rotated and the minister appeared behind a trapdoor, Rick had to suffer from the man's dribbles for another fifteen minutes before getting several of Al's locations. With the wind on his face and the heat in his chest, he drove to St. Peter's Yard, near the train station, to look for Al. He parked the Ninja behind a water tower, took out a crowbar and went down a side street toward an alley. The minister said Al might've gone to the abandoned toy factory on the alley's left side. Why hadn't the Mouse avoided the slaughterhouse? The factory had shut down three years ago and drug addicts had been visiting the place until last year when some psychopath started dissecting vagrants.

At the street corner, a roar startled him. To the right, Mitch the demented Vampire on a Road King winked at him. The psycho adjusted his leather jacket and raised his semi-automatic shotgun.

Rick dropped his crowbar. Ran down the alley. Just as the Road King roared. By the time he reached the abandoned chocolate factory, tires were screeching and the motorcycle was probably turning into the alley. He threw himself through the factory's broken window. A pane cracked and shattered.

Several rats scattered from a drum. After a blast, a ridgepole cracked and collapsed. Dust swirled as he crawled along the wall toward the corner. The front door flung open. Mitch stepped in. After reaching a stairway, Rick went down the steps just as a bullet plunged into a cabinet near the wall. In the cool darkness, he reached the bottom, then turned on the flashlight. More rats scattered. In the middle of the room, a skull leaned against several rusted drums against the left wall. Cobwebs blocked the way and he swung the flashlight to clear a path. He almost slipped on the dusty floor as he wound his way around the drums that reeked of spoiled eggs. Just as he passed the last drum, a shelf collapsed and lifted a dusty fog. Then silence, no gunshots and no footsteps on the stairs. Deeper into the basement, he reached another stairway leading back to the main floor. He climbed the stairs and at the top, pushed open a trap door. Light flooded through the opening and he had to close his eyes. The sky beyond the trapdoor welcomed him into a yard behind the factory. A motorcycle roared away. A minute later, he tiptoed along the wall to the alley, then poked his head around the corner. Well, Mitch and his Road King were gone. The freaky vampire. Brushing his hair and straightening his clothes, he stepped into the alley, shards and splinters scattered on the ground, and approached the abandoned toy factory, just opposite the confectionery.

He looked around the alley before entering and pointed his flashlight at the dusty room. Sure enough, Al's head sat on a picnic table among empty soda cans, the beggar's eyes fixed on Rick.

CHAPTER 8 – JO-BETH

Jo-Beth yanked out the three knives from the center of the target and walked until she'd gone about twenty feet. Then turned around. "God grant me the serenity to accept the things I cannot change..." She threw a knife and it hit the bull's-eye. "Courage to change the things I can..." She threw another knife and it again hit the bull's-eye. "Wisdom to know the difference." She threw the last knife, pretending she was aiming at her manager's forehead, and it landed between the first two. Yes, the darn sun would rise tomorrow.

Billy McGee, her balding landlord, cheered under a tree ten feet away and scratched the cross on his forehead, then pulled up his pants zipper. If she had another knife in hand, she'd throw it at the clown.

"Ain't saying nothing but a reminder the rent's due." Billy scratched his Adam's apple and flicked away the dirt.

Jo-Beth lit a carcinogenic stick, and puffed out a plume of smoke into the humid air. The nicotine calmed her and restored a moment of peace. After the Bostonian had told her about the killing at the train station, she couldn't concentrate on her job, dropping several dishes and serving liver to a vegetarian. She called the sheriff's office about the casualties but the police wouldn't release any details.

The warm evening breeze against her damp skin, she imagined embracing and kissing Rick. For the past several weeks he'd been staying away about four to five cursed nights a week, probably with another lover, a whore no less. Now, she couldn't recall his scent.

"You got wind of them queers gotten put out of their misery? Well, I reckon them—" Billy said.

Jo-Beth dropped the cigarette butt onto the ground and trampled it, as if crushing her landlord's head. Humming "Amazing Grace" to drown out Billy's rant, she wiped her shoes on the mayor's election poster. Gus Davis had aged. When she met him seventeen years ago, he had a full set of hair and no beer-belly. She'd given birth to Lucy-Jane three months earlier and he'd moved from Dallas three years earlier and was navigating his real estate agency to record earnings. That day, he came for lunch at Jacob's Café after selling a million-dollar house on Main Street and he ordered chicken fried steak with extra mashed potatoes. When his gold cufflink glittered in her eyes, she flirted with him and he invited her to dinner that night to celebrate his win. She bought a low-cut red dress and a matching pair of high heels and went to the Heaven Steakhouse for dinner. He described how he'd helped his client save twenty thousand dollars by paying off the house inspector.

Jo-Beth promised to leave her husband and waited for him to divorce his wife and marry her. She'd take over the mansion and his wife's role. She'd loiter in department stores, shop for clothes until noon and nap in the afternoon. But he didn't leave his wife and his son. He would run for mayor, and the small town residents frowned upon divorces and other moral lapses and expected its mayor to honor his family.

One Sunday, she waited across the street from the Church of Paradise, hoping his wife would curse an usher or shout at their son. After the service, Gus came out holding his son's hand and kissing his anemic wife.

Why couldn't she have that life?

She went to Safeway and bought a gallon of cheesecake ice cream and a bottle of sleeping pills. Within an hour after gorging the soul food, she checked into the emergency room with a bellyache and stayed overnight in the hospital. After returning home, she flushed the sleeping pills down the toilet.

She prayed for a miracle, that the wife would divorce Gus Davis so he'd marry her and that he wouldn't abandon her as her mother had.

But he did.

One Monday morning, Gus's assistant ambushed her and informed her the mayor didn't want to see her anymore. In front of the spotted mirror, facing her pear-shaped figure, she waited for tears. But they also abandoned her. For a week, she couldn't eat, drink or sleep. She went to the psychiatrist and began taking Prozac, her buddy to this day.

Two months later, she had an affair with a retiree who owned several buildings near City Hall, but after finding out he'd given the properties to his son, she left the geezer. Through the years, she had other affairs but never found a man worthy of her. Until she met Rick.

\#

Jo-Beth picked up the circular saw and opened the trailer door but hesitated to enter. Only the couch and TV would welcome her. She carried the saw into the God-forsaken trailer that reeked of mildew and stale onion. The air irritated her throat. She coughed. Dropped the doctor's report on the counter and carried the saw to the kitchen where a fly was buzzing over the dishes in the sink. Still had to cut a piece of plywood to replace a cabinet door. She'd asked her dear Rick to fix the crappy cabinet but the board lay on the kitchen floor for three weeks, blocking her path whenever she had to grab some damned pizza or soda.

When would God grant her the life she deserves? After dropping the saw on the scarred floor, she grabbed a can of beer from the refrigerator. Last night, she'd again eaten dinner alone, macaroni and cheese and Prozac, and hadn't cleaned the damned dishes afterward. While watching *I Love Lucy* reruns and drinking whiskey, she'd fallen asleep on the sagging couch, dreaming of Rick leaving her for Lucy-Jane. This morning, a sickly broadcaster had woken her with news of the police finding more body parts.

She phoned Rick, but didn't expect him to answer. He might've already ditched her, embracing a slut and driving to Florida, where they'd scorch their skins on the beach.

In the bedroom, Rick's scent almost calmed her. Posters of creepy rock stars whom she didn't recognize decorated the walls and his T-shirts and shorts covered the discolored floor. His computer monitor displayed, "Go to Hell."

And on his bed, Lucy-Jane's pink bra.

Jo-Beth dropped the can, the beer splashing on his clothes and her sandals. She picked up the bra reeking of Lucy-Jane's perfume.

Oh God. The slut really slept with her Ricky.

She fainted.

CHAPTER 9 - ERNST

Under the morning sun, Ernst crossed Angel Road, eating a raisin oatmeal muffin. A man approached to sell marijuana, but he declined. According to the directions, Dick's lair should rest along an alley off the road. He would help Mr. Demir—agent or mobster—as long as the man located the money. His father had hated Muslims and he vowed to be different. He had several Muslim friends until 9/11, after which he struggled not to equate them with terrorists. The proprietor might be toying with him and he might not find the homeless man. Still, he had to trust the man. He had to locate the money and ransom Lee-Ann.

Beyond a pawnshop with a spray-painted door, down an alley, a beggar leaning against the wall extended her blistered hand. He handed her the half-eaten muffin. But the woman didn't move until the food touched her hand. He left the stench while the beggar nipped on the pastry, picking up the crumbs as they dropped onto the ground. Near a nook, a homeless man lay on the ground and several flies buzzed over him. He asked for Dick, but the vagrant didn't answer or move. Was the man breathing? A machete beside the body scared him and he scurried down the alley. Had to leave the stench of Paradise. He passed two women rummaging through a trashcan and reached a makeshift tent below the graffiti of a lobster and a steak. Amid the aroma of pizza, the canvas flapped in the morning breeze.

He called for Dick and waited. Noise emerged from the tent but no one responded or came out. A minute later, he called again and a voice told him to get lost.

"You Dick?"

"Get the hell out of here."

"I need your help."

"Can't."

"It's important."

"Don't bother me."

"I can reward you."

"How much?"

"Twenty dollars."

"Fifty."

"Deal."

"Get in."

The zipper along the middle of the canvas opened and Ernst bent down and crawled into the tent reeking of cat urine. His palm crunched a roach. A balding man, whose hair swayed in the breeze and eyes squinted at Ernst, shoved the pizza into his mouth. Mud, oil and tomato sauce on his face.

The homeless man at the train station.

Ernst wiped his hands, pushed aside the pizza box and asked for Al's location. Dick narrowed his eyes for several seconds before saying, "Dunno."

"But Mr. Demir said—"

"Who?"

"Al."

"I know him. Just dunno where."

"But you must got some idea."

"The Mouse got too damn many hideouts."

"Tell me."

"Fifty dollars."

Ernst gave him the cash. Dick sniffed the bills, then took out a flashlight and examined them. He blurted out about five locations, slipped a slice of pepperoni pizza out of his jacket and bit into it.

"Now, buzz off."

After writing down the locations, Ernst showed Lee-Ann's photo and said, "I'm also looking for her. Lee-Ann Russell. Have you seen her?"

"Nope."

"You sure?"

"Nope, she ain't Lee-Ann nobody."

"You know her?"

"She's Lucy-Jane. Lucy-Jane McIntyre."

"What? You sure?"

"You trying to insult me? You think I'm a numbskull?"

"No, I'm—"

"Get the hell out of here." Dick reached for the crowbar on his right.

Ernst gave him another fifty dollars and Dick said Lucy-Jane lived with her mother, Jo-Beth, in the trailer park near Noah's Beach. The mother worked at Jacob's café and rented a trailer in the middle of the park from Billy McGee.

"J.B.'s the best knife-thrower in town, so don't you mess none with her. But Billy's the worst scumbag, worse than the mayor, so you can kick his fat butt."

Lucy-Jane McIntyre, not Lee-Ann Russell.

No, impossible. Dick must be lying. But sure enough, she sometimes responded to her name as if she had forgotten it for a second.

"Check with J.B.," Dick said.

Ernst wrote down the addresses of Jacob's Café and the trailer park, then took out his cell phone and showed Rick's photo.

"You know Jo-Beth's beau?" Dick said. "What a catch for her, eh?"

A week ago, when Rick phoned to say that Lee-Ann had been kidnapped, Ernst couldn't digest the man's words. In the common area children were laughing and playing, the giggles and guffaws reminded him of the frozen dinners on the balcony before her smiles warmed his heart. The smell of butter wafted through the air from the apricot ginger scones cooking in the oven. But he no longer delighted in the aroma. When a lark chirping on the balustrade soared into the sky, he closed his eyes and the air glided over his skin like happiness over his life. Beyond the apartment complex, a siren blared along the street.

Before receiving Rick's call, he was going to visit her in July or August. The news burst his dream and Rick's voice rang in his ears until two sparrows on the balcony's balustrade sang to each other. When he picked up the phone, Rick asked for fifty-thousand dollars to ransom Lee-Ann. To show his love, Ernst agreed to bring the money in four days. The ransom would drain his savings but he had to win Lee-Ann's heart. While going to the bank to get the money, he crashed into a pick-up truck on Burlington Turnpike and trashed his car.

He rented a car for four days and returned it at Logan Airport before going to Paradise with the ransom. As he boarded the flight for Charleston, he vowed to save Lee-Ann and win over her.

But he had lost the ransom and Lee-Ann turned into Lucy-Jane. After counting another fifty dollars for Dick, he left the makeshift tent.

CHAPTER 10 - PERRY

When Sheriff Todd Perry woke up on the sofa around noon, the midday heat was squeezing through the blinds. Under the ceiling fan he turned to look for Grace. Several minutes later, he took off his T-shirt to wipe the sweat from his chest. Last night, after taking a sleeping pill, he had drifted into another world and dreamed of walking on the beach with Grace, a breeze playing with their clothes and the waves whispering and soothing his soul. They were walking into eternity.

He woke up.

He shut his eyes but couldn't return to the dream. Just the heat irking him.

After finishing the glass of whiskey on the coffee table and having a cigarette, he took a shower. While cold water splashed over this skin, he yearned to touch Grace. He could find her but he couldn't walk up to her and introduce himself. If only he had taken a lock of her hair.

While he was brushing his teeth and a molar was throbbing, his deputy called.

"Hey boss, I found Al's head on a picnic table. The rats were trying to have a picnic."

Todd rinsed his mouth, then thanked the deputy for the update and asked for pictures of the head and the factory. After hanging up, he probed his gum. He had a root canal just six months ago. When would he lose all his teeth? Lately, his knees ached whenever the weather changed. His body was decaying, but what had he done with his youth?

He put on his beige shirt and gray pants and as he adjusted his tie before the mirror, he smoothed the creases around his lips.

In the café downstairs, he bought a blueberry muffin and a cup of coffee. Then drove to New Heaven Cemetery and lunched under the shade next to his former deputy's headstone. During the past year, he had often sat here to have breakfast or lunch and mull over the cases. As he ate his muffin, the grass blades swung in the wind and he felt like a ten-year-old again. But unlike that boy, he no longer wished his mother to watch the grass with him. If she were alive, he wouldn't let her defile his sanctuary. But he wished to share his peace with Grace. When the caretaker strolled down the path sipping a carton of skim milk, he greeted the old man. A crow cawed on a branch above the headstone and he threw a rock to scare it away. The wind whispered through the foliage, until a car coming down Main Street disrupted the peace.

After finishing the muffin, he put an hourglass on the headstone and with his laptop searched through the FBI database for the dead gay couple's identity. A hate crime, he was sure. An old lady walking along the path greeted him and thanked him for getting her cat down a tree. He didn't recognize her but had saved a cat earlier last year.

Two days ago, while he was eating a slice of cherry pie, his deputy stepped into his office and reported two bodies and a head in the train station. After finishing his pie and having a cappuccino, Todd went with the deputy to the parking lot, prepared to examine body parts. Sure, there was the bobble head, which matched the body parts found later that night in the cemetery. But the two bodies, the killer had only hacked with an axe and, unlike the Vampire, hadn't cut them into pieces.

The laptop showed the gay couple's profile: they lived near New York's Coney Island and worked in a halfway house in Bedford-Stuyvesant. He saved the shelter's address and phone number, and when the last grain had passed through the hourglass funnel, he strolled through the cemetery to clear his mind. Avoiding the main path and walking among the headstones to the site where he had examined the agent's remains. The yellow tape still marked off the area near the fence where mounds rose from the ground. As expected, the crime lab didn't find any fingerprints on the plastic bags. And those on the agent's possessions belonged mainly to the deceased. But the psychopath taunted the police by making the agent into a bobble head and putting it in the parking lot.

Todd walked through the police line and up a mound, sipping his coffee. Were federal agents watching his every step? The recent killings would draw their attention and they would arrive sooner or later. But his men hadn't detected these outsiders. Since the agents hadn't announced their arrival, he suspected they didn't trust him or his men. On the mound he surveyed the Paradise cityscape, the Church of Paradise and City Hall to the north, and the Sheriff's Office and the ocean to the east. The agents might be hiding anywhere in town, but he would recognize him or her, he was sure.

Not the Bostonian. Too silly. Then again...

Mr. Demir, the proprietor who had saved Grace from the lowlifes. The poise, the confidence, the gaze that drilled into his heart.

Todd finished his coffee and threw the cup into a trashcan, then took out an hourglass. The sand rushed through the funnel, the seconds passing from his life. A showdown with the agents would come soon.

If only he could love Grace. If only she would love him. If only he had the courage to leave this hell called Paradise.

But here, hell's fire would baptize him and grant him salvation. As he surveyed the clouds gray and low above the ocean, a siren blasted through Melchizedek Street toward Abraham Boulevard to remind him he hadn't gained redemption. When his phone rang, he put the hourglass into his bag.

"Boss, guess what?" the deputy said.

"We've been working for about a year. Have you ever seen me guessing?" Todd walked down the slope, picking up a few daisies by the roadside. He had put some in Grace's room when he left her that night. Had they withered?

"Well, I bet you'd be surprised at what I've just found."

"Another body?"

"About this Georgian high-school girl."

"Don't tell me it isn't a thrill kill. Because I'd question your ability. I smelled the Vampire's odor."

"But this is sensational. Paparazzi-fitting news. The girl, she's Mayor Davis's latest mistress."

Gus Davis had committed statutory rape with the sixteen-year-old girl. Todd suspected the mayor of having affairs with several underage girls, but couldn't find evidence to nail him.

"I know you want to be the next mayor," Todd said.

"Come on, boss, have some faith in me."

"I don't need faith; I need facts. I'll believe you when you show me the evidence."

"You in for a video tonight?"

"Only something I can't rent from Red Box."

"I found the DVD on my desk this morning. No name or address on the envelope."

"And you thought it's from your girlfriend?"

"Actually… remember last week's parade? Anyway, but the videos shows Davis with that Georgian girl in his bedroom from April 1st to April 30th."

"And you thought I'd be interested in viewing it?"

"Guess we should start preparing a deluxe chamber for him," the deputy said. "After all, he's the mayor."

"Guess you should start preparing your election campaign for mayor. That way, you get to be my boss."

Todd would walk up to the ogre's front door and put handcuffs on his wrists. He would charge him with statutory rape and interrogate him about the girl's death. He would crush this enemy before confronting the FBI agents. After he had hung up, he went to meet Cassidy, to prepare for the coming transaction and check whether the preacher had bought more Rohypnol.

CHAPTER 11 - ERNST

After having a bowl of oatmeal in Paradise Burger, he drove his rental car to the Church of Paradise and expected to arrive a few minutes before the service would end. In front of the white cathedral whose spire soared into the heavens and whose glass façade displayed the Crucifixion scene, a Shangri La in the desert, he got out of his car. While the notes of "Amazing Grace" vibrated through the metal gate. A man in the churchyard was tending the barbecue pit and another setting up the picnic tables.

He passed the signpost *Welcome to the Church of Paradise* and entered the foyer where a breeze fanned his face and body. Applause leaked out of the sanctuary. On the bulletin board were photos of church activities. A balding man in a white suit—the man who had cowered under the bench in the train station and probably Pastor Cassidy—was breakdancing on the sanctuary stage under neon lights and playing Romeo on an outdoor stage. Billy was shoving away an usher while several men held him back. A middle-aged woman—the waitress at the diner—wrinkles around the corner of her mouth, was throwing knives at a target. And Mary-Lou Kensington, whose gentle face reminded Ernst of morning glories, was playing the piano during worship service.

What if Mr. Demir really was a mobster? What did he want with this woman?

Then he saw it. The ring on her finger, with the same initials. She was the masked woman pointing a gun at him.

Had she kidnapped Lee-Ann? What did Mr. Demir want with her?

He walked to the doorway—get out of here—but stopped before the heat. A moment later, he turned around and marched into an oval auditorium where three screens above the stage broadcast Pastor Cassidy's trimmed mustache and gelled hair. At the arena and on the side balconies, the audience stood and cheered as the minister waved his hands and bowed. A man, rather than Mary-Lou Kensington, played the piano.

Ernst slipped into the back row where an old man was snoozing and two boys were playing Angry Birds. When the minister gestured for the audience to sit down, Ernst walked toward the aisle to leave, but sat down behind a man clipping his fingernails. He would stay in the air-conditioned room until the service ended.

Pastor Cassidy in an Armani suit raised his right arm and pointed at the congregation as his gold cufflink glistened under the spotlights. The screens above him magnified his features and highlighted the mole on his left cheek. "My dear brothers and sisters, before you leave, I've something I want you to listen to and to take to heart. Something all-important. Guess what?" He wiped his cheeks with his handkerchief. "Listen to what I got to say. Listen to what I'm urging you to do. Something that'll affect your lives profoundly."

"First, you gotta vote for Mayor Davis for a second term, to reelect him to the office so he can keep restoring our community. Especially during this critical time. Yep, the recovery is just around the corner and jobs are coming back but we gotta have the right man for the work. Ain't that right? Our good mayor comes to worship whenever his busy schedule permits. And today, he's with us."

A round-faced rosy-cheeked man in his late forties rose in the amphitheater's front row and waved, while the audience clapped, some sang a song Ernst didn't recognize. The minister continued, "And second, you also gotta vote for Sheriff Perry for a second term. He's probably hard at work investigating the recent crimes, damned nasty stuffs." He wiped his eyes with the handkerchief and gave the benediction.

Two men flanking Davis pushed aside the approaching fans and the mayor bobbing his belly wobbled toward the stage and shook hands with his supporters as they filed past him. The minister walked to the sanctuary entrance and shook hands as the audience left.

"My dear chap, I didn't expect to see you here." Mr. McDonald walked up to Ernst and shook his hand. "I was jet-skiing and guess what, next to me was a shark. Fancy that. Lucky the fellow wasn't around when I was surfing."

Mrs. McDonald tapped her husband's arm and pointed to Pastor Cassidy who was waving at them. The tourist and his wife excused themselves and approached the minister who guided them to a corner and after glancing around, whispered to them.

Ernst followed the pianist to the hallway and asked about Mary-Lou Kensington, but the man didn't know why she hadn't come to the service today. When the McDonalds left, Ernst thanked the pianist and walked toward the sanctuary to look for the minister, but before he reached the entrance, the waitress with crow's feet around the corners of her eyes stepped in front of him and said, "Have you found Ricky?"

He was about to reply when Pastor Cassidy emerged from the sanctuary and said, "Oh, bless you, my son, glad you're here to worship with us. Stay for some food. Praise the Lord for barbecue ribs." He grasped Ernst's hand in both palms.

The woman coughed and left and though Ernst turned to follow her, the minister said, "Come, let me show you a magic trick." When he passed the bulletin board, Ernst pointed at Mary-Lou Kensington's photo and said, "I know her. She gave me direction yesterday."

"You sure don't sound like a local. Well, never mind where you're from. The Lord's house welcomes one and all. I'm Pastor Cassidy. You can call me Sid. As you can see, we're decent, God-fearing folks down here. Not like some other places."

"She part of the worship team?" Ernst said.

"She's a decent pianist. But you know, if I didn't have to give the sermon, I would've played the piano. Better than her."

"I want to thank her."

"Never mind that. Come on, let me show you something." Pastor Cassidy led Ernst into the sanctuary and told him she serves as a deacon and leads the music ministry.

"I didn't see her."

"Sometimes, she and I would play duets. Too bad today——"

"Where can I find her?"

"You taking a liking to her?" In front of the Baby Grand, the minister adjusted the seat and rolled up his sleeves.

"She looked——"

The minister was about to land his fingers on the keys when his hand stopped as if flaunting his fingernails. "How did she look?"

"Tired. Like I said, I'd like to visit her and thank her."

"Well, you'd be tired too with a son like hers." The minister played "I Left My Heart in San Francisco" but stopped and said, "You like her, don't you?"

"I just want to thank her. Is that so hard to understand?" Should whack the minister's head with the bench.

"Yep, you do like her."

"What if I do?"

"Poor woman, four years ago her boy graduated from high school. Couldn't find a job. No way, not in this economy. At first, he really worked at finding one. But after a year, he gave up and just stayed home all the time playing *Candy Crush* on his phone. Real sad like."

"All the more I should visit her and let her know I appreciate her help."

"Haven't seen the kid for three years. What a shame."

"You probably don't have time to visit your members. At least I can visit her and her son so you'd be spared of a visit."

"Of course, he isn't the only one. Only half the graduates in the past four years got jobs. The rest, well, they either stayed home or left town. The lucky ones flip burgers in McDonalds." The minister shut his eyes and tilted his head and played "It's Not You, It's Me."

"Reverend, I'm in a hurry so I'd appreciate it if—"

"It's your lucky day. She's a single mom."

"How can I find her?"

"What's the hurry? Here's another one of my favorites. How'd you like it?"

When Ernst asked for Mary-Lou's address and phone number, the minister played "You Light Up My Life" and said, "What a shame. The boy should've taken photography. That way he can work at his mom's model agency and meet some pretty girls."

"How can I contact her?"

"Hey, why are you really looking for her?" Both hands on the keyboard, the minister tapped the C note with his index finger and the staccato echoed in the sanctuary. "Are you a gangster? Does she owe you money? I want no part in it."

Ernst showed several photos of Lee-Ann and said he'd like Ms. Kensington's opinion. The minister reviewed them and said, "Wow, awesome. Maybe you should ask her if she's hiring a photographer. She only has freelance guys slaving for her. And this girl looks familiar."

"Do you know her?"

"You a private dick?"

"Just want to give her a surprise visit."

"Hey, what's your name again?" The minister tapped an F sharp note. "Show me a photo ID."

"What'd you mean?"

"ID."

Ernst gave the pastor his driver's license and the man copied his name and address on a notepad, then said, "I'll let her know you're looking for her. If she wants to see you, you'll know."

He shouldn't have agreed to help the restaurant owner. He shouldn't have stepped into this church or talk to this minister. *Someone come ask the minister for a prayer, please.* But all the parishioners had left the auditorium.

Taking back his driver's license, Ernst said, "Actually, I'm looking for her mother."

"Mary-Lou? I didn't know she has a daughter. Well, well, well, that'd be a surprise. Sneaky girl, this Mary-Lou." Pastor Cassidy played "You Are So Beautiful."

"No, Jo-Beth. Jo-Beth McIntyre."

"Oh, well. Just to let you know, I'm not one of those fire and brimstone preachers. I wouldn't have excommunicated her from the church."

"Go ahead and excommunicate anyone you want to. Just tell me where to find her, can you?" Ernst wiped the sweat from his cheeks, raised his hand as if to pluck the mole from the minister's cheek, but lowered his palm and wiped it on his trousers.

"J.B. sings in the choir. A great singer and a devout member. Of course, to lend the choir a hand, once in a while I'll sing solo. And I do sing a mean 'Amazing Grace.' Want to hear?"

"But where can I find her?"

"You playing with me?"

"What do you mean?"

"That's what I want to know."

"I just want to talk to her."

"Weren't you talking to her?"

"You mean the lady in the hall?"

"I think it's the heat, boy."

Or your voice.

"Anyway, J.B.'s talent is knife-throwing. You don't want to mess with her." Pastor Cassidy bent down and squinted at the photos. "Now that you mention it, I see some resemblance. Yeah, I believe she has a daughter but don't recall seeing the girl. Probably never comes to church. Yeah, think her name's Lucy-Jane."

Ernst took the photos.

Lee-Ann. Lucy-Jane. Why? Why hadn't she told him her real name?

Rick, as Jo-Beth's lover, should know the daughter's name, but also called her Lee-Ann. Ernst's hands trembled as he returned the photos into the envelope and Pastor Cassidy, after wasting more time with another tune, led him out of the sanctuary and gave him a church brochure.

In the yard, the aroma of barbecue ribs irritated him. Church members throughout the lawn were eating ribs, drinking beer and soda and watching football on a portable TV. Three picnic tables in the center displayed corn, baked beans, paper plates and plastic forks. And beside the apse eight men and women were tending the four barbecue pits. Some put hot dogs on the grill. Some flipped the racks of ribs. Others heated up the baked beans. The smoke rising into their faces.

Amid the scent of charcoal, Ernst choked and coughed—should leave the heat and return to his hotel. A flock of birds flew in formation overhead toward City Hall.

A man handed him a plate of corn, beans and ribs, the spicy barbecue sauce tickling his nose. How would he recover the ransom? The men and women in the yard chatted and laughed from a different world. Alone he had to rescue Lucy-Jane and escape with her from the heat.

"It's a quiet town," the minister said. "You'll dig it. Maybe after you've found your friend, you'd want to stay here. We've got barbecue every Saturday whenever the weather permits. And the weather's quite decent here, except for an occasional hurricane. But hey, you'll always find the church here."

In a corner of the yard, Jo-Beth McIntyre was throwing knives at a target, the children around her cheering and clapping their hands. Ernst excused himself and ignored the minister's jabber. Jo-Beth threw three knives, her eyelids drooping halfway over her eyes. One. Two. Three. They landed in the bull's-eye. She threw the fourth one and it landed in the center of the other three. The children screamed and jumped up and down and several asked to throw the knives, but she wouldn't let them.

After the children had scattered, he walked up and took out Lucy-Jane's photos and was about to inquire about his lover, when Jo-Beth, dropping her knives onto the lawn, seized his sleeve and tugged it. "Did you find Ricky yet? Where's he? Where's Ricky?"

"I called him, but he still hasn't returned my call." Ernst backed away but the claws wouldn't release his sleeve. He protected his Adam's Apple with his free hand so she couldn't choke him again.

"You gotta find him." She seized his forearm and dug her nails into his skin.

Ernst shuddered and pulled away his arm, but her nails had slashed his skin and left five marks.

Jo-Beth cussed and threw a knife into the bull's-eye. "You looking for Mary-Lou, right?"

"Do you know where she is?"

"Find Ricky and I'll let you know."

"Tell me now."

"Sixty bucks then."

"That's steep."

"Then find Ricky."

"Forget about it." Would the proprietor reimburse him for locating Mary-Lou Kensington? He also had to look for her, but he had suffered enough with the minister and refused to haggle with Jo-Beth.

"Won't find her without me." She extended her hand. She tapped her foot.

He took out his wallet and counted fifty dollars. She grabbed the bills, counted them, and gave him a location in a trailer park.

"I want the money back when I find Rick," he said.

"If you do, but I doubt it."

When Jo-Beth walked toward the target, he showed his lover's photo and inquired about her. She took the photo, ripped it into four pieces and threw them into the air and said, "Dunno."

Ernst raised his fist, but restrained his muscles.

"Haven't seen her for days," she said. "She comes and goes as she pleases."

"Aren't you worried?"

He told her about the kidnapping and she pulled the knife from the target and wiped it with a cloth, then said, "You're a sucker."

"I don't like—"

"Listen and be smart."

"I want to find her."

"She's probably trying to dupe you."

"No, she won't."

"I know her better than you do."

"She cares about me."

"You rich?"

"She's your daughter."

"I suppose it's possible someone kidnapped her if her latest lover's rich."

"She loves me."

"But you don't look rich."

"Someone kidnapped her."

"If you say so."

"Didn't you receive the ransom note?"

"You poor man."

His phone rang as Jo-Beth picked up a knife.

"Hey, better come down to the station," Sheriff Perry said.

"What happened?"

"But not now, I'm freaking busy today. In the evening. Seven."

"Did something happen to Lucy-Jane?"

The sheriff hung up and Ernst stared at the knife in the bull's-eye, trying to decipher the tone and the unspoken words. Before he left, Jo-Beth gripped his arm again and inquired about the phone call.

After Ernst had relayed the sheriff's words, she dropped her knife, which stabbed into the lawn, and said, "No, no, it couldn't be."

Jo-Beth crossed the churchyard and the street and entered a white Corolla. Her car sped down the street, the tires screeching against the pavement. Ernst rubbed his arm and left the church, while the men near the TV roared and hugged each other. A touchdown.

CHAPTER 12 - WOLFGANG

Wolfgang shifted his weight onto his rear foot. Isaiah shouted, stamped his feet and raised his shinai to strike. Then swung at his *men*. Wolfgang parried, struck his friend's right kote. They sparred, shinai striking shinai. Taps mixing with shouts and stampings, the symphony echoed throughout the gymnasium. They parted, raising their weapons at shoulder-level, and Isaiah's breathing matched his footfalls.

Five years ago, Wolfgang had tracked a human trafficker, Kay Emil, to El Paso and monitored her meeting with members of a Mexican prostitution ring at an abandoned oilfield where the rigs had collapsed and the cactuses withered. Isaiah, ignoring the team leader's order to wait for the signal, charged into the ranch to arrest the criminals but stumbled onto a dozen guard dogs Ms. Emil had planted to secure the compound. They charged at Isaiah and he shot them, alerting the criminals. Wolfgang led his team after the human traffickers but Ms. Emil escaped in her all-terrain vehicle, leaving only a dried red rose, an insignia of the Elysian Fields, an international human trafficking organization. Isaiah had bungled several operations, but Wolfgang recognized his skills and dedication and kept him on the team.

When Wolfgang shifted his shinai and mentioned the Red Rose Incident, Isaiah said, "I want to obey you," and quoted Kahlil Gibran: *Your pain is the breaking of the shell that encloses your understanding.*

"Thanks a lot."

"It's not you; it's me." Isaiah raised his shinai and stepped to the right.

"You said that to the pimp you shot in the shoulder last October in Nashville." Wolfgang turned to face Isaiah and protected his left side.

"I wouldn't have disobeyed you if I didn't respect you."

"The psychopath we captured in early January wanted to stop killing. But that didn't help his victims."

"So, when are you transferring me to the IT department?"

"I can't have you jeopardizing the other team members' lives."

"To be or not to be, that is the question."

"You're an FBI agent, not a moral philosopher."

"I know. I know who you'd rather have on the team. Kerstin. You think she's a better shooter."

"I would rather have you without your quirks."

"Too bad. You chose friendship over career."

"Are we trying to save the world just to compensate for our guilt?" Wolfgang stamped his left foot and raised his shinai, ready for another attack.

"If you believe in good, you wouldn't be here. Right?" Isaiah shifted his weight from his right foot to his left and brought the shinai behind him. "Maybe we should consider staying here to run this restaurant. We'd still be an A-team. You cook and I count the pennies."

Isaiah's shinai pressed against Wolfgang and as sweat dripped down his forehead to his cheeks, he tilted the shinai to the right and prepared to execute uchiotoshi-waza. If only he had a similar counterattack against the human traffickers. The sunlight had moved closer to them and he turned his back to the sun. He had to seek the higher ground against his foe.

"Have you ever had that urge when an idea possesses you and you have to act? Like eating to satisfy hunger and having sex to satisfy the need." Isaiah also tried to gain the upper hand.

"I wanted to kill the man who had killed my father," Wolfgang said. "Not from an idea though, but a feeling. And yet, I wanted to rise above—"

"Aha, then you have. Then you understand. Not a feeling, not anger or hatred or lust or love. Nope, an idea, that something should be, that it had to be. That you had to right a wrong."

"Are you ready to commit a crime thinking it is a virtue? Are you going to be a lunatic believing you are a savior?"

"Hey, lunatics may be the only ones who can save the world. Take it or leave it. Kiai!" Isaiah stamped his foot and lunged at Wolfgang, the shinai slicing the sunlight through the window. In the gust the rose petals from Isaiah's floral arrangement flew red in the air.

#

When Wolfgang led Kerstin and Ida into Eden Botanical Garden's atrium, where the orchids' fragrance welcomed him and several Russian tourists were taking photos of the fountain, a stout man in a panama greeted him.

"Well, it's you. Fancy seeing you here." McDonald greeted Kerstin and shook her hand. Then patted Ida.

Winston McDonald, the round-faced tourist with a mustache, and his wife had come to Akdeniz for lunch two days ago. Wolfgang had chatted with the man about Hampshire, where he had gone with Kerstin and Ida for three months last year.

The tourist fanned his face with the panama and his Mickey Mouse watch reflected the sunlight onto a nearby glass wall. "I say, did you see those peonies? Aren't they adorable? I was in China once, Shanghai, and—"

When Ida chased a yellow swallowtail to the cymbidiums, Wolfgang excused himself and followed her, thanking her for giving him the pretext to escape from the tourist. He had waited an hour for Ernst to show up before leaving the restaurant, but Isaiah rushed him through the hallway to the dining room. While waiting to buy the tickets, he checked whether the agents had found any traces of Grace. None, a word that expanded the void in his stomach and nauseated him, a word that was guiding him to the edge of despair.

The butterfly fluttered from the cymbidiums to the bog orchids before playing with the stamens of a white lily. He lifted up Ida so she could see the pattern on the butterfly's wings. A figure entered the back garden, but when he looked in the direction, only the bamboo columns stood near the entrance.

"You spoil her." Kerstin walked up and wiped Ida's forehead and cheeks with a handkerchief. The sun shone through the windows onto her face and mists from the fountain sprayed onto her cheeks. She was going to take Ida to the beach, but the little girl asked Uncle Wolfgang to keep his promise and take her to the botanical garden.

"She's happier than when we were in Disney World."

Was Kerstin happy to see him?

After Ida was diagnosed with leukemia, Kerstin had taken her to Orlando every Christmas and made her sushi every Saturday and last month she bought her an iPad.

Wolfgang stepped under a palm tree and put down Ida. But he couldn't find a shelter from life's storms, the downpours and the gusts and the occasional tornadoes.

Kerstin pushed back her hair while leaning forward and studying the lilies.

Wolfgang followed Ida to the jasmine's purple-tinged white petals gleaming under the sun and savored the wispy fragrance, which purged the images of body parts from his mind and the scent of despair from his soul.

"I'm so afraid of not spending enough time with her. I'm so afraid." Kerstin made way for two boys chasing after a monarch.

"I'm glad you and Ida came," he said.

"Aren't the peonies pretty?"

Would she have come if Ida didn't ask?

"I want to spend more time with her alone," she said.

"Ida likes me."

"I know."

"I like her."

"I know."

"And life is too short to be stifled by guilt." Wolfgang followed Ida into the back garden where the bamboo columns had partitioned the space into a maze and lilac's fragrance was wafting through the air. "Isn't it a joy for the three of us to be together?" He treaded among ferns that flanked flagstone paths and admired the rhododendrons red, white and pink among yellow primroses. While Grace and the other girls cried for help, his help, to escape from the inferno.

"She likes you more than she likes me." On a flagstone Kerstin drove away a mosquito and studied the rhododendrons.

"But she doesn't." Wolfgang caught up with Kerstin and held her sweaty hand. "The good times we have together, they are the icings on the desserts."

"I guess Ida's leukemia would be the main course." She took out a handkerchief embroidered with a peacock and wiped his hand.

They reached a pond where water lilies spotted the surface. Near the edge, a kusamaki shaded a stone engraved with Japanese characters for pagoda. He studied the tree and the stone to center his mind and heart but they drifted. The sound of Grace's harmonica seemed to waft in the air.

"You are a good man." Kerstin crossed the zigzag bridge to the pagoda where Ida was waving at them.

Kerstin had to let go of her burden before she could scale the peaks. Beside the balustrade, Wolfgang surveyed the pagoda's green pyramidal roof with sweeping slopes and up-turned eaves. He had traveled to Hangzhou's West Lake after his sister's rape and toured similar ones. In the pagoda, he studied the lotus's pink-tipped petals raised toward the sky as if offering a prayer. A prayer Wolfgang had said as a boy—before his father's death, before his sister's rape, before entering the FBI.

Am I a good man?

He turned his head. A figure darted behind the bamboo trees. He didn't see the face.

Ida crossed the bridge and when she was looking at a rock, Kerstin said, "Before coming here, we visited the grave."

Eight years ago, after Kerstin divorced her husband, he began drinking and would arrive late to his office and within a month he received the termination letter. One day, the police found his body in the Thames.

"I chose. He died," she said. "Simple cause and effect."

He understood her pain. He wrestled with a similar guilt. Wolfgang leaned against the balustrade and a frog's croaks seemed to respond to the stream's gurgle.

"I asked for the divorce but I still cared about him."

"Do you see that drop of dew on the side of the lotus petal?"

"Sometimes, I wish I were a different person."

"Do you smell the lilac in the air?" he said. He could escape from everyone else except himself. His emotional burdens were his fields to plough and irrigate and fertilize until the day he could reap the harvest.

"I don't know if I would've divorced him if I knew I was pregnant."

Wolfgang threw a pebble into the pond and the ripples swayed the lotuses. Her departed husband would always be the better man, having died and perfected himself through death, his image would shine in her heart until she passes on.

He couldn't compete with perfection.

"I didn't want to hurt him. Certainly didn't want him dead."

Life is too short to envy, just as it's too short to hate. Let me love and treasure you. I'll be happy if you value me as you did him.

"I'm so afraid," Kerstin said.

Let's be afraid together. He crossed the bridge to the pond's edge and looked for Ida but didn't find her.

A void expanded in his stomach. No, please, no. That figure, that figure lurking in the shadows.

Kerstin yelled for Ida. No reply. She rushed onto the flagstone path and called again.

Wolfgang ran down a different path around a wall of bamboo stalks and was scanning for footprints on the flagstones and the soil when Isaiah called. His friend said Ernst had found Kensington's hideout and agents were monitoring her moves but they hadn't found Grace or the other girls. He thanked Isaiah and ended the call, turned a corner and passed the daylilies. His heart pounded against his chest and sweat dripped from his back. As Kerstin called Ida, he found a red rose under a rubber tree.

The Elysian Fields.

His legs weakened. His stomach churned. His head spun and he almost fell.

A shot echoed among the bamboo stalks. A groan, curt and subdued. The conch Ida had given him fell onto a flagstone and he almost stepped on it. On a sunny day last summer, he was holding Ida's hand and walking along the beach...

CHAPTER 13 - PERRY

When Todd stepped into Paradise Burger, Cassidy the preacher was singing the "Toreador Song" from Bizet's Carmen and customers had turned their heads to listen to the performer.

On Independence Day two years ago, Todd was at Babel Park watching the firework and smelling the gunpowder when he came upon Cassidy juggling, tap-dancing and pulling rabbits out of hats to wow children and seniors. A con man passing through town for a few bucks.

He had the deputy watch the con man, then returned to the office and searched through the police databases across the country. He found out the man had served five years for running a prostitution ring in Atlanta. He returned to the park and, after relieving the deputy, invited the entertainer to dinner and discussed a joint venture. Cassidy came to town to recruit delinquents for his new operations, but after three glasses of brandy and a rack of barbecue country ribs, shook hands with Todd. With more than ten years of experience ministering in churches, the entertainer applied for a position in the Church of Paradise, which had lost its pastor more than three years ago. A month later, Todd attended Cassidy's ordination and after the ceremony, the minister introduced him to Mary-Lou Kensington. Todd had Kensington set up the model agency as a front to kidnap young women and sell them into prostitution in France, England, and Japan.

On Labor Day, they met in Cassidy's office again, to celebrate their successes. Todd poured the champagne and after taking a draft, he counted the stacks of cash for his team members. Kensington stacked the bills into piles and suggested ways to reduce the risks. The preacher grasped the stacks and sang and danced around the room, and said the money would fund his retirement in the Riviera.

Unlike Cassidy, Todd wasn't funding his retirement. The image of his mother undressing before a stranger gnawed at his psyche and threatened to eat away his sanity. Each time he sold a woman into prostitution, the transaction purified his soul and baptized him a new man, each time offering a burnt sacrifice.

After kissing Grace on the cheek, he had traded one nightmare for another and had to save her from the monster inside him. Her breathing and her fragrance haunted him even as he examined the body parts in the dumpsite. He would dream of her and wake up, sweat dripping down his forehead and soaking his T-shirt. Having found the real Todd Perry, he despised the fiend and vowed to destroy it.

To sleep without take sleeping pills, for once.

"Hey, I missed you." Lily-Rose, the redheaded cashier, whose nose-ring was swinging as she talked, grabbed his arm and brought him back to Cassidy's theater where the aroma of barbecue ribs mixed with the entertainer's melody.

Every time he came to lunch at Paradise Burger, Lily-Rose would refuse to charge him for the food and if her manager found out, she would pay the amount. If he refused, she would yell at the customer behind him.

As the crowd applauded the entertainer, Todd pulled her behind the counter and said, "Did you see the Vampire or the Werewolf?"

Mitch had begun terrorizing the town last summer, but only started killing when Luc the Werewolf arrived in October. Todd had searched through the FBI databases but failed to find any files on Luc and had to rely on Mitch's profile to predict their behaviors. Should he have rescued Mitch from the Atlantic Ocean ten years ago? No, he wouldn't hesitate to do it again.

"Nah, you must've scared the shit out of them." She held his arm and giggled. "You want me to find those losers? I've got ways."

"Stay out of trouble." He ordered a cup of black coffee and insisted on paying for it.

"You can take me out to dinner. Or to Eden's Joy." She slipped the bill into his pocket and poured him a cup of coffee at the fountain.

Last Friday, she had asked him out, but he said he had to file several reports. He didn't. He worked until ten o'clock on weekdays and when he wasn't working overtime on weekends, he met with Cassidy and Kensington to review the minister's prospecting in Texas or Alabama and the proprietor's latest models and discuss potential clients and coming deals.

He took the cup of coffee and approached Cassidy who was bowing to his audience's applause. A teenage girl approached and hugged the entertainer.

Beware of the lecher and sadist.

They would've met in the church dungeon if the entertainer hadn't rented the sanctuary to a traveling troupe. Extra income to renovate the church basement. Todd suggested New Heaven Cemetery, but Cassidy wouldn't step into the cemetery even before the body parts showed up. Anyway, the preacher had to sample the new menu at Paradise Burger.

"You just missed the show. Not everyday you get to see a live performance of the 'Toreador Song' in Paradise." Cassidy slid the French fry into this mouth.

"Get a life."

Lily-Rose stepped out of the kitchen and handed him a Paradise burger. He thanked her and while she returned to the register, he opened a door and stepped into the meeting room beside the men's room. Cassidy entered with fries and shut the door. Todd set an hourglass on the table next to the window and after removing the wrap, bit into the burger.

A sedan parked in the handicapped space, its doors opened and two boys jumped out of the car. The mother chased after them. The father locked the doors and followed them. A picture of an American family.

A lie.

Todd never knew his father, who had paid his mother to have a son he didn't want. She didn't want him and kept him only to receive welfare. Whenever a stranger walked into his mother's bedroom, he'd wonder whether his father was returning for service. After his mother had contracted AIDS and continued to receive men, he warned the bald man who'd given him his first hourglass. But the man just smiled at him. Whenever a family with two parents, a son and a daughter, and a dog came on TV, he would curse the producers for the propaganda. He became sheriff to prevent those lies from perverting Paradise and fight against the government, the Church, the Mafia, and other corrupt organizations.

"I bumped off that agent. Like it?" Cassidy closed his eyes and thrust a handful of fries into his mouth, munching for half a minute before slurping the soda to wash down the food. The preacher folded his hands behind his head. "Damn, I'm disappointed. I went to all that trouble. You should've guessed it. My handiwork."

The surgical cuts—the bones severed at the joins and no hesitation marks—sure, he recognized Cassidy's handiwork.

"You're a mega-moron of the highest order," Todd said.

Last month, Cassidy strangled a girl in his bed and Kensington had to take the body to the crematorium. He should have arrested the preacher. First, he had to find a replacement. Cassidy, like any performer, not to mention psychopath, was drawing too much attention. The preacher had killed an agent and the FBI would be looking for the entertainer.

"Hey, Sheriff, I trust Kensington. She says he goes, so he goes. If you can't stomach this kind of stuff, then get the hell out of town. I'm sick and tired of you small town boys thinking you can play in the big leagues."

"And a sick bastard. Listen, preacher, I won't let you jeopardize our operation."

Todd would treat this case as another thrill kill and search for a scapegoat, but with any evidence pointing to the entertainer, he wouldn't hesitate to arrest him. Of course, Cassidy would die before he could say a word to the FBI and the evidence would point to the dead preacher as the human trafficking ring's mastermind. All activities would stop after his death, and Kensington and Todd would live *normal lives*. He sipped the coffee and planned his countermoves. He would send an officer to attend Sunday services and monitor Cassidy ...

"Hey, man," Cassidy said, "you listening or what? I said, if the agents are onto us, we got to make some changes."

"Did your brain just power up?"

Last month, a parishioner accused Cassidy of sleeping with his wife and punched him in the gut. After groaning and twitching for a minute, the preacher in tears begged for mercy and said she seduced him. Several days later, he expelled the man from the church and probably would've hired thugs to cripple the man, if Todd hadn't threatened to fry him in the electric chair.

A young woman crossed the parking lot, her strides reminding Todd of the dismembered Georgian girl, who had entered New Hollywood Model Agency in late March carrying Cassidy's invitation letter. Kensington was preparing to take her to the preacher the next day when a psychopath killed the girl and dismembered the body. At first, Todd suspected the preacher, but after studying the jagged cuts from a machete, he recognized Mitch's handiwork. An intern from the mayor's office revealed that Davis had flirted with the girl at Eden's Joy and they left together around midnight. Now that he had received anonymous videos showing the mayor having sex with the girl, he would arrest the lecher for statutory rape. He would've done it a year ago if the mayor's lover hadn't turned eighteen a few months earlier.

Without evidence that the mayor had paid Mitch to get rid of the Georgian girl, he would still have to catch the Vampire to implicate the mayor for murder. But ever since the thrill kills had begun, he couldn't locate the delinquent, though officers had been monitoring the mayor's mansion day and night.

Mitch had led the debating team to a statewide championship before dropping out of school to terrorize the town. Two years ago, Cassidy had even praised the teenager for leading the youth group in church and bringing in a dozen teenagers. But soon Todd arrested more than half of that group for helping the Vampire kill a dozen elderly men and women, and he vowed to capture the delinquent whom he had taught to swing the bat and hit homeruns.

Might Cassidy be mentoring the Vampire?

As the young woman disappeared down Heaven's Way, Cassidy shut his mouth and Todd drank another draft of coffee and said, "If you want to be behind bars, I'll arrange a cell."

Cassidy wouldn't need it. Todd will personally bury him alive.

He took the fries from Cassidy and finished them. "Ask the buyer to move up the meeting." *After that, adios, preacher.* He took out his organizer and set up a reminder to have Kensington help look for the preacher's replacement.

"You do that. I just talked to him this morning after worship. A real pro. You'd never imagine this guy smuggles women across continents."

CHAPTER 14 - WOLFGANG

Wolfgang picked up the conch. He ran down the garden path. Heart thumping. Hair tossing. Hand reaching for his gun.

The Red Rose. The Elysian Fields.

He faltered, kicking a stone, but regained his balance, thinking of Ida and Kerstin, going to Magic Kingdom with them, having ice cream beside Epcot Center.

He still had to stroll along the beach with Ida, picking starfish for her.

Footsteps thumped ahead. A woman holding a bloodied left arm darted in front of him. Mary-Lou Kensington, the figure he had seen earlier, the woman who had taken Grace from him. Grace, who was waiting for him to save her. Yes, alive and waiting.

At the garden exit where the lilacs bloomed along the path, he almost crashed into Mrs. McDonald, who was holding Ida's hand. "Are you looking for this little girl?"

"Are you okay?" He embraced Ida, who gave him a quartz pebble. In the atrium, tourists were rushing out the exit. No sign of Kensington.

He thanked Mrs. McDonald, who patted Ida and left through the front door. Kerstin ran toward him, sweat down her cheeks. She rushed to Ida, embraced her and buried her head in her daughter's bosom. While a security guard rushed a group of boys and girls out of the botanical garden, some were still chatting and laughing and teasing each other.

"I heard the shot," she said, "and I thought—"

"Everything is fine now."

After Kerstin had led Ida out of the botanical garden, he looked around but couldn't spot Kensington in the garden. Who might've been shooting at her? He contacted Isaiah to check whether any agent had come to the botanical garden. None. The agents were waiting outside Kensington's hideout, waiting for her to return. He requested that Isaiah get the surveillance video from the botanical garden and monitor the hospital for anyone checking in with a gunshot wound in the arm, though he suspected Kensington would only go to a *trusted doctor.*

He had looked forward to taking Kerstin and Ida around town, but now, he would get them tickets on the next train out of Paradise, away from the heat and humidity and the criminals. Had Ida seen anything? After searching for the shell casing and not finding it, he left just as the police sirens blared in the distance.

#

At noon, they lunched in the food court at the corner of Bliss Parkway and Jerusalem Avenue, where a crowd had converged upon the stalls, and they had to sit on the bench next to the playground to eat their pulled-pork burgers and French-fries. Wolfgang would have preferred to eat on the terrace under a palm tree facing Bliss Park and the ocean. But Ida couldn't take the heat.

After folding the piece of paper, which she had been scribbling with crayons, Ida handed him the drawing and played with two other girls in the playground. Beside him on the bench Kerstin said, "I was looking into my brother's death before coming to Paradise."

"You never mentioned..." He grabbed a napkin and wiped his mouth.

"He was the man who raped your sister." She sipped the green tea. In the playground, Ida bounced on a balloon.

Wolfgang dropped the cup of chai onto the floor and the liquid splashed away from the bench, dozens of brown strands reaching toward a hamburger wrapper next to the trash bin. He had been reading Thomas Merton's *No Man Is an Island* when the police phoned and said his sister had been raped. A distant moment stored in his memory, ready to resurface at a smell or sound. Kerstin bent down to wipe the floor. He grabbed the napkins from the bag and stooped to join her.

If only he had stopped Hilda from getting drunk in Georgetown after breaking up with her boyfriend...

She picked up the cup and put the bundle of soggy napkins inside. "I was going through the documents and looking into his murder when I saw your sister's name." She wiped her hands and glanced at Ida running around the plastic slide. "At first, I wanted to keep it from you, but I could not. How could I?"

No wonder he bumped into her and her husband near Lorton Prison several days after someone had castrated Hilda's rapist in prison. And to think that he wouldn't have met her if her brother hadn't…

As Wolfgang threw the napkins into the trash bin, a frowning pimple-faced teen came over to mop up the liquid. Wolfgang apologized but the boy just grumbled and swung the mop back and forth.

"We weren't close even before he immigrated to the U.S." Kerstin took out a tissue to wipe her cheeks. Her lips moved as if to speak but she just wiped the back of her neck and turned to watch Ida play hide and seek with the other two girls.

He reached for her but she backed away and said, "I'm sorry."

After mopping the floor, the staff member dragged the mop and bucket back to the storage closet. On the bench next to them, a teenage couple was kissing each other. He should get away from the chatter and laughter and elevator music. He should just sit on the beach and stare at the sea, and contemplate the hisses of the waves and the whispers of the winds.

"Maybe destiny does trump personal freedom. I have struggled to assert my choice over fate, but…" Kerstin rubbed her forehead and walked toward the playground, stopping outside a souvenir shop where seashells lay on a display behind the window.

It isn't your fault. You are you and your brother was a rapist. Wolfgang followed her to the seashell display and opened his mouth but no sound came out and he struggled to form the syllables that seemed afraid to leave his mouth. Would this build a wall between them?

The phone rang.

Isaiah informed him the human traffickers would meet tonight for a deal. Wolfgang ended the call and opened Ida's drawing, a sketch of a woman shooting another with a gun. No, not Ida. His hands shook. He dropped the drawing. He grasped the gun beside his ribs. His fingers brushed the conch inside his pocket. He reached for Kerstin, but she was rushing over to the playground where Ida had fallen.

CHAPTER 15 -RICK

On a hot evening last August, Jo-Beth took Rick home for the first time. While he approached the shabby trailer that was her sty, Lucy-Jane in a black miniskirt stepped out of the trailer and headed toward a limousine parked along the road.

"Slut."

So she's Jo-Beth's daughter. He was cursing his fate and hadn't focused on her, but when the mother *greeted* her daughter, he turned to the girl, to study her eyes, the gleam of hope and despair. She glanced at him as she entered the limousine. At that instant, he should've run toward her, hugged her and taken her away from this hell-town. Walking up to the trailer, he vowed to build a life with her.

Well, that night, while he had sex with Jo-Beth, he thought of the girl. Afterward, he left the bedroom and waited in the living room smoking a pack of cigarettes. But the girl didn't return. Later, he found out she'd gone to a motel to meet the mayor.

#

After finding Al's head, Rick went to several alleys and dumpsites to interview homeless men and women about the Mouse's latest activities. All dead ends. He drove his motorbike over the ramp and somersaulted in the air, vending his frustration. Where might the expired Al have hidden the dough? Maybe the killer took the money.

When Lucy-Jane didn't answer his call, he cussed and came to the trailer park. He parked his Ninja next to a tree, then strolled under the twilight, sucking his cigarette. While the wind pushed against him as if to prevent him from confronting Jo-Beth.

Sure, Rick came to Paradise to find money and love, expected to fail as he had in Atlanta and New Orleans. Then, when he met Lucy-Jane, he dreamed. Really dreamed. Fifty-thousand dollars would confirm his faith. But hell, he hadn't touched a single stack of the cash and now couldn't even locate dear Lucy-Jane.

Trekking through the woods, he imagined Jo-Beth maybe tying up Lucy-Jane again and whipping her with a belt. He sped up, kicking pebbles into the distance, swinging the crowbar.

Near the trailer, a crow on a branch cawed as if to warn Jo-Beth. He imagined Lucy-Jane walking out of the trailer to greet him. He'd hug his sweetheart and kiss her in front of her mother.

A crash inside the trailer startled him. Behind the kitchen window, Jo-Beth was chopping the pumps he'd bought Lucy-Jane. He clenched his fist, ready to crash in and punch the hag's chubby cheeks and stop her from destroying his lover's mementos.

The day he moved in with Jo-Beth, he entered the trailer to find Lucy-Jane polishing her nails. Even before he put down his backpack, Jo-Beth complained that the *slut* couldn't even cook scramble eggs. He soothed the mother while peeping at the daughter who smoked a cigarette.

That evening, during dinner, Jo-Beth ordered her daughter to clear the closet to make room for Rick's clothing. But he had a cardboard drawer and wouldn't need the closet. Still, Jo-Beth insisted. Throughout dinner, Lucy-Jane didn't say a word. That night, lying beside Jo-Beth, he heard the girl tossing and turning on the living room couch. She left the trailer after midnight and didn't return until dawn.

The next day, he asked Jo-Beth for money to buy accessories for his Ninja. After finding out her shoe size, he bought Lucy-Jane a pair of pumps and put them next to her stilettos. Sure enough, that evening, the girl left the trailer wearing her new pair of shoes.

The next day, when he woke up at noon, he found a bowl of beef stew on the kitchen table. He licked the last drop from the bowl. He took his Ninja to the landfill and after lifting off a makeshift ramp, somersaulted into the air. When the vagrants crowded the dump, he left and went to Eden's Joy for a drink. To celebrate a new life.

On Columbus Day, after Jo-Beth had left for work, Lucy-Jane came into his room. She took off her clothes and slipped into bed with him. He kissed her. They made love. Just like that. He held her for half an hour. Then she kissed him and left. He lit a cigarette and held up his pendant—a cross. What would be her first words to him?

Lucy-Jane's lips warmed him even as Jo-Beth threw the pieces of the pumps into the trashcan and took the girl's picture off the wall. She cursed her daughter. She smashed the frame against the counter. She ripped the picture into a dozen pieces and burned the scraps on the stove.

Go ahead and burn the pictures. He didn't need them to remember Lucy-Jane's face. *Just you wait. I'll have the last laugh.*

The fire burned Lucy-Jane's picture. Soot drifted into the living room. When Jo-Beth turned off the stove and walked toward the door, Rick stepped away from the trailer and darted behind the tree. The trailer door opened and she poked out her head and peeped left and right.

The crow cawed again and after slipping out of her home, Jo-Beth bent to pull out a cart from under the trailer, then rushed inside. Within a minute, she dragged a garbage bag out of the trailer. While heaving it down the steps, she slipped and rolled onto the ground. The bag thumped against her right leg. She cussed and raised her leg to kick the bag but stopped and cursed Lucy-Jane. Then heaved the bag and dumped it onto the cart and wiped her forehead.

Had she stolen plates, pitchers and pans from Jacob's Café again? More like a piglet or several chickens.

After heaving for half a minute, Jo-Beth rushed inside and within a minute slung another bag onto the cart. She bent over and grasped the cart, panted for a minute before entering the trailer. After filling the cart with five bags, she sat on the steps, pressing her right hand against her chest. Several minutes later, she pushed the cart along the dirt path to her car, parked twenty feet away.

Probably taking some loot to sell on the black market.

Jo-Beth loaded the bags into her trunk and returned to dump another five bags onto the cart. Rested for about ten minutes and loaded them into the trunk. After the third load, which she put in the back seat rather than the trunk, she pushed the cart under the trailer and drove off.

Where was Lucy-Jane? Probably gone or Jo-Beth wouldn't move the loot.

He should go into the trailer to check for Lucy-Jane, but really had to follow Jo-Beth, who'd reap a profit from her cargoes. He ran toward his motorbike just as a prostitute left Billy's trailer and cursed her customer.

Rick jumped onto the Ninja and sped away as Jo-Beth's car left the trailer park. He followed her car onto Church Street, turning off the headlight and keeping a distance. Just as he passed Heaven's Way, his phone rang.

Lucy-Jane.

But his phone showed Jo-Beth's name. Should he answer the call or force her to tell him about her business deal? Sure, she'd tell him. But better to step up to her after the deal and yank the money from her hands. Of course, he would tell Lucy-Jane what he'd done so they might celebrate.

"I'm happy."

Those were the first words to Lucy-Jane after he made love to her at Devil's Point. They were sitting on the sand naked. The October breeze cooled his skin as he puffed his cigarette and the Atlantic waves crashed against the shore.

After his mother at last divorced his father, he danced naked near a lake and sang "Hallelujah to the Lord." She moved to Nashville and would take him to concerts almost every week. Amid music he didn't understand, he'd hold onto her hand. Why were the crowds yelling at the performers? He'd steal beer from the man jumping up and down beside him. On Sundays, they'd attend church and a bully would yell at everyone from the stage. He really didn't understand the man's words or his fury but to be sure, he avoided him and his voice.

And whenever his head ached as if about to crack open, his mother would hug him and kiss him. He didn't like his mother calling him Ricardo Maria Collins—what kind of name is that—but he still liked her voice. He'd call her Isabella rather than Mom. Hell, if only life would really remain like that.

But his father returned after divorcing his second wife, Jo-Beth. He took Rick, not to the concerts, but to football games, where the fighters in armors and helmets boxed each other with their shoulders but sometimes their fists. Rick didn't like the fights and preferred the concerts. His father would show him how to change the motor oil or replace the engine filter or the brake pads. When he learned to play the guitar, his father shouted at him just as the man in church did at the audience. And he avoided his father's bad breath and body odor like the devil. He'd stay in his room when his father returned from work smelling like motor oil. He'd avoid those darkened fingers when they reached for him. His headaches worsened after his father returned and he had to take painkillers. Why the hell did he have these headaches while others didn't? Neither Isabella nor his father could tell him, just that he had them even as a baby.

Now, the migraine attacked him just as he passed Eden's Joy. Yeah, he would've gone into the tavern to buy a drink if he weren't tailing Jo-

Beth and her profit. He was slowing down to take a painkiller when engines roared behind him. Two Road Kings sped toward him, one rider pointing a 9mm Intratec semi-automatic handgun, the other a 9mm semi-automatic rifle. Damn, the Vampire and the Werewolf.

His life fleeing before him, Rick cursed it. He and Lucy-Jane were just planning for a better future. A life where they would love each other on the beaches under the sun. A life without Jo-Beth and Paradise. A single bullet from either Mitch or Luc would end his revelry.

It's so not fair.

Rick dodged into an alley. A nearby display window crumbled and shards showered on the sidewalk. He shouted at the beggar who had extended his hands. Sidestepped the man. Knocked down a trashcan. Almost slamming into the wall. Papers were flying into the air. A cat shrieked behind him and scurried down the alley, while a shot echoed between the walls. Two bullets clanged as they hit the trashcan and the wall. He turned into another alley and parked the motorbike. After shutting off the engine he took out the crowbar from the toolbox and hid in the dark, waiting for the gangsters to leave. Should've bought a gun in last month's gun show outside town.

The engines roared among the alleys and he couldn't identify the direction of the sounds. A shot echoed between the walls. Someone screamed. Then, just the engines sputtering.

On a similar night five years ago, he was walking down an alley in Atlanta smoking a cigarette...

As the motorcycles roared out of the alley, the scent of gunpowder and garbage thick in the air, he rubbed his forehead and focused on the stench, trying to wipe away that Atlanta night's memory. Rotten mushrooms. Sour milk. Orange peels. Someone moaned while a breeze whooshed through the alley.

Rick returned to his Ninja and pushed it out of the alley onto Church Street. To the left, shards paved the sidewalk. A group of men and women huddled outside Eden's Joy chatting and drinking beer, some pointing at the shards. A siren moaned. While across the street a car passed by, the driver thrusting his head out of the window to gaze at the debris.

Rick called Lucy-Jane. But she didn't answer. *What's going on?* He was going to call Jo-Beth but decided to drive down Church Street toward Jacob's Café, hoping she had gone there for a cheeseburger and milkshake before selling the loot. He was about to leave when someone called, "Just a second there, night rider."

Sheriff Perry opened the car door, got out and walked toward Rick and said, "Awesome bike."

"Wasn't me. They tried to waste me also."

"Your license."

Rick took out his wallet and handed him the driver's license.

"How come I dunno you?" Sheriff Perry took his license and glanced at it, then at him.

"I've never been arrested."

"Only means you've never been caught."

"I haven't committed a crime."

"Turn around and face the wall."

"Why?"

"Because I say so."

Rick was trembling. That night five years ago when he was forced to become a man. He didn't want to turn around but Sheriff Perry's gaze pierced into his heart. He faced the gray wall next to the barber and squeezed his legs together. His knees shook.

"What're you afraid of? You think I can do anything I want, don't you?" Sheriff Perry said.

That night, he'd just finished his shift at the fast food restaurant and was strolling back to his apartment when an officer stopped him at a street corner, just as Sheriff Perry was doing. The lawman shoved him into the alley. Turned him toward the wall, where someone had drawn a phallus. As he stared at the drawing, the policeman frisked him, then pushed him against the wall and pulled down his pants.

The migraine numbed his pain with pain. He was lying on the ground. He got up, pulled up his underpants, pulled up his pants and walked down the alley.

In a similar alley facing the wall, with Sheriff Perry behind him, Rick shivered and his bowels moved but he controlled his bladder to avoid humiliating himself. Every muscle in his body was contracting.

"Maybe I can. Maybe." Sheriff Perry handed him the driver's license. "Go on. Get out of here. Go back to your lover or girlfriend or boyfriend."

He ran away from home at fifteen, left Nashville and traveled to Atlanta, where he worked to begin a new life. He changed his name to Rick Dougherty and applied for positions in male escort agencies but they wouldn't hire someone only fifteen years old. So he begged in the street for a while but when the drug dealers threatened to chop off his fingers and toes, he found a job in a fast food restaurant.

As Rick drove along Church Street and tried to wipe away the images of Atlanta, Jo-Beth's car left Charleston Diner's parking lot and stopped at the red light. Just like that, slipping in front of him. A police cruiser was straddling across two parking spaces in the lot. He parked his motorbike behind a car and waited for the traffic light to change. Inside the diner, two officers were polishing off barbecue ribs and gulping beer. He walked to the rear of the cruiser, stooped down, and took out a knife and just like that plunged it into the rear right tire and under the hissing cut along the rubber. After the air had escaped from the tire, he whistled and left. Sure enough, the headache was fading. Every time he slashed a police cruiser's tire, he'd save a few painkillers. The air would smell fresher and he'd tread lighter. Catharsis. Rebirth. Baptism by misdemeanor.

He'd never told anyone about the Atlanta incident, not even Lucy-Jane. One time, after they'd made love behind the bushes in the park, he opened his mouth to tell her about the specter haunting him through the years, to share in the one secret haunting his dreams and to seal their union. But no, in the end, he just kept the nightmare inside his bosom.

No, he'd tell her the secret tonight. To perfect their love.

After finding the ransom, they'd leave Paradise, his prison these past two years, for the island under the sun. He'd videotape their life there—drinking coladas and watching the sunset on the beach, dancing past midnight in the tropical clubs and surfing during the winter—and send the tape to Jo-Beth and he'd request a similar video from the hag.

When the traffic light turned green, Jo-Beth's car crossed Martyr's Way, into the dumpsite. He drove his Ninja across the street and parked it behind a tree.

Lucy-Jane had learned about sex not from Jo-Beth but through an affair with her history teacher. She was going to tell her mother about the affair, to relish in the latter's trauma. Too bad Jo-Beth found out before the girl had a chance to reveal it. After Lucy-Jane had told him the story, he fought to tell her about his ordeal, but he couldn't recount the colors and sounds and odors and sensations of that Atlanta night. He just couldn't relive the sky falling and hell rising.

While trying to dislodge the past from his memory's crevices, a crow on the tree branch called him back to the present. The wind lifted the stench out of the dumpsite and he had to cover his nose with a handkerchief Lucy-Jane had bought him. Her perfume wafting into his nose.

Jo-Beth opened the trunk, pulled out a small bag and flung it into the side of the garbage mound. A dog barked in the distance as the trash bags flapped in the wind. A minute later, she got into her car and drove away.

Rick, holding the handkerchief against his nose, rushed into the dumpsite after her car had left, stopping at the spot where she'd discarded the bag. He rummaged through the mound and found the black bag against several gray and white ones. While the dog barked, he pulled the bag from the mound and set it on the ground.

Something light, two items.

He untied the bag that reeked of blood without taking off his gloves. His heart drummed against his chest and he opened the bag but couldn't see inside. He shone the flashlight into the bag.

Two breasts.

He dropped the flashlight. His heart pounded and his head ached. But he didn't vomit. No crows were cawing. Only a dog was barking.

Several minutes later, he picked up the flashlight. Again beamed the light into the trash bag. The light highlighted the blood along the cuts. He couldn't recognize these breasts though he could Lucy-Jane's in his dreams.

Those weren't Lucy-Jane's breasts.

He held the flashlight with his teeth and retied the trash bag, his fingers trembling. If only he could maybe hold Lucy-Jane, her body warming his. Several minutes later, he flung the bag onto the mound. Leaving the dumpsite, he stepped on dung, but just continued to walk toward his Ninja before he puked.

Those really weren't Lucy-Jane's breasts.

CHAPTER 16 – JO-BETH

On Independence Day last year, Jo-Beth was picking up the dishes from a customer who didn't leave any stinking tips when Rick, her dear angel who had brought sunshine into her life, walked into Jacob's Café smiling at her. She'd prepared to suffer another day but through his smile she enjoyed the cloudless blue sky outside the diner. She left the dishes at the table, where the flowers' fragrance aroused her, and followed him to the booth to take his order. Outside, a bird was chirping. *Let me sing and dance for you.* His sparkling eyes deposited a seed of love inside her bosom that no devil could purge. Her life had taken a turn. He ordered a club sandwich and asked about her job and her life in Paradise. As she walked away to place the order, he pinched her buttock and she giggled. She gave him an extra sandwich and when he paid the bill, he asked her out. She accepted the date and while humming, "Oh, My Darling, Clementine," crashed into another waitress and knocked the dishes from her hands.

She left work early to buy a pink dress and went to the spa to prepare for dinner at Heaven Steakhouse. That night, he told her about his adventures in Atlanta, Houston and New Orleans. After finding out he'd arrived just a month ago, she volunteered to show him around town. After dinner, they walked around St. Davis Square and she showed him City Hall. He gave her his number and asked her to call him, then kissed her on the cheek before returning to his hotel. That night, she dreamed of marrying Rick and starting a family, having a boy and a girl, of moving to Atlanta and living in a single-family house beside a lake. The next day, she bought a lottery ticket.

Six weeks later, Rick showed up at the diner and, sure enough, asked her out again. She accepted the date and took the rest of the day off to have a facial, a mud bath and a perm. She bought a new dress but wore the pink one again, to remind him of their first date. They had lobster and white wine at a restaurant near St. John Square just behind Babel Park.

Afterward, they went back to Rick's place and made love until daybreak. She called in sick and slept until noon. When she woke up, the birds were singing in the balcony. The aroma of fresh bread drifted into the room. Her wrinkles in the bathroom mirror stared at her. Why would Rick want her?

When she found out he had less than ten dollars and would have to leave his condo in a week, she thanked God for the providence, gave him five hundred dollars to buy new clothes and invited him to live with her. She didn't want him to meet Lucy-Jane, but needed him by her side every night. So she took the risk. When he thanked her, she embraced him and told him she loved him above everything else in the world. That was true.

Whenever she woke up alone, she'd jump out of bed to look for him, thinking he'd left her for another woman. The sun would cease to rise without him. She had to earn more so he'd stay with her and even marry her. Soon, her doctor prescribed Prozac again to control her depression. Then she took a second job and bought him the Kawasaki Ninja he'd dreamed of having since he was a teenager. She waited for him to say, "I love you," and propose to her.

As Gus's mistress, she'd saved about ten thousand dollars, but so within six months, she gave all the money to Rick. When the second job couldn't bring in enough money to keep up with the expenses, she thought about robbing convenience stores with him, like Bonnie and Clyde. That'd be something.

#

The evening that she found the slut's bra in her lover's bed, she collapsed onto the floor and wailed for several minutes before going to the kitchen to swallow her Prozac. Lying in bed, she couldn't sleep. She ripped apart the bra and itched to strangle her daughter. Whenever she closed her eyes she'd imagine them making love in bed. She lay awake until dawn, calling in sick at sunrise. The knot in her stomach drove her to take more Prozac. She'd expected Rick to leave her and suspected he was sleeping with her daughter. The bra sneered at her. Rick was deserting her just as her mother had done when she was bearing her father's child. She pulled a knife from the rack. Just a stab to earn peace for eternity.

Why had the same shit repeated again and again, after decades? A roach; she was a roach.

Her mother, her father, her therapist, Gus Davis, and now Rick. Everyone took turns deserting poor her. She, like everyone else, only wanted happiness. But she'd lose Rick just as she'd lost everyone else. She couldn't hold on to him anymore than she could Gus Davis. And life would end without him. She drank a can of beer to fill the void in her stomach. But it didn't. At that moment, she resolved to kill him and then herself.

But on Sunday, when the Bostonian said Sheriff Perry had found more body parts, Jo-Beth no longer had to kill him or herself. Like having solved the problem last night. But of course she left the Church of Paradise. After passing the Sunday brunch crowd across the street, she got into her car. Several boys were playing *Angry Birds* on their tablets and leaning on her car, but she shooed them away and drove into the street where a pigeon waddled away from the front tire. She really ought to leave town. But no, she still had to return home.

She'd leave this hellhole only with Rick.

When she slammed against the steering wheel, the horn blasted through the quiet street. A bulldog barked at her as she drove past a colonial with a raised porch. Approaching the park, she checked for police cruisers. None. So she edged her car into the park and surveyed the surrounding. No one in the park. She parked in her usual spot and tiptoed toward the trailer, her heart banging against her chest.

She opened the door. She peeped into the trailer. No one. She tiptoed into the living room that reeked of bleach. That spot in front of the couch; she still imagined Lucy-Jane lying there. Jo-Beth stepped into Rick's bedroom and picked up her daughter's bra, which she'd torn into four pieces. Tears again rolled down her cheeks.

Oh, Ricky, my dearest Ricky, I need you.

Lucy-Jane had taken Gus Davis from her and was going to steal Rick. She tolerated the slap in the face, but wouldn't allow the slut to seize her only reason to live. No, the girl had crossed the line.

This meant war.

#

Jo-Beth stepped into the bathroom, which reeked of bleach, blood and guts. The fifteen bags of her daughter's body parts in the tub prevented her from stepping into it and taking a bath. She took the bottle of

Prozac from the cabinet. Maybe she ought to swallow the whole bottle and end the nightmare. But she didn't have the strength to commit suicide. Even more, she didn't want to die next to her daughter's body parts.

God, grant me the courage to change the things I can.

Last evening, having found Lucy-Jane's T-shirt in the bedroom, she swigged whiskey. Outside, Billy cussed when he passed the trailer.

At 7:00 p.m., she went into the bathroom and vomited into the toilet. After rinsing her mouth, she called Rick. But he still didn't answer his phone. Must be having dinner with Lucy-Jane. They'd probably be going to a motel later. In the kitchen, she sharpened the knives and stabbed one into the stinking cutting board, vowing to rid the world of the slut. She cried. Could Rick hear her? But even Billy the clown didn't knock to check on her. Nobody gives a damn if she lives or dies. Toward sunset, she wiped her tears and cleaned her face of mucus in the bathroom. She raised her fist to punch the face in the mirror, but when her knuckles reached the glass, she just cried. And this time, even the tears abandoned her. She sat on the toilet, stared at the ceiling light. What ought she to do? She pressed "1" on her phone but ended the call before the ring.

Oh, miserable me.

Jo-Beth took the bottle of Prozac and pressed it against her forehead. Then opened the bottle and counted the pills. Then put the cap on and flushed the toilet. At 9:00 p.m. in the kitchen, just as she picked up a glass to take the bottle of Prozac, the lock clicked.

Oh, Ricky.

She dropped the glass and got up, banging her knee against the table leg and bending down in pain for a second. But she rushed out to the living room to embrace her lover, her jewel.

The door opened. Lucy-Jane entered.

Jo-Beth stopped in the middle of the living room and almost toppled onto the floor. That slut had stolen her lover, had destroyed her life. Not once, but time and again. And so she regained her balance as blood rushed to her arms and legs. Her chest heated up. She charged at her daughter, who turned her head just in time to receive the fist.

Jo-Beth threw her body at her daughter. They knocked down the desk lamp and the end table and crashed onto the floor. Lucy-Jane struggled underneath the weight but couldn't break free and she bit the mother's forearm. Jo-Beth pulled her arm away. Grabbed her daughter's neck with both hands. She squeezed and squeezed and squeezed.

Oh, Ricky, I love you. I love you so much I'd do anything for you.

Lucy-Jane gurgled. The girl's fists pounded her ribs and the finger-nails dug into her arm. But she squeezed and squeezed and squeezed. Trying to squeeze the pain, the anguish, and the fear from her body. Trying to squeeze the misery and the failure from her life. She squeezed and squeezed until Lucy-Jane's fingernails released her arm. Then, she squeezed for five more minutes before letting go and wiping the sweat from her forehead with the back of her arm.

Ricky, I love you.

She closed Lucy-Jane's eyes and went into the kitchen, opened the re-frigerator and took out a single-serving frozen pizza, inserted it into the microwave oven and pressed for two-minutes. While the microwave was heating the pizza, she made iced coffee. Sitting on the stool she cut the pizza into quarters. As she ate the pepperoni pizza and sipped the coffee, Lucy-Jane was lying sideways in front of the couch, her head twisted to-ward the front door. Just dispose of the body in the woods. But just a second, the police had discovered body parts in dumpsites, landfills, and local parks across Paradise in the past month.

After finishing the pizza, she took out the pack of ground beef and put two handfuls into the pan, then grabbed a package of sloppy-Joe fla-voring and mixed the powder with water. After cooking the ground beef for three minutes, she drained the oil and mixed in the sloppy-Joe sauce, cut two slices of tomato and three rings of onion and put them on a hamburger bun. When the ground beef simmered, she added the patty.

Jo-Beth took a can of beer from the refrigerator and returned to the stool. While eating the sloppy-Joe burger, she studied Lucy-Jane's fea-tures. As sluttish as when she was alive. She drank the beer to down the food and took another bite. When she had finished the burger, she took a shower in the tub.

Ax or saw? The circular saw would work better.

#

Jo-Beth should've dumped the bags last night so she could bathe now. But no, she'd have to finish her work before relaxing in a hot bath. Putting away the Prozac and cleaning her hands, she changed to a T-shirt and jeans and tied her hair into a chignon. She grabbed a bag...

God grant me the serenity to accept the things I cannot change...

Jo-Beth was fourteen when her father came into her room and mo-lested her. At first, she didn't know what he was doing but endured the pain. But when her mother ignored her complaints, she turned to her father for comfort and looked forward to holding and kissing him. He would love her and wouldn't abandon her as her mother had.

Then her belly grew and her friends congratulated her for being pregnant and asked about the father. The boys in school wooed her. She'd flirt with them but wouldn't sleep with them.

When her mother threw her out of the house, she cried for two days in the front yard and pleaded for her father to rescue her, waiting for him to come and say how much he loved her. She apologized for her sin and asked her mother to forgive her. But the door never opened. Her father never came to rescue her. He abandoned her just as her mother had. She loitered through the streets and alleys of Charleston to beg for food. For several days, she stayed under a bridge just two blocks from home, waiting for him to sneak out and bring her food. But he never came. She went to a shelter, where she waited for her father to reclaim her. Five months later, after she'd given birth to a son, she put the baby on a church's front steps.

After a homeless man had tried but failed to rape her, she slit her wrist. But she failed to kill herself. As she was recovering in the ward and eating the meatloaf and mash potatoes, she looked for a knife to try again after leaving the hospital. But she started an affair with a social worker and abandoned the idea.

A year later, finding out her father had died of AIDS from visiting a prostitute, she sought out the woman and thanked her, asked for a picture and had kept it ever since. She hated her father not so much for raping her as for abandoning her. As for her mother, she never knew what happened to her.

… courage to change the things I can…

After she'd loaded the fifteen bags of body parts into her car, she drove along Church Street toward the dumpsite beyond Martyr's Way. She stopped outside Eden's Joy. Get a Bloody Mary. No, better finish her work before taking a break. Soon after she'd passed the tavern, screams echoed through the street and display windows on both sides cracked and the shards collapsed onto the sidewalk. When two motorcycles roared down the road, she drove into Charleston Diner at the corner of Church Street and Martyr's Way, parked the car and went in to have a strawberry sundae while sirens screamed and police cruisers sped past the diner. After finishing the sundae, she bought a chocolate milkshake before hitting the road.

In the dumpsite, Jo-Beth checked around for vagrants rummaging through the garbage. Only a dog was barking nearby. She took from the backseat the bag with her daughter's breasts and flung it onto the garbage heap. In front of the garbage she sipped the milkshake. Then left.

84

When she reached the landfill along Martyr's Way, she parked her car just inside the fence. After taking the bag with the head, she walked past a trash pit and rounded the garbage heap. A refrigerator was leaning against the trash. She opened the door and threw the bag inside.

While strolling away and sipping the shake, a thump startled her. She dropped the shake, twitched around, searching for crows and rats among the heap. Only three dogs roamed near the fence.

She hurried away, glancing back every fifteen seconds. Then another thump. A refrigerator door closed. She dashed away from the heap and ran beside the pit until she reached her car. As she started the engine, a figure waddled out of the heap. She backed up her car, exited the landfill and sped down Martyr's Way.

CHAPTER 17 - ERNST

Ernst met Lucy-Jane at the end of March, when the Canadian wind had just left Boston. He had taken three days off without traveling, after helping a multinational conglomerate buy a biotech startup in Somerville and signing the contract the day before. On Wednesday, after baking a green tea Swiss roll, he drove down Route 128 South under an overcast sky. He and his brother used to picnic under autumn foliage beside Walden Pond, the red maples reflecting in the still water. But on that March day, the trees were leafless. At Wellesley College, he parked the car just as a group of students crossed the lot, backpacks over their shoulders and books in hands. With the air cold and moist against his face, he took his backpack and walked across College Road toward Lakeside.

His brother had dated a Wellesley sophomore while studying at Boston University and would visit her every weekend. After they had broken up during the spring of 2001, his brother continued to visit the campus on weekends. Ernst tagged along to ease his brother's pain. The latter would stand at Tupelo Point under the gray birches and survey the sails racing in Lake Waban, and begin to talk about how he and his former girlfriend had walked hand-in-hand along Lake Edge Path. His brother would stop in mid-sentence and turn to gaze at the Galen Stone Tower rising into the cloudless azure sky. What was the girl like? He couldn't assemble his brother's words into a story. He couldn't understand his brother's feelings. A gray stillness flowed through his heart.

His brother graduated later that year and went to work for an investment bank in the World Trade Center. Ernst didn't visit the campus again until his brother died a few months later on 9/11. He returned a week after the disaster and visited the campus about once a month, strolling along Lake Edge Path under the sweet gum's orange-red foliage. His brother and the girl hand-in-hand, what would they have been thinking and feeling? On Green Beach, with sails in the water, he looked for the girl who had broken his brother's heart. Before the white birch, squirrels crouched folding their hands but Ernst looked past them toward Tupelo Point where weeping willows no longer swept the lake and sweet gum foliage no longer colored the water. The previous September, young couples whispered under the shade while the lake murmured a distant tune.

Now, beside the pepper-bush blossoms at Lakeside, he ate an eggplant sandwich and drank carrot juice. How fragrant the sweet gum in autumn. But no sails dipped into the lake to brave the March wind that incited ripples against the shore. When two students walked past and scared away the squirrels, Ernst finished his carrot juice and strolled along the lake toward Tupelo Point. The sun warmed his skin though a breeze lifted from the lake. He searched for a sign to guide him ever since his brother passed away. Two years ago, he walked on the same path but under the summer sun, when he met a student studying by the lake and they talked about her major, neurobiology. He inquired about the functions of the neocortex and the temporal lobe and she explained the vision's ventral and dorsal streams. She inquired about discounted cash flows and he explained various ways to value a startup, including the founders' characters and skills. Before leaving, she gave him her phone number. But he never called.

He walked toward Tupelo Point past the dogwoods' red twigs and the birches' white barks. Would he meet another girl? He only came upon squirrels along the way. Toward the right, a bird soared above the Galen Stone Tower across the ashen sky.

Across the lake, a figure stood at Tupelo Point. He squinted to identify the tree but when a breeze brushed on shore, her hair rippled under the white birch. He drew near. Her cheek pink against the blue-green water, the same blush as that of the neurobiology student. As he approached, she turned to gaze at him as if expecting him. He found the signpost.

She was Lee-Ann for the past two months, but now, Lucy-Jane. At Tupelo Point, she talked as if she had known him all her life.

"I want to leave Paradise," she said.

"I'll help you." He told her about losing his brother on 9/11.

They passed the Slater International Center and strolled along Lake Edge Path toward Green Beach while the breeze continued to frisk her hair. At the beach, shoulder-to-shoulder with her under a white cedar whose scale-like needles swayed to the wind's rhythm, he searched among the grayness above the water for an image in his dream.

She grasped his hand. As the wind whispered and the lake rippled, he sniffed the air's moisture, her hand warm and soft against his fingers. Time passed. Let the moment last forever. For the past eleven years he had been wandering around Lake Waban looking for her. This girl. He had come to know each gray birch, each white cedar, each sweet gum and each turn on the Lake Edge Path before finding her.

That evening, beside his apartment's sliding door, under the purple twilight he ironed his shirts and trousers. Beyond the balcony the bare maples around the common area, their branches' shadows matched the wind's rhythm and jitterbugged on the ground. Their dances that of the bare trees along Lake Waban. Amid the wind's hissing, Lucy-Jane, her pink cheeks reflected against the turquoise lake and gray sky. Was he dreaming? But the steam hot against his face pained him as no dream could.

Ernst turned to the photo of his brother at Tupelo Point. Who would have talked to Lucy-Jane if the World Trade Center hadn't collapsed? The phone jingled on the coffee table. He pressed the iron onto the trouser to deepen the crease as steam hissed past his face. The phone rang again. He pushed the iron along the trouser leg. The phone rang a third time. He stood the iron on the board and pick up the phone from the coffee table. After sipping the chamomile, he answered the phone.

Lucy-Jane's voice chimed through the phone speaker.

"I want to hear his voice before going to sleep," she said.

He hadn't considered tuning his dream with her voice. He might already be dreaming. On most nights, the sound of silence would fill his mind and heart. He unplugged the iron. Her voice and her laughter caressed his heart and her gaze glided across his face as if searching for a mole or a scar. She thanked him, for spending time with her, for showing her Wellesley College's campus.

"I would've liked to study there," she said.

"Stay in Boston," he said.

"Would you show me around town?"

"Yes." He hung up his trouser. "Faneuil Hall, Harvard Square, The Common."

"Good night."

After cleaning the dishes, he rested on the easy chair in front of the balcony. He held the key chain she had bought him at the campus bookstore. That night, he didn't sleep.

#

In his apartment, Ernst sliced the Chinese mushrooms and diced the shrimps for his siomai as the melodies of Yanni's *Love Songs* emerged from the stereo. After mixing the chopped scallions, garlic, carrots and water chestnuts with ground pepper and sesame oil, he added the Chinese mushrooms, the shrimp bits, and marinated ground pork. He peeled a wonton wrapper from the stack and put a spoonful of the mixture in the center. Then gathered the edges around the filling as he pleated the wrapper and flattened the top. After making twenty, he put them into a steamer, lowered it into a pot of boiling water and set the timer for twenty minutes. He poured Worcestershire sauce into a container. Ida would delight in the siomai.

Eighteen years ago, bank robbers shot his parents while they were cashing a check. After he and his brother had moved to their grandmother's home, he learned to cook. The routine helped stabilize life after his parents had departed. At first, he made Swiss rolls and cheesecakes. When his brother and grandmother praised his cooking, he cooked lasagna and paella. Later, he prepared lunch and dinner for them.

After checking the siomai, he took out the bottle of Shiraz he had bought Mr. Demir, to show he didn't hate Middle Eastern men.

His father had killed a Turk while still in Frankfurt, never paying for his crime. Ernst only learned about the incident after the family had moved to Boston. The next day he ran away from home and stayed in Reza's place for a week. He confided him about the crime while sleeping on his friend's bedroom floor. When he returned home, he still despised his father for hating Muslims and for killing an innocent man. For four years, he didn't speak to his father. He didn't know why his father hated Muslims and didn't ask. After his parents had died in the bank robbery, he regretted not having forgiven his father.

He'd never be like his father.

After 9/11, he avoided Muslims and fled from his anger and hatred but at night, lying in bed, he would imagine concrete and steel collapsing onto his brother.

So, that's why he hated Muslims. I'm just as despicable.

After steaming the siomai, he packaged ten into a Styrofoam box. Once, Reza had wanted to try one until finding out it has pork. Ernst pushed the rack of apricot ginger scones into the oven. Had to mend that rift with his friend. He cooked linguine alla pescatora, steaming the scallops, squids, clams and mussels and mixing them into the Marinara sauce.

He had to exorcise the demon. He had to free himself.

He put two plates of pasta and two sets of utensils on the table. The empty chair. The untouched food. His brother would gobble down pasta while he sampled its texture.

After lunch, he left his apartment and drove to Akdeniz to deliver food and information.

#

What a relief Mr. Demir wasn't at the restaurant when he delivered the information. He had to continue to look for Al and the money, and Rick. Under the evening light, Ernst listened to Yanni's "In the Morning Light" while walking from the parking lot toward the sheriff's office. At the main entrance, the neon sign across the street cast his shadow onto the ground and four girls in miniskirts sang as they entered the nightclub. A police cruiser charged out of the parking lot, its siren blaring down the street. At the security checkpoint, he put his wallet and keys into the tray and passed through the scanner. The receptionist at the front desk was checking in a middle-aged couple from Atlanta waiting to identify their dead daughter. He gave a tissue to the weeping mother.

While he was signing in, the deputy pushed a drunkard through the front door and the man vomited onto the floor.

"Okay, no problem. The cleanup will cost you a hundred dollar," the deputy said. "We can add that to your fine."

With the receptionist's directions, Ernst took the elevator to the third floor and, stepping out of the cage, he shut his MP3 player, then strolled down the hallway where imitation gas lamps guided his path. Passing the deputy's office where a Scooby-Doo poster decorated the door, he reached the sheriff's office at the end of the hallway. On the door, Eleanor Roosevelt's quote greeted him: "The future belongs to those who believe in the beauty of their dreams."

Did the sheriff really believe in it?

He knocked three times.

"Enter."

In the office that smelled of sandalwood, the neon signs across the street flickered and cast intermittent shadows on the desk. The sheriff was on the phone but beckoned him to sit down on the chair before the desk. He pulled the chair and sat in front of the four hourglasses on the desk.

The sheriff rummaged through several piles of body part photos and picked one up, while speaking into the phone speaker. "I don't think they'd want to see what's left of their daughter. Just show them the bag of belongings, which we won't need. Be there in fifteen minutes." He ended the call and said, "Nasty business. Just between you and me, I like finding the bastards. But talking to the family member, that sucks. Are you looking for a job?"

"No, just the beggar."

"You mean the money."

"Same difference."

"Well," Sheriff Perry said, folding his hands, "in that case, it's been nice knowing you. Have a good day and enjoy your flight back to Boston." He extended a hand and Ernst stared at the veins on the back. *Shake it and leave or spit on it?*

"But I thought—"

"That's your first problem: always assuming."

"But you promised."

"That's your second problem: always trusting."

"But Al—"

"He's dead."

"You must be mistaken." *I don't believe you.*

"You want to see his head? Sorry, you don't have the clearance level." The sheriff grabbed the courier bag on a side shelf. "Please confirm this is your bag. But I need it for the investigation."

Ernst slumped in the chair. He picked up the second largest hourglass and slammed it on the desk and sand flowed from the top bulb to the bottom one. Lucy-Jane was waiting in an abandoned shack and praying for him to rescue her but he didn't have the money.

Sheriff Perry turned the hourglass around and wagged his index finger. "You've already used up five minutes. You don't get another fifteen."

"I need the money."

"We all need money."

"It's a matter of life and death."

"Who did you steal the money from? Some gangsters in Boston? Only criminals carry so much cash."

Ernst raised his hand to block the neon lights and told the sheriff he brought the money to ransom his kidnapped lover. Sheriff Perry, who was flipping through the body parts photos, dropped them and leaning forward, grabbed Ernst's lapel and pulled him onto the desk.

"Did you just confess that you've been lying to me? I don't like people lying to me, especially when it involves a crime."

"No, I didn't lie." *You're the liar.*

"Yeah, you did."

"I'm looking for the money. I just didn't—"

"Nice try. That kind of deception doesn't work with me. Who'd you think you're, coming to town and playing me for a southern fool?"

"I just want to rescue Lucy-Jane."

"I don't care if you're trying to rescue your ass from the alligators."

The sheriff pressed him against the table ledge and his cheek almost touched the hourglass and its inscription: *Carpe Diem.*

"You have to look for Lucy-Jane." Ernst struggled to free himself, but the sheriff's claw refused to loosen and the table ledge jammed into his chest.

"Don't tell what I have to do." The sheriff released him and typed on his keyboard. "Lucy-Jane McIntyre. Doesn't she have a mother? Why didn't she report her missing? One week already and she still didn't know her daughter's missing?"

"How should I know?" Ernst inhaled the sandalwood scent and straightened his shirtfront. "You have to."

The sheriff tapped the hourglass and said, "Your time's up."

"Will you look for Lucy-Jane?" *What kind of a policeman are you?*

"Get the hell out of my office. I don't want to see your face again."

The phone rang and the sheriff picked up the phone and pointed to the door. Ernst shoved away the chair. Incompetent fool. He itched to grab an hourglass and smash it on the floor. But no, he mustn't spend the night in a cell. *Find Rick and look for the ransom.* If only he didn't have to work with Rick, but… He turned around and as he walked toward the door, the sheriff said, "Shit, damn idiots."

Ernst opened the door and was stepping out, when the sheriff passed him and dashed out of the office and disappeared down the hallway.

CHAPTER 18 - WOLFGANG

In the humid evening air, Wolfgang walked to the corner of Heaven Avenue and Martyr's Way as a coupe passed. Across the street, sycamores shaded two abandoned trailers in the park where Kensington would be bringing the girls to meet her clients. Isaiah disguised as a beggar was leaning against a tree outside the park and drinking lemon water under the twilight. Farther down the street, three agents in a sedan were eating sandwiches and monitoring passing cars and pedestrians. Wolfgang had called in the agents monitoring the Church of Paradise and they were waiting for his orders to charge into the park.

An agent called to inform him Kensington had driven a van out of the Church of Paradise and stopped at the trailer park near Noah's Beach. Wolfgang told the agent just to monitor her, even when she and her partners were loading the girls into the van.

Two hours ago, the FBI laboratory, after analyzing the hair inside Grace's pump, had relayed the DNA report and a name: Kay Emil, the human trafficker who had eluded Wolfgang five years ago. The revelation confirmed his suspicion that the Elysian Fields was maneuvering behind the scenes. He didn't reveal that Mary-Lou Kensington is Kay Emil. Else, Isaiah would try to redeem his previous failure.

Who tried to kill Kay Emil? Kerstin? She wouldn't, even if she had come to capture the fugitive.

He unfolded Ida's drawing. She had seen the shooter and drew the picture. Would the woman come after her? Never, not Ida. He had to protect her. His agents were guarding Ida after the hospital had released the girl but he wouldn't relax until he locked up that woman. Kensington had probably seen her shooter so he looked forward to catching the model agency owner. A shadow flitted before him and he almost slammed into the lamppost, but tilted his body to avoid the pole. His palms sweated and his head fevered. He called the agent guarding Ida and only after confirming the girl was napping in her room did the breeze warmed his face.

While Isaiah scratched his cheek, Wolfgang wiped his palms on his pants and returned to the van to check the monitors surveying the abandoned trailer park. He took out the phone to call Kerstin but after dialing three digits, he cancelled the call and picked up his copy of Kahlil Gibran's *The Prophet*.

And stand together yet not too near together;
For the pillars of the temple stand apart,
And the oak tree and the cypress grow not in each other's shadow.

Were he and Kerstin standing in each other's shadows, stifling each other, preventing each other from growing?

He was flipping through the book unable to focus on any passage when his agent tapped his shoulder and pointed at a monitor. A silver van turned into the park and stopped between the trailers. He dropped the book, zoomed into the license plate and checked the registration in the FBI database. The Church of Paradise's van. He called the restaurant and sent an agent to the church to monitor the minister.

Kensington got out of the van, her arm bandaged, and surveyed her surrounding for ten seconds before checking her watch, lighting a cigarette, and tapping her foot.

Wolfgang directed Isaiah and the agents in the sedan to monitor the roads. He picked up Gibran's book and was about to read, when a beige camper pulled into the trailer park and stopped next to the van.

Kensington took a draft and threw away the cigarette butt. When she walked up to the camper, a masked man in polo shirt got out of the car to shake her hand.

Wolfgang alerted Isaiah and the other agents to prepare for action. As a siren blasted through the night and an ambulance raced down Martyr's Way, he assigned four agents, at his signal, to charge into the park and protect the girls.

When the masked man pulled out a briefcase from the front seat and put it on his camper's hood, Kensington stepped forward and reached for it but the man pointed to her van. She walked to the back of her van, opened the doors and shouted several times. Grace, her hands tied behind her, walked out of the van dragging a chain. Five other girls followed her as the chains on their ankles chimed.

Wolfgang dropped the book. Leaped out of the seat. Almost calling out Grace's name. His knee banged into the monitor stand knocking a remote controller onto the floor and he fell into his seat.

Grace, hold on, I'll be there soon.

He rubbed his knee and opened the holster beside his ribs, his fingers trembling.

Isaiah asked for permission to attack but Wolfgang told him to wait for the girls to enter the camper before rushing the human traffickers. If someone started shooting, the girls would be caught in the crossfire.

Isaiah ignored the order. And charged into the park. Wolfgang ordered him to stop, but Isaiah, gun in hand, continued to run toward Kensington and the masked man.

After directing his agents to secure the area around the trailers and protect the girls, Wolfgang left the van and charged toward the park, the warm air stifling him. A car was heading down Heaven Avenue toward Martyr's Way but the agents stopped it and told the driver to turn around. When Wolfgang reached the intersection, a shot echoed through the night and several crows flew off the tree branches. No, please, not Grace. He faltered almost crashing into a lamppost but grasped and leaned against it. After ordering two pedestrians to stay down, he crossed Martyr's Way and reached the fence. Near the van, Kensington was holding Grace hostage. Two agents at the park entrance pointed their guns at her but didn't approach. The other girls prostrated on the ground but he didn't find Isaiah or the mask man.

"I want to speak to your leader Demir," Kensington said, "Don't play any tricks or the girl gets it."

Wolfgang raised his gun. Blinking and clearing a speck from his eye. He wiped away the tears. He steadied his hands. Only one shot. No second chance. Why weren't there second chances? He aimed. He blinked. He fired. The shot rang for a second. His heart beat against his chest. The seconds stretched into minutes. His mind raced into the future, predicting the bullet's arc. Hit or miss? Would she make him pilaf? Would he bring lilies to her grave? Maybe spicy lamb gyro. Maybe roses. Then again, maybe neither pilaf nor gyro, neither lilies nor roses, just one steady step after another to the end. Walking into the coffin and resting in peace.

Mary-Lou jerked and dropped her gun, but before the agents reached her, she ran toward the landfill beyond the park.

Wolfgang ran along the fence, hoping the bullet hadn't injured Grace. He reached the entrance and kicked a tree's raised root and almost fell over, but steadied himself and continued to sprint toward the trailers. The fifteen seconds: an eternity. In his mind, Grace was playing the harmonica and drawing the magnolia tree, the notes and the strokes, the melodies and the colors. He passed the camper. Grace shivered on the ground, red smeared across her chin. He knelt down. He picked her up. He had failed his sister, but he mustn't fail Grace.

Please be all right. Please don't get hurt.

He wiped the dirt from her face and her dress. Blood had smeared her right cheek and shoulder and he checked for a bullet wound. His hands trembling and his fingers clinging with dirt and blood. She held his arm, steadied his hand, and said that she wasn't hurt, that she hadn't been shot, and that the blood belonged to the other woman. That he has saved her. He continued to search for the bullet hole until she repeated her words, which dispersed the image of his visiting the mortuary to identify her. He wiped the sweat from his face, relieved that he hadn't failed.

Not this time.

The agents helped the other girls and soon reported no injuries. He directed them to escort the girls, including Grace, to the hospital, to check for rape and internal injuries.

After opening the briefcase and finding stacks of blank notes, he asked the agents to check the fingerprints and the strands of hair in the camper against IAFIS and CODIS and the Interpol databases. Then he contacted the two agents running after Kensington. They had lost her among the garbage heaps and would continue to search the area.

When Wolfgang stepped on a paper scrap, he picked it up and found a note with a red rose insignia.

I can hand you your father's killer if you help me identify and eliminate the Red Rose.

Kensington, a.k.a. Kay Emil, had lured him here with the previous note. Could she really identify his father's killer? Was she really trying to eliminate one of her own? Or was the Elysian Field just setting a trap for him?

Ernst, who looked so much like his father's killer, had to be related to the man. He arrived at Paradise not by accident. Had Kay Emil planned everything?

While he was directing several agents to secure the van and the camper and take them to the nearest FBI facility, a shot boomed farther down the trailer park and birds scattered from trees into the sky. The echoes moaning an elegy. He ordered three agents to follow him but before they took a step, another shot echoed through the night, a reply

96

chasing after the initial mourning. Wolfgang led the men through the woods toward the park's northern part where no streetlights shone. The darkness inviting them to death. He took out a flashlight and trudged through the sludge listening for disruption in the wind. He approached a clearing where the stars shone on waist-high weed and the air reeked of manure. Shadows flitted on the weed and the breathing beyond the trees reached him.

He signaled with his flashlight. A beam of light replied. After signaling his men to watch the treetops and bushes beyond the clearing, he tiptoed toward the light. Just as he reached the flash, Isaiah stood up, his left hand holding his bloodied right arm and said, "We were ambushed." He pointed at the agent lying on the ground, the man's face half-buried in the mud. "We were chasing the scumbag..."

The muscles under Wolfgang's eye twitched and he raised his fist to punch Isaiah, but smelling the decay in the air, he just cracked his knuckles. After ordering the agents to secure the area, Wolfgang bent down and checked the fallen agent's pulse. None. Another damn mistake. More ammunition for regret. No disruption in the wind; no twigs cracking on the ground; no one was hiding nearby. He held out his hand and said, "Gun and badge."

"Boss—"

"Now."

Isaiah stared at the hand for several seconds before giving up his gun and badge. After handing over a watch, he trudged across the clearing into the woods.

Wolfgang stooped next to the body and held his head in both hands. At least, he saved the girls; he saved Grace. The stench of manure mixed with the fragrance of magnolia and he couldn't separate the two. He called for an ambulance and when the three agents returned, he directed them to go to the hospital and protect the girls, who might be able to identify Kensington's accomplices.

He should call Kerstin. He should report the loss and wait for his replacement.

He left the trailer park and walked down Martyr's Way until reaching Jerusalem Avenue where he followed the street to his parked car outside Akdeniz. The moisture in the air weighted down upon his skin as the death of the agent upon his heart. The heat was oppressing him and he had to flee from Paradise. To purge futility from his heart, he drove to Bliss Park and strolled along the boardwalk, the waves rumbling along the shore.

Near Noah's Beach, where several lanterns swayed near the water, he inhaled the night air that smelled of the sea. He sat on the sand to clear his mind, to regain his calm, to reassure his faith in humanity. Four teenagers carrying electric lanterns picked starfish near the water. The darkness beyond the surfs drenched him with peace. The same darkness that invited him to death.

He still had to nab those criminals. He still had to redeem his failure.

Eleven years ago on a winter day, after the policeman said over the phone that his sister had been raped, Wolfgang left his apartment and roamed the streets of Washington for three hours before locating the hospital. After fifteen minutes he entered the lobby. He checked the directory and paced the hospital corridor for another two hours before walking into his sister's room and embracing her and crying with her.

He could have stopped the rapist.

That day, he had vowed to stop rapists and murderers and psychopaths. Four years later, he joined the FBI to fulfill his vow, to prevent sexual assaults against men and women, boys and girls. He would roam the streets on dark nights and hunt for predators in the alleys. He would search through the FBI databases under the fluorescent light and reconstruct the crime before daybreak. He would dream of defending his sister in a dark alley or an abandoned building. And those dreams drove him through the night beyond a case's seeming dead end.

Earlier in the day, beside Kerstin, he was about to embrace her and say he no longer hated her brother, when Isaiah called and interrupted him. Anyway, someone had murdered Kerstin's brother after castrating him. He could neither punch that rapist's jaw nor shake the man's hand. His sister had married and was working at the United Nations to fight human trafficking. So why should he continue to box the phantom and let it poison his life? Now, on the beach, he took out his phone and pressed the digits, but after dialing the number, he ended the call.

After examining the watch Isaiah had given him—a Mickey Mouse watch—he rebuked himself for failing to identify the criminal. He called his agent to study Winston McDonald's file in the Interpol databases.

CHAPTER 19 -RICK

Not finding Jo-Beth's body-parts-mobile next to the trailer, Rick walked past the dwelling and through the woods to the other end of the park. Under the dim light, a squirrel bobbed along the tree trunk, a dance to celebrate the night. The air reeked of manure until he exited the park at Church Street, where he headed east toward Noah's Beach.

Nope, those weren't Lucy-Jane's breasts. No way, no how.

She wouldn't die and abandon him. He still had to tell her about the cop raping him. He still had to take her to the Bahamas. To live out the rest of their lives.

Passing the railroad, he crossed Bliss Road while the wind rushed out of the ocean and the air smelled of salt. A night he would make love to Lucy-Jane on the beach, if he could find her.

A pop, like a firecracker, startled him. But no one was around. No car was coming down the road. Just the wind and the waves.

On the boardwalk he strolled alongside the beach until reaching the stairs, then walked down to the sand. The waves roaring against the shore used to calm him and soothe his migraine. But tonight, the ocean's calls depressed him as he treaded through the sand among starfishes.

"I'm the mayor's mistress." Those were Lucy-Jane's first words to him as they watched the sunrise on the beach. If she hadn't known he was sleeping with Jo-Beth, he would've introduced himself likewise. He embraced her and their shared identities, similar grief and similar hope, the camaraderie of the underdogs, a fellowship in suffering.

Lucy-Jane began her affair with Gus Davis a year ago, when she was seeing her history teacher on weekends. In the school's yearend production of *Grease*, she played Sandy and received the Best Actress Award. When Mayor Davis shook her hand during the award ceremony, she knew he wanted her. The next day, she received a message from his assistant, inviting her to dinner at Heaven Steakhouse where he had reserved the dining hall for the night. She seized the opportunity. The mayor, more than her history teacher, could help her escape Jo-Beth's sty. That night, they ate dinner and danced in the restaurant, then went to a hotel.

After she'd begun an affair with him, Mayor Davis bought her a BMW and hired her as a summer intern in City Hall. She asked for a condo but he just rented an apartment in his aide's name and visited her every weekend. She'd return home two or three times a week to steal money from her mother. Sure, she despised the mayor's lips and hands but enjoyed her new lifestyle and urged him to divorce his wife. Of course, the lecher wouldn't.

After Rick and Lucy-Jane had begun their affair, they planned to blackmail the mayor for statutory rape. Rick hired a local gumshoe to take pictures of Davis and her. The dick set up surveillance cameras at her apartment and tailed the lovers to restaurants and shopping malls. But one night, the mayor's henchmen crashed into the private eye's office, broke his right leg and blinded his left eye. They even burned the office and destroyed all the evidence. When the gumshoe left the hospital in a wheelchair, he headed for the train station and fled town.

Lucy-Jane was going to skip town. But after Rick had found out the gumshoe didn't reveal his identity, he insisted that she stay in her apartment to avoid suspicion. He'd hide in her closet to protect her. But Mayor Davis never came. He sent a messenger to break up with her and she had to leave the apartment the next day. Rick soon found out the mayor had a new mistress about Lucy-Jane's age, but of course he didn't try to blackmail the mayor again.

Approaching Devil's Point at the tip of Noah's Beach, he longed to hold Lucy-Jane's body, kiss her lips and tell her how much he loves her. Just as he had done when she first introduced herself. The waves crashed against the reef and thundered in the darkness, the booms echoing around him. He'd locate the dough, he had to. Then the muscle below his right eye twitched and he search for shadows among the sand. He inhaled the sea air and picked up a starfish just as Lucy-Jane would every time she found one. She'd throw the creature into the water and wish it good luck. He held the starfish, hoping she'd appear to fling it into the ocean.

Then, he heard it. The clothes flapping. He turned and opened his arms. And waited for Lucy-Jane to walk into his bosom and kiss him. But he only embraced the sand swirling around him and caressing his face and hands.

Yet, something was flapping. Not his clothes. He closed his eyes and approached the sound. One step. Two steps. He walked toward the opposite shore. Something was flapping on the other side of Devil's Point.

He opened his eyes and a body lay on the sand, the hair fluttering in the wind, the eyes closed and the expression peaceful. A dried red rose on her chest. The woman seemed to be sleeping but blood was oozing from her forehead. Mary-Lou Kensington. Shot point-blank. Not Mitch and Luc's handiwork.

He backed away. The waves boomed against the shore. One step. Two steps. He turned and ran toward the boardwalk, the wind resisting his every step. He checked the sand for footprints but found none.

While the waves continued to thunder behind him, he ran through the wind toward the boardwalk. He tripped. His face crashed into the sand and he sucked in a mouthful before he lifted his head. He spat out the sand. Got up but fell again as he lifted his foot. He cussed and staggered to his feet. He shivered in the breeze, but ran toward the boardwalk. Sand had seeped under his T-shirt and pants and into his shoes but he ignored the granules. Just focused on running. When he reached the stairs, his shin kicked a step and he groaned in pain. He limped up the stairs onto the boardwalk, empty except for a squirrel munching a stick of French fry.

He crossed Bliss Parkway and the railroad track. After stepping into the trailer park, he stopped to catch his breath. Turned around to check for shadows in the dark. Seeing none, he dashed through the woods towards Jo-Beth's trailer.

Was that a sound? He kept running among the trees. A breeze brushed against his neck. And a force thrust him to the side and onto the ground behind the bush. He opened his mouth but a hand covered it. The image of the officer raping him in the alley replayed in his mind and he wetted his pants. He raised his fist and punched a tree trunk.

"If you want to live, keep quiet."

A man's voice whispered in his ear as he wriggled and kicked. He couldn't bite the hand covering his mouth. He couldn't free himself. A slap on his face and his head spun and tears rolled out of his eyes.

Oh God, no. Not again.

"I'm letting go of my hand. Don't bloody shout."

When the man released him, Rick just stared at the air and the officer's face kept flashing through his mind. He drooled as the man turned him to lie on the ground. A round-faced man with a mustache, his face bleeding, was tightening a bloodied handkerchief around his left arm. He'd seen the Englishman in the train station after meeting Ernst. The man pressed on his shoulder and told him to stay down. A squirrel jumped from a branch to the next tree but jerked in midair and went limp and it dropped onto the ground and twitched several times.

"Bugger." The Englishman ducked under the bush and raised his gun, which Rick hadn't noticed before.

Next to the dead squirrel, Rick psyched himself up, but his head was still spinning and a damn headache was really twisting his reasoning and emotions. Before he could focus, the Englishman dragged him toward Jo-Beth's trailer.

"We have to get out of here."

Rick opened his mouth but could hardly make a sound. So he just crawled along the ground beside spittle and cigarette butts. While the Englishman huddled down and moved sideways. A twig scraped his face but he kept crawling. They reached Jo-Beth's trailer and the Englishman, grasping his wounded arm, leaned against the stairs.

"I'm out of here. This has nothing to do with me." Rick found the cart Jo-Beth had used to move the body parts. After the breeze calmed him, he crawled up the steps and looked for a path to avoid the shooter's bullets. But before he reached the door, the doorknob sounded a note and dented. He rolled down the steps and landed facedown on the ground, the stench of urine nauseating him.

"I need your help," the man said.

"I need my help more."

"This is life and death."

"Mine."

"I just need you to deliver a message."

"I'm not a courier."

"Be a good Samaritan."

"I'd rather be a live scoundrel than a dead hero."

"I can reward you."

"How much?"

"One hundred dollars."

"You think I'm a beggar?" Rick raised himself to walk away but spotting a dead rabbit, he squatted and checked for shadows among the trees. The leaves nearby swished and an owl hooted in the distance. Damn annoying owl, which last year had hooted until late autumn.

"Stop fannying around. How much do you want?" The Englishman peeped through the trailer and aimed his gun at the darkness.

Rick flipped the bills in his pants pocket and said, "A thousand dollars." He would use the windfall to locate Ernst's bills. And if Jo-Beth had murdered Lucy-Jane, he'd need the money to avenge his lover.

Those breasts weren't Lucy-Jane's.

"That's a jolly expensive service."

"Not as expensive as your life."

"I don't have the money."

"Okay, that's fine. I don't want to haggle. I respect your decision if you believe your life isn't worth a thousand. Adios." *You can go to hell for all I care.*

"Wait."

"Like I said, don't want to haggle."

"I don't have the money with me. But if you deliver my message to the lady, she will pay you the money."

"Not sure I want to take that risk. Maybe I should just mind my own business."

The Englishman gave him a hundred dollars and his ring. "Here, take the money. That's all I have. You will get the rest when you find the lady."

This man was just a crook fleeing from the goddamn law or another crook. *Why should I trust your words?* Rick took the ring and examined it. "You know I'm risking my life, don't you?" I'll deliver the message only after receiving the money from that lady.

The Englishman scribbled on a piece of paper while it fluttered in the wind. Then handed Rick the note. "She will know this comes from me when she sees the ring." Instructing Rick to go to the hotel on Heaven Avenue at the other end of town. "I will wait for her outside New Heaven Cemetery. I will draw the shooter away so you can sneak toward the parking lot."

"Who's the lady I'm looking for?" Rick touched blood on the cart. The breasts in the dumpsite, those weren't Lucy-Jane's breasts. While petals showered from a nearby tree, he dropped to the ground and covered his head with his arms. And took a painkiller. Just as he slipped the note into his pocket, his phone rang and the ditty sounded through the darkness. He cursed Jo-Beth.

After two minutes, when no shots cracked the trailer's windows, the man said, "Ask for Kerstin, Kerstin Becker."

CHAPTER 20 - PERRY

Under the morning breeze, Todd pocketed the DVD starring Gus Davis and his mistress, the Georgian high-school girl, and got out of his car. At the ten-foot gate in front of the mayor's palace, two armed guards asked for his identity. He showed the arrest warrant and asked for the mayor. One guard took out his phone and whispered into it for two minutes before letting him through. He strutted along the driveway between two rows of elms. Would the next mayor inherit this palace beside City Hall, a bonus for fleecing the town? Sure, he'd lose a trusted lieutenant, but he'd like to have his deputy as the mayor. Two years ago, when he arrested the mayor's nephew for rape, Davis took him to dinner and hinted at a promotion to town treasurer if he should lose some evidence. Todd regretted not having brought a cassette player to tape the conversation so he could send the recording to the district attorney and repay the mayor for his kindness. But even with the evidence, the mayor would bribe the jurors and the judge into an innocent verdict. This time, Todd would put the mayor behind bars in the state penitentiary and end the legal jujitsu. He had sent copies of the DVD to the district attorney and her seven assistants. Just in case.

He probably wouldn't have enough money or clout to influence all of them.

At the end of the driveway, near a limousine, a mustached man in John Lennon hairdo and dark glasses wobbled down the marble steps and led him into the palace. Stepping into the Mafia boss's den, he touched the gun around his waist and said, "I like your mustache. And I like even more your hairdo." He had shot more than a dozen hit men during his career and today might add another to the trophy list.

"When did you start working for the mayor?"

"Just a month or so."

"Haven't I seen you somewhere before?"

"Not unless you've been to New Orleans."

"If you say so."

In the foyer, the mayor's portrait greeted visitors, and on the ceiling, a surveillance camera beside the chandeliers pointed at him. A valet asked for his hat but he waved the man aside and sauntered down a rose-scented hallway where more portraits of the mayor greeted him. At the end of the hallway, a maid handed him a glass of bourbon.

After calling his deputy to keep an eye on *Mr. Lennon*, Todd went through the cherry-wooded double door into the guestroom where several African masks along the walls confronted him. Passing two armed guards behind the door, he put the glass on the marble table. The mayor, cigar in his right hand and a glass of whiskey in his left, was wearing a wig and sunglasses and reclining on his easy chair, watching the stock market updates on the TV above the fireplace. Most stocks had risen on the economic news and the mayor was smiling at the TV screen.

"How's Mitch?" Todd stepped before the full-length mirror beside an African mask and adjusted his hat and tie.

"What're you insinuating?" The mayor flicked the ash off the cigar and sipped his whiskey.

"That you're a model father."

"Haven't seen him for years."

Todd picked up the newspaper and said, "Hiding your bald head and beady eyes won't help. Tomorrow, you'll be front page news."

"You brought a cake to celebrate?" The mayor pressed the remote controller and changed to another financial news channel.

"I guess you can call it a celebration."

The mayor called his stockbroker and bought a thousand shares of a technology stock. Just trade online and save a few dollars on commissions. Of course, Davis should worry more about adjusting to life in jail.

"Hate to ruin your day, but I got some bad news." Todd stepped between the TV and the easy chair and studied the Mayor's face. The cheekbones were protruding and the chin had receded.

"I don't harbor crooks in my house. You can search all you want. Hell, forget about Mitch." The mayor scratched his forehead with the cigar tip and held his hand over his cheek. "Come join me for lunch. We should coordinate our election campaigns. At least, we got to appear on TV together and endorse each other."

"I guess you've forgotten about your nephew."

"Oh, come on. That's ancient history. Let bygones be bygones. Right?"

I wouldn't believe you even if I have dementia.

The latest poll showed the townspeople favored Sheriff Perry's work more than Mayor Davis's. Todd picked up the glass of bourbon and toasted to the town's wisdom and said, "But I haven't forgotten about the budget you didn't approve. The ten officers I couldn't hire and the cruisers I couldn't upgrade."

"Don't blame me for the prostitutes and drug dealers on the street corners. You're the sheriff."

"I know how they prop up your side businesses. But not for long."

"If you've been tough enough on those beggars and vagrants, they would've migrated from town already. Now I got to hire several trucks to ship them to Charleston. You know how much that'd cost?"

"And I promise you I'll tell the mayor there where the increased population comes from."

"He'd be on state pension next year and probably cruising in the Mediterranean. Why the hell would he care about the city's demographics?"

"Well, you won't be in the Mediterranean anytime soon. Something to dampen your spirit and relieve you of your smugness." Todd took out the DVD and slipped it into the player. "I'm sure you'd be interested in this video." He warned the guards the video would have adult themes and they nodded and stared at the TV.

"Hey, I'm watching my stocks."

The mayor got up but Todd pushed him back onto the chair. Enjoy the show. When the screen showed the bedroom scenes, whiskey spilled from the glass onto the mayor's hand. He dropped the glass. Jumped up and ran toward the DVD player. He fiddled with the buttons, but couldn't turn it off. The guards approached, but Todd put up his hand and wagged his index finger in front of their faces. While he showed them the arrest warrant, the mayor ejected the DVD and stuffed it into the shredder.

"Hey Sheriff, I got this penthouse condo. Along Bliss Parkway. Ocean view. And I'm looking to sell."

"Can't afford it. Not enough bribes."

"Maybe it's haunted and I'm superstitious. Maybe I want to sell it for a dollar."

"Do you have a few more?"

"Now, look here."

"Not for me. I've sent half a dozen copies of the video to the DA's office. So maybe you have enough condos for her and her team." He finished the bourbon and threw the glass into the fireplace.

The mayor jabbed his cigar into the wall. "Bastard, you think you can leave just like that?" He signaled to the two guards and threw the cigar into the fireplace and they pulled out their guns.

"Of course not, I'm taking you with me." Todd called the servant for another glass of bourbon and requested extra ice, then turned to the guards and said, "You have wives and children?"

"What's it to you?" one said.

"What'd happen to them when you're behind bars?"

"Hey, Sheriff—"

"Cut the crap," Davis said, "and take him into the basement."

"He's going down for statutory rape and if he's lucky maybe murder also," Todd said.

"Seize him."

"Are you betting on him? You decide."

"I'm ordering—"

"Of course, maybe one of you bumped off the girl."

The guards put the guns on the coffee table and informed the mayor they were resigning. As they were leaving the room, Todd reminded them the prosecutor would contact them for their statements.

Todd collected the guns and adjusted his hair in the mirror. "Much better, right? Just you and me. Man to man."

The mayor leaned on the fireplace and wheezed, wiping the sweat from his forehead. After filling a glass with whiskey, he downed it in a gulp, then knelt before Todd and begged for mercy, saying he didn't kill the girl.

Todd grabbed him by the shoulders and threw him onto the divan. In the chair behind the desk, he lit a cigarette. "Okay, I'm listening."

The mayor massaged his forehead for a few seconds before spinning his tale. "On April 31st, after we... you know... the girl stayed for the night but left in the morning. She had an appointment. I think it was the New Hollywood Model Agency or some other outfit. So, you know, my chauffeur drove her back to the motel around ten o'clock. And that's all."

"Maybe you should be a screenwriter." Todd opened the door and took the glass of bourbon from the servant and, after thanking her, shut the door and drank the liquor.

"The motel staff must've seen her."

Davis might've paid the motel staff to lie.

Todd puffed out a ring of smoke while the TV broadcaster announced crude oil prices. The phone on the desk rang and he invited the mayor to answer the call. After picking up the phone and answering in monosyllables, the mayor requested Todd to let the chauffeur drive past the front gate and go pick up the Governor at the train station.

"Stay and wait for someone to arrest you." Todd thanked the mayor for the bourbon and left the guestroom. In the washroom at the foyer, he cleaned his face, adjusted his tie and tilted his hat, studying his teeth in the mirror…

Damn it, the rotten rat, that judge.

He returned to the living room and yanked off the mayor's wig and sunglasses. Then rushed out the front door and sprinted down the driveway toward the limousine at the gate. *Mr. Lennon* was arguing with the deputy, saying he would kick the man's ass.

While they argued, Todd walked up and finished his cigarette. After dropping the butt and trampling on it, he seized the man's mustache and yanked it out. The man doubled over and covered his mouth. Todd grabbed the guard's hair and pulled out the wig.

The deputy took the fake mustache and put it on his upper lip. "No wonder he has to steal from the city treasury. Employing actors and hit men."

"Well, the mayor's bored with his job and wants to play the chauffeur." Todd grabbed the actor's collar and pulled him up. "Nice try, Davis. Guess you want to pick up the Governor yourself. Well, your brother the judge is going down for aiding and abetting."

"Perry, I'll make sure Internal Affairs gets your ass."

"I've wanted to do this for years," Todd said. "It's a dream come true."

"Ah, boss, maybe you need to upgrade your dreams," the deputy said.

The mayor pulled away, but Todd pushed him against the limousine, cuffed his wrists and had the deputy get the surveillance tapes from the motel to check whether the chauffeur had taken the girl there on April 30th.

While the deputy took the mayor to the police cruiser, Todd took out his organizer and ticked off the task. The next one: to talk to Cassidy and give him a dressing down. He didn't want to go to the psychopath's torture chamber, but had to confront him about his failure.

He wouldn't wait any longer. He had to eliminate this liability before finding a replacement. If the preacher didn't fumble again, Todd would plant evidence to implicate him. He would rather jump into the water than have a numskull drag him into it. Damn it, Todd was seeking salvation but still have to dally with the fumbler.

Mary-Lou Kensington was still missing, probably arrested, maybe shot. Without her to take care of the logistics, the preacher would mess up the next transaction.

The night before last, Todd mused about sewing the button on Grace's dress and considered disbanding the ring. Not to flee from the agents but to release Grace from this snare. So she could roam the daisy fields under the cloudless sky. His nightmares would continue, but he would forsake his salvation and suffer hell to set her free. And this morning, when he learned of the fiasco, he typed the resignation letter and searched the Internet for a town in Alabama where he might shoot himself in the mouth. He loaded his gun for tonight's meeting, ready to shoot Cassidy in the heart.

But he had waited for a savior for years, and within days, Demir might shoot him between the eyes and save him from damnation. Another deal might just lure out the man. And he would need the preacher to coordinate the meeting.

He was stepping into his car when the phone rang. One of his men had found more body parts, in the dumpsite and the landfill and in several parks.

Damn it.

He called Cassidy and asked whether the buffoon had dumped any body parts in the local parks but the preacher denied having done so.

CHAPTER 21 - WOLFGANG

Wolfgang was reviewing an agent's interview with Pastor Cassidy, when the front door opened and Isaiah, who had disappeared from the trailer park last night, walked into Akdeniz's dining room and sat on a barstool. According to the minister, every deacon had access to the church and the van and he never suspected Kensington of using the vehicle for human trafficking.

The minister was probably covering up and trying to avoid a scandal.

Wolfgang had the agent watch the church and the minister and he continued to monitor New Hollywood Model Agency and the phone lines and waited for Kensington to appear and lead him to her accomplices. And maybe tell him the address of his father's killer.

After the agent had left, Isaiah adjusted the lilies next to the tap and said, "I know she's Kay Emil."

"You disobeyed my order. Again. But worse, because of your mistake, Sam died. Do you understand what that means? His life, gone. Do you understand what it means for his wife and children, for his mother?" Wolfgang put a photo of the dead agent with his family on the counter. This morning while brushing his teeth and practicing yoga he had searched for the words to comfort the wife.

May I come in? Can we talk? Is this a good time to talk? It's about Sam. It's about your husband. I have bad news. I have some very bad news. I'm sorry. I'm very sorry. I'm really very sorry. Here are Sam's belongings.

"I know you know," Isaiah said. "But you didn't tell and if I didn't check with headquarters—"

"Have you ever considered your actions and their consequences?" Wolfgang poured him a glass of cranberry juice and picked up the photo to examine the smiles in front of Magic Kingdom.

"If you want to fire me, just say it."

"You still don't understand, it isn't about you losing your job, it's about Sam losing his life."

"I shot that guy in the right hand. How the hell am I supposed to know he's ambidextrous?" Isaiah drank the cranberry juice and went to the middle of the dining room to adjust a table that had rotated forty-five degrees.

"You're reckless."

"You hesitated."

"You're suspended."

"Do you think I care about a goddamn suspension?"

"The problem is you don't care about a goddamn anything."

"Okay, just say it."

"I don't want to see you."

"Just say it."

"I should send you back to Washington."

"You're still pissed at me about the Red Rose incident." Isaiah kicked down a chair and walked out of the restaurant. He crashed into an old lady and when he extended his hand, she slapped him. Wolfgang walked out to help her and Isaiah marched down the sidewalk.

#

At the hospital entrance Wolfgang grasped the Styrofoam box for five minutes before pushing the revolving door and entering the lobby, where a young couple was complaining at the reception desk and the receptionist was chatting on the phone. Inhaling the disinfectant-scented air, he climbed the stairs. When he reached the third floor where several nurses rushed a gurney to the operating theater, he forgot the room number. No one was at the nurse station. He passed through a doorway. Wait, the room is on the second floor. Rushing through the swinging double doors, he went down the stairs and at the bottom, kicked a gurney's wheels and toppled it. After straightening it up and putting the sheets on top, he stomped down the hallway but didn't find Grace's room. He asked a janitor for direction, but the man didn't speak English. When he was about to try German, a hand landed on his arm.

Grace greeted him in T-shirt and jeans. He opened his mouth but no sound came out and he just handed her the box. She invited him to the room she shared with two other patients. One was pacing around the room dragging her intravenous stand, the other watching a soap opera and eating a raisin oatmeal cookie. When Grace opened the box, he asked her to try the pilaf and chickpeas.

"Today, I'm checking out." After breaking the wrap, she took out the plastic fork and spoon.

"I know."

"Have you caught them?"

"I will."

Wolfgang picked up the pitcher next to the bed and poured her a cup of water and she drank to wash down the food.

"It's good."

"I made it."

"Will you teach me how to make it?"

"This and others."

While she scooped another spoonful of rice and ate it, he opened his knapsack and pulled out the pair of sneakers he had bought her, then put them down and walked to the window to avoid her gaze. Outside the window, the sun had cast the shadow of the hospital onto the building across the street where the windows reflected the sky and clouds and the sea and horizon. A lone sail drifting across the horizon. He had sailed with Isaiah on the Chesapeake Bay, but those days had scattered among the ashes of time. Now his left knee ached. Could he still challenge the gusts and surfs?

The fragrance of Grace's hair stirred him. She put the half-finished pilaf on a counter next to him.

"He was my first man."

"Please cry."

"Would you feel less guilt?"

"No."

In April of 2001, as Wolfgang and his sister sauntered along the Tidal Basin under a shower of cherry blossoms, she held out her hand to catch the petals and vowed not to let the rapist destroy her future. And she had succeeded. She worked in the United Nations to fight human trafficking, she married a man who loved her and she had a boy. On that day, he also vowed to shed the burden and march toward a new tomorrow. Now, he had to offer his team members' families sympathy.

Grace finished her lunch and brought her dress to him, showing him how the rapist had stitched on a button. He studied the knots and thread pattern on the backside, admiring the workmanship. Even in his dreams, he would recognize the fiend's handiwork.

After she had returned the dress to her bag, he carried her belongings to the nurse station. She checked out. He drove her to Bliss Park and they strolled along the sycamore path. The same trees and sky, and the same air and waves. In another five days, would he be gunning down the rapists and killers or lying in a dark alley?

Glancing at the surfs in the ocean, Grace slipped her hand around his arm. She wanted to write and conduct concertos and symphonies, to immerse in the melodies and forget about the world and its evil.

"I want to lend a hand," she said.

"You did."

"I still have the invitation."

"No."

"Mary-Lou would remember me."

"Never."

"I can go back and help you track their location."

He held her by the shoulders and said, "Please don't."

"I refuse to just sit and be a victim."

When they arrived at Akdeniz, she praised the floral arrangements and he promised to introduce her to the artist. Before the poster of Lake Louise, its surface reflecting the glazier, she revealed her peace and joy. While he poured her a glass of soymilk, she checked the menu and promised to make him pilaf.

"I have your other shoe."

"And the strand of hair?"

"Thank you."

"I was hoping—"

Grace embraced him. She kissed him on the cheek and drank the soymilk.

Wolfgang turned from her face to avoid reflections of his failures in Paradise and Frankfurt and Washington. Just as Kerstin stepped through the front door with Ida, and said, "Something urgent came up. We have to leave earlier."

He embraced Ida. She held him. Tight. So tight that he should defy Kerstin. But he only kissed the girl on the cheek and promised to give her a conch and take her to Rome after her therapy.

CHAPTER 22 - PERRY

After the officer had pulled the trash bag from the landfill's garbage heap, Todd opened the bag and picked up the severed arm. Under dusk's dim light, he examined the cut and noticed the hesitation mark.

Might be the Georgian girl's arm. The hand and fingers were the same sizes. But the cut...

An amateur was trying to imitate Mitch and Luc: a circular saw had cut this arm, not the gangsters' machete. Todd dropped the arm into the bag and walked around the garbage heaps to check for clues.

Damn, a copycat was glorifying the gangsters' methods.

He grasped Cassidy's twisted mind. But this copycat? Al's killer might have dropped the hacksaw and used a circular saw but a criminal would stick with his most comfortable weapon. He told a lieutenant to request the STR test and compare the results against the Georgian girl's profile.

Another sleepless night.

While the trash bags flapped in the wind, in his car he ate the barbecue rib sandwich from Paradise Burger and embroidered the magnolia petals on the handkerchief. He had stitched four flowers and only needed one more. If only he could give Grace the handkerchief. But the FBI agents had either escorted her home or taken her to Washington for an interview. Still, he would embroider it just for her.

Before the transaction Todd had put on a hood and gone into Cassidy's dungeon to check on Grace. Agent Demir had rescued her from Billy and his gang. Would he rescue her again? As he thrust the key into the lock, her breathing seemed to whisper in his ears. He shut his eyes and pressed his ear against the door. After a minute, he pulled the key out of the lock and left the dungeon.

Now, the agents had rescued Grace and she had returned to her life. Perry had taken something from her and couldn't return it or reverse time. He would accept punishment but never surrender to any agent, not even to Wolfgang Demir, if he should be one.

Grace's breaths whispered from that night to this moment. Her hair's fragrance was also wafting through time. He would never see her again but would finish the embroidery to celebrate her freedom. She had escaped from the hell that he couldn't.

Finishing three petals, he put down the embroidery and checked his organizer. The next task: to talk to the halfway house director, the gay couple's manager. He pulled out an hourglass and put it on the dashboard. Fifteen minutes, he would finish this task in fifteen minutes.

Earlier in the day, he called the director, but she had to take a teenager who had attempted suicide to the hospital and brief the police on the incident. Now, as she talked on the phone, she mentioned the boy's name when referring to Luc. Todd waited for her to drink some water. She told him the gay couple went to Paradise to look for their adopted son Luc and stop him from killing his biological father, whose identity she didn't know. The couple had adopted Luc fifteen years ago and raised him as their child. When the five-year-old boy killed cats and dogs, they took him to a psychiatrist. But the boy continued to mutilate squirrels and birds, and fought with other children in school at least once a week. In the sixth grade the school expelled him. The parents sent him to a specialized school, which helped him control his behavior though he remained anti-social. Then, last fall he left home with only a letter informing the foster parents that he would kill his biological father for abandoning him. After Todd had requested a list of residents and workers who had left the halfway house during the past two weeks, he thanked the director and promised to find the gay couple's killer.

The delinquent must've bumped them off when they came to stop him. He didn't dismember their bodies probably out of some minute attachment.

Todd had to locate Mitch and Luc and though he didn't find them in the mayor's palace, Davis must be harboring them. He would search the mayor's other homes. Davis had posted a million-dollar bail and left the jailhouse, but four officers were tailing him to prevent him from escaping to the Cayman Islands. Todd would wait for the mayor to meet his son, then lock both behind bars. When the last grain passed through the hourglass funnel, he marked another task done, took out his notebook and reviewed the next task: meet Lucy-Jane's mother, a Jo-Beth McIntyre, and squeeze information from her.

Night's aroma roused Todd as he drove along St. Jude's Way past the crematorium. He mumbled the questions to pry the mother's thoughts. Cassidy didn't know the daughter, but said the mother serves in his church and is a grade-A knife thrower. And several church members whispered that she had a jobless young lover, a Rick Dougherty.

He picked up the handkerchief from the passenger seat and smiled. He was crafting Grace the gift. But could never give it to her.

But why not? He could find her address and send her the handkerchief.

But she didn't know him and wouldn't want anything from him and he didn't want to frighten her.

At his usual parking space outside Paradise Burger, he scanned the restaurant for Lily-Rose. Maybe, she had quitted. Earlier, while he was waiting for the burger, she had asked him for a date tonight but he said he had to work. If she saw him she would ask again. She was living on the edge and he would persuade her from smoking pot and selling her body and guide her away from the pit. But she wouldn't listen to him even if he were her father.

Todd was about to step out of his car, when Dick in silk shirt and leather loafers, emerged from the restaurant with three bags of food. The homeless man was whistling and skipping.

Lily-Rose wouldn't even give the bum free coffee.

Not seeing her in the restaurant, he bought a cup of cappuccino and said to the cashier, "You must feel generous tonight, giving the bum free food." The man showed him a hundred-dollar bill and said the homeless man had bought three barbecue rib sandwiches, two large French fries and a large soda.

"You sure that isn't counterfeit?"

"I just thought he found a wallet."

"Or robbed an old lady."

"Hey, Sheriff, I just work here."

In the dining area, two teenagers groped each other in the back. If Lily-Rose were working, she would throw them out. Of course, she had tried to kiss him while he was eating.

In a booth by the window, a middle-aged woman with hair on her face and crow's feet around her eyes was reading a letter. He put an hourglass on the table. Five minutes, he would give her five minutes.

She was putting the letter in her purse when he took it. He scanned it with his phone and returning it said, "I apologize for disturbing your night." He would review the love letter later but now studied her expression to construct its content.

"I wasn't doing anything."

"Would Rick need you back soon?"

When she dropped the cup and coffee splashed across the table, he wiped the spill with a pile of napkins while the letter trembled in her hand.

"Was the letter from him?" He gave her his cup of cappuccino and wiped the coffee droplets from the hourglass.

"Did you say Rick?"

"You must want to go back to him right now. Don't worry. It won't take long."

"Nope, he isn't home."

"Oh, is he working late?"

"Do you know where he is?"

"He must be worried about Lucy-Jane."

"What? Why would he... No, no..."

She dropped the paper cup but he caught it before the coffee spilled, then pulled the hourglass toward him.

"After all, he must love her like a daughter."

"A daughter? Nah, she isn't my daughter. She isn't, I tell you."

"Can you explain?"

"The slut."

"Why didn't you report she's been kidnapped?"

"Kidnapped? Did someone kidnap Rick?"

"Did Rick kidnap your daughter?"

"I didn't know she's been kidnapped."

"Then, where's she?" He handed her the cup of cappuccino.

"I mean, yeah, I found out later she's been kidnapped."

"I see. But how come Rick knew about it last month?"

"Did he?"

"Didn't he?"

"You got to help me find him."

"Were they close?"

"What'd you mean?" She banged the cup on the table and the cover flew off, the coffee splashing onto her hand.

"It seems," Todd said, "the kidnapper contacted him rather than you. Maybe the criminal knows something we don't." She knew her lover was sleeping with her daughter. Maybe she kidnapped her.

"No, no. No." Her hand reddened. She tightened her fist and the vein bulged on the back of her hand. "I couldn't reach him."

"And when was the last time you saw her?"

"Might something have happened to him?"

"Last week?"

"Maybe they also kidnapped him."

"Do you feel hot? Maybe it's the coffee." He pushed a pile of napkins toward the red hand.

She wiped the sweat from her forehead and her neck, and said, "Do you know how I knew she's been kidnapped?"

"Contrary to popular belief, I'm not a psychic. I hope that wouldn't lessen your confidence in my ability."

After opening her wallet to reveal the driver's license and a picture, she pinched a piece of folded paper and pulled it from the fold. "Got this last night. Yeah, last night. Then I knew she's been kidnapped. Before, just thought she was sleeping with one of her lovers."

"I'll need that list of lovers." He was about to take the note when he recognized the woman in the picture. His mother in a white dress was posing in her bedroom, a room he had learned to forget. He seized the wallet before Mrs. McIntyre folded it and when she pulled away, he gripped it and said, "How'd you get this picture?"

"She's my hero."

"Your daughter's kidnapping must've screwed your thinking. May I suggest counseling?" Todd gazed at the hourglass his mother was holding and seized the one on the table and almost smelled her scent. "She was a prostitute."

"I know," she said. "My father visited her quite a few times. And she gave him AIDS."

"Oh, now everything makes sense." He released the wallet and took a napkin to wipe his forehead. Another nutcase.

"That's why she's my hero. That's why I kept her picture. Every time I look at the picture, I'd thank her for avenging me." Tears rolled down Jo-Beth McIntyre's cheeks as she took out a picture of a bald middle-aged man. "I hate him." And she put it to her cheek.

Todd turned the hourglass in his hand. The bald middle-aged man who visited his mother after she had contracted AIDS. He bought Todd this hourglass after the previous one had cracked. Todd should've warned him but didn't.

After grabbing the folded piece of paper, he jumped out of his seat and ran away from the lunatic and his mother's picture. His arm hit a trash bin and the hourglass almost flew from his hand. Mrs. McIntyre called after him but he ignored her and charged out of Paradise Burger and inhaled the warm air while sweat poured down his back and images of his nightmares swirled around his head.

He pocketed the hourglass and was unfolding the piece of paper when his deputy called to say he had found Mary-Lou Kensington's body in Noah's Beach.

Damn Cassidy, the sick bastard.

CHAPTER 23 - RICK

After handing the Englishman's message to the blonde lady Kerstin Becker and receiving the cash, Rick left the hotel and took out his phone to call Lucy-Jane, but when he found her name and number, he just stared at the screen.

Oh, Lucy-Jane, how I wish... When he opened the trash bag in the dumpsite, he had recognized the birthmark on the breast. Yes, he'd kissed the birthmark on Lucy-Jane's left breast more than once. On Halloween, when they made love at Devil's Point, he hadn't revealed his secret. Hadn't told her about the rape or shared his fear and anger and hatred. Now, he wouldn't have another chance.

Nope, those weren't her breasts.

Stopping by a liquor store, closed about two hours ago, he threw a trashcan through the display window and grabbed a bottle of daiquiri. In an alley behind Eden's Joy, he lit several newspapers and threw them into an abandoned building. On a trashcan he drank the strawberry daiquiri while the flame rose through the floors. When the migraine refused to leave and a homeless man crashed out of a window with rags burning, he threw the bottle into the flame and went to the dumpsite, where he somersaulted into the air with his Ninja. Still he didn't relieve his headache or heartache.

He went to the cliff he and Lucy-Jane had made love in early November. The magnolias were blooming but he couldn't share the fragrance with her anymore. The water below reflected the sky. He stripped, screamed and jumped off the cliff. The air rushed at him, then the water smacked his face and he plunged into the wet silence. His heart thumped inside his head and Lucy-Jane's voice chanted sweet as a lark's melodies. He remained in the water until his head spun. He surfaced for air, drifting on the water, waiting for the current to carry him into the ocean.

Half an hour later, he swam toward the shore. He should forget Lucy-Jane and just look for the ransom. Yeah, he should skip town after locating the money. And maybe go to Atlanta, Dallas or New Orleans and seduce a rich lonely woman, or just travel to the Bahamas and enjoy life. After tracking down the money, he should retire to a tropical island.

But he couldn't let go of Lucy-Jane. Jo-Beth had taken away the only person he'd ever loved, torn away a piece of his heart and smothered his future. Well, she'd have to pay and pay a hundred-fold. He got out of the water and faced the heaven and swore to avenge Lucy-Jane's death. He'd give up his life in the Bahamas to torture Jo-Beth's mind and soul. And revenge would baptize him into a new man.

Returning to the cliff, he imagined shooting the murderer between the eyes. He wouldn't allow her an easy death. No, he'd terrorize her mind and heart before her final end. He'd design a death worthy of his hatred and grief. And yet, he might just finish her with a bullet or a blade. His head pounded as the migraine seemed to split his skull. He took out a painkiller. No, he wouldn't take it. The pain would strengthen him.

He wrote a note:

Thirty-thousand dollars. St. Peter's Yard. July 4, 2012 at 9:00 p.m. You know it's about Lucy-Jane.

Then went to the trailer park and slipped it under Jo-Beth's door.

#

Rick was handing out Ernst's picture to the bartender at Eden's Joy when his phone crooned out a jingle. He answered the call and said, "Lucy-Jane?"

His beggar friend cleared her throat and informed him Ernst had just left his building at the corner of Jerusalem Avenue and Abraham Boulevard. Rick thanked the beggar and after promising her the reward, left Eden's Joy.

He had to find the ransom and though he couldn't spend it with Lucy-Jane in the Bahamas, the money would finance his revenge. Jo-Beth had created a living hell for him and he'd return the gift. He'd have to pay a few officers to carry out his plot. And he'd maybe have to buy a semi-automatic handgun to haunt and hunt Jo-Beth.

After lighting a cigarette, he puffed out a jet of smoke and stepped out of the alley onto Abraham Boulevard, where the streetlights sparkled under the gray sky, but crashed into a mumbling idiot. They fell onto the ground. He landed on his buttocks and the man on the right shoulder.

"Damn it. Do you have eyes?" Rick got up and rubbed his buttocks. He'd freaking torn his jeans. He reached for the cigarette, but pain drilled into a spot behind his right ear and he squeezed his head with both hands to alleviate the headache.

"You." The man grabbed his T-shirt and pushed him against the lamppost. "Who're you?"

Ernst's cheeks twitched and his lips trembled. Rick gripped the Bostonian's wrists and shoved him against a wall, then straightened his T-shirt, cleared his throat and said, "I'm looking for you." He lit another cigarette and exhaled into the idiotic face.

"Al's dead."

"Yeah, I saw his head. Looks pretty sad. But he sure asked for it. If he can't defend his turf, then he ought not to take such a big bite."

"Now what?"

"Like dah, we hunt for the money. In case you've forgotten, we still need the money to ransom your girl." Rick's heart ached as he mentioned her and raised his fist to punch Ernst, but just rubbed his knuckles and lowered his hand. After retrieving the money, he'd punish the Bostonian for Lucy-Jane's death. But now, he needed the moron to help locate the cash.

"But the deadline."

"The kidnapper called and we have five more days. So, let's get going and find the money."

"The sheriff's looking for Al's killer."

"Whoopee, now we can twiddle our thumbs and wait for the sheriff to rescue her. Should we go to the bar and have a drink?"

"I checked under the bridge, in the dumpsters, near the red light district, but I can't find anything."

"I know. It's dangerous."

"I love Lucy-Jane with all my heart," Ernst said. "You've no idea how it feels like to love someone and wait and wait and wait as she gets deeper and deeper into danger."

Rick raised his hand to reach for the idiot's neck but even as his fingers twitched, Lucy-Jane's laughter checked him. He exhaled to relax his abdominal muscles, puffed his cigarette until his heartbeats settled down. Still, Lucy-Jane's detached breasts, they glared at him and his head throbbed behind his left ear. He took another painkiller, before puffing the cigarette again.

How the hell did the idiot know her real name?

"Your pendant—" Ernst said.

"Don't even think about it." Rick had been wearing the pendant ever since his mother gave him the memento for his first birthday. Once, a thief had reached for it, but he knocked out the man's front teeth and drove him away.

"I once knew someone—"

"Why'd I care?"

"Something important."

"Not to me."

"You may."

"But, I don't." While puffing his cigarette, Rick strutted down the sidewalk toward the red-light district where he would rummage through several shelters. Walking up to his Ninja, he unlocked the toolbox in the back seat, taking out a crowbar and wiping it against his jeans. Raising the crowbar, he exhaled a jet of smoke and said, "Had to be one of Al's beggar friends. I know each one by name." He wiped his sole on the motorbike's front tire.

"What's your relationship to Lucy-Jane?" Ernst said.

Rick passed Casino in Heaven, where a guard stood cross-armed and shouts emerged from the building. He opened his mouth to spit the truth in the fool's face—he ought to—but after considering the result, just said, "Come on. Let's grab something to eat before we kick asses." As soon as he recovers the dough, he'd tell Ernst how he and Lucy-Jane had made love on the beach under the stars. Yep, the truth, nothing but the truth.

"I asked—"

"I heard."

"But—"

"I've told you."

"I want you to look into my eyes and tell me."

"I don't want to look into your ugly eyes."

"I want to know—"

"Ask Lucy-Jane, after we find her."

Hey, buddy, I'm trying really hard to protect you from getting a wounded heart. Got it? So, like get smart and back off.

Rick threw the cigarette butt onto the sidewalk and crushed it with his sole. He knocked twice on the lamppost with the crowbar and walked away from the motorbike, passing a beggar who was vomiting into the trashcan.

"If you want to find Lucy-Jane, then let's go. If not, then go back to Boston and I'll find her myself." Rick supported the crowbar on his right shoulder while grasping the handle with his hand, as if he were carrying a rifle. Passing a restaurant, he smelled barbecue ribs. Should order a rack, but had to crash the beggars' dens before eating dinner.

"Are you in love with Lucy-Jane?" Ernst walked up beside him.

"Cut the crap."

"How'd the kidnapper know to ask you for the ransom?"

"Ask the kidnapper. Don't ask me," Rick whistled at a prostitute who was waving at a Mercedes-Benz. "If I could read minds, I would've found Lucy-Jane already."

"But—

"Focus."

"I have to know."

"Focus on saving Lucy-Jane," Rick said, covering his mouth and checking himself from mocking the Bostonian. "If you can't, get out of my sight. I don't want you to distract me." He coughed to cover his joy. But when he passed a couple kissing under the streetlight, Lucy-Jane's breasts again glared at him and he had to breathe in the warm moist air to relax his muscles. Inside a bar, men were singing, "For He's a Jolly Good Fellow." The music really sickened him.

"I love her."

"I heard."

"I'd do anything for her."

When the sky darkened, Rick pointed at a metal pipe lying near the gutter's opening and said, "Then, pick that up."

Ernst picked up the pipe and swung it, almost tossing it from his hand.

"Yeah, that's right. Be strong for Lucy-Jane." Rick encouraged the dupe to lead the charge into the beggars' den. He slowed down to keep an eye on the pipe, just in case it swirled toward him. The dimwit can't even swat a fly.

"How long have you known her?" Ernst held the pipe with both hands and swung it like a bat.

Not long enough. Rick tasted bile. He spat and spat but couldn't get rid of it.

"She never mentioned—"

A teenager with fangs and shoulder width hair stepped out of a side street, pointed his semi-automatic handgun at Rick and said, "Howdy. Drop the freaking batons, ladies."

Why hadn't the Vampire shot them before opening his mouth?

"We don't want any trouble." Rick lowered the crowbar onto the ground, his muscles twitching. Why the hell was the Vampire following him?

"But we do." Luc, whose mane fluttered in the night air and whose mouth was dripping with saliva, scratched Ernst's cheek with his semi-automatic rifle. "Look like you want a fight. Well, ain't it your lucky day."

The metal pipe shook for about five seconds before dropping onto the ground, the thump echoing in the side street. But the Bostonian's hands kept shaking as he retreated and his back hit the lamppost.

"That's a sweet girl. Come and have fun with us." Mitch the Vampire pointed the handgun into the side street. "In there, y'all."

Rick stared into the devouring darkness between the buildings. His arms and legs in a trashcan. His head sitting on a headstone. Better to have them in the ground or in the water.

But at least, Lucy-Jane died the same way.

Luc shoved him into the alley and pointed the rifle at his nape. That night, the officer had pulled down his pants. Rick staggered forward, the ground tossing like a raft in the ocean.

Run. It's the only chance.

An exhaust fan hummed beside the sketch of a phallus on the building wall. Ernst heaved behind him as Rick prepared to flee at the next intersection. Better to die under a shower of bullets than to have his flesh sliced piece by piece.

"Do y'all know that cowards die many times?" Mitch sprayed bullets into the exhaust fan but it continued to turn. "Damn useless gun."

"Fine with me. As long as I get to waste them a thousand times." Luc knocked down a trashcan and shot at a cat but it fled into a side street. The delinquent thrust his face in front of Rick and said, "Hey, you look nothing like me, brother."

"Should I?"

"Nah, why should you? We only share some freaking genes."

"Not that I'm aware of."

"Of course not, you dumb ass."

Rick gazed at Luc's cheeks and jaw as if looking into the mirror and they reminded him of his mother. Oh mom, you just knocked me off by giving birth to this bastard.

"How's Isabella?" Luc said.

"She never mentioned you."

"Of course not, she gave me up for adoption."

"I'm sorry."

"Too late for that."

"I can help you. Whatever you need."

"Don't expect me to call you 'big brother.' After tonight, she only got one son."

"I can get you money."

"What the hell you blabbering about?" Mitch grabbed Rick and shoved him away from Luc.

Poor Isabella. Miserable Rick. He smelled fried chicken as he side-stepped the overturned trashcan and sought a bottle among the trash to smash Luc's head. But no luck. The intersection was about two-hundred yards down the alley. *I can make it.* He used to run from bullets in Atlanta and New Orleans and he trust his legs. He really ought to walk another hundred yards before dashing for the street. But the closer to the intersection, the less time he had to dash down the side street before the freaking Vampire and Werewolf would reach the corner and gun him down. Ernst's legs probably had betrayed him and the police would be gathering the Yankee's body parts tomorrow.

Yeah, cowards deserve to die many times before their deaths.

Rick's blood pulsed through his arms and legs as the night deepened and a breeze blew through the alley.

I'm faster than that Bostonian. I know I am. It's now or never.

He lifted his left leg but Mitch grabbed his T-shirt and shoved him against the wall. His cheek pressing onto the concrete, just as he had the night the officer raped him. His head ached and his muscles convulsed as the gun barrel pressed against his jaw. When the officer's face surfaced in his mind, he thought about making love to Lucy-Jane at Devil's Point, her skin's fragrance mixed with scent of the salt in the air, her soft lips against his while the waves thrashed. He prayed for a quick death. Ernst was pleading and Rick cursed the coward.

Oh, Lucy-Jane.

"This ain't fun." Mitch shoved him into the middle of the alley where Ernst was shaking and the Vampire pointed down the alley with his gun and said, "Tell you what. I'm giving you a chance. Ain't I generous? Run. Run for your life."

Ernst convulsed and dropped onto the ground. The coward must've fainted. Rick spat at the face on the ground. He wouldn't faint. He'd run though a dozen bullets would catch him in the back. Mitch shouted at Ernst and kicked him about a dozen times. When the Bostonian didn't move, the Vampire sprayed a volley of bullets into the still body, then ordered Rick to run.

Rick spat again. He ran down the alley, toward the darkness. Had to reach the intersection before the bullets touched him. He was running away from home, being raped by the officer, meeting Jo-Beth, seeing Lucy-Jane outside the trailer, greeting her when he first moved into the trailer. His life passed before his eyes.

The wind brushed against his face, howled into his ears. His legs light under the starlight and the melody of "The Battle Hymn of the Republic." For a second, he was running in the Grand Canyon. But he smelled the fried chicken and returned to the alley. Running toward the intersection. The shots rang in his ears. The pain thrust through his body. He went down.

Oh, Lucy-Jane.

CHAPTER 24 - ERNST

Ernst dreamed of kissing Lucy-Jane on the beach. The stars sparkling in the sky and they naked on the sand. Her lips pressed soft against his and the waves hissed beneath her breathing. He drifted to another world as he made love to her.

He woke up. Isaiah slapped his face.

"Okay, Sleeping Beauty, time to get up."

A few stars twinkled in the sky but he lay on the pavement in the side street beside several pools of blood, the spot where he had fainted. But instead of Rick, Mitch and Luc, only Isaiah knelt beside him, shaking him.

"Mitch and Luc?" Ernst said.

"Exorcised. What else do you do to vampires and werewolves?"

"Glad I didn't see it."

"You're damn right about that."

"Thought they shot me."

"If it weren't for me, you'd be dead."

"Who're you guys anyway?"

"Sorry, you don't have the clearance."

"I'm scared that one day you might shoot me between the eyes."

"Possible, but unlikely."

"Not too reassuring."

"It's the truth."

"Did you see Rick?"

"As I've said before, I'm not in the lost and found business. You may want to hire a private dick."

"Is that his blood?"

"You're welcome."

"He may be in danger."

Isaiah sauntered down the alley, saluted a cat on the trashcan, and disappeared around the corner. A breeze wafted through the alley and the cat skipped down the trashcan and scurried into an abandoned house.

Ernst wiped the dust from his jacket and pants and left the pools of blood, running after Isaiah. But when he reached the intersection, the restaurant manager had vanished. He called after him and his voice echoed among the side streets. Several minutes later, he searched for Rick along the side streets, where a rat was bearing its teeth at a kitten, but he didn't find his partner and rival.

The joy, the sadness, the longing in Rick's blue eyes whenever he mentioned Lucy-Jane.

He's in love with her for sure, but are they lovers?

That question gnawed at his entrails. He had to find Rick, not to search for the money, but to answer that question. After retracing his steps along the back streets five to six times he walked toward his hotel. Outside a gambling parlor, cheers and groans chorused through the night. He cut through the air warm and humid against his skin. Lucy-Jane was calling him and he again tasted her lips. He would find her. He had to find her soon. Or he would collapse in the streets of Paradise.

After entering a pub around the corner, he ordered a strawberry frappe at the bar and asked about Rick, but the bartender hadn't seen the man since yesterday. Amid the voices bouncing around the crowded room, he tasted the frappe and called Rick, to find out whether he had made love to Lucy-Jane. But Rick didn't answer. Ernst had to know. Or he would keep guessing and arguing with himself. His stomach churned. The truth and nothing by the truth, even if it should slice and scar his heart. But, no, not really. He finished the strawberry frappe while the singer mumbled the lyric.

A young man in a pink shirt approached and touching his fingers offered to buy him a drink. He pulled away his hand and shook his head. He stepped off the stool and headed toward the door but stopped at the end of the bar and ordered a glass of cranberry juice. A prostitute near the bar flirted with a middle-aged man. How Lucy-Jane had danced on Harvard Bridge while a wind lifted her skirt. Under the Boston sun, a group of Ukrainian students walking toward Back Bay clapped and whistled as they passed her. He had taken a photo of her against the fleet of sails on the Charles, but left the file in his computer.

While he sipped the cranberry juice, a girl plopped down on the stool next to him, ordered a margarita and, her nose-ring touching his cheek, whispered to him, "Do you think the sheriff's gay?" She brushed back her hair, a strip of brunette amid the red hair, to reveal her dimples and blushing cheeks. "He doesn't seem to be interested in women." She put her elbow on the counter and her chin on her palm and stared at the bartender's feet. "Have you noticed it?" Her young face shaded with sadness beyond her age. When the margarita arrived, she drank a quarter and said, "You know, sometimes I wanted to tell him how I feel."

The day after they had met, Ernst took Lucy-Jane to the Kennedy National Historic Site in Brookline and they lunched in a café opposite Boston University's dormitories. Afterward, they crossed the Boston University Bridge and strolled along Memorial Drive, M.I.T.'s dormitories on the left and the Charles River sparkling under the sun on the right. Even now, in the crowded pub next to the nose-ringed girl, that day's breeze seemed to cool his skin again. Just pretend the girl was Lucy-Jane.

He'd soon be holding her body and tasting her lips.

"Maybe you're gay." The girl leaned over and studied his face. "You aren't local. Where're you from?" She finished her margarita and ordered a Tequila Sunrise.

On the last day of March, Ernst had taken Lucy-Jane to a steakhouse to celebrate her eighteenth birthday. As he was driving on Route 1 through Danvers, she said how happy she was and how much she loved him. She should stay. He would buy a house in Newton, just two miles from Needham, and they would live their quiet lives there. On weekends, they would go to Copley Square, Symphony Hall, Newbury Street or Harvard Square. On holidays, to Sturbridge or White Mountains. That night, after dinner, he bought her a chocolate ice cream cake and they celebrated her birthday in his apartment, drinking sparkling wines until midnight.

#

The nose-ringed girl, after sipping the Tequila Sunrise, nudged him and shoved her face in front of him. "You really queer, aren't you?"

"Do you know Rick?" What's Rick's last name? Where does he live and work? How long had he known Lucy-Jane? Had he made love to her?

"Does he like me?"

"Does he love Lucy-Jane?"

"Do you think the sheriff will notice me if I perm my hair and put on high heels?"

Ernst finished the cranberry juice and, squeezing between sweaty bodies, left the pub. Outside, the air had cooled but the moisture still clunk to his skin. A woman in mini-skirt smoked under the streetlight and took money from a middle-aged man. Outside an arcade, five teen-agers drank beer and teasing each other. And at a street corner, two girls giggled and whispered to each other while a musician played his guitar and sang "The Sound of Silence." Somewhere down the street, a group of men and women sang "Sha La La."

He had to find Rick and he had to find the money. *Oh, Lucy-Jane, hang on.* He ran down the street to flee from the laughter and the music, but at a lamppost, he bent over and vomited into the gutter.

CHAPTER 25 - ERNST

In the gymnasium, where kendo sticks lined the left wall, and masks and breastplates the right, Mr. Demir practiced yoga and moved into the *Warrior I* pose. Ernst passed several yoga mats to examine the floral arrangement on the windowsill. More lilies.

How to ask the man to help locate the money?

After fifteen minutes, Mr. Demir arose from the *Child* pose and said, "Thank you for the siomai and the information on Kensington." He was rolling up the yoga mat. "I shouldn't have—"

"What did you do to her?" I need her to find Lucy-Jane.

Mr. Demir stopped for a second and continued to roll up the mat. "Did you bring some wurst? Blood sausages are my favorite though I'll take liver."

"The beggar who stole my money, he's dead. And the money's missing."

"It's only money."

"I need the lousy money to ransom Lucy-Jane. That's what I mean by life and death." Ernst's voice stiffened as he mentioned Lucy-Jane, who was waiting for him, her savior. He wouldn't fail her. He had to rescue her. "I don't care about the money. If I did, I wouldn't be here in Paradise."

After putting the mat behind a tray of kendo masks, Mr. Demir splashed water over his cheeks at the sink and dried his face with a towel. He grabbed a bottle of water on the desk beside the doorway, twisted off the cap and took a draft.

Ernst took out the note with the banknotes' serial numbers. "I thought the information might help catch the kidnappers."

"Do you like the pilaf here? How is it compared to those in other restaurants?" Mr. Demir took another draft and wiped the sweat from his forehead.

"Please lend me a hand. I really don't hate Muslims." He lifted his arm to shake Mr. Demir's hand, not to bargain for the man's help, just to reach out to another soul. But dropped his hand before the proprietor turned around. He couldn't pierce the invisible barrier.

He'd probably spit on Ernst's hand.

"Okay, but why keep telling me?"

"I thought—"

"Did you think I was praying on the yoga mat?"

"No, but—"

"From what my Muslim friends told me, you're supposed to face Mecca."

"I'm sorry." He must've insulted Mr. Demir by labeling him a Muslim before learning about his past, his beliefs or his aspirations. "My father—"

"My father was beaten to death by man who looked like you."

The syllables hammered at his eardrums and the words seared into his mind. The note fell onto the floor while he shook away the image of his father beating the man to death.

No, my father didn't kill your father. Please, no.

"Don't worry. The man should be in his sixties by now. And he's probably still in Frankfurt." Mr. Demir left the gymnasium and walked into the corridor toward the dining room.

Ernst picked up the note and ran after him. Midway in the hallway where a Japanese lantern hung from the ceiling, Mr. Demir entered an office. When Ernst reached the doorway, the proprietor was in an armchair facing a computer monitor on the side table and had raised his hand, saying, "Thirty minutes. I give you thirty minutes."

Should he shake it or give him a high-five? Ernst opened his mouth to ask who had killed the proprietor's father but the words wouldn't come out. Stuck in his throat, checked by his tongue, muffled by his lips. Leave. Forget about the truth. But his legs wouldn't budge. He still had to save Lucy-Jane, his joy and salvation.

"What're you waiting for?" Mr. Demir rubbed his fingers as if asking Ernst for money.

"I only have a hundred dollars. I can go to the bank."

"What'd I want your money for?" Mr. Demir swiveled around in his armchair. "That's one minute. Twenty-nine to go. You're wasting my valuable time."

He studied Mr. Demir's fingers for five seconds before inserting the note between them.

"I have a favor to ask." Mr. Demir removed a can of Oolong tea from the cabinet. "Would you mind having dinner with a girl in a hotel restaurant? I don't want her to eat alone."

"The man who killed your father, his—" Ernst said.

"The girl, her name's Grace. Don't ask me whether she's pretty or not." Mr. Demir opened the can and scooped a spoonful of tea into his mug, picked up the kettle and poured hot water into it.

"My father—"

"Can you do it?"

"Sure, but my father—"

"You can tell me about your father when I retire. I have to help you find those bills." He returned to his armchair, put down the mug, opened his laptop and said, "Now, step outside and shut the door."

Steam whirled above the mug as Ernst struggled to wrest a question from his mouth, but his throat tightened and his tongue slacked.

"What're you waiting for?"

Ernst hesitated. He opened his mouth to ask for the killer's name, but just apologized and left the office and closed the door. Under the Japanese lantern he held his head with both hands for five minutes before walking down the hallway toward the dining room.

Ernst had to ask him. He had to know.

In the dining room, Kerstin was at the bar drinking altbier. When he sat next to her, she poured him a glass.

They drank.

Silence thick as molasses.

Amid the aroma of frilled lamb, he searched the wallpaper's floral-patterns for a word of wisdom, but found none. He waited for Mr. Demir to come out with the information. Or Isaiah to walk in and talk about the philosophy of nothingness and black holes. But the clock on the wall ticked away.

Why didn't they use a digital clock?

"An old boyfriend of mine just proposed." Kerstin finished the glass of beer. "On the phone. He is in Germany."

"Did he send an e-ring? Or, at least some e-flowers?"

"Maybe it would be good for Ida if I remarry."

"She'd want you to be happy." He refilled both glasses and raised his.

"To Ida," Kerstin said.

"To Ida and you and your happiness."

"I was building a wall."

"If we can build a wall, we can also tear it down."

"Maybe I am comfortable with the wall. Maybe I am scared to take it down. For years, it has protected me."

"When you see love waving its hands on the opposite shore, you have to risk jumping into the water and swimming across the channel even though you don't know how to swim, even though the water's freezing, even though an alligator's waiting in mid-stream." Ernst was shielding himself against reality with his words.

"Would I be myself without the wall? And would I have borne the pain of raising Ida? I do not know. I could not know."

"But you're yourself now, with the wall. And when you shed it, you'll be a new woman, still yourself."

"I hate roller-coaster rides. By the end, I usually just want to vomit."

Ernst scrolled through the photos in his phone and related to Kerstin how after his brother had died, he walked alone on a road among dusts and ashes until Lucy-Jane came along and showed him the clouds overhead forming lilacs and orioles and even the Mona Lisa. That was why he had to find her, to find part of himself.

"Have you talked to Sheriff Perry? You know, he once saved my late husband's life."

"I hope he can do the same for Lucy-Jane."

"Have you met Grace?"

"I will."

"You will like her."

"Mr. Demir is just inside."

"You know what is so attractive about her?"

"You just have to walk in there."

"You will, when you meet her."

"He's probably waiting for you to step in," he said. And he'll stop searching for the money once he sees you.

"And you will have to tell me."

What's holding up Mr. Demir?

"Promise me."

"My father killed Mr. Demir's father, a long time ago."

Kerstin finished her beer, refilled the glass and finished the second one in three gulps, the veins in the back of her hand wriggling as she grasped the glass.

"Will you tell him?" she said.

"Should I?"

"Are you ready to?"

"I want to tell him. For my selfish reasons."

"I wish I can lend a hand."

"I want to be his friend."

"And I."

"I'm scared."

"So am I."

Ernst drank his beer. How would Mr. Demir react to the news? The clock ticked. At Tupelo Point an angel had descended to protect him. The front door opened, a breeze caressing his face.

Lucy-Jane, my love, you're back.

He put down the glass. Slipped off the stool. Turned toward the doorway. Ready to hug and kiss Lucy-Jane.

A slender young lady walked in. Light footsteps. Sadness in her eyes.

Kerstin leaned forward and said, "Tell Wolfgang that Isaiah would take Ida and me to the train station tonight. Tell him I do not want to see him. Tell him to take care of Grace." She slipped off the stool and left as the girl greeted her.

You can't run away from your fear, not even if you bring Ida with you.

The girl's eyes followed Kerstin out of the restaurant, into the street, until the latter disappeared down the sidewalk.

"What happened?"

"You must be Grace."

"Let me talk to her."

"She's worry about her daughter."

"I have to explain everything."

"Have a seat."

"It's my fault."

Don't make things worse.

"What should I do?" she said.

Ernst grabbed a glass and poured her beer. "Drink this."

"I don't drink."

"It'll help."

She sipped the beer.

"No, you have to gulp down the ambrosia." He refilled his glass and invited her to sit down at a table, where the peonies bounced under the ceiling fan.

"I'm your date tonight," he said.

"I was planning to make pilaf for him."

"If you don't want to, you don't have to."

"No."

"I can ask Mr. Demir to come instead."

"No."

"What do you want?"

"Did he ask you to chaperon me?"

"Just say the word."

"It'd be my pleasure."

Ernst should excuse himself from tonight's dinner, to avoid staring at his food for an hour and not wanting to eat it, to avoid staring at the girl not eating her food. But he would keep his promise. After finishing his beer, he took her glass and emptied it. While she studied the table's floral patterns.

When Mr. Demir came out and greeted them, Ernst said, "Kerstin has left." The proprietor walked out of the restaurant and glanced around for half a minute before returning and taking a bottle of altbier from the bar. Then, he walked onto the terrace facing St. John Square and Babel Park, and drank the beer. Ernst refilled the glass with beer and followed Grace onto the terrace, and the proprietor said, "At least I have good news for you." Paradise Burger's manager had deposited into Paradise Savings Bank a hundred-dollar bill with a matching serial number. "So you have to have dinner with Grace tonight." He handed Ernst a note with the manager's name and the restaurant's address.

"You won't be able to join us?" In front of the door, Grace gazed at the back of Mr. Demir's head but the proprietor was studying the passersby near the fountain.

Ernst turned around to return to the dining room, but Grace was in his way and he scratched his ponytail. Two boys were running around the fountain.

"Your work's much more important," she said.

"Maybe, tomorrow."

"I don't want to interfere."

"No, it wouldn't."

Ernst drank the beer while Grace studied the floral pattern on the tabletop and Mr. Demir scanned into the street as if searching for someone.

He approached them but turned around and walked to the balustrade and studied the floral arrangement. Three tulips: one facing forward, another the left, the last the right. He touched the flowerpot and with his fingers traced the floral relief.

Ernst mumbled for several seconds and marched up to Mr. Demir and interrupted their silence. "The man who killed your father," he said, "is his name Niebuhr?" The twister would land, to sweep away his peace and joy.

Mr. Demir dropped the bottle of altbier onto the table and turned to him as if appraising Van Gogh's Sunflowers. The proprietor's gaze... Ernst cursed destiny for its child's play and searched for strength to defeat facts, truth and reality. Hot air wafted through the terrace as he dropped his glass.

The glass cracked.

Beer and shards splattered on the tile floor. He knocked down a chair and tumbled onto his right side, his palm and elbow hitting the floor. Grace reached down to help him get up. Beyond the balustrade, a man in striped short-sleeve shirt, the pianist at the Church of Paradise, stopped and while pulling his suspenders and wiping his scalp with a handkerchief studied the scene. When a lady in a floral dress stopped by, the pianist pointed at Ernst and chattered.

Guilt draped over Ernst and clung onto his skin despite his trying to fling it away. He pulled himself onto his feet. Sprinted out of the terrace beyond the balustrade. The pianist and the woman jabbered as he passed. He ignored Mr. Demir's call. He charged down the red-bricked path. His footsteps tapping along with his heartbeat. The hot air against his nostrils almost suffocated him. He knocked the ice cream cone from a girl's hand as he passed a poster urging the townspeople to reelect Sheriff Todd Perry. When a lady talking on the phone stopped in mid-sentence. When a boy bouncing a basketball followed him. When a dog barked at him and pigeons scurried away from him. He sprinted down Main Street. Turning into a side street, he stooped over a trashcan and panted while the scene of his father beating the man enacted in his mind. He wiped sweat from his face as if clearing guilt from his heart. But sweat and guilt continued to smother him. Ernst smoothed his hair with both hands. But strands still fell before his eyes. He shut his eyes. *Oh, Lucy-Jane.* His father's face haunted him.

Footsteps neared. Grace approached, her eyes soft against the shadows under the noon sunlight. Before she opened her mouth, he said, "What do you want to eat?"

"Mr. Demir would like to talk to you later." She put a hand on his arm. "I hope you two can—"

"Let's go grab a burger." Ernst bent his elbow to let her put her arm around his. *He can spit in my face some other time.* He staggered but Grace steadied him. He cursed his existence, then apologized to her.

Forget about the guilt. Forget about the misery. He had to find the thief. He had to retrieve the ransom before the kidnapper runs out of patience and harms Lucy-Jane.

"I shouldn't have come here," she said, "but glad I did."

After passing Mayor Gus Davis's poster with the red word *loser* across his face, they stopped to let six pallbearers carry a coffin out of a funeral parlor. Across the street, two girls no more than ten years old were singing an unfamiliar song, but that melody deposited peace into his heart.

"My father killed Mr. Demir's father."

"Let me talk to him. That is, if he's willing to talk to me."

If Ernst hadn't talked to Kerstin, he would tell Grace to seek her happiness, but now, he pretended not to have heard her words and shut his mouth. Just as he patted Grace's arm, a rear pallbearer slipped and fell and the coffin slanted to the side. Ernst pulled Grace away just in time to avoid the coffin, which wobbled for two seconds before the remaining five pallbearers again balanced it. The fallen pallbearer jumped to his feet to take his position. A *pallbearer* in Ernst's life had slipped and fallen and his world would collapse and his life would crumble if he failed to save Lucy-Jane.

"Everything will be alright," Grace said.

Was she referring to his situation or hers? "I like Yanni's music," he said.

"I prefer Kitaro. When I listen to 'The Silk Road,' I'd imagine myself riding a camel in the desert. Nothing but sky and dunes. Sand rippling down the dunes. And my mouth tasting the sand."

"You're a romantic."

"Just a daydreamer."

After the coffin had passed, Ernst led Grace across the street and said, "You know the feeling when a person you've been searching for a long time suddenly walks into your life?" Lucy-Jane at Tupelo Point was an angel against the blue-green water and gray sky.

"That sense of wonder, shock and excitement? As if you're in a dream?"

"I've been planning to buy a triple-decker in Newton, a quiet town outside The Hub, ah, Boston. Well, not so quiet anymore. But the house I'm interested in is beside a pond and has three bedrooms."

"I share a bedroom with my brothers and sisters and sleep on the upper level of a bunk. So having my own bedroom isn't very important. But guess having one would be nice."

Ernst would build a deck on the second floor to face the lake and on summer evenings, he and Lucy-Jane would dine there, watching the sunset. He would plant daffodils around the house and chrysanthemum on a path to the lake, a cherry tree in the front yard beside the driveway. And build a studio for Lucy-Jane to record her songs.

"Wouldn't have answered the ad and come to Paradise if Johnny wasn't ill with lung cancer," Grace said and leaned on him as they turned right at the corner.

Passing a liquor store before Paradise Burger, Ernst for a second thought Lucy-Jane rather than Grace was leaning on him and he almost stroked her hair just as he had after making love to his lover. But now chestnut rather than blonde hair was brushing against his shoulder. And Grace's eyes couldn't rouse the hope and vision that Lucy-Jane's lips had.

"I enjoyed working under the restaurant's chef," Grace said. "Even if I don't have a prayer of a chance to get promoted, wouldn't have quitted if not for Johnny's cancer."

He offered her money, not that he had much left after draining the bank account for the ransom, but she declined his help.

If Mr. Demir had offered to help...

After his brother had died, he only lived day-to-day and moment-to-moment like one domino pushing the next. He didn't expect next year to differ from the last just as he didn't tomorrow from yesterday. Though the seasons came and went and the stock market rose and fell. Until he met Lucy-Jane at Tupelo Point. Now, as he approached the restaurant, he prayed his dream wouldn't disperse. Grace, as if reading his mind, tightened her grip and huddled closer.

"You have to talk to Mr. Demir." Ernst was referring to the medical facility though Grace might link his words to her feelings for the proprietor. Still, she should seek happiness just as Kerstin should. And Mr. Demir would have to decide between grief and grief and pain and pain.

"Love isn't easy, is it?" Grace said.

"Life isn't easy."

"I'm glad."

"I'm not."

When he stepped into Paradise Burger, the nose-ringed redhead with a stripe of brunette hair was behind the cash register grumbling at a customer. No longer drunk. Last night's verve had fled from her face. Her eyes focused on empty space as she took the cash and counted changes.

When he asked for the manager, the girl filed her fingernails. He called the lady wrapping hamburgers in the back and repeated his request. The manager came out and said, "Are you complaining about Lily-Rose?"

"Just would like to know who used a hundred-dollar bill yesterday."

"Sorry, don't keep a ledger of bills and coins."

When Ernst took out a hundred dollars, Lily-Rose grabbed the bills and said, " Dick Wadlington, that stinking homeless bum." She showed him the surveillance camera video to confirm her words.

CHAPTER 26 - WOLFGANG

A robin was chirping on the sycamore branch when Wolfgang strolled under the tree outside the hotel room. Kensington must've arranged for Ernst to come to Paradise. With the bait, she would've bargained with him for her hunter's head, and probably handed him the Bostonian if he'd agreed. But too late. The assassin terminated her before she negotiated with Wolfgang. Now, he had to find the Red Rose.

Kerstin stepped into the patio that faced the back garden. "You don't have to take us to the train station." Her voice trembled in the warm air as a breeze caressed his cheeks.

You don't have to leave.

The muscles that had relaxed through the yoga half an hour ago tightened again. He opened his mouth but his jaw stiffened. The white clouds against the azure sky accompanied him as he walked up to a magnolia tree beside the patio. But neither the sky nor the tree returned his calm. At the farther end of the garden, a lady in the pool splashed water onto the man next to her as the robin flew off the branch.

He waved to Isaiah and Ida, who were walking out the side gate. To ease the knot in his stomach, he inhaled the flowers' fragrance. A squirrel bobbed past a stone eagle guarding the garden and disappeared into the bush beside the wall but he still tracked the critter through the twigs' movements. A shadow suggesting a phantom.

"Stay a few more days."

On his first date with Kerstin, after bumping into her in Frankfurt International Airport two days earlier, they sat beside the Rhine and shared their experiences growing up in the suburb while a finch chirped on a branch above them. That day, scattered clouds drifted beneath the steel-blue sky as they left a castle. Ida was singing a folk song he had heard growing up and memories of his Frankfurt childhood engulfed him. Joy and grief, laughter and tears, returned to him, even after four years.

Just a few more days.

"Maybe it's better for us to not see each other for now." Kerstin left the patio and stepped into the empty playground next to the pool and sat on a swing. When she and Ida visited him in Washington last fall, he had found them playing on the swings in Rock Creek Park and joined them.

"I think Ida would like to stay a few more days." He leaned against a pole as his arms and legs weakened. Under the blue sky, birds flew in formation, an arrowhead pointing east. He was swimming toward one bank and she the opposite.

"To think about how we want to move forward."

He didn't need any more time. He sat on the swing next to hers and tossed to and fro. "Do you remember the Croat painting by the Rhine?" On their date, they had walked along the Rhine with Saint Bartholomew's Cathedral on the opposite bank rising into the sky and he enjoyed that day more than any other time in Frankfurt. And Ida's laughter at Römerberg still warmed his heart.

She matched his movements and the two swings advanced and retreated together, while the man and woman in the pool laughed and splashed water at each other.

The swing reached the top of its flight. Beyond the wall, across the street, a circular fountain in the park spouted five water jets. "I still remember how happy Ida was eating wurst at Römerberg. She reminds me of my sister, when she was young."

"I cannot forgive my brother for raping Hilda." Before the swing stopped, Kerstin leaped off and landed on the mat.

I've forgiven him.

Wolfgang jumped off the swing and extended his hand, waiting for her to grasp it. His hand shook, weighing on his arm. And sweat wetted his palm. He waited as the sun descended and the shadows of the trees and poles stretched eastward. A lark landed on a nearby branch and chirped a melody the joy of spring and the peace of a windless morning.

Kerstin stared at his hand, then into his eyes and he considered the stranger before him. He advanced. She retreated. Keeping the same distance. Her breath disturbed the tweets.

"You're a good man," she said.

Let me be a good man.

"I have always feared walking into the darkness of my guilt."

We fear less when we have a companion.

"I watched my father get beaten. I couldn't prevent my sister from being raped." The moments flashed before him. In the alley, the man beat his father to death. At home, on the phone, the police told him his sister had been raped. Wolfgang waited for Kerstin to take his hand but if she wanted to fly to her Shangri La...

Where was the boundary between holding onto and letting go?

Kerstin turned and went back into the hotel room. She had plunged into the sea beyond his reach and he had extended his hand but she wouldn't take it, just continuing to flap her arms in the water. He wouldn't force her out of the water, but would jump into the sea beside her.

Wolfgang stepped through the sliding door to find Kerstin folding Ida's dress and putting it into the suitcase on the bed.

He would wait for her to hold his hand.

He picked up the framed photo next to a Bible on the side table and while he was studying mother and daughter in front of Epcot Center, Kerstin said, "Can you check the bathroom for Ida's medicines? I thought I took them out here but I couldn't find them."

You're too stubborn to spread your pain and agony. And you won't let me treasure them like diamonds.

In the bathroom, he found a bath towel on the floor, a tube of toothpaste on the counter and two toothbrushes inside a glass. Two bottles of medicines hid behind a Mickey Mouse hand soap dispenser he had bought Ida the last time at Disney World.

He picked up the medicine bottles and the soap dispenser and as he returned to the living room, Kerstin said, "Did you find them? They are most important."

After he handed her the bottles, she put them into her handbag and resumed folding the light-blue dress he had bought her last Christmas and said, "It hurts so much to love you."

"I'm sorry," he said.

"And I hurt you so much by loving you." She put the travelling bag inside the suitcase and picked up the photo on the side table.

"Forgive yourself." Wolfgang embraced her and kissed her on the cheek.

"Where's the book I bought Ida?" she said. "It's a picture book of flowers."

Wolfgang again checked the drawers but didn't find anything. Searching the closet, he only found an iron board and five laundry bags. Checking the bathroom, he only spotted four towels. But opening the small suitcase, he found the picture book between Ida's T-shirt and her jeans.

Kerstin picked up the picture book and said, "How can I forgive myself for being his sister?" She put it into the small suitcase and picked up the slippers.

Forgive yourself.

He stepped onto the patio. The wind caressed his face and the magnolias' fragrance stirred him. The young couple by the pool was kicking water at each other while music and cheers from the park across the street drenched the air. In another world, he would walk beside Kerstin through the quagmire.

A glitter, like the sunlight reflecting from a mirror, alerted him of the advancing army.

"Down."

The sliding door cracked and a spider-webbed pattern spread through the glass. His left forearm throbbed. Kerstin fell to the ground, thump onto the floor, landing on her shoulder and her back.

While the flowerpot on the patio table shattered, he threw himself onto the ground. Thinking of Kerstin taking a bullet. Praying she hadn't abandoned him and Ida. When he landed on the tiles, dirt showered his head.

Across the garden, a gun barrel sticking out of the East Wing end unit's sliding door pointed at him. The shooter hid behind the door and only exposed a gloved hand.

Kerstin lay on the floor beside a few shards.

He crawled into the room. He stooped and held her. Kerstin had walked beside him at Sea World while he held Ida's hand, while two children passed them soaked from head to feet and Ida clamored to see Shamu. Now, the image retreated and he couldn't recall that day's colors and sounds and smells.

"She doesn't miss," Kerstin said. "She didn't miss."

Blood dripped from his left forearm as he checked Kerstin for wounds, praying the windowpane had diverted the bullet's path, praying she and he would have another chance to stroll along the Thames, to trace another path, to journey into another life.

She rose. She took out her handkerchief and tied it around his forearm. The bullet had only grazed his arm.

"You should give that girl a chance." She grasped his other arm, her hand cold against his.

What if I don't want to?

He held her hand cold and shaking, and checked for blood.

Lifting her jacket, she pulled the slug from the bulletproof vest and, after handing him it, left the room with her gun.

Kerstin, Kerstin, wait. Wolfgang stepped through the doorway, but didn't see her. He ran down the hallway, turning right at the intersection. The door of the East Wing's end unit was open. He sidled into the room, gun in hand. No one. Just a red rose and a bonnet on the bed. Elizabeth McDonald. He checked the bathroom. He checked the closet. He whispered Kerstin's name but she didn't answer. Stepping through the sliding door, into the patio, he asked the young couple at the pool holding each other, "Had a woman come out of the patio?" But they just trembled and glared at him.

Kerstin, where're you?

He ran toward the lobby, where a staff was snoozing on the counter. An old lady on a divan pointed at the hotel entrance. He thanked her. Then pushed through the revolving door. On the sidewalk, several pedestrians sang, "Peace Like a River." A couple tangoed in the street and the liquor storeowner was peddling whisky and vodka. A boy handed out flyers for the Paradise Massage.

Wolfgang looked down both sides of Abraham Boulevard. No Kerstin or Elizabeth McDonald. Only pedestrians ambling toward Heaven Avenue and converging onto Babel Park. Strangers and lampposts and traffic signs he didn't recognize. Music and laughter he couldn't identify. He called Isaiah and told him to keep Ida away from the hotel for at least another half an hour.

After returning the gun to the holster, he walked around the hotel. Inside the gate, the young couple was again frolicking in the pool. He couldn't open the gate.

Kerstin, don't leave me.

While retracing his steps to the hotel entrance, he imagined in his old age driving along Sea-to-Sky Highway with Kerstin and visiting Whistler and admiring the snow peaks. Another life, second chance. He was about to push through the hotel's revolving door when the dancing man dropped to the ground, pulling down his partner. Was the man suffering from a stroke or a heart attack? But blood seeped out of his head. Wolfgang shouted for the pedestrians to stop chatting and laughing, to stop singing and dancing, to drop to the ground, to escape the bullets. While some stared at him or the dead man, while others glanced around, the storeowner groaned and dropped to the ground, the bottle of whiskey shattering beside him. A bullet hole in his left temple.

Wolfgang drew his gun, if only Isaiah were here to show off his shooting skills, and gazed in the direction of the shot, where a row a single story stores lined the street, several cars parked along the sidewalk. He searched for the shooter and his gun among the rooftops sparkling under the sun.

A gun barrel was sticking out of a car trunk, just to the left of the license plate. The gunman inside was shooting the pedestrians. Not Elizabeth McDonald.

Was the shooter aiming at him, but missing him, killed the bystanders? But he didn't expect anyone shooting at him to miss. Certainly not Elizabeth McDonald.

The boy whined. Dropping the flyers. Falling onto the ground.

"Get down."

Wolfgang aimed his gun. Steadying his hands and fingers. *Don't look at the boy. Just think and feel as Isaiah or Kerstin would.* Aiming, sensing the trigger, not worrying about the surrounding or the next bullet, he only sensed his gun, only focused on the target. He swept away distractions, accepting and trusting his skill. Uniting with the gun.

A woman wailed. Several pedestrians ran past him. An engine roared. The carnival music wafted in the air. The shooter was trying to draw attention, but the world was ignoring him.

He focused on the barrel. He pulled the trigger.

The sedan roared out of the parking space and turned at the corner, but left a piece of the gun barrel on the ground.

Kerstin. Where's Kerstin?

He ignored the blood and the bodies and the pedestrians screaming and crying and he entered the lobby where the staff was still snoozing but the old lady had left. Calling for an ambulance with his phone, he ran down the corridor to the room where Kerstin had packed both suitcases, hoping she had returned, waiting for him. But she wasn't there.

Kerstin, Kerstin, where're you?

She hadn't taken a bullet. She hadn't. While he was looking for her in the back garden, screams rose above the carnival music. When a bullet hammered out another spider-webbed pattern on the sliding door, their lattices crossing each other, he dropped onto the floor. It came from the gunman in the car trunk. Not Elizabeth McDonald. In the yard, a woman screamed. Another bullet hit the sliding door and shattered the glass.

Messy shooter. The woman screamed again. He went into the patio, while a car engine roared down the street. The sedan he should've pursued, speeding away. Outside the side gate, pedestrians rushed out of the park, a lady pushing aside a girl and a man trampling on a fallen woman.

The young woman who had been frolicking in the water was crying and twitching by the poolside. The young man lay face down, a pool of blood around his body, some dripping into the pool and tainting the water. While scattered screams echoed through the street, Wolfgang went to the woman and held her shoulders and checked for wounds. After finding none, he asked her several questions but she just sobbed and shivered. He left the woman and turned over the young man. Eyes wide-opened and a bullet through the left temple. He checked the pulse and confirmed the man had died.

The police sirens blared through the streets, the tires screeching to a halt. Kerstin walked up, grasped the woman's hand and comforted her.

Wolfgang embraced Kerstin but she urged him to check the crime scene. He went through the side gate into the street, where a girl moaned and twitched on the ground and a policeman was attending to her wounds. Across the street, inside the park, several men and women lay in front of a stage and their blood colored the marble ground. Blood reeked in the air as a breeze blew from the park. Three police cruisers parked in the middle of the street while their sirens wailed over the sobs and moans. Four policemen checked the wounded and the dead and another two talked on their transceivers.

A policeman picked up a flag, the word "Mitch" below an image of a red vampire bat.

Wolfgang approached a wounded girl, her face and right arm bruised. But before he reached her, the phone rang. He answered the call. Isaiah told him Ida had fainted and he was taking her to Paradise Memorial Hospital.

When a medic brushed past him, his phone fell on the ground and several ambulances had parked next to the police cruisers. The paramedics pushed a gurney toward a wounded boy.

Isaiah's call. Ida was in the hospital. He rushed into the hotel.

CHAPTER 27 - RICK

Rick rested on the ground and faced the starry sky. Just die before the gangsters could torture him. One night about three months ago, he and Lucy-Jane had lain on the beach and counted the stars.

Oh, Lucy-Jane, I love you.

About a month ago, Rick was in Bliss Park devising a plan to swindle Ernst of fifty-thousand dollars while the waves crashed against the shore and helped him think. When Mitch and Luc drove their Road Kings down the boardwalk, chasing a girl into the street. She ran across Bliss Parkway but before she reached the Botanical Garden, they gunned her down. She lifted her face twisted and bloodied, crawled about a foot, then dropped her head. Rick hid behind a sycamore tree avoiding her eyes, and after the psychopaths had taken the body and left, he lay on the ground for about half an hour, staring at the sky. Two weeks later, the newscaster announced that police had found her body parts in Noah's Beach and several public parks.

As he lay in the alley searching for the Little Dipper, waiting for the gangsters to cut him up, just as they had that girl. That'd be fine as long as he was dead. But when he located the constellation, the pain in his back had subsided. That was something, a miracle. He checked the pavement. No blood. Did he become Superman? He picked up a bullet and squeezed the rubber. The goddamn Vampire and the Werewolf were toying with him. They'd torture him before killing him. He couldn't get up and run. His freaking limbs had abandoned him. The gangsters walked up to him.

No, please, no.

"What the hell?" Luc examined his rifle and said, "Supposed to be dead."

"God damn whore monger." Mitch raised his semi-automatic handgun and pointed it at Rick, but before shooting, he glanced down the alley as if searching for a shadow in the darkness.

Rick turned his head. A figure in bowler and trench coat sauntered down the alley, the shadow draping over the wall and the trashcans.

"Waste that whore monger."

Mitch and Luc raise their weapons and shot five rounds at the figure. Rick wrapped his arms around his head to shield from the shell casings. When he lifted his head, the phantom, whose trench coat was flapping in the wind, passed him and kept walking toward the gangsters, the bowler shielding the stranger's face.

"What the hell's going on here?" Luc examined his weapon and at the man. "What the hell do we do?"

The man drew out a handgun. He fired. Luc dropped his weapon and fell onto the ground. Mitch hesitated for a second before dropping his weapon and fleeing down the alley.

The man kicked aside several casings and passed Ernst. When he reached Luc, he kicked aside the rifle and stepped on the Werewolf's wounded arm. A scream echoed through the alley. A cat screeched and dashed past Rick.

"Why were you tickling me with your rubber bullets?" The man rubbed his sole on Luc's wound and ignored the screams. "And quit whining just because I spoiled your party. I hate cry-baby delinquents."

Rick recognized the manager at Akdeniz, Mr. Jefferson, as he picked up several rubber bullets to confirm he hadn't turned into Superman.

"Don't kill me. Don't kill me. I beg you." Luc was wailing and the tears had muffled his voice.

"Okay, okay. Since you prepared the bash, I don't want to spoil your fun. So, let's pick up where you'd left." Mr. Jefferson put away the handgun and cracked his knuckle. "And don't worry. I know the drill. I've practiced."

"No, no, no. Please, please."

Get away from both psychopaths before either one comes after me.

While the restaurant manager pulled out a blade and Luc begged for mercy, Rick crawled down the side street. Dragged his body toward the building. Crawled along the wall. When he reached an air conditioner, a scream shook the window screens and his arms gave way. He covered his ears. The screens continued to rattle and a scream stretched for several seconds. With the air conditioner as support, he got up. Sprinted down the side street, to flee from the next scream. But he had only passed one building when the shriek threw him onto the pavement. Almost cracking a bottle with his jaw. He covered his ears but the phantom seeped into his eardrums and he almost wetted himself. Several stray dogs howled as they passed him.

Rick was about to get up when a figure stepped into the side street from the main road. Maybe a pedestrian or an officer had heard the screams and was checking the alleys. But shouldn't take a chance. He rolled to the foot of the building and crawled behind a container. The pedestrian walked into the side street. He covered his mouth to stifle his panting. Then his ears as another scream echoed through the side streets. The pedestrian stopped several feet from the container. Lit a cigarette. The Englishman's wife was smoking under the dim light. Why had the man asked Kerstin Becker, not his wife, for help? Maybe, the man didn't want the wife to know he was a crook. He waited for the Englishwoman to leave, but she continued to smoke until Mr. Jefferson sauntered down the side street toward her.

"Were you responsible for the beastly din?" The woman flicked ash into the container while leaning against the wall.

"I'd never scream like that." Mr. Jefferson cleaned his blade with a handkerchief. "It's improper and even indecent. As you probably would agree."

If Rick had a semi-automatic handgun he'd also jest. But without even a dagger, he just shivered behind the container and waited for these crooks to leave. His throat itched. *Don't freaking cough.* He swallowed and held his breath. His face flushed and tears tumbled out of his eyes but he covered his mouth as his body shook.

"Jolly good. I would venture to say I have found the suitable man. Though I expected a stiff upper-lip."

"Glad you approve, madam." Mr. Jefferson grabbed his bowler and swung his arm in an arc to bow. "But seizing my prize isn't a good way to start a working relationship."

"You had a shot at Kay Emil, but you dithered, worrying about innocent bystanders. So don't blame anyone but yourself," she said. "Anyway, you should thank me. You probably won't even be here if I didn't tell you that she's in town."

"Well, you've probably checked my references. So you'd know my dos and don'ts. And what'd you do? You exploited it."

"I quite admire assassins with principles."

"An assassin without principles is a painting without vanishing points."

"I wish we have people of your caliber. But jolly glad you are here."

"Bumping off my colleague isn't very nice either."

"That was either him or me. Survival instinct, mind you. I didn't have a choice but to use up an extra billet. My supervisor wouldn't be happy I wasted resource."

"We'll have to settle this after everything's done," Mr. Jefferson said. "How's Mr. McDonald? Wasted any bullets on him?"

"Buggering off for his bloody life. I imagine he's enjoying the adrenaline rush." Mrs. McDonald exhaled a jet of smoke into the air and threw the cigarette butt into the container. "He's the target I want to write off."

"I see."

"Surprised?"

"Not at all. Statistics show that close relations, especially spouses, are the top targets for hired killings. I've done a few. But crimes of passion are messy."

"Not to worry. In this case, strictly business. As you might have ventured, he isn't exactly my husband."

"Well, business associates are the next largest group for such services. We all want to maximize profits, not to mention increase shareholder values."

"And neither of us is a McDonald."

"As they say, a rose by any other name… But I can still call you Mrs. McDonald, right?"

"Elizabeth. I insist."

"Actually, I prefer lilies to roses. It's the purity and elegance. But sometimes all you can get are roses. Bummers."

Rick wiped away his tears. Hoping the assassins would leave before he coughs. He itched to have a cigarette but only pinched his lap to alleviate the craving. Ernst, he must still be lying in the alley. The fool, dying an easy death—as fools usually do—and not having to learn that Lucy-Jane had deceived him and never cared an iota about him.

Lucky bastard.

"I heard you only accept certain targets." Mrs. McDonald pulled a red folder from her handbag.

"I think of it as community service."

"Are you atoning for some misdemeanor?"

"I donate most of my earnings to charity."

"His profile should convince you he's no Pollyanna." She handed Mr. Jefferson the folder.

After accepting it, he said, "I'm sure it wouldn't add to my knowledge. I've no problem bumping him off." Scraping his chin with the folder. "Or you, for that matter."

"You and I, we have a great deal in common." Mrs. McDonald pulled out another folder and said, "My credentials. You may be surprised at my view towards vigilante justice."

Rick should report these murderers to the sheriff. But no, he had to avenge Lucy-Jane, a mission he should sacrifice his life for. How to torment Jo-Beth? He focused. Mr. Jefferson and Mrs. McDonald continued to irritate his ears. A soda can clanged in the alley. A rat dashed toward a building. But before the rodent reached the wall, two bullets pierced its body and it twitched and flipped over. Rick covered his mouth to stifle his groan but his hand shook and smacked his teeth and snot was slithering down his upper lip.

Don't make a noise, please, don't.

"Guess we should have a beer together to chat about our philosophies of life." Mr. Jefferson put his gun into his pocket and, accepting the folder, glanced over the contents. "Interesting resume."

"Will you tell me there are supermen and superwomen qualified to levy justice without the law?" Mrs. McDonald wiped her gun with a handkerchief and returned it to her purse.

"Nope, just that, 'Hell is empty and all the devils are here.'"

"Quite comforting, I must say."

"Got to go back into the alley. An unfinished business. As they say, carpe diem."

"Only give me enough time to go far enough not to hear the din. I'm allergic to loud noise."

"I know a cure."

"I'm not ready to try it now."

"Pity."

"Quite, pity."

"You know, I don't want to mention it."

Mrs. McDonald took out her phone and pressed several buttons and said, "Check your bank account for the advance. Not to worry. If they get me, you will still receive your payment."

"But I thought we'd have a drink at the tavern after the assignment."

"Jolly good. Your round. Cheerio." She stepped back and left the side street.

After Mr. Jefferson had returned to the alley, Rick stood up, his useless knees aching and trembling. He straightened his clothes and combed his hair and limping down the side street toward St. Jude's Way, he covered his ears and ignored the snot dripping from his nostrils. Near an exhaust fan, his freaking knees buckled and he fell against the building wall but grasped the window ledge to prevent from collapsing onto the ground. Steadying himself and standing and waiting for his knees to regain strength. An eternal minute later, he put his foot forward and at the end of the side street, he turned right and staggered down the road, where ignorant pedestrians were strolling under the streetlights.

He went into the nearest bar, ordered a Seven and Seven and down it in three gulps. Then ordered another one but sprawled on the counter for several minutes before continuing the drink. That day, the Georgian girl had screamed and run along the boardwalk and the gangsters sprayed bullets that cut down several branches before hitting the girl. These crooks—Mitch and Luc, Mr. Jefferson and Mrs. McDonald, and especially Jo-Beth and the officer in Atlanta—just violated and butchered their victims.

Shit, even animals deserved better.

When Luc claimed to be his brother, for a moment Rick studied the delinquent's nose and jaw. But no way, this psychopath wasn't his brother. With superior genes, his mother would give birth to decent children. Sure, if he had a brother or a sister when growing up, they could've defended against their father together. But he didn't. And now wouldn't want a sibling. He had lost Lucy-Jane and nothing mattered except revenge.

After finishing his drink, he went into the men's room and washed his face in the sink. Then dried his face, brushed his hair and pressed on the creases on his T-shirt until they disappeared. He wouldn't disappoint Lucy-Jane.

CHAPTER 28 - PERRY

The baseball bat traced an arc across the air and headed for Todd's left temple, but he lifted a lid from the trashcan beside a building's drainage pipe to shield the blow. After a note blasted through the alley, he crashed into the trashcan, knocked it over and fell onto a pile of soda cans while the lid banged against the wall. His right arm was stilling shaking as he got up. A homeless man lay behind the trashcan. He had to wake him up and shoo him away, but the vagrant didn't have a heartbeat.

Under the evening light, Luc the Werewolf, his right eye blackened and blood dripping from the corner of his mouth, rubbed the scar running from his left forehead down his cheek while his other hand swiveled the bat. He whistled a tune Todd didn't recognize while the wind scattered the soda cans.

"Bozo, now you buy it."

"Looks more like some kid kick your ass. You sure your luck hasn't maxed out? I don't want to bust a wounded man's chops." Todd kicked away the soda cans and rose rubbing his right arm.

Todd was getting too old for this.

Luc raised his bat ready to strike, but the deputy sheriff slipped out of the building's corner, kicked the delinquent in the stomach and punched him in the jaw. Luc groaned and dropped his bat as he spewed blood and bounced across the alley. Just as he fell onto the ground, the deputy reached him and kicked him several times in the abdomen.

"Okay, let's not have too much fun here." Todd adjusted his tie and picked up his hat. "Just handcuff him." After putting it on, he took out a mirror to check for scratches on his face. The deputy cuffed the Werewolf and Todd grasped the delinquent's cheeks. "It's not nice to bump off your foster parents, especially when they came to help you."

"Asshole, you can't—"

Todd squeezed the delinquent's cheeks to muffle the voice and said, "On the contrary, I can."

"I'll waste the bastard." Luc couldn't free his face from the grip as more blood dripped from his mouth and the cuts. The deputy punched him in the stomach.

"What's the matter? Spooked by the electric chair? Too late for that." Todd massaged the delinquent's bloodied face until the cheeks reddened. Then let go and rinsed his hands with bottled water.

"Hey, I ain't scared of nothing. Just try me." Luc opened his mouth to bite the deputy's fingers but the latter slapped his face.

"Don't worry, you'll be afraid. In no time."

"Cassidy's a dead man. You can tell the asshole. One of these days, I'll shove his head in the oven."

Todd examined the delinquent's face and recognized Cassidy's features. "Yeah, I can see the eyes and the chin, definitely the chin. But can you sing and dance? You have to sing and dance to be his son."

If nothing else, he inherited his father's pathology.

"You know, you might have dozens of half-brothers and half-sisters." Todd lit a cigarette and blew out a ring of smoke, and when a drunkard stumbled into the alley from Angel Road, he shooed the man away and pointed to a detour. He would hand in the gay-couple-murder report tomorrow to speed up the prosecution and execution. The townspeople had formed several vigilante groups and sought to lynch the Vampire and the Werewolf. Last Monday while hunting down the delinquents, these zealots had shot a bystander in the chest. Todd would prevent other casualties.

"I ain't nothing like him," Luc said.

"Can you switch to another channel?"

"My buddy—"

"Don't worry. Soon, he'll visit you, in the next cell. To keep you company so you won't feel lonely."

"Let me give you a clue."

"No, let me give you a clue. The electric chair will be cushy compared to what you'll experience behind bars." Todd picked up the bat and rubbed the delinquent's facial scar with its tip. "You talk too much. Just like Cassidy. I begin to see the resemblance. Just feel sorry for you, having to inherit his genes."

"You're hunting for Gus Davis, right?" Luc giggled and spat at Todd but missed.

"Okay, since you're feeling generous, tell me where I can find his ass and I'll make it less painful behind bars."

The officers tracking Davis had lost him earlier in the evening and Todd gave them one day to locate the fugitive before firing them. He had set up checkpoints along the roads leaving town and expected to return Davis behind bars, but if necessary, he would pursue the lecher across the country.

"Hey, dude I'm out of here in no time."

"I won't trust your buddy the Vampire if I were you. Never trust a vampire."

"Like it or not, you'll find the mayor tonight."

"Do you know you're the perfect fall guy for the mayor?" Todd squeezed the Werewolf's neck while the deputy held the delinquent in place.

"Do you know why that girl from Georgia got wasted?" Luc said.

"Because you and Mitch are sick bastards."

Todd asked the deputy to escort the Werewolf back to the sheriff's office and squeeze Davis's location from him. Handing his aide the bat. "Feel free to play with it in your interrogation. But don't quote me." Then called an ambulance to pick up the dead vagrant.

When the sky had darkened, he returned to the sheriff's office and ordered his men to prepare for Mitch ambushing the place to rescue Luc. In the security room, he asked the officers to have two pairs of eyes watch every monitor, and to alert him of any motorcycles. In his office, a Paradise Burger set meal was sitting on his desk. He checked with the deputy but the man didn't buy him dinner. When he took out the burger, a note dropped from the paper bag. Lily-Rose sent her greetings and asked him to think of her with every bite. He crumbled the note and threw it into the trashcan and dialed her number but hung up before she picked up the call.

He ate the burger. He drank the coffee. He ate the French fries. He dreamed about Grace, while finishing the coffee.

After lining five hourglasses in a row on the desk, he put a folder before each, except the first. While the neon sign flickered across the street, he smoked a cigarette. An all-nighter to put together the puzzles.

Nothing like working in the office at night. No phone calls. No interruptions from his deputies. His mind clear and calm to focus on the problems. He preferred sitting in his office and solving problems without having to bother with the red tapes, without having to deal with his nightmares. But the image of his mother undressing would torment him and he would have to purge it. In his youth, he would roam Paradise's dark alleys trying to flee from that phantom. Now, he just focused on his work.

At 10:00 p.m., he turned over the first hourglass and took out the handkerchief on which he had woven several magnolias. He threaded the needle with a dark green thread. Turned over the handkerchief and imagined the leaves' positions. After planning all the stitches for the leaves, he pushed the needle through the back of the handkerchief for the first stitch. If Grace hadn't left, he would give her the handkerchief. Now, he would keep it to remember her.

When laughter down the street seeped through the office, he got up and stood by the window. Across the street a group of girls was leaving the bar. As several men approached them, he opened the window and called for the girls to go home. The men dispersed. The girls invited him to join them but he shut the window and lit a cigarette and continued to weave the leaves. In and out; in and out.

He would send her the handkerchief.

After Jo-Beth McIntyre had shown him his mother's picture, the image of his mother undressing before a stranger returned to him every night. Except the stranger had crystallized into the bald man, McIntyre's father. If only he had told Mr. McIntyre about his mother having AIDS, saved his life. Now, he could purge these images from his mind only when he embroidered the handkerchief and thought about Grace. Still, he had to take more pills to sleep.

The end was near.

After the last grain of sand had passed through the first hourglass's funnel, he put down the handkerchief and lit a cigarette. Flipped the second hourglass and grabbed the folder in front. A picture of Al's head. Random cuts through the flesh revealed failed attempts. A sloppy job. The killer used a hacksaw to cut up the body. Probably had stolen the money and tried to disguise the crime as a thrill kill. After finding out Dick Wadlington had used a hundred-dollar bill at Paradise Burger, Todd sent several officers to track down the homeless man and to retrieve the money and the hacksaw. He called the officers, but they still hadn't located Dick after checking several hideouts. Numbskulls. If the officers couldn't locate Dick in the next two or three days, they would probably find his body in the dumpsite. The money would attract urchins and thugs willing to kill for just a hundred dollars. The sooner he finds the money, the sooner he would end the killings. He picked up the letter a beggar had delivered this morning. In the letter, Al said the money would allow him to start a new life. He wouldn't have to steal another wallet from visitors or cheat another old lady of her savings. He would go to Los Angeles, open a grocery store and earn a living. And he would repay Todd's loans though he couldn't repay his generosity and encouragement. He would visit Paradise again and would bring a gift for the sheriff, a gift money couldn't buy.

After reading the letter, Todd flipped through the pictures of Al's head, limbs and torso. What was Al going to give him? A gift money couldn't buy. He would have liked such a gift. Like a kiss from Grace.

He was folding the letter when the phone rang. Lily-Rose invited him to have a drink at Eden's Joy but he told her to go home and avoid trouble and he hung up. After finishing his cigarette, he flipped the third hourglass and took the next folder.

A picture of the severed arm he had examined at the dumpsite two days ago. Not the Georgian girl's. But the cut and skin texture and decomposition matched those of the body parts the deputy had found on the same day. Another girl, another killing.

Not Grace. Anyone else but her.

He still recognized her arms and legs. Also, the cuts didn't come from Cassidy's scalpels. At the crime lab, he tested various saws and found out the killer, stronger than Dick according to the cuts, had used a circular saw. The cut marks on the leg showed the killer's rage. A crime of passion. No other killings had the same cut patterns. He had checked IAFIS and CODIS, but couldn't find any match. Not a prostitute, not a criminal. Jane Doe might be Lucy-Jane. He would send an officer to Jo-Beth McIntyre's place to collect fingerprints and confirm his suspicion, then interrogate potential killers: a lover, a spouse, an admirer, or a rival.

Todd stretched his back. After putting the embroidery into his bag, he went to the men's room and splashed water over his face. In the mirror a scruffy man stared at him. *Who the hell is that stranger?* In the hallway's silence, he stopped in front of the deputy's office to study Scooby-Doo's picture, its two front teeth sticking out like hoe blades. The man had shown him his Scooby-Doo figures, some dating back two decades. Like Todd's embroidery, the deputy's hobby kept the man sane. He bought a cup of coffee at the vending machine, returned to his office and recited Eleanor Roosevelt's quote several times before stepping into the room and closing the door.

After flipping the fourth hourglass and grabbing the next folder, he read the blackmail note Jo-Beth McIntyre had given him. Then flipped through the scanned files in his phone until he reached the picture of McIntyre's love letter. But his farsightedness prevented him from reading the chicken scratch. Damn it, I'm going downhill. He printed the file and matched the scribble with the note's handwriting. So, the lover Rick Dougherty had kidnapped the daughter, and perhaps killed her, and was blackmailing the mother. Not only that, he was going to milk fifty-thousand dollars from Ernst. And only Al the Dead Mouse prevented the kidnapper from succeeding. But Todd found fingerprints at the abandoned toy factory where the killer had left Al's head and they belonged to Rick Dougherty. Perhaps Rick had killed Al and retrieved the money already. And if Jane Doe was Lucy-Jane, Rick must have killed her. Todd would only have to find Rick to solve the three cases. He checked the DMV database and when he saw Rick's picture, he banged his fist on the desk and almost spilled the coffee over the file. The man he had stopped four nights ago near Eden's Joy. The man's address in the DMV matched that of McIntyre. Todd still remembered that face and even if he couldn't find the man, he would locate the motorcycle. He issued an APB to arrest Rick and intended to capture the man by next weekend.

In front of the mirror Todd examined the stubs around his chin. After putting on shaving cream, he shaved while humming "Oh, My Darling, Clementine." But when the image of Mr. McIntyre taking off his mother's clothes returned to him, he splashed cold water onto his face to purge the phantom. And was about to wipe his face when the deputy stepped into the room and said Luc had given him a location and he was going to Paradise Burger to look for Gus Davis in the men's room.

"Did the bat help?" Todd wiped his face and returned the towel on the rack. Why was Davis hiding in the men's room? The deputy tipped his hat and left the office.

Todd flipped the last hourglass and opened the remaining folder. He examined the picture of the dead Mary-Lou, a red rose on her chest. That time, he and Cassidy went to her place to celebrate her birthday. They chatted and had champagne while her son played video games in his bedroom. Her son had stayed in ninth grade for three years and would drop out of high school. She asked him to work at a fast food restaurant but he wouldn't even cook his own meal when she had to work overtime. That night, after Cassidy had left, he stayed at her place and they talked through the night about dreams, regrets and aging, and he might have found a friend. But he wouldn't mix business and friendship. Sure, he trusted her, but he knew nothing about her past.

Had Cassidy eliminated her to cover his tracks? But on the beach, he had checked the bullet hole in her forehead. The preacher hadn't killed her. An assassin had eliminated Todd's partner. Clean and professional. He collected a strand of hair in the sand beside the body and sent it for STR analysis.

What does the rose mean?

Her enemy probably had located her and eliminated her. Of course, the FBI or a vigilante organization might be targeting his ring and getting rid of his comrades one by one.

He had searched IAFIS using Mary-Lou's fingerprints but didn't find a match. Same with Interpol. She probably had plastic surgery and altered her fingerprints and he had to wait for the STR results. Once, while they were drinking in Eden's Joy, Mary-Lou told him she had worked for an international human trafficking organization but had left that group to free-lance. Maybe she was running away from her former colleagues but he couldn't identify the organization. So, he searched through the police databases for the red rose insignia. While he was sipping his coffee and waiting for the result, an officer rushed in with an envelope and said a beggar had handed him the letter. The beggar said a masked man had given him a hundred dollars to deliver the envelope to Sheriff Perry.

After the officer had put the envelope on the desk, Todd opened the drawer and put on a pair of plastic gloves. Had someone sent Anthrax for his birthday? How thoughtful. He pressed on the envelope and after confirming only a piece of paper inside, he cut the lid with a letter opener, slid out the letter and read the mayor's suicide note. Sifting through a drawer, he found a previous letter from the mayor and matched the signatures between the two documents. But the mayor wouldn't kill himself for crimes such as statutory rape or murder. Not the man's style. Davis would spend his last penny on legal fees and bribes to get acquitted. He wouldn't give up on his life even if he only had an iota of a chance. Todd inserted the letter and the envelope into a plastic bag and asked the officer to take it to the crime lab for fingerprint analysis.

He took his hat and an hourglass and left the Sheriff's Office for the restaurant he dreaded. Lily-Jane would complain that he never went to Eden's Joy with her. As he pulled his car out of the parking lot, the deputy called and said he was chasing Mitch through Bliss Parkway and needed backup. Todd dispatched three cruisers to help the deputy and continued toward Paradise Burger to look for Davis's body.

CHAPTER 29 - RICK

Rick climbed up the apartment building stairs and passed a woman whose perfume almost knocked him out. Reaching the second floor, he walked along the hallway to the left end unit and pushed the ringer, unsure whether or not Ernst had expired in the alley last night.

After resting for a whole day, this morning he'd returned to the alley and only found the rubber bullets and shell casings and bloodstains on the pavement. No yellow tapes around the area or reports of Ernst's death.

He rang the bell again. Could he still tell the man how he'd made love to Lucy-Jane at Devil's Point?

Ernst opened the door and, after staring at him for a moment, said, "You must be him."

"I'm not him; I'm me." Rick slipped past Ernst and strutted into the apartment where about a third of a green tea Swiss roll sat on the coffee table. He opened the refrigerator in the kitchen to grab a beer and found a carton of wimpy soymilk. "Give me a break. You a man or a mouse?"

"Let me see your pendant." Ernst picked up the Swiss roll and cut him a piece.

"Get your own." He took the cake and bit into it and said, "And Lucy-Jane didn't give it to me." While chewing, he opened the oven. A rack of Chinese dumplings.

"I've seen it before."

In the living room, he dropped into the sofa facing the plasma TV and put both legs on the coffee table. "We got to brainstorm. To find the dough."

Ernst told him Dick had used a stolen hundred-dollar bill at Paradise Burger. Rick dropped his feet onto the floor, jumped up and said, "Damn it. That jackass of all trade." He'd asked Dick about Al and the fiend had pretended not to know the beggar's whereabouts. He missed the deception in those homeless eyes and swore to kick Dick's ass.

An oval-faced young lady in T-shirt and shorts opened the bedroom door. Glanced at Rick and hesitated for a second before closing the door.

"Well, guess I came at a bad time. Didn't mean to interrupt you."

"It's not—" Ernst said.

"I got it. It's lonely here."

"She's—"

"Just a fill-in?" Rick didn't mind Ernst having another girl but still had to reveal his intimacies with Lucy-Jane and jab the Bostonian in the heart.

"I love Lucy-Jane."

"Guess you won't be looking for her." Rick gobbled up the Swiss roll and wiped his hands on his jeans. Then wrote on the notepad "IOU" and signed his name. Ernst had told him about sly Dick. So Rick no longer needed the outsider's help.

Why didn't the dope ask about her alias?

"I love Lucy-Jane."

Rick folded his hands before the reddened face and nodded for several seconds before patting the Bostonian on his shoulder and saying, "No need to run it by me. I got it. I'll tell her."

"I love Lucy-Jane."

"Do I look like I'm deaf?"

"Her name's Grace."

"I didn't ask."

"I'm coming."

"What's it to me?" Rick checked his hair and jacket at the entryway mirror. "Thanks for the cake." He opened the door and smelled crayfish gumbo in the hallway. While he and Lucy-Jane were plotting to swindle Ernst, they'd gone to a seafood restaurant and he'd had crayfish gumbo. Now, the memory grieved him as that of health would a sick man.

Ernst grabbed the metal pipe next to the front door and waved it before his eyes and said, "I'm tagging along."

"You sure you don't want to chow down some cake with your honey before beating the shit out of the creep?" Rick ought to reveal his relationship with Lucy-Jane but with that metal pipe swinging back and forth, he would delay the revelation.

They arrived at the landfill, Ernst riding in the Ninja's backseat, several times almost falling off the motorbike. Rick dabbed some cologne on a handkerchief and wrapped it over his nose and mouth. To fight against the stench of spoiled shrimps and rotten eggs. Then took out the crowbar and strutted into the landfill, where several crows were rummaging through a Styrofoam box. Swinging the crowbar and whistling, "London Bridge is Falling Down." While Ernst held the pipe above his shoulders and treaded on the dirt. Beyond a garbage pit, a dune rose into the air. Rick had only gone to Dick's hideout three or four times but still remembered the entrance behind the dune, through a rusting refrigerator.

"I know you love Lucy-Jane," Ernst said, the pipe shaking in his hands.

The sun was baking Rick's face and his forehead was dripping with sweat. His shirt wet against his back. He kicked aside a milk carton. Skipped over the puddle of milk. And approached a dunghill where a dog barked and scurried away.

"I know you made love to Lucy-Jane."

That first time, Rick made love to Lucy-Jane, as if they'd known each other a lifetime. Now, only memories of her. He slowed down and watched the pipe while Ernst, skipping over patches of dung, walked around the dune.

"She loves me and I'd never let you have her." Ernst faltered a step and almost trampled on dung but after scattering the flies, his foot landed an inch beside the pile.

Rick gripped the crowbar and went behind the dune. He could kill Ernst here, in the landfill, in Dick's hideout. And frame the homeless creep for the murder. But he'd have to use the pipe or a weapon inside the hideout rather than the crowbar. The girl in the apartment had probably spotted them leave together and he'd have to invent a story for the police. Walking up to the refrigerator, he planned his moves. But he didn't have time to mull over each step. The crowbar shook in his hands just as the pipe in Ernst's. Sweat rolled down his arm onto his glove and the crowbar, and his heart beat faster and faster as if about to leap from his chest.

"We'd planned to get married." Ernst rushed forward to push away the refrigerator but it refused to move.

Rick approached Ernst from behind and opened the refrigerator door, a hole in the back leading into darkness. A stench emerged from the hideout and Rick had to cover his nose and breathe through his mouth. But Ernst rushed in, the pipe leading the way.

"I love her," Ernst said.

Rick took a step but stopped and walked away. Lit a cigarette and puffed the smoke into the air. A jet cruised above the skyline and plunged through clouds under the blue sky and the hot wind patted his face.

He took another puff. Mulling over his plan. If Dick killed Ernst, the latter would no longer bother him. If Ernst killed Dick, then the Bostonian would have to go to jail. Rick waited for the outcome, to enjoy the moment, but Lucy-Jane's death hung over his heart. Several times after making love to her, he'd wondered whether he'd sacrifice for her. Through her death, he'd confirmed he loves her. Now, he'd sacrifice his future to avenge her death.

No sounds, shouts, clangs, crashes, alms bowl shattering or bone hitting flesh or pipe hitting bone. He puffed his cigarette. Rubbed his sole on the dirt. More silence. He dropped the cigarette butt onto the ground. Kicked it onto a trash bag.

Ernst screamed. Then, silence. Rick gripped the crowbar and waited behind the refrigerator door for Dick. After five minutes, no one came out. Inside was as silent as a vacuum.

Rick twisted his neck to loosen several bones. Then took out his flashlight and stepped through the refrigerator into the stench. He shone his flashlight. Ernst sprawled on the ground, the pipe and flashlight beside him. No blood. Kneeling, checking Ernst's pulse, he found out the dunce had only fainted. A rat scurried across the room as he beamed the flashlight. He rubbed the handkerchief against his nose. Tiptoed toward the back and lifted a blanket lying against the wall. Only to find a straw mat and a hacksaw beneath. He checked the bowl and the plate in the basket. But found no food. He beamed the light onto the left wall. Soda cans and bottles sprawling beside the wall while scraps of paper hung on the wall. Dick's notes of his errands and deals with other homeless men and women. But Rick didn't understand the stench, even for Dick.

He beamed the light onto the right wall.

Lucy-Jane's head rested on the ground.

He dropped the flashlight. The light shone on Ernst's face, still twisted from seeing Lucy-Jane's head. Rick dropped onto the floor. His limbs trembled, his head spun, and his breathing rapid but shallow.

Then his head ached. Migraine. He took out a painkiller and swallowed it. Sitting on the floor, holding his head with both hands, murmuring Lucy-Jane's name while her head was facing him in the darkness. Jo-Beth probably had dumped the head in this landfill. And Dick, too stupid to think about the police finding the head in his hideout, picked it up as a souvenir and put it alongside his bottle collection.

In the darkness, Lucy-Jane's head beside him, Rick's head throbbed. He had kissed her soft lips and fragrant skin. Ten minutes later, he shone the flashlight on the head. The hair draped behind the head and the eyes looked into empty space. The mouth closed but the lips beginning to rot away.

"I love you." Lucy-Jane had whispered to him, in the trailer and in their apartment and on the cliff and at Devil's point, and now those words gnawed at his guts and pounded on his head.

Rick buried his head between his knees. Shedding tears. Not caring whether or not Dick would step in at any moment. He'd stored the pain in his bosom and now had to expel it and tell her head of his agony. But he dared not look at her peaceful but decaying face. Flies buzzed around him but he cried and cried until he drained his emotions, tired his muscles. Then, he rubbed his eyes.

My love, I'll avenge you. I'll make Jo-Beth's life so miserable she'd take her own life. I swear.

After having a cigarette in the dark, he picked up the metal pipe. Aimed at the back of Ernst's head. He should kill him for sleeping with Lucy-Jane and he had only to hit once to end the Bostonian's misery. She had to suffer the man while she was in Boston seducing him. She deserved to swing the pipe and release her pain. She sacrificed herself for their happiness, but that happiness had fled. She, dead; he, alive but miserable. His hand shook.

He swung hard. But stopped before hitting Ernst's head. Then dropped the pipe onto the ground. After picking up the flashlight and crowbar, he searched the hideout for the money, but as he suspected, Dick had hidden the money elsewhere.

He shred the notes and smashed the bowls and plates. Left the hideout and closed the refrigerator door. Retracing his steps to his Ninja, saying goodbye to Lucy-Jane's head. Near the gate, magnolias danced on the branches as if celebrating a new day. To be sure, a new life for Rick.

#

Rick called his streetwise friends to track down the homeless man's whereabouts. Went to the dumpsite to somersault in his motorbike. Crashing several times into the trash heaps and bruising his left leg. But still couldn't drive the image of Lucy-Jane's head from his mind. The lifeless eyes, the pale face, the drooping lips. Haunting him even among the stench. He cursed Jo-Beth. Lay among the garbage bags and wept for an hour before receiving a call from his *eye*. She'd spotted Dick in the abandoned toy factory in St. Peter's Yard. He sped down Martyr's Way and ran two annoying red lights. But while he was driving down Angel Road, honking at a stray cat, the *eye* called again to inform him Dick had left the toy factory and taken a cab. She gave him the cab's license plate and he called the only cab service in town and asked about the vehicle. At first, the dispatcher wouldn't reveal the cab's location but when Rick told her he was an officer chasing after a crook, she released the location. He arrived at City Hall just as the cab was about to leave. The driver told him Dick had gotten off at the Church of Paradise.

At St. Jude's Way, Pastor Cassidy in a Polo shirt was shuffling cards on a tabletop while about a dozen passersby hovered around the table. Rick asked the entertainer whether he'd seen Dick.

After moving several cards, Pastor Cassidy looked up and said, "Hey, Rick, come here. I want you to check this out."

"Dick. Have you seen him?"

"What's the rush?"

"He's around here somewhere." Rick ignored the entertainer—didn't have time to entertain the clown—and marched down St. Jude's Way where four boys were playing soccer in front of a liquor store and an officer was writing a parking ticket.

Before he had walked the length of the church, Pastor Cassidy called him and ran toward him. "Hey, wait up. I just saw Dick."

Rick stopped. Itching to punch the entertainer. Leaning on the wall, the pastor hunched and panted for a minute before saying, "Did you know he was sporting an Armani suit? Wow, must've won the lottery."

"Where's he?"

"Why are you looking for him?"

"It's important."

"You two up to something again?"

"It's life and death."

"It's always life and death."

"He copped my money."

"Hmm, that's intense, isn't it?"

"Will you lend me a hand?"

"You bet I'll lend you a hand. I always help people in need. Was I ever not a Good Samaritan when you needed help?"

"Then, where's he?"

"Answer me."

"No, no. Of course not."

"Now, that's better."

"Dick—"

"Oh, yeah, he took off that way." The pastor pointed to the alley behind the church.

I'll come back to burn all your props.

After thanking the pastor, Rick hurried down the alley along the church. The homeless man's cologne nauseated him. Hell, he'd thrash the creep until the bum begs for mercy. Stepping on a burning cigarette butt, Rick slowed down. And listened. Noise around the corner of the church. He tiptoed toward the corner. Reaching the building's edge, he poked his head out. Down the side street, Dick hunched in front of the church backdoor and was picking the lock with two metal strips. A poodle was sniffing at a backpack in front of the door.

Rick picked up a pipe, ready to confront the greedy bastard and retrieve his money, money he should've gotten days ago if it wasn't for the slimy beggar and the toothless homeless man. Dick unlocked the door and picked up the backpack. Now, you get it, you son-of-a-bitch. Rick raised the pipe and was about to rush out when pain seized the back of his head.

Stars swirled around his head. Nearby a crow cawed. Then darkness engulfed him as he fell onto the ground.

CHAPTER 30 - WOLFGANG

Wolfgang was holding Ida's hand and licking the ice cream cone when the speaker announced the train's arrival. A group of migrant workers and an old couple stood up and walked toward the platform. Ida grasped his hand and licked the ice cream cone and Kerstin picked up the luggage and said they had to go. He didn't want to let go of Ida's hand, not after she had fainted in City Hall while with Isaiah. What if he couldn't see her again?

He finished the cone and following Kerstin walked Ida toward the platform and when he emerged from the waiting lounge, the heat slowed his breathing. By the time they reached the platform, the train had rolled into the station and several passengers were exiting the coaches. When he approached the train, he hugged Ida and promised to visit after her treatment and she reminded him to accompany them to Rome later in the summer. He held Kerstin's hand and said, "Take care of yourself and Ida." Earlier, when they arrived at the hospital, Kerstin had held his hand until the doctors came. If only he had held onto her a bit longer.

"Take care of her." Kerstin kissed him, then took Ida's hand and boarded the train.

In the evening heat, a chill spread through his body and he shivered. Following them along the platform as they move into the carriage, he almost crashed into a couple kissing beside a display. He waved his hand and Ida hers until the train moved. Under the twilight, the shadow of the train draped over the platform and slithered away. He stepped on the retreating shape, hoping to stop the train but the shadow just slipped away. He chased the shadow until reaching the end of the platform. The tail of smoke drifted farther and farther away, until he couldn't distinguish it from the evening clouds.

Ida, please be safe.

After returning to the waiting lounge, where re-election posters of Gus Davis and Todd Perry decorated the walls, he stepped into the diner to buy a cup of chai. In a booth, Dick Wadlington was having filet mignon and a bottle of Chateau Margaux. The homeless man in an Armani suit had shaved and cut his hair but wasn't using a knife and a fork to eat his steak.

Wolfgang stepped onto Angel Road amid the train's rhythm. The silhouette of the skyline hung under the purple clouds as he followed his shadow toward the parking lot. Let the days cascade into the week when he would visit Ida. The taxis glided past him and the flag flapped above the building and the smell of the ocean drifted like dream fragments fleeing the morning light. His steps matched the wind's rhythm. When he reached his car, a note flapped under the windshield wiper.

The bitch taking potshots at you earlier in the day. Hey, want to know where she's hiding? Bring two-hundred bucks to Paradise Burger. Order a barbecue rib burger and drop in the booth next to the lady's toilet.

When he arrived at Paradise Burger, he grabbed the spicy lamb gyro and Greek salad Grace had made him and he stepped into the restaurant where an old couple was eating burgers near the entrance. At the counter, where Lily-Rose yawned and greeted him, he ordered a veggie burger.

"No veggie burgers. Think you're in New York or what?"

"Grilled chicken burger."

"Sold out."

"What do you have?"

"Barbecue rib burger."

"I'll just have a coffee."

"One barbecue rib burger coming right up." She leaned forward and whispered, "Don't worry. It's on me. Just take me out to Eden's Joy when I get off."

"I'm busy."

"Never mind that. Just grab a seat. I'll bring it over when it's ready."

She shouted at the boy beside the oven to make a barbecue rib burger as the manager talked on the phone in front of the drive-through window.

Wolfgang crossed the dining area. The old couple had finished their meal and was walking out the door. In the booth next to the lady's room, he put the note on the table. Outside, shadows flitted in the parking lot.

He had to find Elizabeth McDonald tonight and strangle the human trafficking ring, then leave Paradise and return to Washington. He would hold Ida's hand and give her a seashell and take her to Rome, to the Sistine Chapel, to the Basilica, to the Roman Forum. Of course, life would change after this assignment.

He called Isaiah and asked him to help monitor Pastor Cassidy. "He's dirty. If not human trafficking and prostitution, then robbery or money laundering."

"Sure, what's a minister without a crime. That'd be Napoleon without hair," Isaiah said. "What about my shield? What about my rod?"

"No and no."

"Ah, so you don't trust me. They say trust is the sentimentality of fools toward their friends. So either you don't want to be a fool or you don't consider me a friend. Either way, I'm disappointed. I thought you're both a fool and my friend."

"You're right."

"But without my rod—"

"I'm busy. I have to eat the lamb gyro and Greek salad."

"But you said you'd share it with me."

"I changed my mind."

"What just went down?"

Wolfgang ended the call. Grace had bit her lower lip while watching Isaiah prepare the spicy lamb. She learned to make the gyro in four hours. He opened the bag and smelled the spices. If only her tenderness would nurture his soul. Why did he still prefer the path into the desert?

Just as he took out the gyro and salad, a shadow cast over him. Grace, she had found him. But Lily-Rose sat down opposite him, pushing the barbecue rib burger and coffee toward him.

"Hey, what's up with that? Coming in here with food. That's against store policy."

He gave her the burger and said, "My treat." Then pushed the note in front of her and sipped his coffee.

She picked up the note and said, "So, you really a Mafioso?"

"Maybe."

"And will you take me to Eden's Joy?"

"No."

"Don't be so sure."

"Where's she?"

"Where's the dough?"

172

After putting down the coffee and taking the gyro and salad, he got up and walked across the dining room. He would return to Akdeniz and have the meal. Perhaps Grace would stop by to share it.

"Hey, wait up." Lily-Rose caught up with him and grabbed his arm. "I need the dough."

"Not really."

"Okay, I want the dough."

"Give me the information. I go check it and I come back to give you the money."

"That's not fair."

"It isn't."

"Hey, I know you need the tip."

"Maybe."

"You seriously a Mafioso? Wish to goodness that we got real Mafioso here instead of cuckoos like Mitch."

"The location."

"Such a cold man. You and the sheriff are two of a kind."

"Thank you."

She said the woman was hiding in the Davis Plantation outside town. "She an agent or what? Will you actually put the kibosh on her?"

After leaving Paradise Burger, he retraced his path along Isaac Boulevard, anxious to confront Elizabeth McDonald, who had executed Scotland Yard detectives, CIA agents, and apostates of the Elysian Fields, throughout Europe and the U.S. He called Isaiah and asked for four agents to go to the Davis Plantation. When streetlights disappeared and Isaac Boulevard became Esau Road, shadows hovered around the headlights and mosquitoes, moths and dragonflies darted around the light. In the distance, three spires pierced through a row of trees into the darkening sky, their silhouettes merging with the purple-black clouds. The crickets chirped their iambic dirge while the wind swooshed among the foliage. His fingers tingled and he breathed to steady his heartbeat. After the road had winded to the west where the trees disappeared, the mansion's façade, its wrinkles crisscrossing its surface, emerged under the last lights. A twenty-foot gate beside the granite walls guarded the colonial revival mansion. He turned into a dirt road beside the house, willows shading the path and fireflies darting in the dark, and parked the car in the woods, beside several eucalyptuses. Outside his car, the fragrance of primrose greeted him as he confronted the mansion's Palladian windows and the darkness inside. After putting on his gloves and taking his handgun and infrared goggles, he lurked toward the side entrance's fifteen-foot wall where a surveillance camera swiveled back and forth above the door. Then hid behind a tree and put on his goggles, preparing to face an enemy that Isaiah was fitter to defeat, peace descending into his mind and heart as the silence and the solitude of the woods deepened in the night. From that calm center, his guilt and anxiety retreated into the void and he accepted life's grief and turmoil.

A light flickered in the woods. Twigs cracked in the distance. Footsteps gnashing the ground. A figure emerged. A teenager, fake fangs coming out of his mouth and hair over his shoulders, his features resembled Cassidy.

The youngster tiptoed toward the gate, his gait unsteady, waited and watched the surveillance camera until it swiveled to the opposite direction. Then approached the gate, punched the code in the pad and entered the garden.

Wolfgang rushed toward the gate and before it closed, held it in place and waited for the teenager to approach the side porch, waited for the camera to make another round. He stepped through the gate. Closed it. Hid behind the bush waiting for the youngster to slip through the door, waiting for the wind to muffle his steps.

"Who's there?"

A flashlight beamed at the bush. Wolfgang froze. The bush flittered and a shot echoed in the night. Before the sound had died, the flashlight pointed at a dead squirrel on the ground. The guard cussed and walked away. After the camera had swung back and forth several rounds, Wolfgang sidled along a row of oaks and stepped onto the side porch and passing two pillars approached the side door, the crown pediment above shielding the fanlights. He entered a sunroom at one end of a hallway, where an amphora stood below a Monet painting. Down the hallway, a stairway led to the basement. Noise rose from below, voices and laughter.

He descended the stairs to the basement that smelled of roses, the scent spurring his nerves and raising his alert. The corridor, which bent to the left after twenty feet, led him into a family room with three sofas, a coffee table and a fireplace. A row of amphorae lined the shelves against the right wall and the corridor continued on the other side of the room.

The calm of death and the silence of oblivion stifled laughter from the first room along the corridor.

Behind the door, two men were watching TV, probably laughing at a comedy routine, perhaps a *Seinfeld* rerun, a show about nothing. He stepped into the opposite room where Mayor Davis's portrait guarded the room and a folder lay on the desk, as if waiting for him. After closing the door and turning on the light, Wolfgang took off the infrared goggles and opened the folder. A photo of Pastor Cassidy. Another of the murdered gay couple with a pimpled teenager, the youngster who had just sneaked into this mansion. He scanned the latter photo with his phone and sent the image to Isaiah, expecting to have located the couple's murderer, either Cassidy or the boy.

When the door across the corridor opened, he shut the light and put on the goggles. Two figures emerged from the room chatting and laughing, one carrying a shotgun, the other an assault rifle. He waited until the laughter had faded before taking off the goggles and going across the hallway into the other room.

The mayor's portrait also guarded this room, a velvet sofa facing the plasma TV on the wall. Remingtons, Glocks and Colts lined the left wall while a saber, a scimitar, and a katana decorated the right one. A case of 9mm magazine on the coffee table. On TV, a handsome teenager with blue eyes and an aquiline nose was electrocuting the naked mayor with a homemade generator and Davis was screaming and wetting his pants. The father was begging for mercy and the son was requesting that the old man beg for death. After several minutes, Mitch put a noose around the mayor's neck and pulled it through a pulley on the ceiling. Wolfgang was about to take the DVD from the player when outside glass shards jingled onto the floor.

The shadow of death and of evil accented his guilt of not having arrested the human traffickers when he had the chance. Opportunities lost and through the Butterfly Effect, pain and grief and suffering.

Several taps resounded in the hallway. He shut the light, put on the goggles and drew his gun. Mitch was holding a shotgun when he groaned and fell onto the floor. His friend hid behind a sofa and sprayed bullets down the hallway, where a figure, like a phantom, dodged behind the wall and sprinted down the passage.

Elizabeth McDonald. Must be her. Lily-Rose hadn't lied to him.

Wolfgang extracted the disc from the DVD player. Left through the backdoor, slipping through the doorway into a chamber reeking of blood, checking for bodies among the holding cells but only finding a skeleton. Several more taps sounded through the wall. On the other side of the chamber, a door opened to a carpeted hallway with oil lamps, wallpapers displaying Harley Davidson bikes through the years.

At the end of the hallway, he entered a room whose door was ajar. Inside, a mattress beside the wall and a dried red rose on top on two photos: of Mary-Lou Kensington and of Winston McDonald. Wolfgang picked up the rose. He and Isaiah had almost captured Kay Emil, a.k.a. Mary-Lou Kensington. Her photo crossed over with a black marker and she assassinated. Elizabeth, also a member of the Elysian Fields, had killed Kay Emil, eliminated the fugitive who had failed her charge several years ago. The model agency owner must have known the assassin was coming after her and she kidnapped Ernst's girlfriend to lure the lover here. She was probably going to kidnap Ernst and bargain with Wolfgang to deal with the Red Rose for handing over a man who resembles his father's killer. But in the end, she couldn't avoid the assassin's bullet.

He checked under the mattress and found a third photo, of Kerstin walking out of Scotland Yard toward her car under a gray sky. She wouldn't collude with Elizabeth McDonald and must also be a target. His hands shook and the photo fell onto the mattress. Elizabeth had shot at them, at Kerstin, earlier in the day. His mind whirled with images of Kerstin and Ida on the train. He called Kerstin but she didn't answer and he left a message alerting her that Elizabeth McDonald was after her, not him. He picked up a paper bag next to the mattress and put the rose in it. And would capture Elizabeth before she had a chance to harm Kerstin.

When he returned to the TV room, the magazines still lay on the coffee table but several bullets had punctured the door and rays of light seeped through, Mitch and Luc and their random violence confronting the orderly executions of Elizabeth McDonald.

In the family room, drops of blood spotted the floor and bullets had ripped open the sofa, split the coffee table and etched a relief on the door. Under the dim light Wolfgang again felt death lurking beyond the walls, in the shadow of darkness. The hunter waiting for the prey.

A breeze stirred like a phantom amid the wind, a photon disturbing the space-time continuum.

He aimed. Shot at a shelf. The bullet piecing the drywall.

Footsteps on the stairs. Not thumping, but tapping, as if afraid to ruin the carpet.

He pursued. At the bottom of the stairs no footsteps or breathing, only darkness and death.

Was Elizabeth thinking of a loved one, someone who meant the world to her? Did she only have her gun and her rose to accompany her through life and crime? Was she thinking of the millions of Euro in her Swiss bank account, perhaps planning to retire to the Maldives next year?

He went up the steps. He would miss Kerstin and Ida, and even Isaiah, if he should meet his end. The sense of evil thickened as he reached the first floor.

Silence as thick and oppressive as the Paradise heat greeted him. The assassin was determined to earn her fee and flaunt her skill.

Yes, Isaiah would envy him, would've begged to come.

Wolfgang didn't care to gamble his life to defeat an enemy and toot his horn. He crossed the hallway. Surveyed the sunroom. He might not walk out of here. Just never imagined he would die in a mansion.

As he stepped through the side door amid the crickets' chirps, a breeze stirred and a crushed stone crackled and he regretted his mistake. Should've stayed inside to admire the Monet. How many mistakes might a man make before reaching his quota?

He dropped to the ground. Aimed and pulled the trigger. He wouldn't have a second shot.

How he wished to see Kerstin and Ida one last time. How he wished to bid Grace farewell and a happy life. How he wished for a spicy lamb gyro.

CHAPTER 31 - PERRY

Todd had walked the path from the parking lot to Paradise Burger hundreds of times, but tonight the smell of barbecue ribs repelled his nostrils and the humid air irritated his skin. He had sought his true self for more than twenty years and when he found his self, he couldn't recognize his surroundings. Perhaps, that true self just couldn't identify with the flowers along the pathway or the French fries inside the restaurant. Perhaps he didn't belong in Paradise.

Inside Paradise Burger, a lady was ordering a barbecue pulled-pork burger with extra sauce and a large order of French fries. Lily-Rose didn't look up. Just pouting and searching the panel for a minute before locating the button to enter the order. Amid the elevator music, a tattooed biker near the window munched a Big Mouth Burger. Ketchup had splattered on the tissues near the soda fountain and a fly was buzzing around the trashcan. Lily-Rose yawned and spoke into the microphone to place the wrong order. The lady cussed and left the restaurant.

Lily-Rose raised her head and moved her lips but spotting Todd, her eyes sparkled and she swallowed the sound, ran to the side and came around the counter. She hugged him and kissed him. He raised his hand to shove her aside, but only back away and said, "Take it easy."

"Thought you were bent."

"I couldn't go to Eden's Joy. Too much work. Probably another all-nighter."

"Okay. But you came here to tell me."

"Actually—"

She hopped onto a stool, put both elbows on the counter and her jaw on both her palms, and said, "Hey, Sheriff, got any job in your place? Seriously, I'd rather work near you."

"Only if you're interested in picking up body parts. They're popping up like weeds." Todd's hands shook as he adjusted his hat so it slanted toward the left. To avoid her gaze, he checked the biker, who just bit into the burger and sipped the soda.

"Jeez, aren't you gonna catch them? Like it seemed they've been going at it forever." She threw a piece of gum into her mouth and chewed. "Seriously, if you got a business on the side, I'd like to lend a hand. And cross my heart, I promise I'd do a groovy job."

"Maybe try Gus Davis. He's always hiring pretty girls." Why hadn't the restaurant manager fired her? Todd had known her when she was in high school, when she looked forward to the future, when she aspired to become a nurse and care for others. If she had known how to pass exams, not cheating but just using the tricks to get the right answers without understanding the subject, she might've become a caring nurse. As a five-year old, he like a million other children had wanted to become an astronaut. And a dozen succeeded despite life. Just not Todd Perry.

"The pig."

"And stay away from pigs." He ordered French fries and promised to notify her of any openings.

"I'll do anything." She scooped a cupful of French fries.

Nope, you wouldn't.

"Someone's paying me to be an eye," she said. "I think a gangster. But I don't mind working for you instead."

"Like I said, stay out of trouble."

"You worry about me?"

He took the food and left the restaurant. The sky had darkened but his shadow was still draping over the fallen magnolias beside the trashcan. The wind was hissing among the leaves. How long could he continue to traffic young women before getting caught? He wouldn't go to jail. He would shoot his way out of a jam and either escape or die. When he reached his cruiser, he waited for an FBI agent to emerge from the shadows and arrest him. *Who're you anyway?* The deputy called and said he had lost Mitch and would come by the restaurant. After ending the call, Todd stepped inside his car and took out the French fries. Eating his midnight snack while waiting for a psychopath to dump body parts into the trashcan outside the restaurant. After arresting Mitch, he would get Cassidy the sadist to help interrogate the gangsters.

When the deputy arrived, they approached the men's room beside the restaurant. The deputy asking whether he had ever vomited when examining a body. Todd shook his head. The first time he faced a severed head, he was enjoying a Texas barbecue ribs burger. So he finished his lunch before examining the head. No use working on an empty stomach. The deputy shrugged his shoulders and sipped his coffee. When the man flipped a coin at the entrance, Todd called "heads." The deputy smiled when he didn't have to open the door. Todd finished his French fries. Wiped his hands with a napkin. Adjusted his tie and hat. He opened the door to find Gus Davis dangling from the ceiling by a rope, his tongue sticking out and his eyes rolled backward. Todd climbed on a toilet and cut the rope while the deputy held the mayor. When the body dropped, it dragged the deputy onto the floor. Todd checked the body's pulse and found none. The pliant muscles showed the man had died just about two hours ago. He told the deputy to have the coroner focus on the red marks on the neck for the post-mortem.

When Lily-Rose stepped away from the counter, he went in the restaurant and ordered a barbecue pulled-pork burger, returning to his car just as the girl came out of the restroom. He munched on the burger. Why didn't Mitch cut up the body? Perhaps an ex-employee, rather than the son, had killed Davis, to avenge the humiliations from the mayor. Todd would have to check the mayor's will to locate the suspects. A car pulled up to the parking space in front of the restaurant and a couple got out of the car and walked into the dining room. Ernst and Grace.

Todd dropped the burger onto his lap. The pork scattering on the seat and the barbecue sauce draping over his pants. He grabbed the door handle. His other hand squeezed the cup and the cap flew onto the dashboard and coffee spilled onto his lap. He opened the door. The bun and the pork dropped out of the car but the coffee was scorching his leg.

When a stray dog came sniffing at the food, he kicked it across the parking space and its head crashed against the trash bin.

He shut the door while the dog whimpered and scurried away, its tail between its legs.

Grace should've left this hell called Paradise.

He grabbed a bundle of tissues from the backseat and wiped the coffee and barbecue sauce off his pants. Pain traveled from his thigh to his shank but didn't distract him from his fever. The Bostonian had probably given up on the ransom and his previous girl.

Rather than ordering food, Ernst chatted with the manager and showed a photo. The manager shook his head but Lily-Rose pointed at the photo and nodded, and the Bostonian handed her several greenbacks.

Is he an undercover agent?

The stationmaster had spotted Ernst arriving in town on June 1st, the same day the deputy found the agent's body parts. He might be replacing the deceased man or investigating the death. Of course, Todd could defeat him just by snapping his fingers. And wouldn't hesitate.

Nope, Ernst didn't have the balls.

Wolfgang Demir had saved Grace, and he should defeat Todd and save his soul. But damned it, life sneered at Todd. He had gotten drunk in Eden's Joy when the Turk turned out to just own a restaurant and sell pilaf. Yet, Todd had faith and hope that Demir might be a gangster boss, and he had sent several men to watch the restaurant.

Had to be a front.

While Ernst was ordering the food, Todd attached a GPS device under the back bumper of the Bostonian's rental car. After returning to his cruiser, he took out the floor mat and dumped the barbecue pork onto the ground. Grace was eating French fries at a booth. Ernst, after talking to Lily-Rose, joined Grace.

Todd waited.

A jetliner roared across the sky above the City Hall spire as the streetlights sparkled in the night. He selected a Simon and Garfunkel album and "The Sound of Silence" calmed him.

When Ernst and Grace left the restaurant and drove off, Todd tailed them. Only a few cars loitered in the evening streets, but outside a disco, the line had extended to the street corner. The warm humid air agitated him as he checked the GPS receiver screen for Ernst's car. When a bug smashed against the windshield, he turned on the wipers to sweep it away.

After Ernst had stopped his car outside Akdeniz, Todd drove down the street past a traffic light and parked behind a BMW. Then leaned out of the window to face the restaurant. His heart thumped against his chest as hope surged through his veins. Salvation extended its hand and beckoned him and he slapped the steering wheel almost pressing the car horn.

In half an hour, when the air cooled, Wolfgang Demir drove up to the restaurant and got out of his car. Grace emerged from the restaurant and handed him a lunch box, her eyes smiling at him and her lips trembling out bliss unfamiliar to Todd. Oh, her supple lips and fragrant hair. He punched the steering wheel. Grasped the door handle.

Step out. Cross the street. Walk up to Demir. Fight him till death, hand-to-hand and man-to-man.

Instead, Todd sped down the street, ran a red light, honked at a pedestrian and shoved himself into a tavern that reeked of sweat and beer.

He ordered a Screwdriver and drank at the bar while voices undulated and bugged him to hell. A middle-aged lady in a low-cut dress was twirling alone under the dim lights. The waitress was stooping over a table and talking to a customer near the dance floor. A man and a woman, their faces hidden in the dark, were whispering in the booth near the restrooms. A young couple was arguing at the bar.

After finishing the vodka, he ordered a Moscow Mule. When a brunette came to chat with him, he imagined Grace's eyes and lips on the lady's face. He blabbed about Gus Davis's romances and raised his glass to toast to Grace's having found a field of daffodils. So he drank and he choked on the liquor and shed tears. When the lady gave him a napkin, he wiped away his tears and his saliva.

He wanted to possess her, not love her.

How could he love when he had never experienced it? He gulped down the scotch to numb the pain but his handicap, like life, sneered at him. The lady's mouth opened and closed but he didn't understand her words.

"Who's Grace? Your wife? Your mistress?"

He sweated. He should leave the tavern, instead ordered a Manhattan and drowned himself in the whiskey. The voices, the music, they nauseated him. His heart throbbed in the saline air as the image of his mother surfaced onto his mind. His head pounded and the heat choked him. When he looked up, Lily-Rose rather than the brunette was talking to him about love and loneliness, lust and passion, dream and illusion. She grasped his hand and asked to go to a quieter place but he declined and ordered two Tequila Sunrises.

After taking a sip, he said, "I hate the weather here. Always dampen my skin, not to mention my spirit." His mouth discoursed on bullshit. He had to invite Wolfgang and Ernst to jail for several days.

"Why are you smiling?" Lily-Rose said.

"I like philosophizing about the weather."

He wiped the sweat clammy against his forehead and finished his drink. Her elbow on the counter, her cheek on her palm, Lily-Rose talked about how her former boyfriend had run off with a high school dropout.

He took her hand and led her to the dance floor and, while her body caressed his, he pretended to be holding Grace.

"I can't really love anyone," he said.

Lily-Rose kissed him and leaned her cheek on his chest. Bodies brushed against him and the heat nauseated him. When they returned to the bar, he had a Seven and Seven before leaving with her.

At the entrance, the humid night slammed against his face. Return to the tavern for another drink. But Lily-Rose insisted on going to her apartment. They went into a liquor store and bought a bottle of Jack Daniel's, and they drank it on the quiet sidewalk. A beggar lay on the ground, flies hovering around the body. One day he might lie in some alley, drunk, ill, or just plain dead. Lily-Rose lit a cigarette and blew out rings of smoke while he drank the whiskey. When he had finished the bottle, the town spun and he struggled to keep standing. After puking, he fell onto the sidewalk, pulling down Lily-Rose, who was laughing while she dropped the cigarette and hit the ground.

On the sticky sidewalk, he leaned against a pet shop's front door and dropped his head between his trembling knees. Next to him Lily-Rose drank from the empty bottle. He waved his arm as if to fence with Wolfgang Demir. Grace kissed the damned proprietor. He puked again. Then kissed Lily-Rose and fell over.

#

The phone woke him up. Naked in bed, not with Lily-Rose but a blonde girl, not in his apartment but in an abandoned courthouse's renovated guest bedroom. After he had agreed to transfer the women to this abandoned courthouse in St. Peter's Yard, Cassidy renovated the building. They built a holding cell in the basement but Todd prevented the preacher from moving his equipment into the chambers.

The ringing wouldn't stop. After covering the girl's body with the blanket, he pushed away the bra and picked up the phone from the floor. Through the phone speaker, Ernst panted and muttered about his lover, a hideout and a head.

Todd entered the bathroom and splashed water on his face. The same stranger in the mirror stared at him. After focusing, he shouted into the phone, "You deaf or something?"

"Dick Wadlington."

"Didn't I tell you to back off?"

"I'm in his hideout."

"Hey, Miss Marples, didn't I warn you not to meddle with the investigation?"

"He got the money. Maybe he butchered Al."

"Go harass Scotland Yard and leave me alone."

"Listen—"

"You listen. Stay away from *my* investigation." What was the blonde girl's life like before coming to Paradise? What were her aspirations and her plans to realize her dreams?

"I've found Lucy-Jane's head. Oh pissa, found her head in Dick's hideout."

My lucky day. Another head. Screw them, got to focus on those Fed agents.

Todd was about to ask Ernst for the location when the call ended. He called the deputy and requested a squadron to raid Dick's hideouts and locate the missing girl's head. In front of the mirror, he sneered at the demon on the other side, waiting to escape from hell. Should free this girl. But then he would have to kill Cassidy and he still needed the psychopath.

Todd was knotting his tie when Cassidy knocked on the door and after entering invited him for champagne and Swiss cheese.

"Guess what I left in the church dungeon." In the control room, Cassidy flipped several switches on the control panel next to the bookshelves and the surveillance monitor showed the worship hall and church offices.

"Do you know your son Luc wants to do you in?" Todd said. "I don't blame him."

"That's a damn lie. A damn lie, you hear me? He ain't no son of mine. I'll sue the freak for libel."

"I'll just dig out his mom and ask her how her son was conceived."

"You blackmailing me?"

"So you better pray it was just a one-night stand."

The preacher flipped a switch and the monitor displayed a dungeon cell. A man, in an Armani suit and leather loafers, lay face up, blood over his face and clothing.

Who the hell had he whack this time? Todd focused the camera on the head injuries and grasped the gun around his waist. Violence, all the preacher knew was violence. And never think about the consequences. Todd could pull the trigger without lifting the gun from the holster. He could eliminate the pest by pulling his finger. But he preferred to set a trap for the preacher. The fiend should have a chance to save himself.

Thank you. I'll nail you with this. Todd raised his thumb at Cassidy and congratulated the preacher.

"Hey, what the hell you gonna do?" Cassidy said.

CHAPTER 32 - WOLFGANG

The bullet passed through Wolfgang's right arm as he dropped his gun and landed beside the two dead guards, the pools of blood around their heads creeping toward him.

Beyond the fence, a thud echoed.

Elizabeth dropped her gun.

He grasped his gun, and aimed, and pulled the trigger. Not to wound her but just to prevent her from picking up her gun, to avoid taking another bullet.

Footsteps retreated, the crushed stone whining in the dark and a twig broke. In the dim light, he detected shadows outside the gate.

As he was getting up, motorcycles roared and the delinquents' shotgun and semi-automatic rifle tapped out their chorus in the night. Wolfgang retreated behind a bush trimmed by bullets and listened for the source of the sounds, but before he aimed his gun, several shots replied the teenagers' taps.

His agents had arrived to sweep away Mitch and his buddy. Wolfgang knelt beside the rosebush. Then took out the crushed conch from his pocket and the fragments slipped through his fingers and scattered on the dirt. He had broken Ida's gift and no mending would make it whole. He punched the dirt and buried the fragments. No second chance. When his arm throbbed, he bandaged the wound and walked out to meet his comrades, who had chased the delinquents beyond the woods, leaving only dozens of shell casings, bullet-riddled barks. He had survived the assassin, and even wounded her, but only capturing or killing her would stop the gun from going after Kerstin.

#

When Wolfgang woke up in the morning, a wren was singing and sunlight warmed the wound that Grace had helped bandage after his return to the restaurant. But he recalled the shadow of Elizabeth's bullet as it pierced through the heat and his arm, a bullet determined to draw blood even if it couldn't drill through the heart or the brain. While he was dressing despite the pain in his wound, Grace called to say she would come to the restaurant around noon and make him pilaf. After meditating for half an hour, the calm mixing with random thoughts, he made green tea and stepped into the dining room where Sheriff Perry, straightening his beige shirt and adjusting his stripe tie, bade him good morning and handed him a warrant to search the restaurant. He took the warrant while the deputy combed his mustache and the officer next to the register polished his holster with a handkerchief.

"I thought the FDA has agents to inspect restaurants. Are they making you do it because of the budget cuts?" Wolfgang, after reading the warrant, adjusted the pot of lilies at the bar, the petals beginning to wilt, perhaps waiting for Isaiah's tender care. The human traffickers probably had identified him or Isaiah and struck back, harassing them with the sheriff's visits.

Go ahead, make your move and show your tail. Then my turn.

For the first time, he found in the sheriff's eyes steel doors protecting the secrets of that soul. He preferred not to step on the sheriff's toes but wouldn't hesitate to crush any human trafficker—minister or sheriff or mayor.

"We received a tip. And since it's your restaurant, I decided to visit myself." Sheriff Perry adjusted his cowboy hat and directed his men to search the restaurant. "Don't worry about it. We get tips all the time. Some people have too much free time."

"We don't have rats here, not even roaches, maybe a fly every so often."

The sheriff was challenging him to a game: Prisoner's Dilemma. The officers hurled pots and pans in the kitchen, probably rummaging through the shelves, perhaps nibbling on spicy lamb, but he had hidden his laptop and the case profiles in the ceiling vault, and no one opened the vents or tore down the dry walls.

"Like I said, you're really blowing away your talent running a restaurant. The first time I saw you, I expected you to be—"

"Would you like a pilaf dish?"

186

"If not a mobster boss or a drug lord, then at least an agent. FBI or Interpol." Sheriff Perry leaned forward. "You got the patience; you got the self-control. And I'm sure you got the killer instinct." After putting his cowboy hat on the table, he cleaned his teeth with a toothpick.

"The special today is the Putlicanli Pilav. The eggplants are very fresh."

"Tell me you're a drug lord here for business expansion. You know, geographic diversification." The sheriff placed the holster on the table and polished the gun with a cotton cloth.

"You won't need that here."

"Not for you. It's for them." He pointed at his men, one sniffing at a bottle of gin and another checking the bills in the register. "You know, got to keep them in line. Show them who's the boss and all that crap." He ordered the officers not to steal any liquor or money, pointing the gun at the one counting the bills.

"How's the investigation on the thrill kills?"

"You still have a chance to impress me. Just show me your shield."

"I'm not from the Mafia. Just have to impress you with the pilaf."

The sheriff returned his gun to the holster and said, "I heard you make a mean spicy lamb gyro."

"It's not on the menu. And if I serve it in a Turkish restaurant, I'll probably get into trouble with the Greek community."

"There's no Greek community here. In fact, there's no Italian community, no Chinese community, no Muslim community. But we have Tex-Mex food here. Well, more Tex than Mex because there's no Mexican community here."

When the deputy returned to the dining room with a bag of white powder, saying he had found the heroin inside the rolled-up yoga mat, Wolfgang nodded to acknowledge his foe's first move and examined the sheriff to determine whether he had ordered the deputy to plant the drug.

Check, but not checkmate.

The sheriff kept his poker face. "If he says it's heroin, then it's heroin. Believe me, he's resident whiz on dope, like a bloodhound." He picked up the plastic bag and sniffed three times.

"You won't find my prints on the bag." Wolfgang worried more about exposing his identity and therefore jeopardizing the investigation than going to jail and sleeping with local drunkards for a few nights. The human traffickers had either discovered his identity or suspected he worked for the FBI. Or, Cassidy might have noticed Isaiah tailing him and tracked an agent to the restaurant. Then again, perhaps a racist was trying to frame him and the sheriff just needed a warm body to fill the cell until he jailed the psychopath scattering body parts around town.

"No need to explain. Being a mob boss is a respected profession. Beats being a pickpocket." Sheriff Perry strapped the holster onto his belt. "But if you're a G-man, then better wave your shield."

"I can only tell you the heroin wasn't inside the mat when I rolled it up half an hour ago." Wolfgang finished his green tea and took out his phone to call Isaiah. The more Perry persuaded him to show his badge, the more he suspected the sheriff of investigating his identity and looking for terrorists. Whether or not the lawman was selling women into prostitution, Wolfgang would have to check his background and prepare to parry his blows.

Know your enemy and yourself. Should rely more on Sun Tsu's wisdom than on Murphy's Law.

"You saying I'm lying?" The deputy reached for Wolfgang's neck, but Sheriff Perry clawed the man's wrist—some variation of jujitsu—and twisted downward. The deputy screamed and knelt down beside the table as sweats rolled down his forehead and saliva dripped from his mouth.

"Well, you just got a pass to the slammer." Sheriff Perry released the deputy's wrist and waved for an officer to collect the evidence. "But before we hit the road, I'll have the special. Extra rice, please. And don't worry about the tip." He took out forty dollars.

CHAPTER 33 - ERNST

Ernst woke up in the dark. Smelling blood and rotting flesh. He must've just escaped from a nightmare. No, he was looking for Lucy-Jane and finding her head at the foot of the wall.

He sat up. "Rick. Rick. Rick." No one answered.

Blasted stench. He crawled around for the exit. Found the flashlight he had dropped on the ground. Oh, Lucy-Jane's blank face. His hands trembled as he tried to switch on the flashlight and he dropped it. After picking it up again, he flashed the light at the floor, avoid the head and those eyes. On the ground, scraps of papers lay next to shards and splinters. After about a minute, he inhaled and shone the light at the foot of the wall. And he dropped the flashlight. He held his head with both hands. His heart drumming against his chest and pulses paining his head. He panted and panted until the foul air filled his lung and nauseated him. He picked up the flashlight for a third time and thrust the light at the wall. The head on the ground gazed at the ground two feet away, the eyelids lowered and the lips relaxed.

Those eyes had smiled at him at Tupelo Point. Those lips had kissed him on a moonless night. He had shared with her a part of him he hadn't with anyone else. But Lucy-Jane had left and she had taken a piece of him away. He didn't accept the Socratic proof of the soul's immortality but treasured his psyche. Now, part of that had disappeared. The light swayed up and down around the head and the blank face flickered into and out of the darkness.

After he and Lucy-Jane had celebrated her eighteenth birthday in his Woburn apartment, after they had finished the bottle of champagne, she took off her clothes and led him into the bedroom. They made love in his bed amid Yanni's music. The bed caressed his body, the air calmed his mind, and her body warmed his soul. As he drifted between dream and reality, not caring where he ended up, she thanked him for the birthday present. After she had fallen asleep, he stayed in the living room and scrolled through his phone and gazed at the photo of her blowing the candles, her eyes twinkling from the light. At that instant, he grasped his brother's joy at dating the Wellesley student and his heartache while gazing at Lake Waban from Tupelo Point. If he had experienced such a moment earlier, he would've called the neurobiology student. That night, he watched the photo until dawn broke and prepared pancake and scramble eggs.

Ernst displayed Lucy-Jane's photo on his phone screen. Compared the photo with the head and found nothing in common. After dropping the phone into his pants pocket, he stretched his hand to reach for her face. Love fled into the past. His fingers stop about three inches away from the decomposing epidermis. Her skin had been warm and soft against his body. Her laughter warped by time faded into the past. Half of him had departed as thorns and thistles escorted him toward the end. From now on, the green tea Swiss roll would sting his taste buds. Yanni's music would vex his ears. Their future lost, aborted before birth. He took out the snow globe. Put it next to the head. But he returned it to the backpack. *Take it to her grave.*

He beamed the light around the hideout and searched for clues to Dick's whereabouts. Picking up the paper scraps and trying to read the handwriting but not understanding the hieroglyphics. He kicked aside the hacksaw and overturned the mat and blanket but didn't find anything underneath. After searching through the place without finding a single clue, he shone the flashlight on Lucy-Jane's head and bid farewell.

He'd avenge her. He promised with his life.

He drove to Eden's Joy and ordered a Long Island Iced-Tea. He would buy a gun in the morning at a nearby gun show. With gun in hand, he would hunt down Dick and kill him. He would avenge Lucy-Jane without Rick's help, to show he loved her more than Rick could ever aspire to, even after she had left them. When a prostitute approached him to solicit business, he waved her away. After another six drinks, the bar spun and the bartender was mixing drinks upside down. He shut his eyes and spun into a void.

#

In the evening, after having curry lamb and naan, Ernst went to the jailhouse and at the prison gate invited the guards to drink whiskey laced with Rohypnol from a street dealer. He sipped the chamomile tea and ate the apricot scone as the guards dropped off the chairs one after the other.

After shaking the head guard thrice and calling him to wake up, Ernst detached the key chain from his belt. Unlocked the gate and stepped into the holding cells reeking of blood and mildew. In the first cell to the left, a young man missing his right arm was reading a comic book. In the second cell to the right, a middle-aged woman was twisting a Rubik's Cube.

How to face Mr. Demir? He stopped. When the woman solved the Rubik's Cube, he dragged his feet forward. In the fourth cell to the left, Mr. Demir as if praying was in the child pose. Ernst straightened his shirt. He scratched his head. Should he leave before the proprietor gets up? But his legs wouldn't move.

"I want to let you in and serve you some pilaf." Mr. Demir sat in the lotus position, his hands on his knees.

"Get out of here." Ernst grasped the bars.

"About my father and your father."

"Isaiah told me what happened. It's a no-brainer someone set you up."

"Do you believe in the sins of the father?"

"Don't you worry about Grace? You have to protect her."

"Shouldn't you be taking care of her?"

"Get out and do it yourself."

"Life is full of twists and turns."

Ernst shook the keys and said, "In that case, let's try another way."

"I've been chasing fugitives for years. And I know I don't want to be one."

"Well, you want to jump off the cliff or fight the cannibals?" Ernst inserted a key into the lock but it didn't fit.

"I want to discuss my father's death."

"Can you forgive me?" Ernst inserted a second key but it also didn't fit.

"I've been trying to forgive your father."

"But still wouldn't forgive me." Ernst inserted a third key and it unlocked the gate.

"I still have no clue what I have to forgive you of."

"I'm his son." Ernst screamed and his voice echoed throughout the cellblock.

The woman with the Rubik's Cube called after him and said, "Hey, try the Cube. It can cure you of being anyone's son."

"You want me to forgive you for being a son," Mr. Demir said. "That's beyond my power. If you believe in a God, ask him or her or it."

"But I can't forgive myself." Extend the cursed arm. Shake Mr. Demir's hand. But he didn't give himself the pleasure of that friendship.

"Yes, a problem, a serious problem. And you'd have to resolve the issue."

"Don't you hate me?"

"Do you know what I hate? I hate not being able to help a drowning boy. I hate not being able to retrieve a baby from a burning house. I hate sitting in jail while girls are being kidnapped and forced into prostitution."

"Then just say the magic word, Alibaba. Something like 'open sesame' would do."

"But no, no more mistakes, no more girls taken due to my hesitation."

Ernst sprinted down the aisle toward the front gate, ignoring the young man ranting about having found salvation in the graphic novel. He locked the front gate beside which the guards were still snoring on the floor. Then, reattached the keys onto the man's belt and looked for Sheriff Perry.

#

The future belongs to those who believe in the beauty of their dreams.

No, the sheriff, so aloof and no nonsense would hiss such dreams. Facts and evidence, not dreams and chimeras. Having annoyed the sheriff earlier, he had to make amends before persuading the law enforcer to release Mr. Demir. Had to play the humble fool. But before he cooked up a strategy, the door opened. Amid the scent of sandalwood was the sheriff's raisin-face.

"Why are you eavesdropping?"

"Just admiring the quote."

"And I'm George Clooney."

"Mr. Demir's innocent."

"Only if you admit to planting the dope."

"He's a good man."

"We're all good men or women, but some better than others."

"He helped me find out Dick stole the money."

"But he didn't lend me a hand to nail those scumbags butchering the townspeople, so that evens things out."

"If you get how much he cares about that little girl Ida."

"Then, I'd be a psychiatrist. And wouldn't have to suffer you."

The sheriff hung below the quote a canvas embroidered with magnolias, the blossoms fleecy over oblong green leaves. Who had smeared the canvas with her sadness and given her feelings to this callus? He didn't ask about the sheriff's romance. The latter beckoned him to enter and closed the door.

"I've something to talk to you about." Sheriff Perry opened the drawer. Taking out a plastic bag with a piece of paper. Some scribbles on it.

"Someone framed Mr. Demir."

"You'll be interested in this." The sheriff put the bag on the desk and turned an hourglass. "You can stand there until time is up, or you can help nab a butcher."

Both palms on the tabletop, Ernst leaned forward, thrusting his head toward the sheriff. "I thought you're a Solomon. I thought you're a Perry Mason. I thought—"

"Cut the crap." Sheriff Perry breathed into his face. "Listen to me. That drug dealer's going down and I'll make sure of it. So just ditch it and lend me a hand to nail your lover's killer. Now, set your butt on the chair."

He had failed to save Lucy-Jane. But no more mistakes. Isaiah had to force Mr. Demir out of his cell. Perhaps put him under and carry him from jail.

He walked to the door. He opened it. The canvas with the magnolias was sad as Lucy-Jane's face. He took a step. But retreated into the office. Shut the door. He returned to the chair. Half of the sand in the upper bulb had tumbled down into the lower one.

"I know you want to help Demir, but facts are facts and we found dope in his restaurant." Sheriff Perry waved the plastic bag with the note inside.

"Anyone might've planted the drug inside."

"Don't think we don't do our police work. We're checking for fingerprints."

"Of course you won't find any. Even I know not to leave fingerprints when I try to frame someone."

"Don't get too smart. We don't like wise guys down here."

"You just don't like me."

"Give me a break. First, you're obsessed with finding the greenbacks. Then you're obsessed with saving your honey. Now, you're obsessed with freeing Demir. What's it with you? If I'm a psychiatrist, I'd be interested in psychoanalyzing your fetishes."

Sheriff Perry showed him the note and asked him to identify the handwriting. Ernst read the blackmail note but didn't understand it.

Just testing me? Or setting me up?

He pushed the note away, but wait, the handwriting looked familiar. The sheriff might be looking for more evidence against Mr. Demir but Ernst didn't find the proprietor's bold and straightforward handwriting on the note.

"Mrs. McIntyre received this note several days ago," the sheriff said.

This handwriting... He took out the scrap on which Rick had written *IOU*, and placed it next to the blackmail note. Same handwriting. The sheriff showed him Rick's photo to confirm the culprit.

Sure, Rick lusted after Lucy-Jane and feared losing her. Sure, he had seduced her, but kidnapped and killed her? No way he hated her. Yet, the blackmail note. So the scoundrel had kidnapped her. Rick might've put her head in the hideout to frame Dick, then took Ernst there to taunt him. He had to avenge Lucy-Jane. The kidnapper had killed her just to cheat him of fifty-thousand dollars. He would've given the money to get rid of him and would've found a way to provide for Lucy-Jane. But no, Rick had crushed his dream and he had to repay the fiend in kind, no, with interest.

"Here's my theory," the sheriff said.

The deputy entered to inform the sheriff that he had found Dick in the graveyard, bruises all over his body but especially around his head. The doctors had saved him but didn't wake him from the coma. The lieutenant promised to send in the report before saying, "A real bummer," and leaving the room.

Ernst pushed the hourglasses to the side. "Guess you'll have to do an about-face on your theory."

Sheriff Perry put the hourglasses back in place. "Guess again, it only expands my theory." Lighting a cigarette. Walking up to Ernst. Puffing smoke in his face. "Here's my theory, my expanded theory. Rick and Dick are in cahoots. They snatched your girl. They called the sucker, that's you, to bring the ransom."

"Thank you for the compliment."

"Believe me, you've earned it." The sheriff blew another ring of smoke in his face. "Things didn't go as planned. And of course, things

194

never go as planned. That's why there's no perfect crime. And no matter how sharp the crook, how flawless the plan, how careful the execution, some dork always makes a boo-boo and spoils the whole shebang. Just like life."

"You were saying their plan going amiss."

"Along came a beggar Al. And he copped their money. By the way, you're the dork, not Al. He's the Mouse."

"Thank you for updating me on the case," Ernst said. "Since you're Sherlock Holmes reincarnated, you'd know someone's trying to frame Mr. Demir and you should stop the charade." He swore to kill Rick and avenge Lucy-Jane. But before going after the killer, he would help free the proprietor and return a favor. He rose from the chair. Wouldn't waste anymore time with the sheriff. He would go to Akdeniz to find Isaiah.

"Of course, Dick found Al and got back the greenbacks. And he might as well bump off the Mouse for making waves. Rick and Dick got the money and killed your girl. Happy ending. But not quite. They clashed over the money and Rick tried to do Dick in. I would've deduced this last part because it happens nine out of ten times. And the tenth time, well, they're arrested before they strangle each other."

As Ernst opened the door and admired the embroidery, the sheriff said, "Don't even think of interfering. I warn you. And I'm watching you."

Go ahead and watch all you want. See if you can stop me. Rick is mine.

Ernst left the office, about to slam the door, but the deputy walked around him and entered the room.

"Hey, Chief, we got a problem."

"You're beginning to impress me."

"Our friends at Internal Affairs rang and they'd be coming over in no time."

"Damn it. Did any of you bastards take bribes or frame some dumb ass? If I find out you did, you numskulls, your interviews with those vultures will feel like a Hawaiian vacation, compared to the ordeals from me."

CHAPTER 34 - WOLFGANG

Wolfgang had extended his hand, hoping Ernst would shake it and forgive himself, but he didn't call after the man dashing down the hallway, running away from his guilt, from a past that shadowed him and tortured him day and night. Ernst would calm down and return with siomai, and would flee from that phantom feeding on fear and grief and more fear.

An officer, probably a human trafficker, had planted the heroin to thwart his investigation but he trusted Isaiah to find the culprit and gather the evidence to prove his innocence, to welcome him back to Akdeniz with his floral arrangement and the aroma of spicy lamb.

He opened the Styrofoam box and ate the blood sausage Kerstin had prepared before leaving Paradise. Chewing and savoring and daydreaming. Last year, when he visited her in London, she made him blood and liver sausages and he made her and Ida pastitsio with extra tomato sauce. At night, they dined on the apartment terrace facing the Thames. During late summer, they traveled to Hampshire and visited the Winchester Cathedral and the residences of Jane Austen and Charles Dickens. Beside the lime tree at Steventon Rectory Wolfgang held Ida's hand and imagined the view from the house as Austen wrote *Pride and Prejudice*. The scent of rain wafted in the air. On their return, Ida requested that he travel with them this summer to Rome. And he promised he would.

I will.

He ate another blood sausage in his cell. How was Ida handling the chemotherapy? He should stay with her during the treatment. She hated vomiting and feeling nauseous and losing her hair. He promised to take her to Rome and to Venice after the treatment and the recovery. He finished the sausage. He would take a leave after this assignment, a month to stay with Ida during her recovery and to take her and Kerstin to Italy.

Whatever the future might hold for Kerstin and him, he would care for Ida and she would grow into a brave and intelligent woman. At her age, beside the Rhine he had yearned to grow up and make a difference in the world. Now, after thirty years, in the jail he reached back to those days along the Rhine for wisdom. The lark on the window ledge chirped, as if reminding him that wisdom comes not with words but with pain.

He wished to stroll along the Thames holding Kerstin's and Ida's hands. He wished to rejoice with Kerstin when she caught a murderer. He wished to watch Ida marry a caring and confident man. When he had told Kerstin about his dream, she held her cheek in her palm and glanced at the Thames as if searching for a reply. He held her hand and waited until the sky darkened and a fog drifted over the water.

He was holding his cheek in his palm and thinking about Kerstin in her Scotland Yard office reading a new case, when Sheriff Perry stepped into the cell with a lunch box. After putting the box on the table and sitting opposite Wolfgang, he said, "Who are you?"

"I've asked that question time and again." Wolfgang opened the lunch box to find a spicy lamb gyro. "I'd wonder how much my skin color, my nose's angle, my cheek's contour, in short, my genes, define me."

"When I dig into someone's history, I'd always scoop up one and all, even the dirt he or she had forgotten or hadn't known yet. I promise you equal treatment." The sheriff picked up the book Wolfgang had been reading and flipped through the pages. "Poetry, so you like poetry? I once read some esoteric bullshit, something about the beauty of love. I decided then and there never to have these mental dopes contaminate my mind. I like you, so I'm telling you. Flush the arsenic down the toilet before it poisons you."

"Do you believe that your thoughts, emotions, and experiences define you more than your eye color? That your fears and wants drive you more than your genes?" Wolfgang dug into the gyro while examining the sheriff's fingers slender and manicured.

"You can't hide from me, not on earth, not in heaven, not in hell. Once a man buried himself in a coffin with an oxygen tank and a pick to hide from me. Well, I found him because his heart still beat and his blood still circulated." The sheriff played with his manicured fingers, then folded his hand and tapped the table.

Wolfgang downed the food with water and pointed at the sheriff's cuff button. "Nice stitching." He had studied the stitches on Grace's dress and now recognized the same handiwork in the sheriff's cuff button, the threads crossing the center to form Xs.

"You're beginning to impress me. Not many people can appreciate how special this stitching is." The sheriff unbuttoned his cuff and turned it over to reveal the same X pattern.

"What other hobbies do you have besides sewing?" Wolfgang imagined those delicate fingers stitching a button but didn't detect the lust and violence he had found on Cassidy's lips.

"Still haven't told me who you are. Like I said, hope you're from the Fed or Interpol. Don't mind if you're from the KGB." The sheriff rubbed the stitches several times before buttoning the cuff. "People who read novels are able assassins. And those who read poetry, well, either they're romantics or they're psychopaths. I hope you're the latter. Being a romantic is so dull. You see, I have great aspirations for you."

"I don't wish to be your enemy."

"You will. I promise you will."

"I'd like to have someone sew me a button." Having stumbled onto the clue—a clue Grace had helped locate—Wolfgang had to track it to the rapist and human trafficker. Grace was smiling at him through her trembling lips. He had to nab the criminal, crush that serpent's head, redeem her from her suffering. Sheriff Perry, who had tortured the deputy and belittled his other subordinates, who carried himself as if he were above the law, gazed beyond Wolfgang and the cell, perhaps rummaging through the past for a moment when the beauty of the sunset had touched his soul. Was he trading women for profit?

"Is the guy out of town or dead?" Wolfgang was determined to sniff the trail even if he had to chase the man across the country or the globe. He would seek justice for Grace and the girls sold into prostitution. He would redeem himself for his mistakes, which had led to his agents' deaths.

"Forget about the tailor. That button will soon be the last thing you have to worry about." Sheriff Perry adjusted his striped tie and said, "Usually I don't wear a tie. Down here, we're all informal. Can't stand those northerners with tuxedoes and cufflinks and silk shirts."

"You don't need to destroy me to save yourself," Wolfgang said.

"But you need to destroy me to save me."

"You found the wrong person."

"I see you more clearly than you see yourself. What the hell's spooking you? What the hell's holding you back?"

His father dying in the alley. His sister lying in the hospital after being raped. His agent's body parts strewn in the cemetery. Grace tied up inside a container, waiting to be sold into prostitution. Wolfgang's fingers twitched and sweat dripped down his forehead. His free hand reached for Sheriff Perry's neck while his other hand continued to hold the gyro.

"Now we're getting somewhere." The sheriff smoothed his tie and watched the hand approach his neck. "You should thank me for the therapy session."

When the fingers tightened around his neck, Perry smiled and warmth glowed from his cheeks. Joy and peace. Wolfgang let go, bit into the gyro and relished the lamb. He had walked into caverns more than once and followed the wind to the light. The man before him, with his broken soul, was groping for a hand to lead him out of darkness. "Who sewed your button?"

The sheriff knocked the gyro from Wolfgang's hand and pointed the gun at his nose. "Like I said, if you don't destroy me to save me, I'll finish you off." His eyes pleaded for destruction, for death, for salvation in hell.

Wolfgang extended his hand to touch the broken soul, but just picked up the gyro and wiped the tabletop with a napkin. How many people could he help? How much failure could he take? He bit into the gyro. Had his guilt affected his taste buds?

"Make my day, " Perry said.

"If I were you, I wouldn't do that." A man in black suit and sunglasses opened the cell door and showed his badge. "Internal Affairs. You're to hand us your deputy."

"My deputy's a numbskull. You don't want him, you want me." The sheriff returned the gun to the holster and adjusted his tie.

"Maybe next time. You can take a rain check."

The sheriff combed his hair and ordered the prison guard to bring Wolfgang a cup of chai and left humming, "Oh, My Darling, Clementine."

Outside the window, a sparrow flew from a branch and soared into the sky. Wolfgang finished the gyro. *Follow the bird and fly out of the cell.* After a night in jail, he wished to stroll along the beach or in the park at will. Neither the beach nor the park attracted him. Rather, being able to go there and beyond, being able to go on, from Frankfurt to Washington to

London and beyond. Where no walls would limit his steps, no fear would limit his ideas.

But reflecting on Kahlil Gibran's words in *The Prophet*, "And thus your freedom when it loses its fetters becomes itself the fetter of a greater freedom," he practiced yoga to clear his mind. How could he prevent freedom from shackling him? He was in the child pose mulling over Gibran's wisdom but worrying about Grace when the prison guard opened the door and took him to an interrogation room where the light had dimmed and the smoke hadn't dispersed. The air still reeked of sweat and blood. Was Sheriff Perry going to give him another spicy lamb gyro, an imitation substituting beef for lamb? But the Internal Affairs officer appeared with the sheriff and inserted a disc into the DVD player. In the video, the deputy-sheriff slipped heroin inside the yoga mat and asked his lieutenant to unroll the mat.

After finding out about Wolfgang's arrest, Isaiah must have retrieved the video from the surveillance camera and contacted Internal Affairs. Wolfgang had planned to leave the jail by week's end but his friend surprised him by speeding up the release. And neither he nor Isaiah had to reveal their identities.

Sheriff Perry patted Wolfgang on the shoulder and said, "Nice move. And I hope it's your move, so I can forgive you. If not, don't expect to catch any Zs until I'm gone."

"I'm not your savior." He would check the backgrounds of the sheriff and his men to find links to human trafficking and prostitution.

"But whether you know it or not, you've been chosen." The sheriff shook his hand and bid him farewell.

Wolfgang thanked the Internal Affairs officer and went to pick up his books and clothing. Outside the cell, the clouds drifted across the blue sky. He wished to stroll in Bliss Park with Grace—the wind on his face, the surfs against the shore, the air smelling of the sea—and dream of the New England autumn foliage, red and yellow against the turquoise stream. In here, he could still read, reflect and plan, and even think about Kerstin, Ida and Grace, but rejoining the tribe of free men and women, he would visit them at his leisure.

In the lobby that reeked of vomit, men and women rushed into and out of the lobby. Isaiah shook his hand and handed him a cup of chai and a report. "Do I get my shield back?"

He accepted the drink and the folder. "Did you bring me a spicy lamb gyro?"

"Now you get to put this slammer experience in your resume."

Amid the heat pouring through the door, Wolfgang dodged an officer rushing up the stairs and opened the report, while Isaiah told him the gangsters Mitch and Luc didn't dismember the agent. The killer was trying to mimic their signature, but the cuts were clean and precise. A surgeon more than a butcher. Kensington or her accomplice must have killed his man.

"May I get my rod back?"

"You just showed you don't need a gun to get things done. Congratulations." He signed for his belongings at the front desk.

"I need my rod."

"No."

Wolfgang opened his wallet. A picture of Kerstin and Ida standing before Westminster Abbey. Kerstin held Ida's hand but gazed at something behind the camera. Was she thinking of their future, uncertain then as now? He took out the phone and searched through the directory for Kerstin's London number.

Just when he found the number, the phone rang. Ernst called to inform him Grace is missing.

The chai spilled. His hand hurt. His heart dreaded. He squeezed through the doorway. Dashed into the heat. Dropping the cup. He looked for a taxi. New Hollywood Model Agency, he had to go there. Had to find Grace.

Should've called to check on her. Should've assigned an agent to look after her. Should've sent her out of town.

But he didn't and didn't and didn't.

CHAPTER 35 - PERRY

After watching the video of his deputy planting the evidence to frame Wolfgang Demir, Todd waited for the last grain of sand to pass through the hourglass funnel and surrendered the subordinate who was only obeying his order. He took the deputy's gun and badge, the man wouldn't rat on him, and requested his attorney to accompany the fall guy to the holding cell and negotiate a light sentence with the assistant district attorney. Naturally, Todd would send the deputy the complete DVD set of Scooby Doo episodes, pay the legal fees and support his former lieutenant's wife and children while the man serves his time. The standard fringe benefits.

After the goons had taken away the deputy, Todd ordered two men to tail Demir and observe Akdeniz day and night. They were to report back even at 3:00 a.m. anyone entering or leaving the building.

After his men had left, he entered the deputy's office, gathered the Scooby Doo collections into a cardboard box and requested a courier to deliver the mementos to the holding cell. He stood akimbo reading the certificate of excellence he had awarded the deputy three months ago.

A shame. Damn good man.

In his office, after drinking a quarter glass of Jack Daniel's and stitching a button onto his pants, he set an hourglass on his desk and checked the police databases for Wolfgang Demir but found nothing. Checked the FBI databases but found nada. If the proprietor were an ordinary Middle Eastern man, the FBI would have his profile. An operative then, FBI or CIA or British Intelligence.

The proprietor's eyes had sparkled while extending his hand toward Todd's neck, but regained his poise as a flame reshaping after a gust. Even when the gun barrel was glaring at his nose, Demir just chewed his food, relishing the spicy lamb. Todd expected to fight a worthy foe, agent or not. Of course, he had to test whether the lawman had a savior's craft and resolve.

Todd opened the blind and the setting sun's rays like snowflakes tickled his face. He opened the window, smelled the magnolia and imagined dueling with Demir in an Old West town. They would face each other ready to draw their guns as the dust dances around him and the dry air chokes him. The quick and the dead. The battle between good and evil. But his mother's face replaced his fantasy and the magnolia's fragrance sickened him. After shutting the window and the blind, he finished the glass of Jack Daniel's.

Let the game begin.

Three nights ago in the abandoned courthouse, after watching the surveillance monitor and studying Dick Wadlington in a pool of blood, Todd pulled out his handcuffs and walked toward Cassidy, but after standing behind the sadistic killer for a minute, he just ordered him to organize the meeting. Dick Wadlington was snooping in the church basement, probably trying to hide the money, but the homeless man had stumbled into the devil's pit. Todd zoomed in to examine the backpack next to the body, the bag's zipper halfway open but the stacks of bills had fled.

"Let's crack open the champagne to celebrate your fifty-thousand dollar windfall," Todd said.

"I swear to God I didn't find any dough."

"You can swear when you're sitting behind bars and I'm counting the bills in my office."

"Sixty-forty. After all, I found it."

Todd threatened to jail the preacher and forced him to hand in the evidence. For fifty thousand dollars, Al had died and Dick had become a vegetable, and perhaps Cassidy would go to jail: the dominoes that Ernst had toppled by coming to Paradise with the ransom.

Todd had visited Dick at the hospital and whispered to the homeless man to wake up and implicate the preacher. Now, the courier bag sat under his desk. Did Cassidy lie about only finding twenty-five thousand dollars? Had Dick hidden the other half in another nook? He was about to count the stacks of cash when his contact at Interpol called and said Mary-Lou Kensington was Kay Emil, an Elysian Fields agent the FBI had been hunting for five years. He looked up the Elysian Field's insignia, a red rose. So, a Red Rose had come to eliminate a deserter. The STR result would identify Mary-Lou's assassin. The killer probably wouldn't come after him, but he still intended to catch the culprit. He would have guessed McDonald but according to the forensics analysis, to shoot at that angle given the man's height, he would have to bend his knees to lower himself by more than a foot. And the strand of hair: a woman's.

As he filed the folder into the cabinet, his new deputy called to report that Rick Dougherty wasn't in his apartment, or Jo-Beth McIntyre's trailer. Todd issued a manhunt for Lucy-Jane's killer and ordered his men to search Eden's Joy and Noah's Beach. After finding the hacksaw in Dick's hideout, he had closed the file on Al, and would the same on the Lucy-Jane abduction and murder case by week's end. After that, he would arrest Mitch for killing his father and the Georgian girl. If Todd had a daughter, he would worry about her ending up like Lucy-Jane or the Georgian girl or even Lily-Rose. But he didn't and he wouldn't. Not in this life.

While he was examining the picture of Lucy-Jane's head, an officer came in and reported the former mayor's nephew had bailed out Luc with a million dollars. *Nephew, my ass.* Todd put away Lucy-Jane's file and went to the security office to check the surveillance videotape. The *nephew*, with a mustache and in a cowboy hat and a neon suit, was probably Mitch playing hide-and-seek. He sent the image to the forensics lab and asked the technician to compare the facial features against the delinquent's picture a year ago. Sure enough, the two faces matched. Todd returned to his office, called the former mayor's lawyer and confirmed the deceased had left his fortune to his nephew, but the DMV database revealed that the young man had registered only two months ago. He sent two officers each to monitor the mayor's palace near City Hall and the mansion just outside town, and directed them to tail the *nephew*. Mitch would build a dungeon, probably in the mansion, and Todd would spoil the Vampire's plan. He contacted the insurance company and coordinated with them to find evidence the rich psychopath had killed his father.

In the FBI database, Todd pulled up Luc's birth certificate, which lists Isabella Collins as the mother and Buck Cassidy as the father. So, the Werewolf didn't lie when he claimed to be the preacher's child. Should he stop the Werewolf from killing his father and reserve the preacher for a manhunt?

He combed his thinning hair, put on his striped tie and cowboy hat and adjusted his hat until its tilt aligned with the stripes of his tie. His phone rang. His new associate called from Eden's Joy to tell him she had picked up Grace. She would take a cab and bring her to his house. When he hung up, his heart pounded as if on his first date. He would see Grace again. Her cheeks' contours would appear beyond his dreams. But her face, her hair, and her breathing would haunt him day and night. Leaving the police station, though the heat was engulfing him, he shivered from the anticipation, the excitement.

He drove his Cadillac out of the parking lot and almost ran down an old lady crossing the lot's entrance. Swirling the car onto the left lane, he sped down the street, running through a red light. His hands shook from a chill burning through his muscles. And as the last sunrays disappeared from the horizon, the building, the cars and the pedestrians blurred into shadows and rushed past his car. The night was swallowing up the town and darkness was engulfing him.

Todd drove into the garage and got out of the car. He slipped on a scrap of paper and landed on his wrist. The pain shot through his left arm and he lay on the floor facing the recycle bin. He laughed. A minute later, he scrambled up and dusted his trouser legs. Then picked up the newspaper on the driveway and shut the garage door. In the living room, Grace curled up on the sofa like a fetus. His associate had left a message that she would return before dawn.

After carrying Grace into the bedroom, he laid her on his bed. Did she shudder? Would she wake up and see him? His heart pounded against his chest as he waited on the bed's edge. He had never let any girl see his face and might have killed anyone who had. But not Grace, not even if she should walk into the police station and identify him as a rapist and human trafficker. Would she look at him? But when he caressed her cheek, she didn't open her eyes.

Water had condensed on the windowpanes and the vapor obscured the night outside. Once in a few minutes, a car would pass under the streetlight and a shadow would crawl under the vehicle. But no pedestrians were strolling in the humid air.

After Wolfgang Demir had botched the deal, Todd had rejoiced in Grace returning to her life, though that life had changed, though she would carry the scar through the years. But when she went to the proprietor's apartment, Todd should've walked up to the unit and kicked down the door, crushed Demir and snatched her from those talons.

Now, she was in his bed. He kissed her on the cheek. Her fragrance and her breathing...

CHAPTER 36 - ERNST

Ernst was eight when he met Mr. Collins and baby Ricardo in Falls Church, Virginia. His parents had bought a townhouse near Leesburg Pike and the Collins just moved into the community. Ricardo was eleven months old when Mr. Collins first held him outside the townhouse. A chubby baby with a dimple. Mr. Collins, a mechanics, wasn't working when he first met him but soon found a job at a local garage. He befriended the family and after school played with the baby. His brother spent his free time in the library reading Robert Louis Stevenson and Arthur Conan Doyle and never stepped into the Collins' home. One autumn day when the foliage had reddened and a cool wind slithered through the windows to lift the curtains, Ernst went over to play with Ricardo while Mr. Collin stepped out to buy milk. He was rocking the baby in his arms sing "Mary Had a Little Lamb" when Ricardo slipped from his grasp. Falling onto the floor. The towel brushed against his forearm. Ricardo crying. The cool breeze against his face. His heart beat against his chest. He froze. The baby dropping. Hours seemed to have passed before the baby hit the floor. He covered his ears but the baby had stopped crying. And wasn't moving. He watched. And watched until he bent down and grasped the baby, limp in his arms. The curtain was dancing in the wind and he opened his mouth but couldn't speak. Alone for what seemed like hours before the baby cried. A wail pounded on his eardrums. When Mr. Collins returned, he told the man about the fall. The father took Ricardo to the hospital but after some examinations, the doctor didn't find any injury. The parents never rebuked him. But he had nightmares: baby Rick slipping out of his arms. Falling, falling, falling onto the floor.

#

In the dark narrow stairs, Ernst regretted not having killed Rick decades ago, not having saved Lucy-Jane from her killer. Even those many years ago, he had sowed the seed of failure, which he was reaping now. Its fruit bitter in his mouth, riling his stomach.

He stepped into Benjamin's Fight Club, a.k.a. BFC, and smelled sweat and blood. Just after showing the invitation, he ran into a bald man with a dragon tattoo on each arm and bounced off the steel-like chest. The man flexed his pectoral muscles and bearing his teeth, seized Ernst by the shirtfront and lifted him off the floor.

Dangling from the claws, Ernst punched. *Make my day.* He had to release the pain of losing Lucy-Jane and the frustration of failing to protect Grace. He missed the bald man. He had come to Paradise to rescue his reason to live. Now that he had failed, he lost his direction, not just in Paradise, but also in The Hub. For more than ten years, he had roamed around Lake Waban looking for his other half. After finding Lucy-Jane, he prepared to start a new chapter in his life, but just after the prologue, the story ended.

He fell onto the floor as two security guards approached the bald man and invited him to leave. The thug lifted his foot as if to trample on Ernst, but after glancing at the guards, just grunted and left the club.

On the floor, his buttock ached. Should've shaken Mr. Demir's extended hand and befriended the man. Losing Lucy-Jane had taken away his compassion and revealed how few friends he had. But he held on to his guilt, so as not to suffer the withdrawal pangs. Apologize to Mr. Demir. But before that, Ernst had to find Grace. He had failed Lucy-Jane. He had to save Grace. He wouldn't flounder again. Not one failure upon another upon still another.

The baby slipping from his arms. Dropping onto the floor…

He shook his head, got up and dusted himself. He squeezed through the crowd as a roar echoed through the room and he searched for the clown who had talked to Grace before her disappearance. In the center of the gymnasium, two men fought on a stage while the crowd cheered and howled. Blood and sweat had smeared the fighters' lips and knuckles and bruises covered their faces and chests.

At the bar where the bartender was cleaning a glass, he bought a glass of martini.

On the day Lucy-Jane left The Hub, Ernst had taken her to Harvard Square for lunch. They had Thai food. He ordered the Garden Duck. While drinking her martini, she said, "I may return here." "You can stay with me," he said, "And take your time to look for a job." At Logan Airport, he kissed her off. "See you in two or three months."

Now, at BFC Ernst drank his martini. He would never see her again. Would never try the Garden Duck at the Thai restaurant again. The bartender chatted with him about the Facebook IPO but he just inquired about the clowns. The man pointed to the back of the gym where benches lined the wall and Ernst thanked the man and took the martini.

After slipping past three women goading on the fighters to hit harder, he reached the back of the gym where a bookie was taking bets from half a dozen clowns on a bench. The bookie blocked his path and solicited his bet. He shook his head, walked around the man and approached the clowns who were doubled-over in laughter.

When they straightened up, Ernst showed Grace's photo to a neon-nosed clown. "Have you seen her in the carnival yesterday?" The clown studied him, turned to his associates and scanned the photo.

"None of us went to the carnival the past three days."

"But there was a clown."

"Go talk to Pastor Cassidy."

"Is he a clown?"

"President of the Clown Club. Schedules us for the carnival." The neon-nosed clown signaled the bookie to come over.

Ernst thanked him and finished the martini just as the crowd roared and booed and he had to cover his ears. One fighter prostrated on the stage and struggled to get up. A man in a cowboy hat cussed and threw his half-eaten hot dog onto the floor and stamped on it. Ernst walked around him and squeezed through the crowd toward the entrance. He stepped on something mushy. A young lady pushed him toward the stage. More cheering as two other fighters stepped onto the stage.

The crowd split and two guards carried the fallen fighter through the opening. Blood hid the face that reeked of spoiled fish. After the guards had passed, the crowd converged and pushed toward the stage.

Ernst struggled against the current, inching toward a wall filled with the fighters' photos. A bookie called for bets while his assistant handed out the forms. At a nook near the bar, Kerstin and Mr. McDonald were whispering to each other. She nodded while Mr. McDonald handed her a file.

No, she wasn't having an affair with that married man. She had mentioned an old boyfriend proposing to her, German, not English.

Ernst inched along the wall toward them. He would sneak behind them and eavesdrop on them. A mousy teenager hissed, approached and showed him Rohypnol but he continued walking along the wall where a waitress/prostitute was soliciting a young man. By the time he reached the bench, Kerstin and McDonald had left. He should inform Mr. Demir. He had promised to contact the agent when he should see the criminal. But he didn't want to implicate Kerstin.

Near the entrance, she and McDonald pushed through the crowd. He was approaching them when an old lady shoved a flyer into this hand. A gun show outside town. Just what he needed. He shoved it into his pocket and pushed toward the entrance.

By the time he reached the doorway, they had left. He escaped the scent of sweat and blood and rushed up the narrow stair into the night-street where prostitutes had lined up to solicit customers. Down Melchizedek Street, among the crowd under the streetlight, Kerstin walked toward Main Street.

He passed a teenager break-dancing on the sidewalk and a man playing guitar and singing, "The Sound of Silence" and treaded along the curb toward Kerstin, who waved for a taxi outside a real estate agency. He reached her as a taxi stopped in front of her.

"Why aren't you with Ida?" Ernst said.

"I wouldn't be here if I didn't have to." Kerstin let the taxi leave.

"Mr. McDonald's a wicked man."

"Do not believe everything you hear."

"Is he your old boyfriend?"

"I love Wolfgang, more than you can understand."

"Mr. Demir asked me to report back if I see him."

"You do what you have to do," Kerstin said.

"Don't throw your life away."

"There are things you do not understand."

"Love? Okay, but I know the people I care about."

"I am sorry you lost your girlfriend."

"That's why I don't want to lose another friend."

"Please do not talk to Wolfgang about this."

She held his arm and he pulled away but didn't refuse her request. *Mr. Demir, come and save me from this dilemma.* But only the waitress who was soliciting the young man passed them. Kerstin waved for another taxi while he scratched his ponytail.

"I have to return to Washington," Kerstin said. "Ida will start chemotherapy tomorrow."

"Don't do this if you love Mr. Demir." Ernst said.

Kerstin was about to step into a taxi when her phone rang. She picked up the call. She listened. She looked at him. Then fainted and fell onto the pavement.

CHAPTER 37 - WOLFGANG

Nine years ago, after the jury had convicted his sister's rapist, Wolfgang went to Lorton Prison and the warden, Isaiah's buddy from high school, after showing him how to beat someone without leaving bruises took him to the criminal's holding cell. Then handed him the phonebook and left the room.

Wolfgang put the phone book against the rapist's abdomen and squeezed his fist. He pulled back his hand and shouted. But couldn't punch the rapist anymore than a soldier could shoot an enemy waving a white flag. He wouldn't cross the line separating man from beast. Wouldn't fling away his integrity and plunge into the viper's chasm. He had helped the police catch the rapist and sought justice for Hilda. But his sister had cast off the trauma and was dating a Bosnian who had escaped the holocaust. She hadn't let the rapist destroy her life and Wolfgang wouldn't his integrity.

But one morning, the prison guard found the rapist prostrated on the floor bleeding below the waist. Castrated. The International Society of Vigilantes claimed responsibility. Wolfgang didn't rejoice at the news, only vowed to catch the murderers.

\#

Wolfgang entered Davis Municipal Park and, amid the music of the Beatles, searched for the palm reader. Two men wrestled on the mat nearby as the crowd whistled and cheered the contenders. After leaving the sheriff's office, his hand scorched and his head fevered, he had gone to New Hollywood Model Agency to search for Grace and found a note directing prospects to the palm reader at the Annual Davis Municipal Park Carnival.

Several days ago, when he told Grace he had watched a man beat his father to death, she sketched the Tidal Basin, the cherry blossoms showering on the water, and handed him the amulet against guilt and remorse. Now, passing a clown who was blowing a balloon, he experienced the blossoms' beauty, but it mingled with decay. Youth cut short by death. After passing a shooting gallery, he walked around a Ferris Wheel. Would Grace walk up and show him another sketch? Perhaps of snow falling on a cedar trail, the white serenity of winter.

He was approaching the palm reader's tent, a yellow flag flapping on top, determined to stop Grace, when his agent called to inform him Elizabeth McDonald worked for the British Secret Service. Must be a mistake. He asked her to check the Elysian Fields, delve into each member's profile and look for double agents. After hanging up, he entered the palm reader's tent that reeked of incense, only to find a cracked crystal ball and several torn Tarot cards. He stepped on a folded piece of paper: the invitation letter to the model agency. Grace had come. She had been taken. He was too late. He had failed. Again. He crumbled the letter and dashed out of the tent, bumping into a girl.

"Grace."

He embraced her.

But it wasn't Grace. The redhead in a pink low-cut skirt smiled and embraced him. Lily-Rose, his informant.

"Playing hide and seek with your girl? Seriously, you surprise me. Like I thought you're the all work, no fun kind of guy."

He let go of her. He paid her two-hundred dollars. While she smiled and kissed the bills, he showed her Grace's picture and asked for information, hoping for a miracle. She shaded her eyes. He tilted the picture to avoid the sun's glare. She squinted for several seconds before saying, "Yeah, seen her here gabbing with a purple-nosed clown. Maybe four hours ago."

Under the Ferris Wheel, a red-nosed clown was taking pictures with two girls. A green-nosed clown munching a chilidog on a bench.

Where had the clown taken Grace?

Wolfgang scanned the park for surveillance cameras. Someone must have seen them leave. He still had time to locate her, to rescue her before the next transaction.

"Don't worry. I'll help you find her. But first, you got to buy me a drink."

A band, its members dressed as hamburgers and hotdogs, was playing "It's Not You, It's Me," as Wolfgang followed the girl to the makeshift bar and phoned Isaiah, asking him to check the surveillance cameras around Davis Municipal Park.

He bought two glasses of Long Island Iced-Tea and inquired about the purple-nose clown but the bartender shook his head. He sat at a table next to the dance floor, where a shirtless man was break-dancing under a reggae tune. He should have accepted Ernst's help to escape from jail. Might have stopped Grace from throwing herself into the lion's den.

Across the table Lily-Rose talked about Sheriff Perry's quirks and defects. When he inquired about him, she cursed the lawman, finished the drink and left, shoving aside a man who had just stepped into the tent looking for a seat.

Amid the smell of barbecue ribs and among the crowd with a Merlin, a Don Quixote and a Henry VIII, he took out the picture of Kerstin and Ida in front of Westminster Abbey. Would he be able to spend more time with them? If only life had taken another route. But the next time in Washington, after Ida's chemotherapy, Kerstin would break up with him, he was sure. How would he mend the rift with Kerstin when they traveled on divergent paths? No matter what, he would visit Ida and take her to Rome and Disney World.

Just as Wolfgang located a surveillance camera above a nearby tent, his phone rang.

"St. Peter's Yard. June 12th, midnight."

"Grace?"

"St. Peter's Yard. June 12th, midnight."

"Where're you?"

"I did it for you, so you can catch them. Catch them and save the girls. Do it for me."

"I will rescue you. I promise."

"I won't let them sell me. I'd take my own life before they do it."

"Please sketch the view from Devil's Point for me, as a gift."

"I love you."

Grace hung up.

The phone displayed "unknown number." He requested his agent to track the last call to his phone. The voices and laughter and even the heat was fading away, leaving him in a vacuum, in his own world. He picked up a handful of peanuts and was tossing them in his hand and mulling over his next move when Perry sat opposite him and pushed a Manhattan toward him. After putting his hat on the table, the Sheriff adjusted his tie and gulped his Seven and Seven.

Wolfgang pressed his left palm against the table to avoid shaking, but crushed the peanuts in the other hand as he imagined Grace whispering his name in a windowless dungeon, the damped chill seeping into her bones.

The sheriff put an hourglass on the table and the sand poured through its neck but Wolfgang, after flinging away the crushed peanuts, turned it around and the sand reversed its flow, emptying into the bottom bulb in ten seconds.

Perry cracked his jaw and finished the Seven and Seven and, after wiping his lips with the back of his hand, threw the tumbler onto the floor, and it cracked into pieces. Wolfgang grasped his tumbler as smoke drifted from the barbecue pit into the tent. His eyes smarted but he drank the Manhattan.

"I don't lose." Perry flipped the hourglass upside down.

"This time, you may want to."

"You'll destroy me even if you don't want to."

"I will destroy you even if I don't have to."

"I pity you."

"But you will destroy yourself even if you don't want to."

"You're my savior."

"You're a lunatic."

"Accept your destiny." Perry grabbed a handful of peanuts and shoved them into his mouth and gnawed at them.

"Are your nightmares still gnawing at your soul?"

Perry's fist landed on the tray and the force launched peanuts across the aisle onto nearby tables. The ladies at the table behind Perry burst into laughter as they whispered to each other and pointed at two men walking down the aisle.

"Grace."

That syllable reminded Wolfgang of Grace's lips soft against his cheek and he tightened his grip on the tumbler, the liquid spilling onto this hand. The drumbeats from a band vibrated through his bones and his hands shook.

"I have her," the sheriff said.

The filtered sunlight cast Perry's shadow ephemeral on the ground while the young men at the table beside the bar sang "You Are So Beautiful." Wolfgang grasped the hourglass, shook it and flung it onto the floor, where its shards mixed with those of the tumbler. The corner of the sheriff's mouth twitched and twitched and twitched as the shards scattered on the floor. The veins on his forehead wriggled. He adjusted his tie. One eye blinked. Then, he smiled.

"I left her in my bed."

The music faded but the ladies behind Perry cheered at the two men who had taken off their T-shirts and were competing with each other to lift barbells. Wolfgang's right hand lifted Perry's tie and his left gripped the neck while a singer crooned "I Left My Heart in San Francisco." In his mind Grace groaned. He had let his father be killed; he had let his sister be raped; he had let his agent be murdered; and he had let Grace be raped and raped again. As sweat dripped down his face and a ring resounded in his ears, he gripped the trachea and the sheriff's face reddened as if encouraging him to squeeze harder.

Perry took out a mirror and combed aside the hair fallen over his forehead as the ladies behind him whistled and clapped their hands and the crooner's base note trembled for almost ten seconds.

Wolfgang couldn't breathe. He had to close his fist. Crush that throat. Relieve the grief, the anger, the hate welling up in his abdomen and bosom. To avenge Grace's suffering, to rid the land of the serpent, to offer salvation for the world.

Sure, he would be the savior.

But Kerstin and Ida, their voices soothed his soul. They would be waiting for him after Ida's treatment.

And Grace, her hands warmed his and he reached across his memory to touch her hair, soft and fragrant as the magnolias.

I did it for you, so you can catch them. Catch them and save the girls. Do it for me.

Her only, and perhaps her last, request. Wolfgang tightened his hands while Perry grinned and trembled, the sheriff's breath fanning his face. A group across the tent was singing, "For He's a Jolly Good Fellow" while a couple jitterbugged on the dance floor.

What did it matter if he crushed this psychopath and his associates? He had to save Grace. He wouldn't fail her. And this criminal will lead him to her.

I promise to catch them. I promise to save the girls.

For Grace. While pain traveled from heart to abdomen, Wolfgang released Perry and waved to the waitress, ordering two Screwdrivers while the sheriff gazed into the mirror and straightened his shirt and tie. The young men near the bar cheered the couple on the dance floor while the ladies behind Perry invited the shirtless men for a drink.

Lily-Rose stepped into the tent and talked to the bartender for a minute before turning to watch the dancing couple.

After the waitress had brought the drinks, Wolfgang touched glasses with Perry, while Lily-Rose smiled and raised her glass toward them.

"To our destruction," Wolfgang said.

"To my salvation."

To Grace.

Wolfgang drank the Screwdriver and a void swallowed the haunting images in his mind. The noise faded and Lily-Rose's face blurred. He even found peace in Perry's look as he surveyed the path toward the end and if he stayed on course, he would cast the sheriff into hell. And then…

Perry drank the Screwdriver, spilling some over his chest as his hand shook and the air vibrated under the band's music. Lily-Rose raised a thumb at them.

"To damnation, yours." Wolfgang finished the drink in three gulps and slammed the tumbler on the table and the vodka stung his throat. Death would save Perry from hell but behind bars, the psychopath would suffer the purgatory he deserved.

"Do you know what it feels like to be born again? To get a whiff of the roses after ditching the cesspool? To give ear to the brook gurgling after fleeing from the screaming loonies? I'm counting on salvation. You saving me. Me being a new man." Perry finished his drink and wiped his mouth, combed his hair and put on his hat. Then tipping his hat, he walked to the bar and greeted Lily-Rose. She pulled his tie and tried to kiss him but he backed away. After whispering to her, he took her out of the tent.

Wolfgang took out the handkerchief Kerstin had given him and wiped his forehead. As he held his head in his palms, the audience clapped and the dancing couple walked to the bar and ordered drinks. Perry, in his delirium and ecstasy, would falter and Wolfgang had to seize the chance to tighten the net. He would save Grace before she took her life and he would embrace her and kiss her.

He would thwart Perry from peace and rest. Block his paths to salvation. Force him to journey into hell, to relive his nightmares seven days a week, to commune with his demons daily.

The band was playing Kenny G's "The Joy of Life," when his phone rang. He picked up the call hoping Grace had found out where she was. "Ida's departed," his sister said over the phone. He dropped his phone as five couples and a group of teenagers danced on the floor and the saxophone's notes vibrated in the tent.

It couldn't be. It must be a mistake.

He ran out of the tent. Looking for Ida. Unsure of his direction. Not finding his phone, he returned to the tent and bumped into a couple on the dance floor. He approached the bartender and asked for his phone, but the man just gave him a glass of lemon water.

When Wolfgang found his phone, his sister had ended the call. He dialed her number, but ended the call and left the tent. Amid Kenny G's music, he lost his direction and crashed into a clown. He raised his fist to punch the green nose, but after cussing, just ran toward the Ferris Wheel.

Ida, Ida, pleases, no. Talk to me again. Smile to me again. I promised to take you to Rome and Florence and Venice. I promised to take you to Disney World again. I promised to give you the seashell. Please let me keep my promises.

CHAPTER 38 – JO-BETH

In Billy's bedroom Jo-Beth took off her bra and opened the top drawer to look for the trailers' deeds. Not there. After shutting the drawer, she was about to open the lower one when she spotted the closet in the corner, its door ajar. A slit of light landed on a wooden handle. Billy crooned in the kitchen, then cussed and cursed at the cabinet. She stepped aside from the roaches crawling over a slice of pepperoni and tiptoed toward the closet, hoping to find the deeds. If she found them before Billy came into the bedroom, she wouldn't have to touch the clown.

Opening the door, she found a bloodstained ax, its handle leaning against a wall. She stooped to study it. Dried blood had caked the blade. *Oh my God, like did he kill someone?* She shut the door, almost banging it. Then returned to the bed and picked up her bra. Before she gathered her clothes, Billy entered the bedroom.

Billy dropped his pants and kicked his socks through the bedroom doorway. Then waddled toward the bed and, following her gaze at the cross on his forehead, said, "Bet you wanna kiss it." When he put one foot onto the bed, she shoved him away and asked about his childhood.

"Ain't got no time, babe."

He climbed onto the bed, so she just pulled a knife from her pile of clothes and pressed it against his Adam's apple and like insisted on knowing his childhood.

"Why in hell you but care?"

Jo-Beth pressed the blade into his goose-bumped skin. She'd thrust it into the hairy chest and get rid of the shaggy face forever.

"I declare you gone batty."

The coward cursed her before telling her he'd grown up in a foster home where his foster-father would force him to toil in the farm for sixteen hours a day and to sleep in the barn with the cows and horses. Once, when he smoked a cigarette from his friend, the brute branded a cross on his forehead with hot iron to punish him for his sin. Since then, he'd dream of the devil branding him with a hot iron and he'd wake up screaming in the middle of the night. And his foster-father would brand crosses on his back to exorcise the devil. He went to the church where his father was a deacon. Had an affair with the pastor's daughter. But she dumped him after falling in love with a local millionaire who had just lost his wife. Just when he was about to run away from home, his foster-father, in a rally, shot a gay man in the head and went to prison for twenty years. Billy sold the farm and left Charleston and he hadn't seen his foster-father again.

"Only God damn break I got in this shit-life."

He might be the baby she'd abandoned on the church steps. Or he might not. She didn't know and she didn't care. She had to leave the sty before this clown got hold of the ax.

He shoved aside her arm. Charged at her. Grasped her neck with both hands, his eyes bloodshot. "You're dead, bitch."

The claws clamped around her neck and she struggled for air. She pulled his hair and removed several strands. But he just tightened his grip and screamed and growled like a wounded dog. The blood throbbed in her head. She gasped for breath. Then grabbed the other knife from the pile of clothing. Swinging an arc, she slashed both his forearms. He screamed and let go as blood dripped along his arms. Then stepped back and slipped on his pants and crashed onto the side table, falling onto the floor.

Jo-Beth grasped both knives in one hand, picked up her clothes with the other, and pointed the blades at him. Ready to throw them at the hairy chest.

"You gonna pay for this. Just you but wait." Billy got up, smearing blood onto the side table. Rubbed his head and wobbled toward the kitchen. Tripping on his socks and falling on a slice of half-finished pizza.

Jo-Beth should cut him up. First her daughter, then her landlord. No, she just had to hold Rick and forget about the past week's ordeals. Leave Paradise and flee from the body parts strewn across town. Squeezing the hilts, she approached Billy. Where should she slice first?

But she left his trailer.

In her kitchen, she opened a bag of potato chips and threw a handful into her mouth. Then washed the food down with coke. Outside the window, the squirrels played on the branches. She wanted to imitate them and dance through her youth.

Billy would probably kick her out of this trailer tomorrow.

After finishing the potato chips and three cans of coke, she picked up Sheriff Perry's business card. She should call the sheriff to report about the ax, but not until she got a hold of the deeds. Her cold hands trembled and she dropped the card. Sure, she still hated Lucy-Jane for stealing Rick from her. But regretted killing her. She should've just disown her and let her roam the streets. Now, someone knew about the killing and would call the police to arrest her. No, she didn't want the electric chair. But she feared even more the blackmailer. She didn't deserve this. After all she'd suffered. Poor Jo-Beth. She held her head with both hands. How did she keep screwing up her life? Her father wouldn't rescue her. Collins had divorced her. Gus Davis had dumped her for a younger woman. She really tried to find something attractive in herself, something worth loving, but damn it, she couldn't. Others had realized that sooner than she had. She leaned on the table. *Rick, return and help me.* He was probably looking for Lucy-Jane and surely would have to return.

She'd studied the sheriff's expression when he was examining the blackmail note. Had he suspected her? He'd taken Lucy-Jane's belongings, probably checking for fingerprints and DNA, but hadn't contacted her again. Sure, she'd avoided leaving any fingerprints. But might've left hair or dandruff on the bags. And the sheriff might wonder about the trailer reeking of bleach. Really, she should escape from Paradise. But still so, so had to wait for Rick to return.

Jo-Beth pulled out a knife from the rack and put the blade against her wrist. One slash and she would end her pain. She wanted to fix her life with such a simple stroke.

God grant me the serenity…

Something rattled outside the door. She dropped the knife onto the table. Froze and listened. Her fingers twitching. Maybe Sheriff Perry came to arrest her. The steps retreated. Maybe Billy came with his ax but changed his mind. After five minutes, she walked to the door and opened it. Heat rushed into the living room. But no one was outside.

She was about to close the door when a folded piece of paper, fluttered at her feet. Please, please, not again. She twisted her neck. Rubbed the sweat from her face. She gasped for a minute before bending and picking up the note. The paper fluttered in her hand. She closed the door and dropped into the couch. Staring at the note for about half a minute. Then unfolded it and read it.

Sure enough, another blackmail note. But the date had changed to June 12, tomorrow. And the blackmailer specified the alley in St. Peter's Yard.

Jo-Beth looked at the ceiling and waited for thirty-thousand dollars to drop onto her lap. A fly circled around her head and buzzed in her right ear. She flicked her finger and sent the pest into the windowpane.

God grant me...

Billy the pest was blackmailing her and she had missed the chance to get rid of him. A slice through that Adam's rotten apple and she could sing Hallelujah. She grabbed another can of coke and stared through the window at his trailer. Scenes of her life scrolled past her mind's eyes. After finishing the coke, she crumbled the can and threw it into the trash bin.

She was taking back her life.

Toward the evening, she took the two knives. Put on a pair of gloves. And left the trailer, marching toward Billy's place, hoping he was drinking himself into a stupor.

She was half way to the blackmailer's trailer when a motorbike roared away from the parking lot. A plume of exhaust blocked her view. Rick? After the smoke had dispersed, the empty street confronted her under the evening sky.

She crept to the trailer. Listened for Billy's voice. Then circled to the rear and tiptoed toward the backdoor. A column of ants marched through the opening. No sound. She peeped through the window next to the door. No clown. After a minute, she stepped on the ants, tiptoed through the doorway and almost slipped on a soiled sock.

The kitchen reeked of spoiled food and underarm odor. She coughed and thrust her head through the doorway to breathe. Sprayed perfume on her palm and rubbing it against her upper lip. Then returned to the kitchen, where roaches were crawling out of the sink. She navigated among pizza crusts and beer cans toward the living room. A thud startled her. She was about to throw a knife when a rat scurried into the bedroom. She kicked aside the underwear and went into the living room where four posters of naked women greeted her. Roaches paraded on a coffee table, circling a piece of peanut butter sandwich. She scattered the pest with her knife and examined a picture of two men embracing each other. Where had she seen those faces? She tiptoed over an unfinished hot dog, entered the bedroom. Socks and underwear, T-shirts and pants covered the bed and the floor. Sure enough, Billy had left the trailer. But the ax was still inside the closet.

Jo-Beth was about to pick up the holster on the bed when a branch outside snapped. Beyond the window, a squirrel was climbing a tree. Aha, those faces in the picture. She left the bedroom grinning and called Sheriff Perry.

CHAPTER 39 - RICK

Rick woke up in the alley behind the church. Pain in the back of his head spread down to his neck. The sky had darkened but the pipe was still lying beside him. He tried the wrinkled back door. Locked. No light inside the church. He tried the front door. No luck either. After searching the byways around the church for three hours and unable to ferret out the louse, he returned to the empty apartment where Lucy-Jane smiled at him from the picture on the TV stand. A damn solid void in his stomach. The walls that had echoed her laughter, they only reflected silence and he foresaw his days and years gray along the cinder road. Just like a nomad wandering the desert. He opened a bottle of whiskey. Swigged a quarter bottle before walking into the bedroom to sniff the sheets. Her familiar scent. He took the framed picture from the nightstand. Her warm body against his. Her smile grieved him just as her scent pained him. Leaning against the headboard, he drank the whiskey. Somehow, falling asleep, despite the images, despite the headache, but he kept finding her head in his dreams.

#

Rick lifted the crowbar from the motorbike's toolbox and marched to the back of the Church of Paradise. Picked up a rock and threw it through the mosaic window beside the back door. The rock broke the windowpane and dropped into the church while glass fragments showered on the cobblestones. No shouts or footsteps inside the church. No one turned on the light. So he plunged the crowbar into the windowpane three times to clear the glass fragments. Then crawled through the opening.

He pointed the flashlight down the church's corridor and grasping the crowbar as if holding Lucy-Jane's hand he tiptoed alongside the wall.

In the apse, he turned on the lights. A book on magic tricks and a deck of cards lay on the bench. Perfume. Lily-Rose's. After turning off the flashlight, he put the crowbar on the bench next to Magician Cassidy's treasures, which he'd burn soon enough. Then walked up to the cross at the opposite wall and grasped the top and bottom and rotated it. Just as Cassidy had done. The wall swung open. He picked up the flashlight and crowbar and walked into the compartment. A stairway led downstairs. He pressed his foot onto the first step, expecting a creak. The light below turned on and he froze. Not a sound, not even a sickly rat squealing. And no shadows against the wall and floor. After two minutes, he took the second step. And walked into the cellar. The concrete walls emitted a piercing chill. He opened a steel door at the farther end of the room. Behind it, a narrow corridor with gates on the left and right. The stench of blood and puke made him sick.

This afternoon, when he woke up, the TV newscaster announced that Dick was in a coma in the hospital after the police had found him in a dumpsite. Rick suspected the homeless man had buried the money inside the Church of Paradise before meeting his doom. He called a sergeant at the sheriff's office and found out the police hadn't retrieved the ransom.

His legs shook as he staggered down the dungeon's stinking passage. When he reached the first gate to the left, he shone the light through the opening. Bloodstains covered the wall. A sick butcher, this entertainer. In the second cell, a sandal lay on the floor, a witness to some earlier cruelty. Outside the last cell that reeked of goat cheese, he bent over, ready to vomit and expel the turmoil in his stomach. But after a minute, he straightened up and just exhaled. And pointed the flashlight into the cell. After covering his nose, he stepped over a pool of puke and into the cell. He passed several blotches of blood. And sure enough, on the wall, Dick's insignia: a circle enclosing an isosceles triangle enclosing a circle. With his camera, Rick took pictures of the insignia and the pools of puke and blood.

He took several more pictures but couldn't find the money. He returned to the apse and checked for other hidden compartments. None whatsoever. Likely, the pastor had found the stash and claimed it for his retirement. Rick wasn't about to leave empty handed, not when he had to avenge Lucy-Jane's death. And no entertainer cum minister was going to foil his plan. He went to Pastor Cassidy's office. Took out two metal strips and thrust them into the keyhole and, feeling the teeth and latches, opened the lock. Pictures of the pastor performing in City Hall and at local theaters and nightclubs decorated the walls. A black cape hung on the clothes stand and the wand lay across the desk. Rick opened the desk drawers, unlocked the cabinet drawers, rummaged through the shelves, but just couldn't find the freaking stacks of bills. He knocked on the walls and pulled away the framed picture of the pastor in City Hall. There it was, a safe. He put his left ear against the door and turned the knob clockwise until it clicked. Then turned the knob counter-clockwise and then clockwise and opened the safe. He checked his watch: missed his record by five seconds. Inside the safe, a picture, three vials of Rohypnol and five stacks of cash: twenty-five thousand dollars.

He put the money into his knapsack. Then picked up the picture. His mother was kissing the pastor outside the Nashville Rock and Roll Hall of Fame. The pastor had the same beady eyes and lizard lips, but hadn't begun to bald. Rick might've seen him at their house, maybe twice.

No way was it a dream. Isabella was really pregnant.

To be sure, if he'd grown up with a brother, he would've protected him and they would've been best friends. But he never knew what happened to the baby until Luc claimed to be his half-brother. He still wasn't sure whether the Werewolf was lying to him, but wouldn't want a psychopath for a brother anyway. He slipped the picture into his pocket, locked the safe and covered it with the framed picture of the pastor's City Hall debut.

Rick turned on the pastor's computer and entered "Isabella" as the password. So, the entertainer still thought of her. That was something. Among the files, he found videos of the pastor raping drugged girls. Not only a killer, but also a rapist. After locating the pastor's email address and password, he accessed the holy man's account and sent the dungeon's pictures to Sheriff Perry with a message explaining the insignia and describing the direction here. The videos needed no explanations.

He shut the computer and the light. Outside, the streetlight cast the shadow of a tree onto a barbecue pit. Two squirrels chased each other around the tree. Beyond the front yard, on Main Street, only his Ninja parked next to the lamppost. He left the office and closed the door.

#

After having the Big Mouth Special at Paradise Burger, he drove his Ninja to the trailer park to deliver a second blackmail note. He demanded that Jo-Beth deliver the money tomorrow night instead of on Independence Day. Under pressure, she'd panic of course and call him. And her trembling voice would soothe his heart, for maybe a day. She'd lose her job, drain her bank account, and live in the street. He'd wear her down until she collapses. Sure, he'd like to kill her tomorrow night. But he just might maybe bring a girl to the trailer and maybe make love to her. Then leave the lingerie on witch's bed.

He delivered the note and slipped behind a tree smoking, reminiscing about the first time he met Lucy-Jane, and just damn cursing the murderous old hag. When Jo-Beth came out, he really, really should go over and punch her in the face. But he waited. He savored her expression as she found the note. Yeah, she'd call him.

Outside his apartment, Rick found a package. Lucy-Jane probably had bought an appliance. So he took it into the apartment. His lover's picture on the TV stand, it made his head ache, so he went into the kitchen to have a painkiller. Then hovered over the sink, trying to puke. But he didn't. After drinking some beer, he went back to the living room. Opened the package. An electric guitar: black with orange-red swirls. A present from Lucy-Jane. He plucked a string and the note resonated in the apartment.

The day Lucy-Jane returned from Boston, they went to Heaven Steakhouse to celebrate a new life. He had ribeye steak and she had prime rib. And they had a bottle of Merlot.

"I'd like a diamond necklace for Christmas," she said.

"You bet. We'll be able to afford it."

"Just kidding. I'd rather we have a house."

"Oceanfront, of course."

"And you can have your electric guitar."

"I'd rather save the dough for your diamond necklace."

They toasted to a new life, with enough money for dignity and decency and even nobleness. After finishing the main course, they had cheesecake for dessert and Lucy-Jane's eyes twinkled under the light.

Now, after finishing the beer and throwing the can out the window, he strummed the guitar in front of her picture, trying to play a song. But so he didn't know any songs, not even "London Bridge is Falling Down." He raised the guitar to smash it on the nightstand but then huddled it. The silence of his sobs mingled with the owl's hoots outside the window. Taking out a songbook from a shelf, opening it on the bed and picking the "Sound of Silence." He'd play the song. But he of course couldn't read the freaking scores. So he left the guitar and the songbook on the bed. And went to the kitchen for another can of beer.

He read the shopping list on the refrigerator. Lucy-Jane was going to buy him a leather belt to replace the one about to split into two. Also, dishwasher liquid, toilet paper and honey-roasted peanuts. Sure enough, he found only a spoonful of dishwasher liquid. And in the bathroom, only half a roll of toilet paper. On the toilet seat, beside the beige wall tiles, he drank the beer. Why hadn't they left Paradise earlier? When he threw the damn can into the tub, the beer gushed out and fizzed down the drain.

His phone rang in the bedroom. He rushed out of the bathroom into the hallway. Was Lucy-Jane calling him? Maybe he hadn't seen her breasts and her head. She might still be waiting for him to hold her and kiss her. They might have a second chance. He tripped outside the bedroom, his shoulder crashing against the drawers, and he fell onto the carpeted floor. A strand of blonde hair lay before the dresser. He picked it up as the phone rang again. To remind him of lost time. He got up. Rushed to the nightstand. Grab the phone.

Jo-Beth was calling him, just as he'd expected.

He cursed her eyes and mouth. He cursed her soul. He answered the phone.

"Oh, sweetheart, where've you been? You okay? Can't imagine how miserable I'm, how miserable I've been for days. Oh, sometimes wished I was dead. But I just want to see you. Where're you? I've something dead important to talk with you. Something lousy has happened. A bomb. Just want to hold you in my arms. Just want you to kiss me and tell me how much you love me. Hello, you there?"

"Yeah."

"Oh, Ricky my baby. Called you ten days ago to tell you something. But never mind about that other stuff now. I'm calling about something else. And this thing's dead worse than the other stuff. It's one lousy bomb."

"Okay."

"I'm pregnant. And it's yours. Been trying to let you in on it. Isn't this awesome? Rick? Rick? You there? Oh, you must be so hyped. Aren't you? Aren't you psyched? Let's tie the knot."

"Uh-huh."

"I need you by my side."

"Sure."

"You heard about these body parts all over town? Well, some of them… But maybe should tell you about it when you drop by. Honey, I miss you. This place feels so creepy without you. Don't even want to come back here after work. When can you drop by? Oh, and they're fishing for Billy. They think he's the psycho who did in that gay couple."

"Right."

"Oh, my darling. Someone's been dropping me blackmail notes. Can you believe it? Blackmailing sweet old me. I wouldn't hurt a fly. Well, I mean—"

"What'd they have on you?"

"What do you mean? Billy's got nothing on me, not a zilch. He just wants to scare the bejeesus out of me. He just wants my dough. You know how people are these days, all trying to con you of the dough you don't have. Greed, greed and greed. It's in the air and the water."

"Isn't Billy."

"What'd you mean? How'd you know?"

"Call the police." Rick imagined sweat dripping down her forehead and her heart struggling toward its last beat, toward the eternal rest.

"Are you kidding? No way I can't call the cops. Do you know what you're saying? I'd have to tell them the whole shebang. You know what'd happen to me? Oh, baby, you got no idea what's going down. Come over in a jiffy, will you? I'll tell you the whole jam."

"Not tonight. I'm busy."

"Huh? What'd you mean you're busy?"

"Busy."

"Are you—?"

"I'm busy."

He told Jo-Beth to sell everything she had and prepare the money as the kidnapper had requested. She ought to deliver the ransom on the specified time and location and he'd kill the kidnapper and retrieve the dough. Naturally, they'd claim self-defense.

"Do Billy in? No, no, no. The sheriff's gonna arrest him in a jiffy. You'll see."

"Then let the blackmailer have the ransom. And it isn't Billy."

"Do you think it's Lucy-Jane's kidnapper?"

"Get the dough."

"Don't have any."

"You'll find a way."

"I love you."

He asked for the time and location and hung up the phone. The hag would sell everything she had and didn't have and would deliver the ransom at the appointed time and location.

He called the jeweler, waking up the man. Ordered the diamond necklace Lucy-Jane had wanted for their wedding and said he'd pay for it tomorrow in cash.

For you, my love.

He put on his jacket and left his apartment. As he walked toward his motorbike, his mind searched for a finale to honor Lucy-Jane, a death for Jo-Beth worthy of his hatred and venom. Jo-Beth would walk down the dark alley, put the ransom into the trashcan, and he'd walk up and...

CHAPTER 40 - WOLFGANG

As Ida's container slid into the chamber, Wolfgang held Kerstin's cold hand and said a silent goodbye. Committing the girl's smile and laughter to memory. Promising to hold her in his heart until the day he departs.

"I'm scared," Ida said at the Paradise train station after Kerstin had gone to buy ice cream.

"Let me come with you," he said.

"Nah."

"I can read to you."

"I don't want you to see me like that."

"I want to do something."

"You're coming with us to Rome."

"And Venice."

"Do you like that girl Grace?"

"You're my dearest."

"You should. I like her. I prefer you with mom, but—"

"I won't abandon you."

"I want you to be happy. I'd like that." She hugged him. "I'm scared. But I'm glad I have you."

Wolfgang lifted her urn. He could no longer share an ice cream cone with Ida. If only she had more days to laugh and cry, to succeed and fail, to love and hate. Which if given the time, she would. Unlike he and Kerstin, wasting their years, turning the months and weeks to ashes of guilt and regret. Amid the scent of charcoal, he put a conch into the urn, apologized for crushing her gift. Promised to save Grace and redeem his hours and days.

He would have given his time to Ida. Now, he would squander the minutes and seconds like a fool.

Kerstin picked up the urn and huddled it for several minutes before kissing it and wiping her cheeks. She moved her lips as if speaking to the ash. Her murmur drifted along the hallway while sunlight through the stained glass window shone red on the urn. The furnace roared and heat stifled his breathing. The ceiling unable to disperse the hot air.

What had he forgotten to say to Ida at the train station?

Outside the crematory, beyond the trees and buildings, a cormorant soared through the sky. The peaceful sadness mingled with the mourning silence. After ten minutes beside the car Kerstin said, "Let's go to Great Falls Park." They had picnicked there two years ago under the autumn foliage. Two years and a death ago.

While negotiating Georgetown Pike's curves, Isaiah phoned to tell him Sheriff Perry had raided the Church of Paradise and found video files of the pastor raping the drugged girls but Cassidy had escaped to an abandoned barn outside town. Isaiah had checked the barn when the pastor cum fugitive left to buy food, but didn't find any girls.

Wasn't Perry in cahoots with the minister? Had Wolfgang been mistaken about Cassidy? Was Perry just insane and didn't have Grace? Wolfgang, wishing he were in Paradise to arrange the surveillance, asked Isaiah to continue tracking the minister and the sheriff and arrest them only after locating the missing girls.

When Wolfgang and Kerstin arrived at Great Falls Park in the late afternoon and walked from the parking lot toward the observation deck, she held his hand and he kissed hers while a warm wind swept against his left side and lifted a paper bag. An old man shuffled along the walkway, and on the grass, two boys played Frisbee.

Beyond the observation platform, the rapids of Great Falls tumbled through the rocks, as they had last year and as they would the next. Kerstin leaned against the rail and her eyes followed a bird above the opposite cliff.

Would be nice to scatter the ashes into the Potomac. Ida would like it.

When an old couple stepped onto the platform and teased each other, Wolfgang and Kerstin went to a nearby picnic table. He took out the roast beef sandwiches and the two bottles of water he had bought near the crematory. Next to the picnic table, the birch that had been shedding its leaves during their last visit was blooming under the sun. But the robin that had been singing amid Ida's laughter had left.

They should just mourn her death and celebrate her life.

Under the same sky two years ago, Wolfgang had been eating hamburger and French fries with Ida at this picnic table. But time had passed and they had aged and Ida had gone. While the striations on the tabletop remained. He ate the sandwich. Would the young couple on the gravel path be holding each other's hands in two years? Time that might as well be eternity when spotted with tragedy.

Kerstin ate the sandwich. Put the wrapper into the paper bag. Drank from the bottle. Wolfgang threw the bag into the trashcan and received a message from Ernst, saying he would rescue Grace from the human traffickers. He dialed the man's number but ended the call. How would he stop the fool from flinging away his life?

"We do silly things to show we're still alive." Kerstin crossed the lawn toward the gravel path where a group of teenagers was singing a camp song amid the rapids' roars.

Ida had been chasing a squirrel along the same path two years ago and her laughter still soothed him. As Wolfgang stepped on the mud path, Kerstin took his hand and they strolled under the dense foliage blocking out the sunlight. An old couple was sitting on a rock next to the path and holding each other's hands.

The trees cleared and they walked onto a ledge overseeing the Potomac below. Two kayaks raced against the current while another drifted toward the bank.

Ahead, a rock climber was setting an anchor between two rocks while another was connecting two kernmantle ropes with a carabiner. Wolfgang had enjoyed the view, the cliffs dropping into the canyons, when Isaiah took him and Kerstin rock climbing in the Catskills. That day, she smiled for the first time in months.

"How is Grace?" At the ledge Kerstin watched the rock climbers descend the cliff.

As he surveyed the river downstream where the current bent to the right and the cliffs blocked the view, he mulled over whether to tell her about Perry having again captured Grace. But he kept silent when the wind pushed against his back.

"I'm sorry for wasting so much of your time," she said, "so much of your life."

Would you care for me if it'll give me joy?

While a third rock climber set his anchor, the three kayaks surfed with the current toward the bend in the river. Across the Potomac, on the ledges along the Maryland side, hikers waved at them.

"Let us call it quits." She lifted her head and inhaled the air.

A gust whipped. Wolfgang slipped on the gravel. And staggered on the ledge. Her words repeating in his mind, reminding him he was journeying into a new season of life, a season of gusts and snow and wintry whiteness. But Kerstin grabbed his arm and pulled him back before he tumbled into the Potomac.

"Don't hate me," she said. "I don't want to fail. Please accept my failure."

He grasped her arm and was about to tell her he loves her, when the phone rang. After releasing her arm, he picked up the call.

"You're a mouse. Skipping town when Grace is waiting for you to save her. Now, she'll become a hooker and you'll have that on your conscience for the rest of your rodent life," Sheriff Perry said. "If you're half a man, you'd come back and face me. Man-to-man. Determine the quick and the dead. I'm ready to die. Are you?"

The phone slipped out of Wolfgang's hand but Kerstin caught it in midair and gave it back to him.

"Last chance to redeem yourself and go to hell," Perry continued. "Just to show my sincerity, I've prepared a gift. Your colleagues will probably be calling in no time to tell you the good news."

While Wolfgang searched for words to curse the psychopath and condemn him to hell, Perry hung up. He staggered and leaned against a rock. Gasping. When Kerstin took out a handkerchief to wipe the cold sweat from his forehead, he said, "Take back what you just said."

"First I have to take care of something. My last chance to assert my free will, to make a difference, to redeem myself." She put the handkerchief in her pocket and leaned against the rock. "If this fails, I'll surrender to fate."

Stand by me while I fight Perry and Cassidy and rescue Grace. But Kerstin had to assert her freedom and overcome fate. Had to unshackle her guilt. He would let her go so she could soar into the sky. Perhaps she would return filled with freedom, filled with life. Perhaps not. She wouldn't give up though fog covered her path, and even if she should fail, she wouldn't surrender to fate. And neither would he.

"We have to seize the life we still have," she said.

234

Before Wolfgang protested, the phone rang again and Isaiah told him that the restaurant had burnt down and that probably the human traffickers were waging the war.

"But besides that, something all important I got to talk with you," Isaiah said. "I'm sorry for doing this during your mourning, but you got to come back now. After you've heard what I'm to say, you'll probably cuff me."

CHAPTER 41 - PERRY

Todd put on his plastic gloves and picked up the bloodied ax, and said to his deputy, "Looks like he saved the ax and the fingerprints as mementos of his crime. Probably wants to show them to his drinking buddies."

"Nah, to his lovers," the deputy said. "Probably thinks it's sexy, the bastard."

Jo-Beth McIntyre had called about finding a bloodied ax in Billy McGee's trailer just as Todd was embroidering Grace's name on the handkerchief and pondering whether to take it to her. He was waiting for an assassin's phone call to arrange the killing before Agent Demir's return. Since he would spend more than thirty-thousand dollars for the killer, he had to go over the logistics with the mercenary.

After ending the call, he put the handkerchief into the drawer, gathered five officers, including the deputy, and went to arrest the clown. But when he stormed into the trailer, Billy had fled, leaving four posters of naked women on the walls and the stench of mildew throughout the rooms. To avoid vomiting, he put hand lotion on his upper lip. A picture of the gay couple, their driver's licenses, and two pairs of earrings lay on the coffee table next to a pair of socks. On the couch, roaches were crawling over an unfinished hotdog. He stepped into the bedroom and picked up a holster on the bed and said, "Armed and dangerous." He ordered his men to hunt down Billy McGee, dead or alive.

"You know what I prefer. So get to work. And we'll celebrate in Eden's Joy when we've nailed him."

Several years ago, after Billy's foster father had branded crosses on the boy's forehead and chest, Todd prepared a jail cell for the abused child. Sure enough, during the next few years, he had arrested Billy more than a dozen times for sacrificing a neighbor's dog or cat on a makeshift altar. The last time Todd came into the trailer, he had to fight off an ax to arrest Billy for beating up an Indian, whom the clown had mistaken for a Middle Eastern man.

In the bedroom, Todd lifted the mattress and after scaring away a mouse, he found a DVD between the sheets. Had Billy taped the killing to implicate himself in case someone else tried to take the credit? Todd didn't want to deny him the merit, so he inserted the disc into the DVD player. The video showed Mitch the Vampire enjoying a film of his father with the Georgian girl, then sending the evidence to the police. How had Billy stolen the disk? Anyway, Todd appreciated the lowlife helping him understand the Vampire's plan to inherit the Davis fortune. He searched the bedroom for other evidence to implicate Mitch for killing his father but only found roaches crowding over several pizza crusts and French-fries under the bed. He quitted. Outside the trailer, he called the judge to issue a search warrant for the Davis Palace and sent two officers to take the DVD to the justice and pick up the signed papers. Then contacted the officers watching Mitch and ordered them to prevent anyone from leaving the palace. But they told him the nephew had disappeared. After scolding them for five minutes, he and the deputy headed toward the palace.

"It'd be something if the Vampire went to the plastic surgeon and came out with your face," the deputy said while driving the car.

"Something for you."

"Wouldn't it be something to come face to face with yourself?"

"Then, I'll have to blow my own brains. Yeah, something alright. A new experience." Todd wouldn't tolerate anyone with a similar face and would shoot the guy without warning, criminal or not. He was probably a narcissist or a masochist, maybe both.

"Wouldn't want to zap anyone who looks like you. I value my life too much."

"Just follow my orders."

"But when you decide to make me the fall guy, just give me a heads-up. Will you?"

"You haven't earned that privilege yet. But keep working at it. I see the potential."

"I'll have to consider the retirement benefits from you."

"Just go to New Heaven Cemetery and check out the headstone nearest to the gate and you'd be sold on my generosity."

They stopped at Paradise Burger and Todd bought two Heavens Combos. Lily-Rose was no longer working at the restaurant. The TV above the counter broadcast the manhunt for Rick Dougherty and Billy McGee. He waited for the order and was checking the soda fountain for grime when Isaiah Jefferson, the Akdeniz manager who had spoiled his fun with Agent Demir, approached and slipped a business card into his pocket, and said, "I heard you need help." Then left. Todd ran after Jefferson but at the entrance his deputy blocked the way and said the judge had reviewed the video and would issue the warrant. Todd picked up the orders and left the restaurant. In the police cruiser, he rubbed the business card inside his pocket, but didn't scan it in front of the deputy, who was eating the pulled-pork burger while speeding down Isaac Boulevard.

When Todd arrived at the Davis Palace, he gave the surveillance officers a dressing down before leaning against the car and having the pulled-pork burger. The deputy hummed "The Battle Hymn of the Republic" as he munched his food. When the lawyer came out to shoo them away, the deputy raised his hand to grab the counselor's tie, but Todd stopped him and just tipped his hat and drank his coffee.

"This sidewalk's public area." Todd wiped his lips with a napkin.

"It's harassment," the lawyer said.

"I believe you're harassing us."

When the officers arrived with the warrant, Todd slipped it into the lawyer's coat pocket and entered the palace.

He asked the deputy to check the bedroom and headed into the basement. A chill seeped into his bones as he descended the stairs, and when he opened the door at the bottom, he faced a corridor, light passing through bullet holes in the wall and the air reeking of blood and sweat. When he found a nightlight, he bent down and twisted the top. Under a growl, a section of the wall rotated to reveal another hallway, prison cells on both sides.

Just great, another Cassidy dungeon.

After putting on plastic gloves, he opened a barred gate and stepped into a cell with whips, saws and nooses on the wall and a stretcher in the middle. Shivering from the chill, he stooped to examine a bloodied machete. Mitch and Luc must've used it to cut up the Georgian girl's body. He called his deputy to have crime scene technicians collect the evidence.

Braving the chill, he went into a torture chamber with a workbench in the middle. After rubbing his hands, he checked the scalpels on the bench and found several missing.

Just amateurs compared to Cassidy.

Blood had stained the mattocks, cleavers, awls and handsaws against the left wall. Beside a miter saw with fresh blood on its teeth, he examined the bloodied Harley Davidson gloves and jacket on the table. When he picked up the jacket, a finger and a DVD fell onto the table. Neither Gus Davis's hands nor the Georgian girl's were missing any fingers. This digit must belong to a recent victim. After picking up the DVD, he walked toward the TV across the room and passing the operating table, he almost stepped on urine. Billy McGee, he must be hiding in the dungeon. Todd went to the TV and inserted the DVD into the player. Who did the gangsters cut up this time? In the video, Gus Davis stood on a chair in the public toilet with a noose around his neck. Luc steadied him while Mitch slapped the mayor until he woke up. The Vampire pulled the chair and watched his father struggle. Todd ejected the disc before the video reached the end and smoked a cigarette. He put the DVD into a plastic bag. He would send Mitch and Luc to the electric chair.

Gus Davis got off easy.

Todd stepped over the urine, ready to leave the torture chamber. But blood oozed out of a closet beneath its door. After snuffing out the cigarette in an ashtray, he stepped toward the closet, careful to avoid the blood. He inhaled and grabbed the knob. Turned and opened the door. A force shoved against the door and a figure charged at him. With no time to pull out his pistol, he punched the man, a naked body. But the man fell on him. Pushed him against the table. It flipped over and he crashed onto the floor, the man falling on him. The body pressed him onto floor and he fought to breathe. Though He couldn't free himself. The hairy hand almost touching his face had lost an index finger. He turned sideways and pushed against the floor and the naked body rolled onto the urine. After adjusting his shirt and tie and putting on his hat, he brushed his hair from his eyes and examined the body on the floor.

Billy McGee, besides missing a finger, had been castrated. Todd found a pulse when he pressed his fingers against the drunkard's carotid artery. He lit a cigarette and put an hourglass on the side table and he leaned against the wall and savored the nicotine. The sand fell through the funnel. Had he outdone Mitch as a sadist? When the last grain of sand had passed through the funnel, he called the deputy to get an ambulance. Should he take the handkerchief to Grace and face her hatred?

Todd took the hourglass and left the torture chamber just as the paramedics rushed in to save Billy McGee. Outside the palace, he lit another cigarette and issued an APB for Mitch and Luc.

Better to have saved that Georgian girl than Billy.

#

Across the street from the Akdeniz, Todd smoked his cigarette. The four thugs, whom he had hired, doused the building with gasoline and lit a fire to consume the structure. The door charred. The windows cracked. The sign toppled. The lintel collapsed. The ridgepole folded. The flame crackled and the heat toasted his face. He sniffed the air as if sucking at his cigarette. Demir would rise to the challenge and triumph over his trial despite suffering from the little girl's death. He had to.

At the carnival, Todd had waited for Demir to punch or shoot him, but the agent controlled his fist and proved worthy of a savior.

He had to be the one.

When Grace was lying in his bed, he raised his hand to touch her face. But he didn't. He couldn't. He checked the buttons on her dress. Pulled a blanket over her chest. Put an hourglass on the side table and sat on the armchair next to the bed and as the sand rushed through the funnel into the bottom bulb he dreamed of life with her in an Alabama town. But he had lost that chance, forfeited that right. Still, how much would he sacrifice for her?

When the last grain of sand had passed through the funnel, he checked his watch to confirm the time and took the hourglass and his hat. After he had stepped out of the apartment, his new associate would take Grace to the abandoned courthouse. If he had finished embroidering the handkerchief, he would've woken her up and given her the gift. And released her. But he still had to stitch her name. He would give her the handkerchief under the blue sky, in the cool breeze and amid the earth's fragrance.

"I'll get my noose, I promise," he whispered to her and snuffed out the cigarette butt in the ashtray before leaving the apartment.

#

Todd entered New Heaven Cemetery through the Melchizedek Street entrance and strolled along the walkway under the starlight smoking a cigarette. Puffing out a ring of smoke and humming "This is the Day the Lord Hath Made," in the cool night air.

Last night, when he met McDonald and Kerstin here, he thought she was the Red Rose, but the Englishman said Elizabeth, a British Secret Service agent, had killed Mary-Lou a.k.a. Kay Emil. So that was how

McDonald received the wound on his cheek. Todd should warn him against future associates, but didn't say a word in front of Kerstin. He just arranged to have the final deal in two nights.

Now, under the stars, he leaned against a headstone. The universe had expanded at the Big Bang. From nothingness to existence. When would he, Todd, cease to exist?

He read Jefferson's business card to confirm the time and location. Still half an hour to enjoy the cemetery before taking care of business. After coordinating with the assassin, he would wait for tomorrow's finale. But he wouldn't sleep. Not tonight. Sure, he tried to outwit Demir, but the agent had to overcome the challenge and deliver him—Todd—from Paradise. He hummed the hymn, the melody from his childhood. His mother would take him to church and leave him there until after lunch and he would attend Sunday school and learn the Biblical stories and hymns. He didn't know where his mother had gone until one day when his teacher took him home and he found out his mother was with a customer. But he just hummed "This is the Day the Lord Hath Made" when that customer paid his mother.

Now, humming the melody, he sucked the cigarette and smelled the grass. Akdeniz had burned in the night, a fire purging his soul.

Todd should surrender to Demir, but he had to challenge the agent and force the man to deliver him. He wouldn't end up in hell, forever watching the video of his mother undressing before a stranger.

Earlier in the day, when Todd checked his emails and found a picture of the church dungeon, he took out a bottle of champagne and called his staff to celebrate, but they had gone home and he toasted to Cassidy before the mirror.

In the picture, someone had sketched on a wall a circle enclosing an isosceles triangle enclosing a circle. Dick's symbol. The homeless man had been in the dungeon. The DNA from his hair, blood and urine would verify it. And Todd had Cassidy's surveillance videos. Even as he waited for the assassin, his men were rummaging through the dungeon, gathering evidence to implicate the preacher. Of course, he still needed Cassidy for tomorrow's transaction and so wouldn't arrest him until afterward. Should he shoot Cassidy in the head? Or should he hand the preacher to the FBI after tomorrow's business? A shadow darted behind the shack, but on the hill only branches swayed in the darkness.

He reached a memorial, beyond which rows of headstones bowed. No, no burial.

No one would visit his grave except the grave robbers. Better to be cremated and have his ashes scattered across the land.

He had dropped the cigarette butt onto the ground and trampled on it. Footsteps descended the hill. He leaned against the memorial and grasped his gun in the holster. The footsteps stopped behind the memorial. The heavy breathing annoyed him and he tapped his index finger on the gun. A man behind the memorial was arranging the flowers.

"What's the target?" the man said.

"Wolfgang Demir." Todd lit another cigarette, as Isaiah Jefferson walked around the memorial and stooped down to arrange the flowers.

Silence.

"Do I see cold sweats?" Todd said.

"You sure there isn't a price on your head?"

"I'm impressed."

"I have a clean shot."

"I like the floral arrangement. Wish our local florist can do such a decent job."

"Fifty-thousand."

"Quite steep."

"Take it or leave it." Isaiah Jefferson dusted the area in front of the headstone with the twigs and flung them into a trashcan.

"Would you pass up this one-in-a-million chance?"

"Fifty-thousand."

"What about job satisfaction? It's Demir, your boss."

"Sixty-thousand if you prefer."

"Maybe I should get the Red Rose to do it."

"Maybe I'm giving you an offer you can't refuse."

"I might have a better shot than you think." Todd pressed his hand on his holster and watched the assassin's fingers.

"Only if you're a betting man."

"Do you always bargain so hard?"

"I don't bargain."

"Maybe you should."

"It's been nice meeting you." Isaiah pushed a rock to support the daisies and stood up.

"Tomorrow night at St. Peter's Yard."

"Cash only."

"So, the FBI doesn't pay you enough and you have to earn some bread on the side?"

"Other people watch a movie or go to the bar. Me, I hunt. To each his own, right?"

If anyone could stamp out Demir, it'd be this assassin. Not money, but excellence drove him.

Todd leaned against the memorial and sucked his cigarette, and enjoyed the wind against his face.

Adieu, Agent Demir.

CHAPTER 42 – JO-BETH

After Billy had fled from the law, Jo-Beth entered the fugitive's sty before the police cordoned off his properties. She found the deeds for the three trailers in the lower drawer of the refrigerator that reeked of sour milk.

The next morning, she haggled with a dealer and sold the trailers for thirty-thousand dollars. The government would seize them in several days but like by then she'd already be in sunny Atlanta or Houston with Rick after he'd knocked off the bloodsucker and reclaimed the ransom.

\#

Sweat poured down her face as she drove into the yard and parked her car behind a shack. Across the street, a streetlight next to a water tower lit the sidewalk but behind the shacks, only darkness welcomed her. She really didn't want to come to St. Peter's Yard. But if she didn't deliver the ransom, the blackmailer would probably tell the police about how she'd killed Lucy-Jane.

She left the car with the tote bag. Shivering and dragging her feet. Careful not to step on the night creatures in the yard. Behind her, a train passed by and the sea air roused her. Inches from the shack, she walked around it until the streetlight lit her path. No beggars or gangsters in the yard. She trudged along the sidewalk opposite the water tower. The road passed a side street and turned into an alley between two abandoned factories. The wind whispered through the alley. As if beckoning her to enter. She hesitated.

No light. No Rick.

She checked her watch. Three more minutes. She threw a piece of gum into her mouth and tiptoed into the alley. Shards crackled beneath her feet and resounded between the walls. A cat meowed and darted across the alley and she almost screamed, but covered her mouth with her free hand. While she lurked down the path, a canvas flapped outside the toy factory's third floor window.

She reached a trashcan. Checked its cover. No white mark. She continued down the alley as sweat poured down her back, the darkness engulfing her. Was that a shadow inside the chocolate factory? Through the broken window, only spider webs behind the frame. A rat near the toy factory door squeaked and startled her. She dropped the tote bag. She had to run from the alley, but her legs wouldn't move. Her heart thumped and her chest ached. A dog barked in the distance and she turned her head. After panting for two minutes, she picked up the bag and walked toward the second trashcan. A white mark on the lit.

She lifted the lid. Just as she was about to release the bag, a grunt echoed from the toy factory. She dropped the bag into the trashcan. While the lid shook in the air. When she tried to release the lid, her fingers wouldn't let go.

Footsteps approached. From behind. She couldn't turn around. Neither her legs nor her neck would move. Only her heart thumped. The pain sharpening in her chest. The breathing hissed behind her. A dim shadow cast over the lid. A hand grabbed her shoulder.

She dropped the lid and the clang echoed between the walls and scared away a pigeon perching on a windowsill further down the alley. The gum popped out of her mouth. Her legs froze and her arms twitched while her heart pained her.

She fell to the ground. Next to the trouser legs and the pair of oxfords. She lifted her head. Rick.

She jumped up and hugged her lover whom she'd been longing to kiss for more than two weeks. She held him. She had to tell him about her suffering. Poor Jo-Beth.

He pushed her away. He slapped her face.

"Did you bring the exact amount?"

"Oh, honey, Ricky. I've been thinking of you all this time. I miss you so much."

He backslapped her. "Blow out of here before the blackmailer comes."

"I want to lend you a hand. We can do it together. If they ever nab us, I'll say I did it." Jo-Beth held both cheeks, the pain burning her skin. But with Rick beside her, she could climb Mount Everest.

"Want me to help or not?" Rick lit a cigarette and puffed smoke into her face.

"But I love you."

"I'm going to shut my eyes. I'll count to three. If I see you when I open them, I'll split and you'll never see me again. And that's a promise."

"Rick, I know you care about me. I know you don't want me to be in the doghouse. But I love you."

"One…"

"Oh, do you want to feel your child?"

"Two…"

"Do you know what happened to Lucy-Jane?"

"Three."

"Okay, Okay. I'm taking off. I'm taking off. I'll wait for you in my car."

"No, get the hell out of here and go back to your place."

"But I don't have a place anymore."

"I don't give a damn where you go. Just don't let me see you."

"Okay, honey. I'll go to the train station and wait for you. Just be safe." Jo-Beth kissed him on the cheek. Put another gum into her mouth and walked down the alley toward the water tower. While the canvas above flapped and annoyed her. She should turn around and stay with him. But Rick would shout at her. She stepped on dung but continued down the alley. The warm air fanned her face but didn't dry her sweat. She chewed the gum. Where'd she and Rick go after they'd fled from this hell? Maybe Louisiana, outside New Orleans. Or Texas, the Mexican border, maybe El Paso. This goddamn mess. She cursed Lucy-Jane for bringing her misery.

Pop. She grunted. She collapsed. Her calf throbbed. She smelled cat urine and moaned in pain when she tried to move her right leg.

"Oh, Ricky honey. Help me. Oh, help me."

She pushed up. She crawled toward the alley entrance. The concrete scratched her jeans and the shards pressed against her palms. The canvas flapped as if sneering at her. She pressed a mutilated rat near the foot of the wall.

Pop. Her face slammed onto the concrete. Her left arm throbbed with pain. Blood dripped from her arm and she screamed for help. The bloodsucker had arrived. He would kill her. Should've listened to Rick and left. Now she might not walk out of this alley.

"Oh Ricky, help me. Please save me from the fiend. Please save me from my misery."

No reply. Maybe he was lying in a pool of blood next to the trashcan.

She'd reclaimed Rick by killing Lucy-Jane. She wouldn't lose him to the damned blackmailer. If something happened to Rick, God forbid, she wouldn't flee from the killer. She wouldn't live.

Oh, honey. Oh, Ricky. Please, oh, God. Don't let any crap happen to my love.

Footsteps approached. Rick or the blackmailer? She again called her lover. Her voice echoed through the alley. A night chorus. Again, nothing. When the footsteps stopped next to her, the trouser legs swayed in the wind. She smelled the man's sweat. Turned her head. The tote bag hung from his hand.

Please. Please, Ricky. You've got to be okay. Don't ditch me.

On the day Rick made love to her in Babel Park, he'd held her and told her that he'd love her forever and ever and that they'd leave Paradise for their Shangri La. She held him and asked him to promise never to abandon her. At that moment, she left Paradise's grief and pain and floated in the clouds.

Pop. A cramp slithered through her abdomen.

"Oh, Ricky, honey. Oh, crap." The syllables would journey with her into the void.

A cigarette butt fell beside her. Then the man followed, his face crashing onto the ground and his body twitching.

It was the blackmailer. Ricky promised to get rid of him. And must've rubbed him out. Good old Ricky, her hero.

She recognized the chestnut hair. And the jacket, the one she'd bought Rick two months ago in a boutique near City Hall. She called Rick but the sound muted in her throat. Still, she called him, louder and louder in her mind. After the body had stopped twitching, she turned it over and blood oozed from a hole in Rick's forehead. His eyes stared at her, as if pleading for her to take him away from Paradise.

No, no, honey, Ricky. Oh God, no.

She struggled to sit up. But slipped and fell to the ground. Dizzy, almost fainting, but still struggling to sit up.

She lifted him. She shook him. But he didn't move.

She hugged him. She kissed him. She called his name. But he didn't respond.

Last night, she'd dreamed of sitting with Rick under the stars as the crickets chirped and the wind whispered through the foliage behind them. The fireflies drifted in the air. Of course, he held her and caressed her and whispered he loved her and would never abandon her. Warm and peaceful, she'd returned to her mother's womb. She held him and told him she'd sacrifice everything for him and not hesitate to face sleet and gust. As the stars twinkled in the sky, marigold's fragrance delighted her. But his face turned to her father's and she woke up.

Jo-Beth held Rick as she had in the dream. And whispered that she'd love him forever. Thanking him for giving her happiness. But the stiff body didn't respond. The bloodsucker about a foot away would soon rid her of misery. Let him. She no longer feared death. Or life. Another cramp and blood stained her jeans. She'd lost the fetus but didn't give a shit. She'd soon croak. Should grab the gun in Rick's hand and shoot the bastard. No, he'd kill her before she pulled the trigger. Anyway, she'd lost the strength to kill the impotent knave.

She dropped Rick and smashed her head against the concrete.

CHAPTER 43 - ERNST

Ernst was humming, "Mary Had a Little Lamb" in the abandoned chocolate factory when Jo-Beth walked up to the trashcan beside the window. She took off the lid but held the tote bag above the receptacle. Wrinkles across her forehead and around the corners of her eyes. Her shallow but rapid breathing against the wind's whisper. He lifted the carton and sucked the orange juice through the straw. The tote bag hung above the trashcan shaking while sweat dripped from her forehead. He sucked again. *Drop the bag into the trashcan.* When Rick emerged from a dark corner and startled Jo-Beth, she dropped the bag.

While she was leaving, Ernst put on his noise-canceling headset and turned on the MP3 player. Took out the handgun and unlocked the safety latch. When his hands trembled, he shook them to steady his nerve. He shut his eyes and Yanni's "Once Upon a Time" flooded his emotions. He had made love to Lucy-Jane under the same tune.

Several days ago, after learning that Rick had cut off Lucy-Jane's breasts and her head, Ernst returned to his apartment and studied the psychopath's face on his phone display. Drinking vodka while clenching and unclenching his fist. He had to hate Rick enough to kill him. His love for Lucy-Jane mixed with his grief of losing her. He inserted the magazine into the handgun he'd bought at a gun show, to feel the weight. Locked the safety latch and pulled the trigger several times. Then unlocked the safety latch and slid a bullet into the chamber. He aimed and pretended to shoot. All the while, Lucy-Jane's laughter at Tupelo Point rang in his ears and her fragrance wafted into his nose. The life they might've had. Living in Newton, walking beside the Charles River, strolling in Copley Square, kissing on the porch, making love in the bed-room. The children they might've had, or might not. The trips to Seattle, Rome, and Tokyo. All gone. Rick had taken her away and crushed his dreams before they budded.

Could he take out Lucy-Jane's killer? But if he had to take a life, he would kill Rick rather than someone else. In the sofa, he weighted the gun in his hand. When he walked alongside Rick that night, looking for Dick, he should've swung the pipe and cracked that head. Rick probably ended Lucy-Jane's life, to block her from happiness, to stop her from leaving him. She had died for loving Ernst. *Oh, Lucy-Jane, my love.* He locked and unlocked the safety latch. *Empower me.*

Dawn arrived and welcomed the day Rick would leave the world. After eating a bowl of oatmeal, he printed several photos of Rick and went to the shooting range a block from City Hall. Practicing his aim. He should fling the gun into the sea and leave Paradise on a train. But his love for Lucy-Jane forced him to send a bullet into Rick. He wouldn't forgive himself for not avenging her. He would rather plunge into hell than fail her.

He would kill Rick. For Lucy-Jane.

Now, when Rick picked up the tote bag and pulled out a gun, Ernst cursed those eyes that had seen Lucy-Jane's body parts and those lips that had tried to impress him. After adjusting his headset, he gripped the handgun in his right hand and the carton of orange juice in his left. Notes of "Once Upon a Time" waltzed into his ears. Rick sawing off Lucy-Jane's head and limbs. He sidestepped a plank and several glass shards, then tiptoed to the entrance. Opened the door and peeped into the alley. The lid clang against the trashcan.

Rick, holding the cigarette butt in his mouth, approached Jo-Beth. Ernst left the factory. Under the streetlight, he strolled toward his enemy, who shot Jo-Beth in the leg. The wind whipped a canvas outside the toy factory's third floor window and a cat chased another across the alley and into the chocolate factory. When a train roared in the distance, he almost dropped the gun into the trashcan. He could record Rick killing Jo-Beth with his phone and send the video to Sheriff Perry. But Lucy-Jane whispered to him through the music. *Pull the trigger. Release the hatred. Redeem your soul.*

Rick shot Jo-Beth in the arm and sneered at her. Ernst approached. Careful not to step on shards. He was following the paths of Cassidy and Mitch. He stopped. Still have time to retreat into the factory. But Lucy-Jane, her body parts were rotting. He walked up. Pointed the gun at the perfect white teeth. He would cross the line of no return. He would fling away the law legal and moral and avenge Lucy-Jane. Offer her Rick's life.

For Lucy-Jane. The hell with dignity and the hell with decency.

Rick's mouth froze for two seconds before changing into a frown. His lips still clamped the cigarette butt. He gazed into empty space, as if trying to figure out Ernst's intention.

Ernst lifted the gun. Aimed the barrel at the forehead.

Five seconds later, Rick lifted the bag. Pointed the gun at the cash. But glanced into the distance as if searching for a memory. Was he reliving the joy of cutting away Lucy-Jane's breasts?

Ernst sipped the orange juice. Wetted his mouth. He sensed Lucy-Jane's breath against his neck. He nodded, not to Rick but to her.

"The hag, she wasted Lucy-Jane." The cigarette butt dropped onto Jo-Beth's calf.

Ernst smiled.

Rick nodded.

Ernst pulled the trigger.

The gun kicked, but he steadied his arm to avoid shooting into the air. The pop scared away a pigeon perching on the chocolate factory's second floor ledge. Two cats dashed out of the factory and scurried down the alley.

Rick dropped the tote bag. His eyes gazed about two feet behind Ernst. Blood oozed from the hole in his forehead.

The wind slapped the canvas as Rick fell onto the ground and twitched, his feet kicking away the bag. Ernst finished the orange juice. Rick would regret having killed Lucy-Jane. He had to. In the shooting range, after Ernst had shot the photos to pieces, the face not recognizable, he said, "Don't hesitate. Don't hesitate." He wouldn't fail again as when he had dropped baby Rick. He didn't. He shot at the face just as he had the photos. He succeeded. He canceled his previous failure by killing Rick.

This alley would lead to a new path, toward a new day. He had given up his future by killing Rick, by avenging his lover. He had sacrificed his decency by snuffing out a life. He had tainted his hands with blood and would descend into the ranks of Mitch and Luc. Still, as he dropped the carton at Rick's feet, he said, "Well done." The benefit excelled the cost. Peace drenched his blood. His hand steady and his muscles relaxed. His heart beat pitter-patter but only from the thrill of having avenged Lucy-Jane and of connecting to her through the bloodshed. What twisted justice, shooting down the person he had almost killed nineteen years ago, the man he had despised for being his victim.

He pointed the gun at the twitching body. But didn't want to pump more bullets into Rick. Had he forgiven him? No, too weak and tired to forgive or to hate. Rick would die in his twenties. And Ernst would have to walk down Harvard Bridge alone and lunch at Faneuil Hall by himself, after love and happiness had teased him.

He took out the snow globe from the backpack. Smashed it against Rick's head. To end the killer's misery. He released the globe. It rolled away and he inhaled the fresh air. He had stepped across the border and could never return home. Before him, the desert beckoned.

Oh, my love, through what tunnel would we to travel between the living and the dead to hold each other's hands again, to gaze into each other's hearts? But what can separate our love? Not Rick or Jo-Beth. Not life or death. I'll love you still, living or dead.

When Rick stopped twitching, Ernst locked the safety latch and returned the gun to his pocket. Before he could help Jo-Beth, she smashed her head onto the ground and fainted. He was about to bend down and check her wound when a glass shard cracked.

CHAPTER 44 - PERRY

Todd parked his car three blocks from the courthouse, behind an abandoned water tower. When he got out of the car, the humid air slammed into his face and a fly buzzed around his head. To outwit Demir, Todd had changed the meeting from midnight to ten o'clock. The agent had to rise to the challenge.

Earlier in the day, Mitch and Luc had killed seventeen and wounded twenty-eight in a shooting spree that included two gas stations, two convenient stores and four fast food restaurants. The officers had been running around town trying to catch up with the delinquents but the duo appeared and disappeared like phantoms. They must be retaliating against Todd for raiding the Davis estates and the government for freezing Mitch's assets in several Swiss banks. But perhaps also against Todd for saving Billy McGee, the only victim to have survived the Vampire's torture chamber. Though Todd was leading the manhunt, he continued to arrange tonight's meeting. If only he had captured the delinquents and closed the investigations before attending to the meeting. But now, the criminals meant zilch. He might not live until tomorrow to deal with them or Rick Dougherty. He strolled down the side street toward the courthouse and just looked forward to confronting Demir and witnessing the duel between the agent and the assassin.

Across the street from the abandoned courthouse, he leaned against an elm and faced the gambrel roof and the panel front door. Soon, the bullets would shatter the transom and multi-pane windows. A minute later, he ducked behind the bush and crept to the back of the building. Then passed the wrought iron gate, skipped onto the portico and stepped into the building. Agent Demir was probably monitoring the courthouse and waiting to nab him and Cassidy. He should escape Paradise to find a new life, but he had come. No matter how hard his mind tried to control his legs, his heart directed them here. He came for Agent Demir.

At the lobby, he adjusted his tie in front of a judge's picture. Under a wedge of light through the window, he dusted his shoes with a brush and checked for creases on his shirt with a mirror. As the crickets tapped out their symphony, his fingers tingled and he, a convict awaiting execution, leaned on a headless statue.

That day, at the carnival, when he taunted Wolfgang Demir, he had meant every word he said. When Lily-Rose said she had been passing information to the agent, he asked her to continue the charade.

Outside the courthouse, the crickets chirped and the wind whispered. Yet, no shadows against the windows. Inside, silence thick and sticky against his ears. No footsteps or murmurs. He shut his eyes and sniffed for the scent of the hunter.

Wolfgang Demir had to end Todd's life and grant him salvation. Salvation from his memories and his deeds. Peace enveloped him as he prodded in the darkness hunting his hunter. He wasn't treading on the linoleum floor. He was walking in a field among lavenders, the clouds white against the blue sky. Perhaps, a bullet would pierce his brain the next second and deliver him from hell, searing in his mind the image of the blossoms under the clouds.

He brushed aside the warm air and ignored the fly that had followed him into the courthouse and was circling above his head. When the ceiling creaked he left the light and kicking aside a magician's hat, stepped into a courtroom. Beyond the bar he reached the plaintiff's table and picked up a pair of gloves. After putting them on, he stepped behind the judge's bench and pulled out the handgun he had taped under the seat. Unscrewed the gravel's handle, slid out the silencer and twisted it onto the gun. He had often stood in the witness box but was sitting in the judge's bench only for the second time and if he had another life, he would study law. But first he had to abandon this life.

Returning to the atrium, he climbed the steps. Perhaps, at the top of the staircase he would meet the Agent's gun barrel and receive the bullet.

No more images of his mother taking off her clothes to welcome a stranger. Or his raping the girls from Georgia, Alabama, Mississippi and Louisiana and selling them into prostitution. He had to free himself from his past. And flee from the memory of having raped Grace.

Grasping the handrail, his finger slid over the moldings and pressed a button underneath to set the alarm. Not a creak under his oxfords, only footsteps thudded above him and a mouse squeaked below the stairs. He sniffed the dry dusty air. No body odor. At the top of the stairs, he adjusted his tie and tipped his hat, but no gun pointed at his forehead or temples.

Pictures of Charlie Chaplain and Groucho Marx and John Wayne decorated the walls along the empty corridor. He walked down the passage, toward a film of light spreading through a slit between the boardroom doors. The streetlight cast the shadow of a totem pole—Cassidy's latest obsession—onto the floor. After tonight's deal, he would chop the pole into pieces and burn them in a furnace, just to spite the preacher.

Inside the boardroom, a model train ran along the raised track near the ceiling and Cassidy's parrot, perching on a clothes rack beside the wine cabinet, said, "To be or not to be, that is the question." McDonald faced the door, his left hand pressing a briefcase on the table. The preacher was crouching between two chairs, rummaging through the cabinet under the table and taking out a magician's hat and a wand. Probably preparing to entertain his client. Todd aimed his gun through the slit. Should shoot the preacher in the butt just to prove a point.

The walls, which Cassidy had turned to screens, displayed a view at New York's Battery Park. The Statue of Liberty flaunted the torch between sky and sea while the Staten Island Ferry headed toward the terminal. The waves splashed against the shore. On the left screen, a bird flew past the balustrade into the blue sky. Cassidy had installed the multimedia system to help with negotiations. Todd refused to pay a penny for the trinket they would abandon after tonight but the preacher had laid out ten thousand dollars.

Where was McDonald's bodyguard, Kerstin Becker? He didn't like or trust any face he couldn't see.

Damn Cassidy, the airhead. He'd croak before the face-off begins.

Todd should worry about where the enemy's queen had positioned herself on the chessboard and whether she would capture his pawn. He didn't. He just mulled over the next moves to overturn the tide. Use Cassidy to bait and distract Kerstin. Lure her out and disarm her. But not kill her. He didn't want to ruin his relationship with McDonald. In the dark, he had the advantage.

But did he want to bother with the fuss?

He should just duel with Agent Demir and determine the quick and the dead. Never jeopardize a World Series to win an exhibition game.

Beyond the window, several fireflies bobbed under the starlit sky. Grace, probably at home staring at the same constellations. He pointed the gun at his temple and heartburn gnawed at him. He wished to release her from her pain, but even after he had turned to dust, she would carry her memories through her days.

He was about to check the meeting room again when a gun behind the totem pole pushed against his skull. The barrel shook and knocked on his head.

"Welcome. Did you see the fireflies?" Todd raised his hands above his shoulders, dangling his gun by two fingers. Yeah, Agent Demir was gripping the gun and probably thinking about pulling the trigger.

A hand grabbed the gun and Agent Demir said, "A good night to die."

"I prepared champagne to celebrate."

So, Demir had outwitted him, hadn't disappointed him. Now, salvation. But not yet. The agent still had to dodge Jefferson's bullet and eliminate the assassin—the last trial—before seizing the prize. Then, Todd would charge at the agent and receive his salvation. But if the assassin killed Demir, Todd would have to escape from the courthouse and stay in hell for several more decades.

"I'm ready to step into hell," Agent Demir said.

"Should be glad you can be a savior. Wish I was one." He wanted to save Grace from her pain and grief. But he had given her misery and suffering. Had taken a jewel from her and could never return it. He deserved to stay in hell, but he dreaded that endless path.

I'm sorry, Grace. Still want my salvation. Forgive me.

"Not yours," Agent Demir said.

"But Grace's? Yeah, I know, I know. How I wish." Todd bent over from the pain gnawing at his stomach. He shouldn't seek his salvation, but couldn't tolerate hell any longer. "Do you see the fireflies?" Facing Demir, he thrust his Adam's apple into the gun barrel. "Do you see how gentle they glow in the night? How graceful they drift under the stars?" He tapped the barrel and when the fly landed on it, he flicked it into the air. "And you just focus your strength and energy on the trigger. Have you ever tasted freedom, peace, relief?" Facing the window, he raised both arms toward the stars. Should've spent more nights in the cemetery gazing at the sky. In the darkness, a shadow darted behind the water tower.

"It won't matter if she—" Demir said.

"The covenant, the covenant. You of little faith." Tell him Grace had escaped? No, torture him a while longer. He might break the covenant after learning she had left. "Guess you didn't see the fireflies." He would treasure his last minutes before witnessing the duel between the leader and his subordinate even while his mother's image haunted him and threatened to ruin the moment. Of course, the assassin just wanted to shoot Agent Demir and collect his payment as soon as possible. "Okay, you may shoot now."

At the cue, Jefferson stepped out of the darkness and pointed a gun at Agent Demir, who continued to glance at the water tower as if searching for something in the darkness.

Demir would only find his lost soul in that emptiness. Todd hummed and enjoyed the moment.

"Wish you'd prepared some sake," Jefferson said, "but I'll take champagne. And I want champagne, not sparkling wines, those cheap imitations."

"I won't disappoint you if you don't disappoint me." Todd adjusted his tie in front of a mirror. "Hope you meet your end of the bargain."

"Shall we crash the human traffickers' gala?" Jefferson said. "Wouldn't want to miss the miserable fun, do we?"

"You shouldn't be here," Demir said.

"I'm here," Jefferson said.

"I thought—"

"Don't presume."

"I forgave you for what happened to my sister."

"I appreciate that."

"You're a fine kendo partner."

"The best."

"Do you need some extra cash?"

"Not really."

"I still can't give you back the gun."

"I understand."

"Hey," Todd said, "I didn't pay you to yak. More shooting and less talking." He approached Demir to take the agent's weapon, but the assassin's gun barrel pressed against his temple.

Jefferson shook his head and gestured for him to step back. "We're going to miss the criminal gala if we stay here any longer."

Todd hesitated for a moment before backing away from the agent. Silence filled the room as the shadow of the pole draped over the assassin, who handcuffed Agent Demir's hands and put on the silencer.

"Let's go in," Jefferson said.

"There's nothing in there for you," Todd said.

"I beg to differ."

"Your job—"

"Don't tell me what my job is."

"There's only Cassidy and McDonald."

"You missed the briefcase on the table."

"Believe me, nothing in there you want."

"Get in."

Todd protested but Jefferson seized his collar and shoved him through the double doors and he crashed into the meeting room. McDonald was tapping on the briefcase but seeing Todd, he signaled with his eyes and pointed to a screen to the side.

The parrot said, "A rose by any other name—"

Where the hell was Cassidy?

Todd was trying to understand the signal when Jefferson stepped in, pointed the gun at McDonald and shot him in the forehead. The Englishman bounced back against the chair and dropped onto the briefcase.

CHAPTER 45 - WOLFGANG

Wolfgang got out of the taxi and approached Akdeniz, the embers warming his skin and the scent of soot and charcoal irritating his nose. After kicking aside the burnt beams and ridgepoles, he stepped on the bar top and flipped over the seared sign, the tughra just a patch of charcoal. With his handkerchief, he picked up an Ottoman miniature. Where had his agents gone?

Leaving the heat and debris, he paced along the sidewalk opposite the restaurant until he found several cigarette butts. Perry must have been standing here several hours ago, admiring his handiwork, congratulating himself on the destruction.

Wolfgang had enjoyed making pilaf and practicing kendo and yoga in the restaurant, but now the building had collapsed and only memories of the aroma and the sweat and calm would draw forth joy and longing. He could no longer make Grace barbecue ribs after rescuing her. Ernst would have to make her siomai. The Ottoman miniature had burned and the past was retreating. He had lost Ida and the restaurant and was about to lose Kerstin and Grace. What lay beyond tomorrow? He might or might not capture Sheriff Perry but he had to rescue Grace and send her home, away from Paradise, away from the blood and bullets.

A bird flew between the rows of houses and disappeared behind a tower. *Follow it and soar above the clouds. Find an oasis in the desert or pines amid the Alps.* No, he would trudge through sand and snow.

Just as he was about to call a taxi, a car pulled up and Isaiah stepped out and informed him Sheriff Perry had sent his goons to burn down the restaurant last night.

Amid the scent of ash, Wolfgang looked for the shinai and yoga mats beneath the debris. He would nab Sheriff Perry even if he had to scale the Himalayas or cross Antarctica.

Minutes later, he greeted his team at Paradise Funeral Home. After briefing the members on the sting later that night, he assigned agents to hide in the abandoned factories and in the bushes along the railroad tracks. Then drove Isaiah to the cemetery where his team had set up an observation post. Under a sky blue and cloudless to the horizon, he strolled among the headstones and stopped next to a fifteen-foot memorial and admired the inscriptions. He preferred cremation though his urn would gather dust in an attic.

He would report Isaiah's actions at the trailer park and wouldn't lie about Sam's death. He could resign to save Isaiah's job, but did his friend deserve his sacrifice? Dark clouds hung over his future. If only Kerstin were standing beside him and sharing his struggle. He would've moved to London, to spend more time with her and Ida and care for the little girl whenever her mother had to leave town for assignments. With Ida gone...

Isaiah leaned against the memorial and said, "Remember that time we'd tracked a serial killer from Memphis to San Antonio?" That day, they cornered the criminal in an abandoned church and were going to arrest him, but the man dipped himself in gasoline and lit his lighter. They couldn't save him. The killer had collected his victims' eyes and inserted them into mannequins in his boutique shop in downtown Memphis. After the assignment, Wolfgang rented a cabin in the White Mountains and for a week hiked the trails contemplating the beauty of the rocks and trees, of the mountains and lakes, of the sky and clouds.

Isaiah rotated his head clockwise and then counter-clockwise before saying Perry had hired him to kill Wolfgang. He took out his phone and played the video. "The compensation's quite something. Enough for me to retire for several lifetimes." He had joined the International Society of Vigilantes or ISOV ten years ago and had gunned down killers and rapists who could either hire a team of lawyers to win the case or bribe their way out of prison.

"Who anointed you the executioner?" Wolfgang touched a headstone inscribed with "Beloved Son." *The dead rest but the living grieve*. If he didn't know Isaiah's *extracurricular activities*, he wouldn't have to choose between his friend and his integrity.

Had Isaiah killed, or rather murdered, Hilda's rapist? Wolfgang had hated the man as much as Isaiah had, but he refused to cross the line that would set him above the law. To become a *superman*.

But what if the law wasn't enough?

"Yeah, I have to confess that was a major excuse for joining the group. But don't you think I got a killer's temperament? I was hyped about knocking off that scumbag."

"Don't blame your temperament for your choices. You don't believe in destiny anymore than I do. You choose to take justice into your own hands. You'd been an ace agent because of your temperament."

"You're dead wrong. I don't blame my temperament. I thank my temperament. For making me Isaiah Jefferson. Wouldn't want to be anyone else."

What laws shall you fear if you dance but stumble against no man's iron chains?

Wolfgang mulled over Kahlil Gibran's words as he climbed the daisy-covered slope, and beside the observation post surveyed City Hall and downtown Paradise. Isaiah had done what he couldn't do.

"Know what I just found out?" Isaiah said.

"That you regret joining the assassins' guild?"

"Tom was the mole helping Kensington. That's how she could take Grace from right under our eyes and that's why she or her accomplice had to butcher him."

That was how Kay Emil's first note reached him. But she should've gone for Isaiah instead. He might've killed the Red Rose and saved her life.

Wolfgang put his palms together, bent his right leg and stood on his left. Focusing on a point in front of him, he reviewed the sting. He would walk down the side street toward the water tower and enter the court-house...

"Let's wrap up this job together like the good old days," Isaiah said.

The *good old days* had dispersed just as Ida had left this world. Wolfgang and Isaiah would walk down divergent paths in the future, perhaps facing each other on opposing sides and aiming their guns at each other across an alley. Wolfgang wouldn't request his friend to abandon his path anymore than the other way around. No, they had to choose their own destiny and damnation.

#

At ten o'clock Wolfgang, swept away the humid air, left the train-station parking lot, crossed Angel Road and walked down the side street toward the water tower. The heat weighed upon his heart. As he passed a bakery, someone darted out from the stairwell next to the shop. The streetlight shone on the chestnut hair covering half of the bloodied face. The woman mumbled as if talking to him but she sounded like a wounded animal. Blood soaked her trouser legs down to her feet.

"Oh, Ricky, I love you. I'll love you forever. Don't leave me. Please don't."

The woman charged toward him and when he stepped back, she stumbled forward. He extended his hand to steady her, but she shoved him aside and wiped her face with her palms, smearing the blood from her forehead onto her face.

Wolfgang failed to calm the woman who seemed to have lost her unborn child. He called for an ambulance and contacted an agent to look after her until help arrived.

"Oh, I'm sorry, honey. I'm so sorry. I didn't mean to. Please forgive me." The woman prostrated on the ground and spoke to the lamppost.

Wolfgang left the woman and just as he passed the stairway, a siren sounded along Angel Road and grew louder.

Either he had got the Midas touch or business was slow in the ER.

At the next intersection, Wolfgang spotted a body lying facedown in the alley. He approached and checked for a heartbeat. No pulse. A shot in the head, execution style. But an amateur.

Not recognizing the young man, he covered the body with a nearby canvas. Perry or Cassidy must have killed the witness. But he found a snow globe between two trashcans. Blood had smudged the surface, obscuring the scenery inside. He slipped on his gloves, put a paper bag on the ground, and kicked the evidence into it.

I'm going to regret this.

Wolfgang left the alley and as he walked toward the water tower, the ocean moaned beyond the track, the scent of the sea thick in the air. He had to rescue Grace from Perry's talons.

#

After the gunshot, Wolfgang stepped through the double doors expecting a bullet in Perry's head. Instead McDonald was slouched over the table, blood spreading into a pool. The room reeked of gunpowder.

"Cowards die many times before their deaths," the parrot said.

"Perry's right. Without champagne, this just doesn't feel like a criminal bash. More like a night at the movies." Isaiah glanced at the walls and the model train. "But I approve of the décor. I'd like my bedroom like this."

"You shot the wrong man, you dope." Perry walked to the cabinet as the model train passed overhead, and he pushed the clothing rack against the wall. The parrot cussed while the sheriff opened the cabinet and took out a bottle of champagne.

"I beg to differ," Isaiah said.

"Still, nice shot." Perry poured a glass and drank it. "Well, here's to Winston McDonald. But you can still wrap up the job and get your fifty-thousand dollars. After you shoot, we'll celebrate."

The parrot said, "Shoot. Shoot."

"Sorry about the let-down," Isaiah said, "but you didn't pay enough."

Wolfgang pulled his hands forward and put the handcuffs on the table. Checking the briefcase under McDonald, he found stacks of tissues.

"As you can see, you goofed up," Isaiah said. "Should've offered me ten-million dollars. That would've paid for ten minutes of my labor instead of just five. There's a lesson to be learned here."

"Aha, check." Perry gulped down the champagne.

"Checkmate," Isaiah said.

"Nice play, real nice," Perry said. "But don't you see something missing?"

"Sorry, boss," Isaiah said.

Wolfgang took the gun from Isaiah's hand and after pocketing the weapon, looked around for Cassidy. Where was the minister?

"Are we still friends?"

"Too late," Perry said.

The walls showed a night scene in the woods, the sycamores, birches and poplars casting shadows under the starlight. The crickets chirped among the trees and an owl hooted from deep in the woods. The stars twinkled on the ceiling and the breeze brushed against Wolfgang's skin. He sniffed the grass, but smelled jasmine.

He and Isaiah had joined the FBI together after they walked around the Tidal Basin discussing their aspirations. Wolfgang could succeed in any venture and his friend would likewise. He analyzed criminal behaviors while his friend learned to kick butts. He studied the psychology of sadists, rapists, and psychopaths while Isaiah improved his aim until he ranked number one in the Bureau. Now, their paths were diverging. One to the desert, the other the inferno.

"He's real mad now," Perry said.

"Remember how we busted that drug cartel?" Isaiah said.

"Where's Cassidy?" Wolfgang touched the screens on the wall to search for an opening and his hands pressed on the jasmines. The last time he had smelled the ethereal scent, he was walking through the botanical garden with Ida. Now he had to confront the friend who had betrayed him.

"Hey, boss, thank you for saving my butt time and again," Isaiah said.

"You're going down," Perry said.

Wolfgang should walk up to Isaiah and punch his face but he was too tired to lift his hand. Just rescue Grace, send Perry and Cassidy to prison, and report Isaiah to the Bureau. Then retreat to the mountain or desert to fling away the heat and humidity oppressing his body and soul.

"Well, boss, what have you decided to do?" Isaiah said.

"No way he'd save your butt again," Perry said.

"Since when have you become the resident mind reader?"

Isaiah had saved Wolfgang from an assassin during a raid three years ago. Now, he had to arrest his friend. He was scanning the opposite wall for crevices when the double doors opened and Kerstin stepped into the room.

Kerstin, what're you doing here?

He almost dropped his gun but clenched his fist to control his muscles and focus his thoughts. His heart pounded and his mind raced. She had stepped into his world, of rapists and killers and drug traffickers and double agents, and he couldn't find a spot for her.

"Isaiah," she said, "you just made the biggest mistake of your life. You will regret it."

"Nice of you to finally show," Perry said. "For a second, I thought you'd ditched your boss.

"I know you're angry I handcuffed him." Isaiah picked up the handcuffs. "But as you can see, he got out of the cuffs by himself. It's only an act."

Wolfgang approached the right wall where a stream flowed in the woods. Why had Kerstin come to the meeting? The stream gurgled steady against the crickets' chirps. In another life, he would escape this inferno and stroll along a brook with Grace, her voice against the wind's whisper.

"I would've preferred not to see you here," Wolfgang said.

"Many things we would've preferred but they didn't happen," Kerstin said. "Something else happened and Ida is no longer here."

"Agent, I have bad news," Perry said.

"If anything happened to Grace—" *No, please, no.* Wolfgang's palms were sweating. So was his back. An image surfaced into his mind but he smothered it and gazed at the stream.

"Are you keen on her?" After sitting down, Perry adjusted his tie and set an hourglass on the table.

"Aren't you a bit nosy?" Isaiah said.

"Isaiah, keep your hands up," Kerstin said.

"Have a drink. Maybe that'd steady your nerves." Perry raised the champagne bottle toward Wolfgang.

"Where're the girls?" Wolfgang said.

"Ready for the bad news?"

"Where's Grace?"

Perry rubbed the smudges from the hourglass with a handkerchief and pointed at Kerstin. "She's McDonald's new partner after Elizabeth betrayed him."

"Nice try," Isaiah said. "That won't save your ass."

"He speaks the truth," Kerstin said. "I work with McDonald."

Wolfgang couldn't understand her words, or connect her with McDonald. The parrot's voice and the sound of the model train faded and her words echoed in his mind.

Not her. Not a criminal. Not a human trafficker. It didn't make sense. Elizabeth McDonald, not Kerstin, killed Kay Emil. What was going on? What was Kerstin playing at? What was Wolfgang missing? *Come on, think.*

"What'd I tell you?" Perry said.

"I'm bummed," Isaiah said.

"Not as much as your boss." Perry toasted to Wolfgang and finished the champagne. He folded his hands and leaned back, nodding like a sage.

"I guess Scotland Yard was paying you pittance," Isaiah said. "But then, since you've defected to the other side, I guess we can have the duel after all. I'm ready if you are."

"Where is Cassidy?" she said.

As the ceiling turned navy-blue and the woods lit up, Wolfgang grasped his gun. Shoot Kerstin or help her escape? How could he escape from this stalemate? Several chirps replaced the owl's hooting. The scene changed to a lavender field under an azure sky and white clouds. Yellow swallowtails fluttered above the purple blossoms and a breeze lifted leaves into the air. Amid the breeze and the lavender scent, he dreamed of walking among the flowers and never returning to Paradise. But the parrot woke him from his dream and he had to choose: noose or firing squad.

"Hell is empty and all the devils are here," the parrot chanted.

"Um, before you blow my brains out," Isaiah said, "may I strangle the bird?"

When half of the sand had dropped into the bottom bulb, Perry shifted in his seat and pulled the hourglass toward him. "This calls for a celebration." He rubbed his hands and filled the glass with champagne. "So, Agent Demir, seems like a queen just appeared out of the blue and is about to checkmate. Your move."

"Your gun, please," Wolfgang said.

"Let me explain," Kerstin said.

"You don't have to explain anything," Perry said. "A million dollar is reason enough for anything."

"I got to agree," Isaiah said.

"Your gun." Wolfgang extended his hand.

"McDonald is—" Kerstin said.

"Don't say anything. Just move away from him."

"You don't understand."

"Do as I say." Wolfgang would arrest her and release her while taking her to custody. He would buy a fake passport and she would escape to South America. Then, he would give himself up and go to prison. Under the morning scene on the walls, he welcomed the new day while waiting for the firing squad.

But maybe she preferred to kill Wolfgang.

Kerstin approached McDonald and touched his carotid artery. "Isaiah, you'll pay for this."

"And you chose money over—" Isaiah said.

"Are we getting somewhere with this?" Perry said.

"He's an undercover agent with the MI6." Kerstin slipped her hand into McDonald's pocket and pulled out the badge.

Isaiah had killed a Secret Intelligence Service agent.

Wolfgang released his breath, relaxed his muscles. The pansies fluttered in the breeze. The sunlight warmed his skin. The swallowtails soared into clouds. He had to face the storm.

"Now we're getting somewhere," Perry said.

"It's a trick," Isaiah said.

"I know you are a member of the International Society of Vigilantes," she said.

"And you thought this'd just be a blah deal between crooks," Perry said.

"He's a crook," Isaiah said.

"Look." Kerstin raised the badge.

"May want to haul a few books to the slammer," Perry said.

"I believe Kerstin," Wolfgang said. Isaiah shouldn't have shot McDonald, shouldn't have come to the meeting, and shouldn't have worked on this assignment. But he had. And McDonald had died.

"What else is new?" Isaiah said.

The scene changed to waves of red, orange and yellow autumn foliage slanting down the mountain slope and bobbing in the wind. An eagle soared beyond the mountain ridge toward the horizon. Nearby, yellow and white chrysanthemums paved the mountain ledge. Wolfgang would like to hike through the White Mountains and breathe the fresh air, not face the firing squad.

Should he hand Isaiah to MI6?

"If she says—" Wolfgang said.

"You bet, you prefer that," Isaiah said.

Do I? Do I value Kerstin more than him?

"You made a mistake," Wolfgang said.

"I chose my destiny," Isaiah said.

"Maybe someone tricked you. But this is over."

"I'm not going behind bars."

"You'll have to answer for your action. You're a fool."

"You'll have to blow my brains out."

"You aren't walking out."

"Then, you'll have to carry me out."

"You won't get to the door." Kerstin left McDonald and walked along the table.

"You're telling me." Isaiah backed away toward the door.

"Don't be a fool," Wolfgang said.

"Ahem, can we have some whizzing bullets instead of just domestic spat?" Perry held up the hourglass and the remaining grains of sand slid through the funnel. "The audience is getting bored."

"I might decide to shoot you first," Wolfgang said.

"Make my day."

"Where is Grace?"

"Do you promise to blast me?"

The parrot said, "To thine own self be true."

On the opposite wall, wind had lifted the foliage into the air and they showered down the slope into the canyon. Like the autumn leaves, Wolfgang drifted in the wind. How to stop the duel between Kerstin and Isaiah? How to prevent the bullets from plunging into the screen and destroying the scene?

A scream resounded outside, a crescendo followed by a diminuendo, the tremolo lasting for about ten seconds. Wolfgang's muscles weakened while the echoes repeated the man's agony, but he steadied his hands, refocusing on Kerstin's gun and the hands of Isaiah and Perry.

"Oh well, guess some fool beat us to the grave," Perry said and was about to drink the champagne when Isaiah grabbed the glass and flung it against the wall and the shards showered on the floor. The sheriff pulled out a handkerchief to wipe the hourglass as if daring the vigilante to punch him.

"Never mind the juvenile misdemeanor," Isaiah said. "Let's focus on our struggle between good and evil, between love and justice."

"Agent, I'd rather have you as my savior than this scumbag," Perry said.

"So much for dying wishes," Isaiah said.

"Don't move and keep your hands in the open," Kerstin said.

"Sorry, boss. I guess it's the end of the line." Isaiah threw a piece of gum into his mouth and chewed. "As Kahlil Gibran said, 'For life and death are one, even as the river and the sea are one.'" He lowered his body and slid backward through the double doors.

Wolfgang took a step forward and called after Isaiah, but then stopped midway and said to Perry, "Don't even think about taking your life." He had to save Perry for a life sentence. The sheriff had to rot behind bars and nothing would foil his punishment, his well-earned damnation.

"I'm quite honored," Perry said. "You're letting the hit man go just to save my life." He tapped his fingers on the table as if challenging Wolfgang.

The red, the orange and the yellow danced on the screen.

The model train stopped.

The parrot said, "Parting is such sweet sorrow."

Perry dropped the hourglass onto the table and ignoring the gun, turned to the train, and Wolfgang followed his gaze and was about to alert Kerstin when Isaiah crashed through the door and said, "Get down."

The parrot mumbled a word and dropped onto the floor.

CHAPTER 46 - PERRY

Before Jefferson warned everyone, Todd had known an intruder was approaching the meeting room. He had set the alarm and anyone coming up the stairs would trigger the circuit and stop the model train. Was Lily-Rose coming to report to him? No. After studying the footsteps behind the door, he prepared for a showdown.

While getting the champagne, he had pressed a button in the cabinet to unlock the backdoor behind a screen and he sat down in front of the exit waiting to escape.

He was dropping onto the floor and crawling to the backdoor when the hourglass shattered and the room darkened. A screen cracked. A woman grunted. He slipped through the doorway into the passage. In the darkness, someone thumped below as the tabletop collapsed onto the floor. He groped his way through the passage and tripped over Cassidy's treasure chest. Another thump sounded below. Before taking a bullet, McDonald signaled that Cassidy had escaped through the backdoor. The preacher was probably downstairs waiting with a gun and had tripped over his wand or cape. Todd wouldn't turn on his flashlight and give the preacher a target.

He reached the stairs and grasping the handrail, stepped down with one foot and followed with the other. Reaching the bottom of the stairs about five minutes later. Footsteps sounded outside the building. After turning a corner, he crashed into the door and groped for the knob. While the footfalls retreated, he opened the door. Warm humid air engulfed him and he passed the portico and stepped into the courthouse backyard where Lily-Rose's bicycle lay in front of a shack. The smell of the sea roused him. A train was rumbling through the track. He stopped to check for wounds, but only found two scratches. When no one rushed at him, he strode to the wrought iron fence and slipped through a five-foot hole.

Ten feet away, Cassidy's headless body lay on the ground, his right hand holding a wand and his left a hat. A trail of blood led to the train track.

Damn psychopaths. Taking his prize.

He would've hunted Mitch and Luc and shoot them in the head rather than nabbing them. But now amid the scent of blood, he just bid Cassidy adieu and waited for the juvenile delinquents to come for their deaths. Would Agent Demir come and finish the job?

Agent, you disappoint me. You've failed me and you've failed Grace. If she had to wait for you to save her, she'd be in hell. If you die in there, well, you deserve it.

Todd reached the track where he had last seen Grace. And imagined her riding a train back to Mississippi, to her home, where she would forget Paradise and Todd and the evil drowning this town. She would marry and have children and live to an old age. And she would wonder whether Paradise was only a dream. But the blood and bullets in Paradise had poisoned his soul and he could never forget the body parts. He would soon lie under the ground and rot with scum and trash. The breeze warmed him. He lingered in this spot, where he and Grace, like lovers, had parted. His memory of her, sweet as arsenic, would accompany him into the grave. He smiled. He had given her the handkerchief. A lover's parting gift.

When he turned around, a gun barrel pointed at his eye and he gazed into the dark tunnel. Ernst held the gun.

Well, guess the sun will rise in the west. Come on, make my day.

The bush rustled and Elizabeth, her right hand and forearm in a tourniquet, staggered toward them, her bloodied left hand grasping a semiautomatic shotgun. When she raised her gun, Ernst waved his hand and said, "None of your business. Leave."

"Yeah, it's between us. I've always thought the agent would do the job. Never you, the coward. But don't be so sure I'd be the one kicking the bucket." Todd lit a cigarette and puffed into Ernst's face.

Several hours ago, he had Lily-Rose take Grace to his office where he had donned a hood and waited for her. When they arrived, he dismissed Lily-Rose and took Grace out of the courthouse. Reassuring her he wouldn't harm her. When they reached the track, he untied her and gave her a thousand dollars wrapped in the embroidered handkerchief. He pointed down the track and directed her to the train station. "Leave on the next train." She held the cash as if waiting for him to kiss her. He had struggled for several days. Should he release her? In the end, he didn't let her perish in the brothels. He would've cared for her if he were Wolfgang or Ernst. But he was Todd Perry, condemned to violate the innocents while catching criminals. When she still stared at him, he said, "Get out of here and never come back to Paradise." She should start a new life and not allow the trauma to destroy her life. After hesitating for a minute, she said, "I forgive you," and staggered down the track.

He collapsed onto the track. She followed the track around a bent, trudging from tie to tie, and disappeared behind the trees. The sun baked his scalp while sweat pour down his face and back. Her words, like a curse, sealed his doom. Even if Wolfgang were to capture or kill him, he might not receive salvation. Not when Grace's words lingered in his mind and condemned him in his grave. But he didn't regret freeing her. He savored her words as if drinking from a spring in the desert and would do so again given the chance. Trading his salvation for her freedom, a fair exchange. He wanted to run away with her. But he had released her not for *happily ever after*, but to seal his doom. And she had, by her words. Perhaps, she would inform the police about him and thus save his soul. In case Wolfgang should fail, she might succeed.

And the agent had failed him.

Todd looked into the gun barrel. Maybe Ernst would save him from hell. A single bullet would end his nightmare and set him free. But like Demir, the coward had to prove himself.

"Elizabeth, finish him off if he zaps me. A hundred thousand. I'll tell you where to get your payment."

"I don't care if she kills me. Just want to send you off to hell." Ernst squinted and steadied his aim.

Todd exhaled the smoke. Sure, the Bostonian blamed him for failing to save Lucy-Jane. He sympathized with the lover and would have killed any sheriff who had failed to save Grace from psychopaths like Cassidy. The crickets chanted and the fireflies darted around the bushes, as if they were rejoicing with him. Though he preferred Agent Demir, he accepted the Bostonian saving him from Paradise. Still, if Grace had called the police, he would savor her gift. Closing his eyes, he imagined holding onto her. And almost smelled her hair's fragrance.

"I should've killed Pastor Cassidy before some psycho took his life," Ernst said. "You, I wouldn't spare."

CHAPTER 47 - ERNST

After killing Rick, Ernst leaned against the chocolate factory wall and hid in the dark while Yanni's "Aria" filled his ears. Half a minute later, smoke rings drifted from the building's corner and Pastor Cassidy sauntered into the intersection puffing his cigarette. Turning his head to the two bodies, he stood at the end of the alley for two minutes before approaching them. He kicked them with the tip of his loafer and when they didn't move, he bent down to check the tote bag. After opening it, he whistled and took out a stack of cash.

"Damn, my lucky day."

Pastor Cassidy puffed out a ring of smoke into Jo-Beth's face and picked up the tote bag. Whistling as he retraced his footsteps. His phone rang.

"Yeah, okay, okay. Have them wait in the meeting room. And don't let those girls break loose." He ended the call and rushed toward the intersection, shaking the tote bag.

Thank you, Pastor Cassidy.

Ernst stepped out of the corner as the canvas on the second floor flapped louder. He knelt and found Jo-Beth's pulse stable. From Rick's pocket, he pulled out a phone and called for an ambulance. When the dispatcher asked for his name, he ended the call and slipped the phone back into Rick's pocket.

While humming Yanni's "Reflections of Passion," he tailed Pastor Cassidy, who tapped his heels as he passed a shack, beyond which the water tower rose into the starlit sky. The train station parking lot stood at the end of the side street. He had started his ordeal there and should end it in the same area.

Under the stars, he should be holding Lucy-Jane's hand just as she had his at Tupelo Point. Proposing to her and proclaiming his love. But he had opened a floodgate and joined Billy and Mitch in spirit by killing Rick. He had embarked on a journey to the wasteland. The night, though dark, couldn't hide his crime. And the wind, though cool, couldn't calm his mind.

Ernst had to finish his second task tonight before moping over losing Lucy-Jane and his soul. He had lost her but had to save Grace, encourage her to seek happiness and to reveal her love for Mr. Demir. Behind the water tower, he unlocked the gun's safety latch. The minister emerged, whistling "Amazing Grace," and threw the cigarette butt into the grass. Then passed the water tower and approached the two-story courthouse where a second-story window was casting light onto a nearby birch.

Ernst hid behind an elm around which fireflies drifted as if on water. He mustn't fail and he wouldn't, not after having killed Rick to correct his previous failure.

The minister walked through the wrought iron gate into the portico and after glancing around for several seconds, stepped through the panel door.

Ernst finished the apricot scone and entered the front yard where two Road Kings leaned against a flag post. A spotlight guided him to the portico. A breeze brought the scent of the ocean and a train roared through the nearby track. If only he was riding the train out of Paradise, into a better world. Gritting his teeth, he went through the front door.

The foyer reeked of mold and dust. The farther wall displayed a quote of Martin Luther King, Jr.: "Even if I knew that tomorrow the world would go to pieces, I would still plant my apple tree." He passed the swinging doors and followed the footsteps into the lobby and hid behind the curtain, chewing on a siomai.

Was Isaiah shaking hands with the minister?

Outside, the spotlight cast the shadow of a magnolia tree onto the lobby's tile floor. An owl hooted in the front yard. And the heat seeped through the windowpane behind him. Oppressing him, vexing him, driving him toward the abyss.

Pastor Cassidy, humming "The Battle Hymn of the Republic," emerged from the side door and went to the back of the courthouse, his shadow creeping along.

Ernst was about to follow the shadow through the corridor when Lily-Rose opened the side door with note in hand and said, "Hey, wait up, look at this." And noticing Ernst, said, "What you doing here? Where's the magician?"

Ernst seized the note and read it, ignoring the girl's complaint. A suicide note. Grace's. After reading the note, he tightened his grip on the handgun and pointed it at Lily-Rose but didn't shoot her. She cussed and grabbed the suicide note and retreated behind the side door.

Grace had held his arm. Grace had confided in him. Now, she had departed.

Ernst grasped his gun. Marched to the backyard. He would shoot Cassidy. But his hands shook. His legs shook. And his heart pounded and his chest ached.

Grace, revenge will be yours. I promise.

In the backyard, the minister dropped the tote bag and pulled out a pack of cigarettes from his left sleeve and a lighter from his right. He lit a cigarette under the dim light while an owl hooted and a breeze whistled through the yard. After puffing his cigarette, he sang "I Left My Heart in San Francisco."

Ernst rubbed his palms on the trouser legs and was about to sneak up and shoot him in the head when Isaiah grasped his hand and said, "Don't be a fool like Wolfgang."

"Are you the buyer?" Ernst said, "Are you here for the transaction?"

"Nice thought," Isaiah said, "But I prefer shooting to making money. Though sometimes they go hand-in-hand."

"I have to save Grace."

"Ah, Wolfgang must've infected you with the virus. Let me cure you."

"I still care. I still want to do something."

"That can be cured, too."

"Are you going to kill Perry and Cassidy? We can join forces."

"In ten years, maybe." Isaiah pulled him away from the backdoor. "When Perry and Cassidy come out, they'll be all yours. But now, let me do my job and I'd really appreciate it. When you hear shots, just wait here to see who's the quick and who's the dead."

Cassidy returned from the backyard, hid the tote bag in a hall closet and tap-danced to the lobby. After he had ascended the stairs, Isaiah took the bag and gave Ernst it, then tiptoed up the stairs.

Ernst gripped the gun in one hand and the bag in the other. Why did Isaiah give him the money? Should he crash the party? No, he wouldn't spoil the assassin's plan.

About half an hour later, when a shriek outside startled him, his muscles twitched and almost cramped. He hid under the stairs and pointed the gun at the entrance. Laughter echoed in the yard, but he didn't move to the window to peek outside. Someone chopped wood. Five thuds. More laughter. Ten minutes later, engines roared away.

When he stepped into the backyard, a plume of dust rose into the air. Beyond the fence, a bloodied ax lay on the minister's headless body.

He could no longer kill the minister and he might've lost the chance to get rid of the sheriff also.

No, he couldn't fail Grace as I had Lucy-Jane.

Gunshots boomed on the second floor. Windowpanes shattered and tinkled and glass shards showered on the yard. Flashlights beamed around the compound. When shadows converged on the courthouse, he hid in the shrub beside the railroad tracks.

Perry must survive the shootout to receive his bullet in the head, Ernst's gift to him.

The gun weighed upon him. Should he forgive the sheriff for driving Grace to suicide? Before killing Rick, he might've but now he had crossed the line between the living and the dead and wouldn't hesitate to shoot Perry point-blank between the eyes. No longer would he drop another baby Rick onto the floor; no longer would he fail. Having stepped beyond success and failure.

#

In the railroad track, while pointing the handgun at Sheriff Perry, Ernst put on his headset. Yanni's "A Night to Remember." He chewed another siomai, savoring the pork, shrimp and Chinese mushroom. Execute the sheriff and avenge Grace. Let Elizabeth shoot him afterward.

Grace could no longer win over Mr. Demir's heart. Ernst couldn't even enjoy that speck of warmth. He had to kill the sheriff. Should've done the same to the minister. Lost love. Lost chances. He had lost too much to forsake his last salvation.

"You sure you know how to handle the piece? I'd hate it if I end up blowing out your brains." Sheriff Perry placed an hourglass on the ground and the sand tumbled from the upper bulb to the lower one.

"You swore to protect the people."

"I tried my best to find your lover's kidnapper. But just too damn many killers in town. Okay, that's an excuse. I admit it."

"You betrayed them."

"If you're going to bump me off, shoot me in the back of the head. I prefer that to a hole in my forehead. And please don't make a mess like those gangsters chopping up the bodies."

"You took away Grace's future. She was innocent and deserved a happy life."

Sheriff Perry dropped the cigarette butt. Shoved aside the gun with his nose. Seized Ernst's lapels. "You don't know nothing about her. You don't know how pure her heart is. You don't know how strong her resilience is. You don't know—"

"I know how much she loved Mr. Demir, how much she dreamed of a life with him." Ernst twisted his wrist, trying to point the gun at the sheriff but the barrel only touched the man's hair.

Sheriff Perry threw him onto the track and as his shoulder slammed onto the rail, the handgun flew from his hand and into the bush. His shoulder hurt as a breeze lifted dust onto this face. He sneezed. He crawled toward the gun. But the sheriff stepped on his neck and his cheek pressed against the railroad tie and his lips kissed a crushed stone.

"I have a soft spot for the lad so keep your quid." Elizabeth limped toward the sheriff, pointed her automatic handgun at him. "Any road, I'd rather eliminate you gratis." She had bound her leg wound but blood soaked the cloth.

"I'm getting sick and tire of klutzes and dopes." Sheriff Perry pressed his boot on Ernst's neck. "You're supposed to bump me off. What the hell are you doing under my shoe licking my sole?"

Ernst spat the sand from his mouth and said, "I'm trying."

"Try smarter, not harder." Sheriff Perry picked up the gun and unlocked the safety latch. "I'm getting sick and tired of this game."

"I can help." Elizabeth edged closer, her gun still pointing at the sheriff.

"I don't need your help. And don't think I won't blow your brains." The sheriff pointed the gun at Ernst. "I'll bump him off before you can finish me off, even if you have a third bloody hand."

"Sheriff, I prefer killing you," Elizabeth said. "Sorry, lad, nothing personal."

"That's the trouble with you fanatics," Sheriff Perry said. "You think nothing's personal when everything is."

Ernst shut his eyes. Rick as a baby was falling from his hands and onto the floor. Failures and more failures. He had failed to save Lucy-Jane and now he would fail to avenge Grace. Even in the seconds before his death, one last failure. His epitaph: Here lies the man who failed, in life as in death.

The grooves on the sole and the striations on the tie, they pained his cheeks. Dung's odor, either from the shoe or from the ground nearby, mingled with the smell of the sea. The wind's whisper mixed with a low rumble. Perhaps another train was arriving just in time to crush him.

"You still haven't told me why you harmed Grace?" Ernst struggled to move his jaw.

"I love Grace. But was too late. Realized it only after—"

"I still want to kill you."

"Wish you could. But damn it, you're a klutz. And you deserve to die—"

Perry's face contorted, his hands pressed against his chest and he collapsed onto the ground. Groaning and gasping.

No gunshot. No blood. Elizabeth hadn't shot him.

Only a heart attack.

"I'll do you a favor, gratis." Elizabeth pointed the gun at Perry, ready to pull the trigger, but a head, its blonde hair waving, flew through the air. She dodged to the side while the sheriff gasped on the ground and the head rolled along the railroad track.

Two Road Kings, one on each side of the track, roared toward them, the riders firing a rifle and a shotgun.

On his back, Ernst gazed at the stars. He had killed Rick and avenged Lucy-Jane's death. He had done it. All by himself. He had stopped his heart, smothered his thoughts, and vanquished his future.

He dreamed of a dream interrupted. At Tupelo Point, Lucy-Jane emerged from the mist to greet him again.

Peace. Joy. Love.

CHAPTER 48 - WOLFGANG

Wolfgang dropped onto the floor next to the parrot and shot through the double doors. A grunt responded. The screens shattered. The table collapsed onto the floor. He crawled along the fallen table toward the doorway, careful to avoid the shards. When he reached the edge of the table, the model train fell on the tabletop. He couldn't pinpoint the assassin. The gunpowder wafted in the air and the dust clung onto his skin. He whispered Kerstin's name. She didn't answer. He pressed his ear on the floorboard. Thumps outside the room. He phoned his agents and directed them to surround the courthouse. Where was Kerstin? Where was Isaiah? After a minute, he got up and beamed the flashlight around the floor and found McDonald's body under the table, but the others had fled. He looked beneath the tabletop for Kerstin and Isaiah, but the debris blocked his view.

Should he have his agents chase Perry and Cassidy? Instead, he directed them to search for the kidnapped girls. He would rather save Grace than nab the evil duo. They would destroy themselves sooner or later.

With the screens shattered, he could no longer savor the slope of foliage bobbing in the wind. Even the scent of lavenders had departed. He picked up the parrot and when it didn't move, dropped it among the shards. After pushing the model train onto the floor, he lifted the tabletop to look for Kerstin, but only found a broken cabinet. He pulled out McDonald's body but the man's shoe came off and remained under the table.

An agent in straw hat and polo shirt came into the room and informed him the team had searched through the first and second floors but found nothing, and would be exploring the basement. But he directed the man to look for Kerstin and Isaiah instead. He would go down to the basement and locate Grace. Rescue her and apologize to her. She would see his face rather than those of his agents. Earlier, as he was leaning on the totem pole and waiting for Perry, he vowed to make Grace barbecue ribs.

Wolfgang left the meeting room and went downstairs. Two agents guarded the front entrance and another two a side door across the lobby. Wielding his gun, he went through the door and tiptoed down the stairs, the floral wallpapers reminding him of the minister's outfit. The dust lifted from the steps and a stench attacked his nostrils. The rats squeaked at the bottom of the stairs as he descended into the darkness thick and deep. The air irritated his throat but he suppressed the urge to cough, just shone the flashlight onto the spider webs and scared away the rats.

When he reached the bottom, a corridor led into darkness. Amid the bodies of flies, roaches and rats, footprints covered the ground. He touched a cigarette butt. Still warm. He put on infrared goggles and tiptoed down the corridor. The floor creaked and he stopped to check for sounds. Still only the rats squeaking.

The image of Grace lying dead in a dungeon haunted him. He shut his eyes. He rubbed his eyelids to wipe the vision away. But the pale face resurfaced in his mind again and again.

She was alive.

His phone shook.

He hesitated for a moment before checking the caller. Was Kerstin calling him about having caught Elizabeth? But the screen showed *Isaiah.*

"Well, boss, guess this is it for you and me."

"I'm in the middle of saving the girls."

"Sorry about McDonald. Bad habit."

"Remember, *Your pain is the breaking of the shell that encloses your understanding.*"

"You know, never liked Kahlil Gibran. Too spiritual for me. I'm a pragmatist."

"You could've called at a better time."

"Guess you'll be after me."

"Not me."

"Kerstin, then."

"You may want to pick up Spanish."

"Guess I'll be seeing you around."

"For your sake, I hope not. But I wouldn't mind having tea with a starving artist in Prague."

"Oops, a bummer."

"Perry? Elizabeth?"

"Kerstin's pointing her rod at me and I'm pointing mine at her."

"Let me talk to her."

Isaiah hung up.

Kerstin and Isaiah would have their duel and only one would stand after the dust had settled. He turned around and retraced his path, but after taking two steps, he stopped. Grace. Shouldn't waste even a second. Anyway, the duel would end before he could step out of the courthouse.

He couldn't prevent the disaster. He could do nothing. Not a damn thing. Just standby and watch. As with his father. As with his sister. He would fail. Again. And this time, he would lose Kerstin or Isaiah or both. And he might already have lost Grace.

He kicked the dirt and pushed away the spider webs and the rats squeaked and scurried away. Kerstin's face appeared in his mind as he reached the end of the corridor. Six people sat several feet behind a door, two on the left, two on the right and two in the middle. He grasped the doorknob. The coating came off. Would he have to bury Kerstin or Isaiah? After holding the knob for several seconds, the coating crumbling in his palm, he turned the handle. Pushed the door ajar. Aimed his gun through the crevice. The four figures on the left and right converged toward the center and the six huddled against each other.

Several women screamed while he shone the flashlight to survey the room and search the wall for a light switch. When he switched on the light, more screams. A light bulb hanging from the ceiling lit up the windowless room and a barred gate partitioned the place into two-halves. Behind the gate, six young ladies, some with blackened eyes and bloodied lips, were covering their eyes.

Grace wasn't there.

The gun in his hand quivered as he showed his badge and told them he came to free them. When Lily-Rose slipped her hand into her pocket, he grasped a bar and asked for Grace.

A blonde girl with a bruised face and torn jeans grabbed Lily-Rose's hand and they struggled on the floor while the others screamed. He called for them to stop. But they continued to roll on the floor.

A gunshot went off. The blonde girl groaned and fell away.

Lily-Rose lifted her gun. The other girls charged at her. One seized the gun and another her left hand and the other two punched her in the face and stomach.

Wolfgang pushed the gate. But it wouldn't move. He checked the lock. Unlatched the hook. And tried again. It slid open. When he stepped into the cage, the girls had knocked out Lily-Rose and one was holding the gun.

"Please drop the gun." Wolfgang showed his badge and pointed his gun at the ground in front of the girl, ready to shoot her arm if she lifted the gun. "I'm here to help you."

The girl was shaking and crying. Ten seconds later, she dropped the gun. He tiptoed across the straw-covered floor toward the girls. And smelled sweat and blood and almost vomited. When he reached the girl, he bent down and picked up the gun.

A girl sitting on Lily-Rose wiped the dirt off her face with her hand, and said, "She's... she's... one of them." She punched Lily-Rose in the face and wept.

In ten seconds, he understood her words and handcuffed Lily-Rose. He shouldn't have trusted the girl to spy for him. Another mistake, another girl wounded. He checked the girl shot in the stomach and after finding her breathing shallow, called an agent to get the ambulance. Then searched Lily-Rose and found a key chain on her.

"Where's Grace?" He leaned against the wall and searched the lifeless faces for an answer.

The girl who had taken the gun from Lily-Rose said, "You Agent Demir?" When he nodded, she took a note out of Lily-Rose's pocket and said, "From Grace. Did say but give it to you. Just fore he took her. The bitch did take it from me."

His hand shook. He took the note. He read it. His eyes struggled to focus on the words. His mind struggled to decipher her sentences.

Grace thanked him for taking care of her and for teaching her to make pilaf. She loved him and had wanted to journey with him toward the future. She had wanted him to be her first and only man. She hoped the information would help save the girls and catch the criminals. She would kill herself rather than sell her body. For him, she wouldn't let another man touch her. She wished him the best with Kerstin.

The note rattled in his hands. Then dropped onto the ground. A fever seized his head. Images swirled. Sounds faded. He staggered for two steps before steadying himself against the wall that flaked under his palm. Grace was lying lifeless in a swamp, the flies buzzing around her body and the vultures circling overhead. He had to kill Todd Perry and avenge Grace. Even if he had to forfeit his career and his life.

He grasped the gate. He would look for Grace. And she would sketch the Tidal Basin for him. But whether she was alive or not, he would hunt Todd Perry across the continent and the globe. He would like to find the sheriff deep in the Sahara Desert so without worrying about the law, he could shoot him between the eyes and bury him among the sand. His enemy had given him a mission for which to sacrifice his soul and he would accept the challenge. Hate and anger would empower him.

He released the bars. An agent was resuscitating the blonde girl, and the other girls, including Lily-Rose, had left the cell. He inquired about the girl and his agent shook his head. Wolfgang held his head with both hands and pressed his forehead against a bar. Another girl dead. Another mistake and another failure. He should've suspected Lily-Rose. *Don't blame yourself.* He folded Grace's note and put it into his pocket next to the sketch of the Tidal Basin.

He returned to the lobby and asked about Kerstin and Isaiah. But his agents only shook their heads.

In the front yard, the air reeking of the ocean, pops echoed near the tracks. But in the sky, no firework, only stars twinkling. He was walking toward the train station when his phone rang.

Kerstin called.

"I'm sorry. I knew McDonald was here to catch Kensington and her associates, but I wasn't working with him until Elizabeth tried to eliminate him and he asked me to join. I accepted. Even though Ida would be undergoing chemotherapy. Even though I would have to keep you in the dark."

She and McDonald should have informed him so the teams could work together and avoid the British agent's death.

"The Bureau has the same crap," Wolfgang said. "But I'm glad you're okay. Where's Isaiah?"

"I had to accept. I had to stop Elizabeth from killing him and the girls from getting sold into prostitution."

"I understand."

"Liz Jones," Kerstin said, "is a team leader in the Elysian Fields and has penetrated MI6 about ten years ago and became Elizabeth. When Agent McDonald posed as a human trafficker and came to Paradise to capture Mary-Lou Kensington, who had defected from the organization after botching an operation, Elizabeth volunteered to come along and prepared to kill both the agent and the defector. After you spoiled their first transaction and she killed an agent, she decided to eliminate McDonald as soon as possible and get the FBI off her trail. She failed to kill the British agent but eliminated the defector."

"At least, she respects you," Wolfgang said.

"She's a diligent worker in MI6."

"Wouldn't leave you to Isaiah."

"She would've surpassed McDonald in about two to three years. A shame."

"I'd want someone like her working for me."

"And Isaiah is a fool."

"And the fool?"

"Departed."

Wolfgang would miss Isaiah, his shinai, his philosophical musings, and most of all, his floral arrangements. He would have liked to have tea or wine with his friend in a Roman palazzo amid a sea of pigeons. Perhaps in another life.

"He thinks he can mete out justice as if he were God," she said.

"He couldn't let go of his guilt, just like you and me." He would have to choose between avenging Grace and life with Kerstin.

"Now, I have to do one last chore," she said.

"Wait for me."

"No more guilt. No more hesitation. Life is too short to take on excess baggage."

"Let's do it together."

"I need to do it alone. Please." Kerstin ended the call.

Go after her, help her nab the Red Rose, stand side-by-side and defeat evil. But no, she had to capture the criminal alone, she had to cast off her guilt, she had to conquer herself. And soar into the air.

But when more pops alerted him, he ran toward the station. He had to arrive in time to help her capture the Red Rose. He had to persuade her to share her grief. Under the shadow of the water tower, death loomed murky and thick. Beyond the shack, his shadow met another specter.

A shape silhouetted against the distant streetlight. Emerged from the surrounding darkness. A shadow pointing at him but stopping ten feet away.

Elizabeth McDonald.

Forget about her. Look for Kerstin. Proclaim his love even in a dark night. But he stopped and faced the Red Rose, the death that wouldn't die. He grasped his gun. He could shoot her to avenge Kerstin, to seek justice, to grief his loss. But he tossed the handcuffs at Elizabeth's feet.

"Put them on."

Elizabeth raised her right arm in a tourniquet, then her bloodied left hand holding the shotgun. "You bloody missed. Not once, but twice."

"Put on the handcuffs. We'll bind your wounds before you get an infection." Perhaps Kerstin would emerge from the darkness and declare her love for him. But the silence almost deafened him.

Elizabeth tossed a red rose in the air. Pointed the shotgun at her temple and pulled the trigger.

The flower twirled in the air for several seconds, its shadow dancing on the concrete, before landing on her chest.

Blood trickling out of a hole in her forehead, she lay on the ground next to the bush, gun still in hand. While a breeze lifted her hair and the scent of blood wafted through the air.

What motivated her to hunt down men and women, agents and criminals? Money? Thrill? Challenge? Emptiness? Wolfgang removed the shotgun, put her hands over her abdomen and adjusted the rose so the petals touched her chin. Why had she work for a human trafficking organization? What fears, what hatred, what visions drove her? As usual, no answers or conclusions, only an empty finale, while his questions lingered and aged and faded.

Case closed.

He took out the paper bag and peeped at the bloodied snow globe inside. Ernst had shot Rick point-blank between the eyes, probably to avenge his lover. Wolfgang had taken it to preserve the evidence and was going to call the police. But now, as he ran toward the station to search for Kerstin, he wasn't sure. Just as he wasn't sure whether he would kill Perry after hunting him down. He wasn't sure what he would see in the mirror just as he wasn't sure whether he would see the sun tomorrow. The night air warmed his face.

Grace, will you make me another spicy lamb gyro?

CHAPTER 49 - ERNST

Down the track, Mitch and Luc prostrated on the rails as if kissing the ties, each with a bullet hole between the eyes. Two pools of blood grew around their heads. Near the train station, their Road Kings sprawled next to Pastor Cassidy's head, one wheel still spinning in the air.

Ernst spat out the sand and checked his body for bullet holes. None. Only his khakis torn at the knees. Kerstin had killed the delinquents before they could gun down Perry and him. Elizabeth escaped.

Several feet away, Kerstin, kneeling beside Sheriff Perry, crushed an aspirin on a business card, squeezing together her thumb and index finger. "Open your mouth."

"Leave me be." Perry turned away and continued to gasp, his face turning purple.

Kerstin turned his head around, poured the powder into his mouth, and covered his lips. Forcing the sheriff to swallow the aspirin.

"Can't a man go to hell in peace?"

"Not tonight. You'll help us infiltrate the Elysian Fields. The perfect recruit, a trafficker fleeing from federal agents, looking for a new home."

"I won't, so kill me."

"You will, if you want redemption."

"Shit."

The monster doesn't deserve redemption; he deserves damnation.

Ernst crawled along the track and grasped the gun. Then stood and pointed it at Perry. "You'll die. You have to."

"Drop it." Kerstin lifted Perry onto his feet and supported him with her shoulder. But the sheriff pushed her away and fell onto the track again.

Ernst aimed the gun at Perry. *Lucy-Jane, give me strength. Grace, give me courage.* The police siren in the distance called out his cowardice.

"Pull the damn trigger already, you klutz," Perry said.

"Drop it." Kerstin grasped Perry's collar and carried him over her back. After swinging her leg in an arc to knock the gun out of Ernst's hand, she trudged down the track, the sheriff dangling over her back. One step. Two steps. Toward the darkness.

Ernst picked up the gun but it trembled in his hand and fell onto the track again. He sat on the rail. Held his head. He had shot Rick in the head. The man's groan and twisted face should entice him to pick up the gun and pull the trigger.

But he couldn't. He couldn't shoot Kerstin. Not even if she let him. *I'm sorry, Grace. I've failed you.*

Kerstin marched down the railroad track with Sheriff Perry on her back. Farther down, Pastor Cassidy's head reclined against the rail at the edge of the train station.

When the two pools of blood under the teenagers' heads joined and the scent nauseated him, Ernst dusted the dirt off his shirt and khakis and backpack. Picked up his MP3 player and put on the headset. His right cheek singed. The back of his neck ached. He picked up the tote bag, embraced it as if holding a baby, the bills still inside. He strode over the fallen utility poles to avoid the wires. Then passed Elizabeth's moccasin beside the fallen blossoms. Limped between the rails toward the train station. The air had cooled but sweat continued to drip down his back. The crickets chirped in the bushes beside the platform as he stepped over a branch and approached the minister's head, whose hair was fluttering in the wind and whose eyes stared at several shell casings in the track.

At the train station, Ernst threw the backpack and tote bag onto the platform. Grabbed the top section of the welcome sign that had fallen onto the track. Stood it on its side. He climbed onto it. Crawled onto the platform. Pushed the toppled ad display toward the back where shards from the broken windowpanes lined the floor. Amid Yanni's "To the One Who Knows" he chewed the last siomai.

Where had the police siren gone?

If Grace walked up and smiled at him or Sheriff Perry's head sat beside the pastor's, Ernst wouldn't have to hunt down the criminal. He preferred going to jail and cooking lasagna and borscht for the inmates and prison guards, to fleeing from the police and hunting down the sheriff. Of course, he still would go to Wellesley College and visit Tupelo Point.

A breeze blew dust off the platform and the door to the waiting area opened. Ernst put his hands in his pants pockets, waiting for the handcuffs. Officers probably had surrounded the station. They wouldn't have to worry. He wouldn't waste his strength. He wouldn't run away. He still had to kill the sheriff but he'd have to find another way. If he had hidden the money, he would hire an assassin like Isaiah to hunt down the criminal.

Agent Demir, paper bag in hand, walked past the metal bench toward him, his oxfords crunching glass shards.

One last chance at redemption, to shake the man's hand, to embrace him, before heading to the jailhouse, before sitting in the electric chair.

"The sheriff took several bullets from those gangsters, " Ernst said, "probably wouldn't survive until morning." *Forget about Perry. Marry Kerstin. Or look for Grace, if she hadn't killed herself. Just don't waste your life.*

"Where's Kerstin?"

"Alive. There's still a chance for happily ever after. So don't be a fool."

"You're a fool for coming here. And a greater fool for trying to kill Perry."

"Grace deserved her life and her happiness."

"I'll look for her and won't stop until I find her, dead or alive."

"She would've been happy with you," Ernst said, "you would've been happy with her."

"Paradise is all we have."

"I'm sorry."

"Leave this town and all its trash."

"I never saw Lucy-Jane alive in Paradise. Never got to hold her or kiss her. Everything we have was from The Hub."

"Here is something for you."

"You're the plank I've been holding onto while I drift in this cesspool. I'll always be grateful."

"I want to thank you for trying to save Grace."

"She loves you. I mean love, not lust. You must know that."

He took out a scone and handed it to Agent Demir. "If Kerstin hadn't approached me, I never would've met you. And you would've never helped me."

"Leave Paradise on the next train." Agent Demir took the scone and handed him the paper bag. "You left this."

In the bag, a snow globe: the one Ernst had smashed Rick's head with. He had bought it in Copley Square as a gift for Lucy-Jane and used it to avenge her.

"You're the real fool," Ernst said.

"Maybe."

"And I'd be a fiend to take it."

"Do whatever you want with it."

"Someone may find out."

"Someone will know. Someone is bound to know."

"Then it's goodbye to your career and hello to the slammer."

"There is a Chinese saying, something like: Don't do anything you don't want known."

"Why?"

"Why ask?"

"Like I said, it's foolish."

"There're fools now as there always have been."

"I wish there're more fools."

"And there will continue to be."

"My manager's no fool and the bank's taking over his penthouse condo next to the Longfellow Bridge with a panoramic view of the Charles and Cambridge."

Agent Demir extended his hand. Ernst grasped it. He shook it. The agent's hand strengthened him. He would march into the future. When a breeze swept through the track, he released the hand.

The agent bid farewell. Turned to leave. But the wind changed direction and he raised his head and gazed down the track. Squinting. Frowning. Then leaped onto the track. Pulled out his weapon. And sprinted from tie to tie past Pastor Cassidy's head, the two Road Kings and the two bodies. His shadow bobbing into the darkness.

"Let it go," Ernst said. "Look for Grace." But only the agent's footfalls responded, defying his plea.

What would he do when he found Kerstin helping Sheriff Perry escape? What would she do? Yes, they had to choose their destinies just as Ernst his, with limited knowledge and corrupted data.

At the end of the platform, he held his hands behind his back. Should he take the snow globe to the police station? Another breeze cooled his face. Across the track, flies buzzed around the minister's head.

Well, Pastor, what'd you advise? I wouldn't mind some magic tricks to help me decide.

No advice from Pastor Cassidy's parted lips. But even if the magician spoke, Ernst would prefer the wisdom of the bartender in Eden's Joy. He dropped the tote bag and the paper bag, one on the right and the other on the left, and sat on the platform, his legs dangling over the edge. Several petals tumbled along the track and landed beside the magician's head.

He would return to Boston. To apologize to Reza. To extend his hand and wait for his former friend to shake it. He wouldn't flee until he had shaken that hand.

Ernst displayed Lucy-Jane's photo on his phone. He had kissed those lips. He had been happy. He had lived before entering hell.

I'm lucky to have had you Lucy-Jane, even if just for a short while. I'll love you forever. And I know that wherever you are, you love me also.

He came here to find his lover, to secure life after Paradise. Now, before Pastor Cassidy's head, as he listened to Yanni's "Whispers in the Dark," his dream, his vision had fled. Only his memory, ever fading, remained to create ever-renewing versions of the past. He had to walk into the night, without a destination, unable to see the path.

He hugged the tote bag and the stacks of bills. Perhaps a figure would walk down the track, as had at Tupelo Point on that March morning. In the darkness, Rick the baby was falling toward the floor, its arms and legs flailing in the air, its screams echoing from the past.

###

ABOUT THE AUTHOR

Leonard Seet is the author of the novel *Meditation On Space-Time* and the non-fiction *The Spiritual Life*. His articles and short fiction have appeared in the *Quarterly Literary Review Singapore*, *Banana Writers* and *Pilcrow & Dagger*. Through his writings, he probes the dynamics of existence, including human consciousness, good and evil, and rationality and spirituality.

Visit the author's blog:

http://leonardseet.blogspot.com

www.ingramcontent.com/pod-product-compliance
Lightning Source LLC
Chambersburg PA
CBHW071903020726
47502CB00003B/873